"This well written and captivating book takes you on a journey. You will be happy to have read this book because it brings hope and encouragement to your own life and experience."

Ginger Shingler, retired adjunct professor at
Point Loma Nazarene University,
speaker and Bible study teacher

"Strong, complex characters; very compelling and poignant character interrelationships that twist and turn in many rich and complex directions; beautifully evocative descriptions; and much authentic and compelling dialogue. The subtle and nuanced ways family members, friends, and other loved ones interact on the surface, while their real motives are often thinly disguised, demonstrate some keen insights into human nature as it is both seen and unseen."

Dennis M. Clausen, award-winning author of
Prairie Son and *Goodbye to Main Street*

Where You See Forever

Cynthia G. Robertson

ISBN 978-1-64458-921-2 (paperback)
ISBN 978-1-64458-922-9 (digital)

Christian Faith Publishing, Inc.
832 Park Avenue
Meadville, PA 16335
www.christianfaithpublishing.com

This book is a work of fiction based on things that did happen and many others that the author imagined could have happened. Some locales and characters referred to in this story are based on real places and people, but the names, people, scenes and events and even time sequence are all fictionalized. Some characters as well as many of the events and locales are completely made-up. Any resemblance to actual persons, living or dead, events, or locales is entirely coincidental. Such is the nature of fiction.

Printed in the United States of America

For Aunt Gayle
Who helped keep my eyes on Christ

In memory of my mother

God makes a home for the lonely;
He leads out the prisoners into prosperity,
Only the rebellious dwell in a parched land.
—Psalm 68:6 NASB

Prologue

June 2, 1996
Wheaton, Kansas

As ALWAYS, THE MAPLE and elm trees on Sherman Street play and pull with my memories. Their branches bend and dance in the wind as dancers, the leaves rustling like ballerina skirts. The trees are dancing and whispering now as I turn the car into the driveway. A cloud of sparrows and finches fly up from the bird feeder in the front yard of my mother's house. Their flapping wings sound like faint thunder.

My heart does its familiar beat, beat, pause, pound. Since moving to San Diego fifteen years ago, I've made this trip home many times, but it's always the same with my heart, this pounding, almost painful beat in my chest, pushing the air out of my lungs.

Across the street is the little house where I grew up, painted white now, looking naked. The new owner has taken down the fence and nearly half the trees.

My mother opens the screen door and I run up to her. She has short perfectly coiffed blond hair and deep brown eyes, looking not at all sixty-something. Instead, she looks a lot like my friends in their forties. We hug tight and long, me practically rocking her back and forth in my arms. I can feel the extra softness around her elbows and shoulders, a comfort to me.

Finally, I let go and step back. "Gaw—" I stop myself, remembering what the bar of soap tasted like years ago when Mom put it into my mouth. "Good grief, it's great to see you!"

"Well, likewise," she says. Her brown eyes search my face. It is easy to see the Cherokee in her, the dark eyes of her own mother who

9

died when Mom was only six years old. I always wish I had eyes like Mom's, but instead I got the high cheekbones and thick hair.

We walk into her house together. "Coffee?" Mom asks. Of course.

While she pours the coffee, I look at all the knick-knacks she has saved throughout the years. I touched the tray I had made her when I was eleven years old during summer vacation Bible school with the Salvation Army. I can almost smell the paint that I had used on the tray, and I taste again the mini-franks with chili we had for lunch. Those were good days, enshrouded though they were in mystery. I was always wondering and worried what my mother would say or do next.

In the tiny living room, I curl up on the floral print sofa. Mom comes in with our cups of coffee and sits down in her favorite easy chair. We sit and sip for a while, and I talk about the long hours of travel by plane the day before. Then she reaches behind her chair and hands me a pretty wrapped slender box with a bow. "Happy birthday," Mom says.

I take a long time unwrapping the gift.

"You still do that?" Mom teases me.

"I want to save the paper," I say. I have this idea of saving pieces of wrapping paper and creating a collage with them. Some day.

The gift is a women's devotional filled with Scripture and inspirational notes by women. Mom has signed it, "With all my love."

I feel Mom watching me as I thumb through the pages of the little book. I do not tell her that I am thinking about the years growing up when I did not know if she was for or against me or just did not care. Yet as time passed, I have realized that she gave me, in all irony, the best gift a mother can give: a craving to know God. I've travelled some long roads in looking for Him.

Tears fill my eyes now as I look through the devotional. "Thanks, Mom. It is just what I needed," I say.

We both turn when we hear a knocking sound at the window. Several finches have gathered at the feeder attached to the window and are fighting with each other for their turn. Mom and I laugh and blot the tears from our eyes.

Storms

– 1 –

I WAS A WEIRD kid. I looked forward to going to church. When Sunday mornings rolled around, my mother had my dress and shoes all picked out. While Rita fussed and fumed about getting ready, I was quiet, eagerly looking forward to going to Sunday school and then singing hymns in church. Everyone used to say how beautiful our family was. It was true; my parents smelled and looked good, and my sister and I looked like well-dressed twin dolls.

The ten-minute journey from our little green house in the county suburbs to church was like a little trip to heaven. As soon as we passed Main Street and headed down Fourth Avenue, my sister and I would start sniffing the air.

"Smell it yet?" I asked Rita.

"Mmmm, not yet."

"There it is," my dad said, rolling down our windows.

The heavenly smell of baked bread made my stomach growl as we rode past the Rainbo Bakery. Beneath all that luscious doughy aroma was something else rather sour smelling.

"What's that other smell? Like cider?" I asked, still sniffing the air.

"It's vinegar," Mom said.

"Yuck. Vinegar? For bread?" I couldn't believe it.

"It makes it taste better. And rise, too," Mom said.

I didn't understand all that, but we had arrived at the church parking lot. I grabbed my picture Bible and was out of the car faster than lightning. Mom was still fiddling with her hair, looking in the little mirror she carried in her purse. Rita rolled her eyes and dragged her feet. I started to run up the stairs at the back of the church when Mom caught up with me.

"Hey, where do you think you're going?" she said, her eyes like deep fire.

"Um, I…I just wanted to be on time," I said.

Dad was still putting on his jacket. He was always so painfully slow in doing anything. And yet even then I could feel my heart blow up big with my need for his attention.

"Walk, don't run," Mom said.

Rita glowered at me. "We're never late," she said, heavy-footing up the stairs behind me, not at all eager like me. When I got to the sunny room, my friend Amber was already in the front row, so I sat down beside her. We looked at each other, smiling and giggling like we always did. I'll never forget the first time I met Amber. She was a new girl, wearing a fluffy dress and her bouncy hair up in ribbons. All the kids laughed at her. I patted the seat next to me and we became fast friends.

Sunday school was a social time as much as it was religious lessons, both equally important to me. I wanted to fill my life with friends and make my parents happy, too. I was thrilled when they let me have Amber over for dinner one night. She and I sat next to each other, happy as songbirds chattering and passing the potatoes, Mom and Dad both being kind and Rita being polite enough, grateful for the diversion. When Dad asked me what we would do when the meal was over, I said Amber would go to my room and we would do our homework together.

"Oh, no, you won't," he said, shaking his head, a greased curl bobbing on his forehead. "She'll be going home right after supper."

"But, Daddy, we will be really quiet. You won't even hear us," I said, my heart pounding.

He closed his eyes, shook his head. I looked to Mom. She shook her head, too.

"No more discussion about it," Daddy said.

And that was that.

Amber's own parents were very strict, too, so she did not feel insulted that night. We stayed best buddies; I would go to her house and we'd toy around with her Barbie dolls, braid each other's hair, play Chinese checkers, and eat cookies her mother made for us.

Amber and I would sometimes go to the neighborhood swing set and push ourselves up as high as we could, daring each other to jump, but neither one of us did so. Thirsty and sweaty, we'd run back to her house and guzzle down cold apple juice, our eyes gazing over the rims of our glasses at each other. On a sugar high, we soon erupted into giggle spasms, spewing juice all over.

Our friendship remained giddy and silly until I turned twelve in 1969, the same year that my parents and Rita and I watched Neil Armstrong take his first steps on the moon. It was also the year Dad walked to the altar after the preacher's sermon. I, too, got down on my knees, asking for forgiveness for all my mean thoughts and I accepted Christ into my heart.

But six years later, I rebelled against God because Mom and Dad had told me and Rita to never expect a penny from them or anything else after I graduated from high school. I forgave them easily enough as the years went on, but I am still trying to forgive myself.

*****

Today I have a date with Dad and his wife, Merilee, whom he has treated as tenderly as the roses she grows. And Rita is joining the three of us—the first time in ten years. It's a miracle, really, because her mind still swells with old memories of his heavy-handedness.

As we slide into the back of the maroon Buick, I feel, like I have so many times, as if I am in the presence of God. Dad makes me think of big and enthralling things, like the impossible reality that we are all whirling around in the universe at 1,000 miles an hour on a big beautiful blue round rock. But it doesn't frighten me, that thought; it starts a delicious thrill in my deepest self.

I look at Dad's meticulous elegantly graying hair combed back. Merilee's artistry, no doubt.

"Dad, your hair makes you look like a millionaire from back here," I chirp.

Dad looks in the rearview mirror, making funny faces and kisses at himself. We all laugh, even Rita. He has been making fun of his own good looks ever since we can remember.

He looks at me now in the mirror. "Well, Renee, you're looking good yourself. For thirty-nine."

"Stop it, Dad," I say.

"Thirty-nine forever," he winks at Merilee.

"Oh, leave her alone, Grady," she says, smiling, shaking her head.

"To Bogey's we go," Dad says, winking at me in the rearview mirror. I did wish I looked about ten years younger. The first time Dad ever told me that I looked pretty, I thought I would die of happiness. After Mom and Dad had divorced, Rita and I stayed with Mom, whose new lecherous boyfriend soon-to-become-husband Todd was living at our rented duplex half the time. She forbade me and Rita to see Dad, to which Rita gladly obliged.

One Saturday afternoon when everyone was out, Dad called to speak with me; my heart skipped a beat with joy. We made a date to have lunch the next weekend. At the Big M, he and I having second helpings of everything from the buffet counter, the world tilted on its axis. We talked about music, love, and the big rigs that pulled into the truck stop that day. My father learned to see me in a whole new light that day, as I did him. He became a little less God and a little more human and in some ways, even more frightening to me. Because people hurt other people, but God, being bigger and better, has no reason to hurt people. You would think, anyway.

*****

Merilee, Rita, and I watch Dad now as he pours caramel and fudge sauce over his three scoops of butter pecan ice cream over a split banana.

"Dad, where's the banana?"

Rita and Merilee crack up.

Dad gives us his mock movie-star grin, bobbing his head. "They never give you enough of the stuff to make it sweet," he says.

Merilee kisses him on the cheek. Rita rolls her eyes and glances at me.

We are going to have a good time, I am determined. This is my family. I dip into my own cold creamy Fudge Delight. Heaven in a sundae, to be sure.

Rita and Merilee dig in to their own small scoops of mint chocolate chip ice cream, and we all eat quietly for a few moments. It gives me a chance to watch Dad and Merilee together. With her halo of chin-length light-brown hair, Merilee is pretty in the plain way that fifty-something women can be. She hasn't spent hardly any time in the sun, so her skin is still soft and supple. Her voice is kitteny sweet. I watch as she wipes ice cream from the corners of Dad's lips, smiling, her eyes crinkling.

"I'm starting to get an ice cream headache," Rita says, puckering her mouth.

"Here's what you do," Dad says. "Breathe in with your mouth open, no ice cream, of course, then breathe out with your mouth closed. Out through your nose so it will warm the air."

"Nah, that's okay. I'll suffer and enjoy."

Merilee sighs, puts her ice cream down. "It's so good to see both of you together," she tells me and Rita. "Reminds me of the times when I'd see you girls sitting in church. You always looked so darling. So well behaved, in cute dresses".

"Us cute? I thought your daughter was as beautiful as a princess. I remember I always wanted to look just like her. She always had that perfect hair," I say.

"You girls did look good," Dad says to Rita and me.

I look at Rita who's already looking at me, her eyebrows raised.

Dad clears his throat. "Renee, I've come across something that I think you will really like," he says, his blue eyes focused on me.

"Yes?"

"Remember a young man by the name of Devon? That you liked?"

My heart skips a beat. Even after all these years. I stare at Dad.

"I've got a video of him," he says.

"What?"

"From the Weather Channel. He's a tornado scientist."

17

Devon. Tornados. But of course. I wrote poems about him in my English Lit class when our teacher assigned us to write a pretend eulogy about someone we knew. Of all things, of all people, I wrote about Devon. Somewhere in my head and heart, I got a vision that Devon would be studying clouds and ice and storms, harnessing the ways of the wind. Except that the wind got him one day.

Dad winks at me. "I always knew you liked him a lot."

"Dad, oh, Dad, do you have this tape? Can I—can we—go see it now?"

Merilee laughs. "I think somebody still has a thing for him."

"No!" I take a deep breath. "No. I just always thought—I knew—he would be a great scientist. Knew it when I was fourteen. But nobody believed me."

"All I know is that you drove me crazy with your constant talking about him. Devon this and Devon that," Rita says, raising her eyebrows at me. Though younger than I by just fifteen months, Rita could still make me feel just two feet high sometimes.

"It's okay if you still have feelings for him," Merilee insists.

I can hardly believe what I am hearing. "I don't have those kinds of feelings. I'm married, remember? He'll just always be somebody special." I sigh. "When can I see the video?"

Dad looks at his watch. "In about fifteen minutes. As soon as I finish the last of this chocolate at the bottom, we'll go."

*****

"Good-looking young man, has quite an Adam's apple," Dad remarks like a sportscaster at a baseball game. Devon looks exactly the same on the Storm Chasers video as I remember him from my younger days.

I can't believe we are all sitting around watching the image of a man I wanted to marry and whose children I would gladly have had—even though I was never goo-goo-gaga for kids like most other women are. But I never even got to date the guy, much less kiss him. Given half a chance, maybe I would have turned out like most women—married for good, with kids, growing in love and in the waistline, placid, patient.

On the television screen, Devon stands tall and lanky, dark hair over piercing blue eyes peering through binoculars with a team of tornado chasers speeding in a van on the Texas plains. The camera switches to the van's interior where Devon sits turning knobs and dials on computers and panel boards. "A Number Four coming straight at us from ten o'clock," he says into the radio.

He and the other tornado chasers scramble to get the equipment and cameras ready. The black tube in the sky drops to the ground several miles away from them. The tube morphs and twists on the wind-torn landscape.

I think back to fifteen years ago when Devon had sent me a letter after I'd first written to him. In the letter, he said that he could have fallen in love at the drop of a hat. My heart dropped to my knees when I read that. I would have driven nonstop to meet up with Devon, but I knew he would have smelled the wine seeping from my pores. I was drinking nearly all day to blot out abuses, both past and present. Besides, I was married, not to Mark, but to a poor lost soul who I thought would save mine. So instead of driving nonstop to my first true love, I fell onto the mattress on my bedroom floor and wept sorely, ashamed down to my toes that a jug of wine and a mixed-up marriage stood between me and Devon. Not too long after that letter, Aunt Sophia mailed me a newspaper clipping. Devon had married—his bride was blond, a pharmacist. A pharmacist? He could have had me, a poet, a writer, a photographer. And so the dream of ever talking to him again died forever.

"In all its advances, science has never been able to predict weather, the heart of nature. And I don't think we ever will. The best we can do is make an intelligent guess," Devon says on the television screen.

I sink my head between my knees and watch the auburn locks of my hair fall one by one.

– 2 –

To THIS DAY, SUNDAY mornings have that sparkly-clean feel about them, along with a heightened sense of expectation, something like Christmas. And this day, a Sunday, I am going to the kids' church, a tiny Baptist church on Fifth Avenue not far from where Mom and Rita and I lived together for a short while with Todd, her second husband after Mom and Dad had divorced. As I drive to the church, I refuse to think too much of all the things that I didn't like about that time; instead, I picture all the little good things, me and Rita spending hours goofing around at the playground up the street, hanging upside down from the monkey bars—yes, even when I was seventeen years old, she, sixteen. We would go sky high in the huge swings when the shadows were long, and we could hear the frogs begin their evening anthem. I remember when Mom opened her birthday gift from me of a brand-new coffee percolator; her old one had made horrible whining noises and took forever to brew. I remember, too, the year that Rita and I both were home—as much as it could be called home, that duplex on Fifth Avenue—on Christmas vacation from the Navy and we were both high on life and energy. I had fallen hard for Kurt, a boy two years older than I—he was an artist in the Navy Computer School with me in San Diego. On New Year's Eve that year, Rita and I were home alone, restless, playing music, and after I'd talked to Kurt on the phone and he'd told me he loved me, I hung up yelling and dancing and hugging Rita. We both scrammed from that apartment and went running and skipping up and down the sidewalks, screaming "Happy New Year!"

I smile thinking of all this as I turn into the parking lot at the New Life Baptist Church. My nieces and nephew Evan have been attending here for a couple of years. The pastor is good to them, Heather has told me.

As soon as I open the door of the fellowship hall, I see that Heather is already in Sunday school. She gets up, introduces me, and all the women nod politely at me and then get back to their study. Reading the passages of the Bible along with the other women, I steal glances at Heather. She is completely wrapped up in the discussion, hovering close to the pastor's wife.

When Sunday school is over, kids pour out of one of the class-rooms, and Gemma comes running to me. Evan and Camille emerge from their classrooms, too, and Heather joins the whole troop as we head toward the sanctuary.

Marvin Payne, the pastor, greets me and shakes my hand. "You must be Aunt Renee," he says. I nod, proudly.

The kids and I take a seat in the second and third rows. Gemma scoots up right next to me. I feel like a mama hen with her chicks snuggled up under her. I only wish that Derrick was here with us. He doesn't do church, the kids told me.

We stand and sing "The Old Rugged Cross" all together; I bring the hymnal down lower so that Gemma can see it. She keeps gazing up at me with smiles, and I squeeze her tiny shoulders. I glance back at Camille, Evan, and Heather behind us; Evan and Camille are look-ing around slightly bored; Heather is singing beside the pastor's wife.

When Pastor Marvin begins the sermon, he has us open our Bibles to Ephesians. Again, Gemma motions for me to let her follow along. Gemma is only five years old, and already church is like a second home to her. It must run in the family, I think, remembering how Grandma Bell would hold me and caress my hair when we sat in church together.

I can barely pay attention to Pastor Marvin as he preaches because I am so completely wrapped up in Gemma. She bows her head when it's time for the Lord's Prayer, and I take her little hand in mine. I get the godly goosebumps on my arms and legs. I can hardly believe the grace God has bestowed upon me. He knows where I've been and what I've done, but He forgave me and He calls me His own and has placed me in a family.

*****

21

After church, I drive the kids over to a sandwich shop. It takes nearly twenty minutes for the guy behind the counter to make all our sandwiches. Time goes slower here than in California, much slower, but I do my best to savor the moments, letting the kids tell the sandwich maker what they want. Then off to Crystal Park we go to meet Mom who is waiting for us there. She is already near the ponds, bending down low, talking to the Canadian geese.

The kids pile out of the car and run up to her; the geese honk and strut.

"Sorry, big guy, we don't have any food," Mom says.

"Yes, we do," Gemma says. "Sandwiches!"

The kids and I laugh. A chill kicks up in the breeze. I look up at the sky filling with gray clouds.

Heather looks up, too, shrugs her shoulders. "It'll pass," she says.

"Let's go to the swings," I say. I've always loved swings. No bad memories are associated with them. One of the most special times I had on a swing was with Devon. Yes, Devon.

The kids spill out of my car and Mom's. I get out the sandwiches and big bag of potato chips and half a dozen cans of root beer; Mom, a pan of her famous triple chocolate brownies. We all meet at the picnic bench and start to dig in.

"Wait!" I say. "Let me pray first."

We all bow our heads. I say the same prayer that Rita and I used to recite at dinner time when we were kids: God is good, God is great, we thank You for this food. Amen.

We are all ravenous, talking around the food in our mouths. I rip open the bag of chips and the kids lunge for them. It's all perfect, except I wish Derrick were here. I ask why he did not come.

"He keeps to himself," Evan says, cramming potato chips in his mouth.

"Probably out at the creek," Heather says.

"What's he do out there?" Mom asks.

"Fishing, looking at bugs," Heather answers.

"Bugs?"

"Yeah. It's a Derrick thing. Always has been since I can remember," Evan says.

Evan is right. I think of the first time I met Derrick, in 1990, the year that Rita and Zach got married. Rita and I would both marvel in the weird specimens that Derrick brought into the house. Neither Rita nor I were ever scared, because we both had been a little buggy in our own childhoods. Rita liked to creep up on what she called "cucumber bugs," the little green striped insects that would eat away at the elm trees in the back. Grinning big, she'd pull their little legs off as punishment for their chewing on elm leaves.

"I know you hate them, but even though they're bugs, they don't deserve to suffer this way," I'd plead with her.

"They're horrible and mean and they deserve to die," she'd say.

I was always uncomfortable about that, knowing that she funneled her frustration and rage at the bugs. Still, she did like creeping, crawling things with too many legs and would hold them in her hand, her hair falling over her face as she studied them.

The wind kicks up again, swishing our napkins off the picnic table. Gemma races off to get them.

"Let them be," Heather says, shaking her head.

"Anyone want brownies yet?" Mom holds her spatula midair.

"Oh, heck, yes," Evan bursts out.

Mom raises her eyebrows in question marks over her big eyes. But she lets it go.

"I remember when you used to let Rita and me have your brownies for breakfast, Mom," I say.

"I did?" Mom says, her eyebrows going up again. She lifts up with the spatula a luscious brown square and places it on Evan's paper plate.

"Yeah, we were never breakfast people too much," I say.

"Neither are we," Gemma says, watching Mom dishing out the treats.

By now we are all stuffing our faces with Mom's most excellent brownies. That's what she should name them. I want her recipe box someday.

In the middle of our taste of heaven, a loud boom crackles around us. My hair stands on end.

Heather wipes her hands of the chocolate goo. "Who's with me on the swings?"

I race off with her, laughing as much from the fun as the sugary high we all have. Gemma and Camille are behind us and even Mom. Within seconds, I am pumping my legs to go higher and higher. "Meet you up at the top!" I yell, all bliss.

Heather's and Camille's faces grimace as they work their legs harder. Evan sits in his swing, nonchalant as can be. And Mom just pushes herself off gently. Suspended, swinging, all of us, beneath the clouds growing heavier and grayer by the second. Heather and Camille wave at me as they breeze by me, pretty pendulums. Evan lets out a Tarzan yell; the kids and I echo him. Mom daintily pumps and pulls on her swing, humming to herself. I soar into the sky, pushing my feet against the heavy clouds.

Just then a spackle of lightning cracks across the sky; the voice of God booms like I've never heard. Heather and Camille whoop it up, and Evan does another Tarzan yell. I slow my swinging down and watch Mom looking at the sky. Another finger of lightning scratches across the clouds, another burst of thunder.

"Okay, we need to go. It's not safe now," Mom says.

Camille and Heather jump from their swings, the rest of us slow down toward the ground. By now, great drops of rain are plummeting our heads and arms and hands. It is glorious.

– 3 –

MY HAIR HAS A life of its own. I am glad that I let it grow out really long; otherwise, the humidity would turn these tresses into a mat of curls. Now I simply pull it all into a heavy ponytail. My heart is pounding, not so much from the three cups of bad coffee at the breakfast buffet included with the motel stay but from nervousness. Today is the day I interview Mom and Aunt Sophia. I will not tell them anything of the other day with Dad and Merilee and Rita. And Devon.

With all the commotion starting again in my heart and mind, I am grateful to hear cardinals singing in the trees as I approach Mom and Aunt Sophia waiting on the front porch for me. Aunt Sophia has set out glasses of iced tea. She opens her arms into a big hug.

"Oh, how do you stay so skinny? It's not fair," she says.

"Thanks, but I'm not so skinny. I'm hiding an expanding middle section."

Aunt Sophia pokes around my waist. If it were anyone else doing this, I'd be steaming mad. I don't like people touching me much.

"Where's the fat?" Aunt Sophia jokes. She and I laugh.

I sit down in a white wicker chair next to Mom looking at old photo albums.

"Look at this," Aunt Sophia says, holding up a picture of her and Mom, both nineteen years old.

"It's hard to believe I was so skinny," Mom says.

I look at the photo. Aunt Sophia and Mom are reclining on the hood of her father's Chevy Impala. Aunt Sophia's long legs are shapely and thin, her lipsticked mouth in a pouty pucker like Rita Hayworth. Mom is looking up toward the camera, smiling as though she knows a secret about the photographer.

I let out a sigh, putting down the picture. "You are both beautiful," I say.

For more than forty years, Mom and Aunt Sophia have been best friends. They first met each other in 1954 when they both worked as cashiers at the five-and-dime store. Neither one of them were very popular girls at school because they did not drink or go to any of the dances. Mom met her future husband—my dad—when Aunt Sophia introduced her brother to Mom.

Aunt Sophia arranges herself on the porch swing. "I'm glad we have the photos out. But you know, what we're doing right now? Just sitting out and talking? Your mom and I do this all of the time, Renee. We're still old-fashioned. We don't have to have fancy cars and big houses," she says. She looks at Mom. "We've always had fun, like going on vacations together. Haven't we, Margie?"

Mom's eyes widen in that comical way she has. "Oh, you bet!"

I feel a prickle of envy. "And why couldn't Rita and I have come along on those trips you used to take in the summer, Mom?"

Mom does not miss a beat. "It was an unhealthy marriage. All your dad wanted to do was work," she says.

This does not answer my question, but I know that just getting out of the house was what she wanted to do back then. So she left me and Rita to boil hot dogs for dinner. Actually, with her out of the house, Rita and I could breathe a little easier, that undercurrent of unrest having vanished with Mom. Not only did we feel lighter in our step—even Dad did—Rita could eat the entire meal without gagging. We could actually look each other in the eyes and make moon-faces while we jubilantly ate hot dogs with all the fixings and bowls of vanilla ice cream with Hershey's chocolate sauce. Dad would half ignore my and Rita's chatter in a good-mannered way, looking up at the sky through the yellow-curtained windows. I knew he was daydreaming about travelling by himself, visiting faraway places. He got that same dreamy look when he sat in his big easy chair, staring at the maps in Randall's World Atlas.

Those days when Mom was gone, I felt a freedom like our parakeet Smarty must have felt when we let him out of the cage. During the dog days of August when Mom was gallivanting around with

Aunt Sophia and my Grandma Howell on the beach in Galveston, Texas, I perfected my Hula-Hoop routine in our backyard. I could make three hoops rotate around me, one at the knees, one at the waist, the other around my neck. On Saturday evenings, Dad and Rita and I would eat popcorn while we watched *My Three Sons*. On Sundays, we watched all the TV nature shows like Mutual of Omaha's *Wild Kingdom*. I never had to worry about getting my mouth washed out with soap because I said "golly" when I watched a deer bound away from a stalking lion. Dad either didn't hear or didn't think it was as important as Mom did.

So hard it was to love both of them together. So easy it was to love my father from afar. And so difficult it had been to earn the love of my mother.

Now I look into Mom's dark eyes, glad that time, among other things, eventually made tender my heart for her. I look forward in this interview to finding out what makes Mom Mom.

"We've been everywhere together, so many states," Aunt Sophia says now. "Swimming in the Gulf of Mexico. That should have been your mom and your dad having all that fun."

"Don't I know it," Mom says.

"We did go on a vacation to Colorado once. Me and you and Dad," I say to Mom.

"Was it fun?" Aunt Sophia asks.

I pause for two seconds. "No."

"Really? Now, see, I don't even remember that," Mom says.

Aunt Sophia and I share a look. We're both thinking that it could be two things: the mind's way of purposefully forgetting or the heavy use of pain pills for the last twenty years. Mom has had three back surgeries. I don't know if the cause has been anatomical or ghost pains.

"Mom, we all slept in a cabin. It was kind of pretty where we were, remember?" I said, thinking about Dad driving and having the radio on with Roberta Flack singing "Killing Me Softly," my soul's song that summer.

Mom had been on one of her emotional rampages, laying insults into me like nails through my heart. All the while, Dad continued

27

to drive without a word with his uncanny ability to block everything out. He told me just a couple of years ago that he always regretted that he had never spoken up for me that hellish week. But I don't want to tell any of this to Mom now. Why replant old thistles? I don't want to get even. I just want to get in a good place.

"So was it a bad time?" Mom implores me with her big brown eyes.

"Not really. I remember at one point we were somewhere in a park around Colorado Springs, and Dad got out of the car and we all watched him as he walked around staring at the trees and mountains. Then he got back in the car and said, "Well, if I ever could live anywhere else, it would be here.'"

"He said that?" Mom asks.

"He wasn't happy," Aunt Sophia says.

I understood Dad's meditation in the woods that day. He wanted to be in love with God. Only then could he be in love with anyone else.

"I think he knew I wasn't happy either," Mom says. "If it hadn't been for Sophia, I would have been—who knows where?"

I shift in my seat, wanting to change the subject. "Weren't there times when you two got really angry with each other?" I ask Mom and Aunt Sophia.

"No," they both say.

"That's got to be impossible. Like that time when we moved away."

"But there weren't words between your mother and me," Aunt Sophia says. "We talked with her about it, and it probably got a little old because my grandma and mother were always wanting to know if you kids were being treated right."

"We all were living so close together," Mom said. "But then if things had been just right, that wouldn't have been a problem."

I take a sip of my tea, thinking. I cannot help wondering when things are just right with anybody. Had Aunt Sophia, my grandparents, and great-grandparents not lived within a stone's throw of our house, no telling what would have happened to me and Rita. Love works whether or not things are perfect. In fact, because things are not perfect, love covers a multitude of errors. Love saves lives.

"Well, Margie, can you really ever remember when you and I got really tiffed at each other?"

Tiffed was Grandma Howell's word for getting into arguments.

"No, I can't," Mom says.

"And if we didn't agree with each other, we didn't say anything. Same thing today," Aunt Sophia says.

I find that a bit much to swallow. But Mom nods in agreement.

"If we agree, we really agree. But if we don't agree—"

"Then so be it," Mom says.

"There's not very many people like us," Aunt Sophia said. "The way we get along. There's not a whole lot of people I'd want to spend that much time with either."

"We just have a ball. Laughin' and carryin' on," Mom says.

How true I know this to be. The whole family has always been like this. Laughter was another thing that saved my soul growing in the house right next door. That and singing, all of us jouncing along in the pickup truck. Back then, there was no law forbidding people to ride in the bed of the truck. So all of us women would have the time of our lives making up silly songs in the back of the pickup truck on our little jaunts out into the country. We'd let our voices shake and jumble as we rode along the rutted dirt roads. The men— my dad, Uncle Jerry, Grandpa Howell, and Grandpa Bell—crammed themselves into the cabin of the truck. Those times of going to gather gourds out in the fields or to snoop around the city dump or just to get ice cream out west in the pretty little town of Sterling were the best times. They were times that helped me trust in family.

A blue jay swoops down from a tree and swipes a hair from Aunt Sophia's coiffed hair. After our initial shrieking, we laugh like crazy. And then I hear the lullaby of a freight train starting its way up the track. Good-by-y-y-ye, it wails. The wind starts picking up. I blink back tears. The nameless sadness is burrowing into my heart again. It is time to go.

"I've got to get ready to see Rita and the kids this afternoon," I say.

We hug and then I take off, Mom and Aunt Sophia still on the front porch, watching me as I stir up clouds of dust with my rental car.

I need to clear my head before I see Rita and her kids, my three nieces and two nephews. It takes only ten minutes to drive out to dirt roads stretching for miles across fields and farms. I stop the car by a wheat field, put in a cassette tape of Vivaldi's Four Seasons, turn up the volume, and stretch my arms wide. The violently sweet strains of violin music overtake me, waxing me nostalgic. Why is it that when we were young and full of energy as kids, we did not notice the beauty around us? It must be that we were all wanting the attention from other people, hungry as kittens for it. We couldn't see any further than ourselves. I gaze now over the waves of amber and do a pirouette with my arms outstretched toward my Maker.

*****

By the time I get to Rita's house, I am hungry. I am also anxious about what we will do for dinner. From the time she was six or seven years old, Rita has never been able to eat in front of others very comfortably. The sounds and sights of people chewing upset her, but the real culprit lay in the constant criticisms she endured from my parents. Especially Mom.

While I tended to try and rise to the level of performance that our parents expected, Rita rebelled. The sight and smell of food turned her stomach. It was everything she could do to eat what Mom put on her plate. Sometimes my parents would get so disgusted with her they sent her to her room, which Rita was always secretly happy about.

I turn into the dirt driveway to Rita's house, a shell of the place that used to be Grandma and Grandpa Fraser's house. When Rita and I were kids, Grandpa ran a gas station in front of the house. On days that Mom drove us out here, Grandpa Fraser greeted us, wiping his hands on a greasy rag. His face would crinkle up with a big smile and he'd ask us what soda pop we wanted from his old-fashioned vending machine. It was the only time that Rita and I drank pop. We always asked for a Coca-Cola or Orange Crush, watching Grandpa as he wrenched off the pop-tops of the ice-cold bottles. Then Rita and I would go inside the house where Grandma was invariably watching *I Love Lucy* while ironing mountains of clothes.

But now the front door bursts open, and Rita's five kids come slamming down the stairs to greet me. I bend down to hug them all, my heart blushing as much as the sun has pinked my cheeks. Rita appears in the front door, an enigmatic smile on her face.

"Hello, sister," she says, flipping back her long dark hair. I can really see the Cherokee in her.

I go to her, we hug. I smell soap and something of a burnt nature.

Gemma and Camille are tugging at my shorts. "Where we gonna go?" Gemma asks. I peer down at her and take her hand. Derrick, Evan, and Heather are poking around between the house and the yard.

"Hey, what are you guys looking for?"

"Toads," Derrick says.

"Ahhh, be nice to them," I say. Camille runs off to poke around with the boys, Gemma tagging after her.

"So," I say, looking at Rita. "You hungry? My treat."

Zach comes out the door just then. He walks over to me, arms outstretched. I stand on my tiptoes to hug him.

"Good to see ya," he says.

"And you, too."

"You like a beer?"

"Ah, no, thanks. I'm actually hungry. Was thinking I could take y'all out for pizza or something."

"Let's go inside," Zach said.

"Aunt Renee, look!"

In the moment I take to stop and look back at them, I am hurtling heavenward quick prayers of thanks for the sweet sounds of these little ones calling to me. Though I knew I would never have children of my own, in my wildest dreams as a kid, I had no conception that the love of my own sister's kids would drive me to use my savings to fly out once a year just to feel their little arms around me and listen to their little voices tell me things.

Evan is holding a toad in his hand, with Camille begging for her turn.

I get my camera ready. "Camille, hold the toad real close to your face," I say, focusing in on her cute little pixie face.

She does so. "Okay, now pretend to kiss the toad."

She screws up her face, giggles, and then looks the toad in the eyes. The toad's throat is moving up and down. Camille purses her lips toward the frog and I take the picture. Everyone laughs, and Camille puts the toad down. We all watch it hopping away.

"Hey, Rita, is it okay if I take the kids out for a little while? There's still plenty of light out and I want to take them around and then get hamburgers. That okay?"

Rita does a mock scolding, crossing her arms over her chest and tapping her foot. "Well, I guess," she says mischievously. She turns to Zach. "That okay with you?"

He shrugs his good-natured big bear way. "Sure. Just be back before midnight," he teases.

"Zach and I are gonna get down tonight with some music. Hang out with us," Rita says, looking at me straight on, unnerving me.

"Okay," I say quickly. "Kids? You're coming with me."

I promise Heather the front passenger seat and they all pummel into the car. Their energy magically lifts from me the thin shawl of sadness cloaking me on this trip.

"Where we going?" Heather asks, chomping chewing gum.

"To the world's longest elevator," I say.

"Where's that?" Derrick asks.

"Right here in Wheaton," Heather pipes in, all toothy grin.

"That's right."

The kids all start that giddy half-singing, half-arguing thing that even Rita and I used to do when we were this young. I join in on their mock-bickering while I drive the mile to the elevator. The sun is slanting in so strong that I have to put the visors down for Heather and me. Here it is, six thirty in the evening, and it will be light still for another two hours. I am lapping it up.

I turn into a dirt road that takes us where trucks are lined up behind the elevator. A hum emanates from the long gleaming white structure looming in front of us. A thing of beauty, really.

The kids all scramble out of the car. "What're we doin' here?" Evan demands to know, his eyes scrunched up from the sun shining squarely on him.

"I'm taking a photo of all of you," I say, grabbing my camera. "I want y'all to stand at each of the walls by the elevator. Gemma, you go to the first wall. Camille, you're next, and then the rest of you lined up."

"But wait," I tell Camille who has grabbed Gemma's hand. "You hear that sound? From the elevator? The humming?"

They listen, look at each other, nod.

"That's the sound of the air-conditioning inside the elevator. Guess what happens if the wheat doesn't get cooled," I say.

"Wheat gets too hot?" Heather says, and we all laugh.

"Yes. And that would cause friction and eventually a fire would start. This whole elevator building would blow up."

"Oh, cool!" Evan says.

"Yes, cool," I say, laughing along with the kids.

They all run up to the elevator and put their ears to the building to hear the humming better; I do the same. The sound reminds me of the noise of the ventilation in the old First Church of the Nazarene building on Sunday mornings. I'd hear that groan-like hum and imagine that God was tuning his ear to us.

After I take their pictures next to the big breathing elevator, I shuttle the kids to Dairy Queen for hamburgers and shakes. We sit at the one table outside, and when the railroad bells go off, we all raise our voices to hear each other better. When the freight train makes its approach, the conductor honks the horn so loud that we cover our ears laughing. When the noise dies down a little, I get them to play guessing games.

"What is the train carrying?" I ask them.

"Horse manure," Evan says,

We girls all groan; Derrick laughs.

"Horses," Gemma says, plumping out her pretty pink skirt around her lap.

"Oh, I hope not. There were no breathing holes for them," Heather says.

"Toys," Camille says, barely audible. I smile at her.

"It's probably wood or scrap iron. That's what a lot of them carry around here. But I just love trains," I say, getting dreamy.

Derrick and Evan elbow each other, roll their eyes.

"Don't they have trains where you live?" Derrick asks.

"Yes, they do. But Kansas trains are real special."

And I tell them the story of trains and me and my grandparents and Mom and Aunt Sophia when I was a kid two years younger than Gemma.

One afternoon, when I was about five years old, Grandpa Bell had called Mom and she agreed for all us to go with them and Grandma and Grandpa Howell and Aunt Sophia to go to the train station at Newton. He called Mom to see if she and I would like to join up with them all, including Aunt Sophia. Mom smiled at me often and looked pretty in her floral print dress. When we arrived, we bought donuts at the bakery across the street. Then we went back to the station and sat on the wooden plank benches.

We were all happy as we ate our chocolate frosted donuts. The day was warm and the smell of the wood of the train tracks mixed acridly with my mother's perfume. We heard the cry of the train whistle coming into town.

"Get ready for a whole lot of noise," Grandpa Bell said, laughing. It surprised me because he never said very much. He loved those trains.

Sure enough, when the train came lumbering by, it was so loud we had to put out donuts in our laps and cover our ears. Steam billowed as the train screeched to a stop. As the people got off the train, we went back to eating our donuts. My grandmas, Aunt Sophia, and Mom talked about the clothes that the different women were wearing. I listened to the music of their voices, nearly lulled to sleep by its sound and my belly full of sweetness.

"Want another donut?" Mom asked me. I nodded and reached for a maple éclair. The dough was so soft I was afraid it would melt in my hand as I bit into the creaminess.

All of us watched the train as it moved off the platform and down the track to some other destination.

"Will there be another one?" I asked.

"Oh, yes," Grandma Howell said. "Newton is a train town."

And another one did chug in about ten minutes later, coming in from the other direction.

Grandpa Bell checked his watch.

"It's right on time," he said.

The big black iron horse brought in the smell of oil and grease. A mirage of heat bounced off the tire tracks. I felt warmed by all the busy-ness, the hustle and bustle of everyone. Too soon it was time to go. My mother took my hand and we all walked chattering and making plans to come again soon to Newton.

*****

Gemma tugs at my arm. "We gotta go home now. It's getting dark," she says.

In the car they are all quiet and on the edge of sleep. Except for Heather, who is sitting in the front seat. She asks me if her mother had been with me that day in Newton. I do not know, do not remember. By the time I turn into the driveway at Rita's house, the sky has gone black. I turn off the engine and let out my breath.

Heather stirs the other kids awake, and I get Gemma from the backseat. She takes my hand and walks sleepily up the short flight of stairs into the darkened living room. The other kids follow, mumbling and yawning. They head down toward the basement where they all sleep. I don't like looking down into that dank, dark space.

Rita and Zach are drinking a brand of beer I don't recognize and listening to Fleetwood Mac on the tape deck. "Hey, girl, join us and stay for a while," Rita says, handing me a can of beer.

"Thanks, but you know I don't like beer. Gives me gas," I say.

"Humph, you still drink wine?" Rita asks.

"I do, yes," I say, nervous, looking around the living room. I really don't want to party down.

"Sorry, but we don't have any here," Rita says. "Zach, turn up the music a little."

Zach reaches for the volume control on the tape deck.

"So what's new, sista?" Rita asks.

I tell her and Zach about my adventures with the kids for the day. "I can't thank you enough for those kids of yours," I tell Rita.

Rita gives me one of her enigmatic smiles. Zach puts his arm around her. And then our favorite Fleetwood Mac song comes on, "Gypsy." Rita and I get up and dance and sing to each other around the living room. When Stevie Nicks finishes her crooning, Rita and I sit down, both of us sighing and smiling. Zach hands me a beer; this time I take it. Sometimes having a beer with my sister and her husband is the right thing to do.

*****

There was never any alcohol in the house at 2206 Sherman Street where Rita and I grew up. Except for that one afternoon when we had just come home from school and Mom wasn't around. We were used to her being out evenings on her Avon route, going door to door selling bottles of perfume and nail polish. But it was mid-afternoon and there should have been something cooking on the stove. No sign of her anywhere, so Rita and I snooped around and we discovered a crushed beer can in the living room. She and I looked at each other wide-eyed. Dad would have a conniption fit upon finding such a thing in the house. And then Rita reached down and picked up another beer can. Rita looked at me. "Do you think…"

She didn't have to finish the question because we were both imagining the same thing. About a year before, Mom had developed a friendship with the rough-and-tumble people up the street. They rode motorcycles, smoked, and drank. The man's name was Max, which I always thought would be a name for a dog, and I can't remember now the wife's name, probably because she was hardly ever around when Max and Mom got together.

One day hotter than blazes, Rita and I had to go along with Max and Mom to a lake south of Wheaton. It was really just a mucky green swimming hole. As Rita and I waded out with Max and Mom, I felt a mossy squishiness sliding around my toes and legs and a sickening squirminess in my heart and stomach. I dared not breathe aloud the words, "Who are you and what do you want with my mother?"

Rita and I swam near each other guardedly, silent. For as angry as I could get with her and as much trouble as she could get me into, I was grateful for her sticking close to me then, and in so many other small ways other times.

Now I take a sip of my beer. "Hey, I can't stay long. But there's something I want to ask you," I tell Rita.

"Okay, shoot."

"Do you remember when you and I went with Mom and our grandparents to see the trains at Newton?"

Rita puts down her beer. "I haven't thought of that in a long time," she says.

"So you were there with me."

"Well, yeah, you don't remember?"

I look up at the ceiling fan doing its whirligig thing. Rita stares at me. "Well?"

"No, I don't, sorry. So then what do you remember about it?"

Rita lets out a huge sigh, takes a sip from her beer. "I was hot and miserable," she says, pushing the bangs out of her face. "But happy, too, if that makes any sense."

It does, I think. It really does.

– 4 –

THIS MORNING IS AS luscious as the Snickerdoodle Cookie–flavored coffee I am drinking at Common Grounds, a little coffee place on Main Street. *I am at home here,* I write in my journal. A couple of ladies sitting at a table next to me are sharing a cheese Danish and talking amiably. In a corner by the window are two Amish women quietly chatting. They probably came in from Yoder, the little Amish town just twenty minutes away, where Mom and Aunt Sophia and I like to get sweet corn nuggets and fried chicken. Oddly, I don't ever remember seeing Amish people that much when I was growing up. But every time I've come out for a visit since Rita got married six years ago, it seems I am always coming across them. One year, I saw a whole group of them taking in the sights and sounds of the Third Thursday Art Walk in downtown Wheaton.

The caffeine is buzzing through my veins—I can no longer sit still. I am ready to meet with Mom and Aunt Sophia again.

When I pull into the shade of the trees across the street from Aunt Sophia's house, I can see both of them already sitting on Aunt Sophia's porch decorated with wind chimes and potted plants. I can just imagine Aunt Sophia chirping about how I look as I get out of the car and walk toward them. She always teases me about how I make sure that my socks match with my shorts or shirt. As I walk up the porch, my mother's big brown eyes widen when she sees me. In the old days, she could cut me to shreds with fiery darts from her eyes. But these days, her eyes make me think of cinnamon and chocolate. She stretches out her arms to hug me. Aunt Sophia rushes over to kiss me on the cheek. I can smell her Desert Rose perfume, the same one she's worn for as long as I can remember.

"Hope you don't mind just water with lemon," Aunt Sophia says.

"It's perfect," I say, pulling out my tape recorder and note pad.

Mom asks me how it went with Rita and the kids last night. I tell her about the elevator escapade and the Dairy Queen dinner.

Then I clear my throat, take a sip of the water, and start the cassette recorder.

"So, Mom, what happened in the '80s when you and Todd were married? I mean, did you and Aunt Sophia stay friends?"

Mom reaches for a little plastic flower fan that squirts water from its flower face and brings it up to her face, staring at it as if it were an oracle.

"When I turned around, there were Aunt Sophia and your Grandma Howell," Mom says.

"We both nearly fell over our feet getting over to your mama. We just hugged and hugged," Aunt Sophia says.

"But wasn't there some kind of distance between you and Grandma Howell?" I ask Mom.

"Not really. I'd always thought a lot of her even though she'd been my mother-in-law and things seemed pretty strange for a while after your dad and I divorced."

"We missed her so much because we used to not even get perms unless we did all them together. We didn't cut our hair unless we did it all together. Or even got lunch, for that matter," Aunt Sophia says.

"And this reuniting with each other happened when you were still married to Todd, right, Mom?"

"That's right—1982."

I reflect for a moment. In 1982, I was getting blue-and-green bruises and old at twenty-five years, slipping into the underworld of self-destruction by drinking cheap wine. I was still blaming my past for my present.

Mom jumps into my thoughts. "Remember when we went to Eureka Springs on our way to Georgia?"

"How can I not?"

"You and Rita were scared of Todd, just plain scared. I don't think I realized it then just how much. You two sat in the backseat of that little Datsun and didn't say a word."

Oh, how I wish Mom could have said something back then, twenty years ago. But in a small corner of my mind, I recognized she was probably scared, too. And sick, not even knowing it. In Eureka Springs, we had had breakfast in a small restaurant in the town plaza. Rita and I perused the menu items.

"What's an omelet?" I asked Mom.

When she told me it was an egg dish made with cheese and other ingredients, I decided to order a cheese omelet, and so did Rita. Mom got pancakes. Rita and I tried to wave away the smoke of Todd's cigarette as we ate.

Afterward, we walked around the plaza. Mom said she needed to sit down for a while. She was acting funny, shaky. All of a sudden, she began thrashing about, her eyes rolled back, saliva dribbling out of her mouth. Todd yelled at me to get help, and my legs couldn't go fast enough. I felt as though her life depended on me, yet I was moving as slow as a turtle. When the ambulance did finally get to Mom, I felt just as I did when she was in that strange, hostile place that Dad had sent her when I was five, maybe six years old. Mom had held on to me as long as she could, there in the stairwell of that horrible place that I later found out was a mental hospital. Finally, Dad told Mom to let go of me. He didn't ever want me to cry, nor did Mom, both for reasons of quiet, but I didn't care then. I didn't, couldn't care. And I wailed loud, so loud that it pierced the echoing stillness of the hospital. My mother turned on the staircase, said that she loved me, then she walked on up, pausing to wave at me again. I had a lump in my throat so big that I couldn't eat food for days.

And it turned out that food was what Mom had needed all those years. Real food, not just pancakes, which is what had caused the attack. That long-ago morning in the emergency room in Eureka Springs, Mom looked so weak, trying to sit up straight after the doctor had revived her. He told us that she had hypoglycemia. Had had it for years. That's why she passed out behind the wheel of her car in 1971. That's why she's always had a secret stash of candy in the house. And that's why she used to sneak snacks of turkey all day long after Thanksgiving dinner was over. She had needed nourishment all along.

Insulinoma?

40

"You know, toward the end of their marriage in 1986, your mother had invited us over to dinner where she and Todd lived. His temper was unreal," Aunt Sophia says.

Mom takes a sip of her water, her eyes big and childlike peering over the top of her glass. Her left leg pumps up and down crossed over her right leg. Mom would never had the courage to leave Todd had it not been for Aunt Sophia's and Grandma Howell's support. In many ways, Mom had lived a sheltered life. Leaving Todd and striking out on her own was akin to my leaving home and joining the Navy at eighteen. A familiar misery was usually more acceptable than an unfamiliar one. I knew from personal experience.

It certainly helped Mom that about the same time she was considering leaving Todd, Aunt Sophia divorced Uncle Jerry and turned right around and married Albert, the love of her life. Whenever Albert and Aunt Sophia were around Mom and Todd, Albert wouldn't stand for any of Todd's cussing or lighting up a cigarette. Then one day, Todd went up to visit his parents by the Nebraska line, and Mom took the opportunity to start packing. Albert borrowed a great big construction truck from one of his construction buddies. He and Aunt Sophia garnered the help of his son Leland and his wife, and together they went over to Mom and Todd's house in the evening.

"We were scared to death that Todd would pull up while we were tearing the house apart," Aunt Sophia says. "We piled up that truck so high that there was one rocking chair that we couldn't get it to sit down good, so we put it on top of everything."

She and Mom start laughing.

"And Leland and his wife sat in that rocking chair and rode in it all the way to Wheaton," Aunt Sophia says.

"For real?" I am incredulous.

They both nod, and I bust out laughing, too.

"When Todd did find me later, everybody was around me—"

"Albert would not put up with any nonsense whatsoever—"

"And Todd asked me, 'Why did you do it?' Can you imagine that?" Mom says, blotting a tissue on her eyes.

"But it wasn't nearly the blowup we thought it would be. Now he has a wife who practically leads him around by his nose and tells him exactly what he's going to do and when he's going to do it. She rules the roost. That's what he needed," Aunt Sophia says, smoothing the back of her hair down. She turns her back to Mom. "Margie, is my hair standing straight up in back?"

"No, Sophia, you're fine."

"I don't know about me. I was wondering about my hair," Aunt Sophia says. "No matter what I do to it, it just won't behave."

"Do you want me to spritz some water on it?"

"Oh, please do! I could use a spritzing!" Their laughing mingles together with the chatter of sparrows in the trees behind us.

For a few minutes, Mom and Aunt Sophia and I engage in a spritzing war with the flower fan.

I sigh, full of gratitude and a sense of being complete. But it is time to go.

"Rita is expecting me at her place tonight for dinner. Can we do this again in a couple of days? I'm seeing Amber tomorrow."

Aunt Sophia's face falls. "Amber."

Mom smiles at me. "Whatcha goin' to do?"

"Take her for a drive somewhere with her daughter. When I come into town, it's like I'm her ticket to fun. Nobody else will spend any time with her."

"I admire you. I don't see how you could be so patient with her," Aunt Sophia says.

I can understand why Aunt Sophia would think that; Amber really is in another world, having to be put away in a mental hospital. Yet I couldn't see how I could not be so patient with Amber. Because I understand exactly what it means to be locked away from the world.

*****

The day that Amber told me that she was having to move with her family to Missouri, I thought God was making a cruel joke of our friendship. I just couldn't understand why he once again would take love away from me. Was I born with a curse? Amber was more resigned about her parents' decision. The last few times she and I were together, we had promised we would write each other all the time. But I was already spending so much time doing homework every night and writing in my journal, and then I had to go to bed with the chickens—as my mother liked to say—when there was still light in the sky at eight o'clock at night. On weekend mornings, so as not to wake up Dad, at least that's what Rita and I would tell ourselves, Mom would make me and Rita stay in bed so late that we got sweaty under the sheets. Rita and I missed more than half our adolescence because we spent it in bed or Mom kept us at home away from other kids our age. Going to church on Wednesday nights became a big night out, for me, anyway. I don't think Rita liked going to church.

On our last afternoon together before she moved away, Amber and I gave each other hugs and promised to write each other. We went into the kitchen and had lemonade, peering over the glasses at each other, choking and spewing out the cold liquid when we burst into giggles. Her brothers and parents just shook their heads at us as they hurried around the house with big boxes and crates.

I cried for the first couple of nights after Amber's news, eventually accepting that her moving away was just another letdown. Junior high drama soon kicked in at the rambling brownstone Central Junior High School where I was all gaga over Mrs. Knapp, my high-heeled social studies and English teacher, and sat in the back row with Devon and made car crash noises with him. Best time of my life, worst time. Began to get confusing concepts about whom I could love. Got a major crush on Mrs. Knapp and on nights when Mom was out on her Avon routes, I'd tell Dad about all the things that she had talked about in class and how she encouraged me in my writing. She was the first person who said that my writing was good enough to be published. Dad had met her at the Parent-Teacher Night and so he knew what she looked like, how she acted.

Those nights when Mom was out, Dad would cook hot dogs for me and Rita, and we'd slice the dogs in half, press them onto Rainbo Bread, dab on lots of pickle relish, squeeze mustard and catsup on our sandwiches and then chow down. We three were chatty-happy,

Rita and I teasing Dad about how much relish and mustard he'd put on his sandwich. I'd tell him about all the things that Mrs. Knapp talked about in social studies, and I'd look up at Dad to watch his reaction. He'd eat his hot dog sandwich, crunch a couple of Guy's Potato Chips, and tap his foot a couple of times on the floor, all the time looking out the window, dreamy-like. I secretly hoped that my teacher would become my mother. It was fun in a sad way, the three of us eating and talking because we were keeping it quiet from each other about how Mom drove us crazy.

But when I fell hard for Devon, when he went magically from boy to man almost overnight, everything had a different vibration. My friends tittered and whispered among themselves and spread it like wildfire that Devon and I were an item.

Fourteen-year-olds who bloom suddenly in love writhe in their own private hell. If they speak of their love, they are condemned. If they don't speak, they become feverish and skittish. I fell into both of these traps. Each evening after my homework was done, I wrote in my diary that Dad had brought home for me as a surprise one wintry day at suppertime. There were snow flurries behind him and cold wind rushing into the kitchen as he placed in my hand the little maroon gilt-edge-paged journal—with its own key. Mom looked at Dad like he'd lost his mind, but I thanked him, nearly breathless with emotion. No hug, because he didn't do that. If I had known how to bake a cake or cookies or brownies—if Mom had been willing to teach me the dozen times I'd asked her—I would have made my father something chocolatey and delicious and then relish the way he'd close his eyes and tap his foot against the floor as he took a bite of my gift to him.

That first evening with my new diary, I had a place to pen all of my sufferings, naming my little maroon book Jolene, taking the example from the Anne Frank who named her diary "Kitty." I'd read the famous diary the year before during Christmas vacation. Mom had been on one of her emotional binges and was stark raving mad about my and Rita's sniffles, but especially mine. She said that I didn't blow my nose enough. So she assigned me to write one thousand sentences, "I will blow my nose when I need to." In between the laborious handwriting of the words, sometimes doing them by columns of sentence fragments, like "I will blow"—I didn't catch the irony of that until years later—or finishing the last part of the last sentence first, in between all that, I'd sneak reads of *The Diary of a Young Girl*. Hungrily, I swallowed all the words and the emotions of Ann Frank, of her being in love with Peter and closed from the outer world. I was completely at home with her in that diary of hers. In my little maroon book, I wrote about the injustices of my own little world, about how other kids my age would bully and ridicule me about my feelings for Devon.

News about romance in junior high school spreads faster than wildfire, but my romance with Devon was just an imagined one. I had wanted to invite him to the Sadie Hawkins dance, and he was hoping I would ask him, but my parents said absolutely not. When I gave him the unfortunate news, Devon reported that his parents did not want him attending the dance either. So—both our parents were strict. But I had a feeling that his parents were loveable. With all his accomplishments and scholastic achievements, from winning the regional science contest with his feeding-aspirin-to-rats experiment to rousing audiences with his fantastical violin performances, his parents had to have been encouraging.

Yet all my miseries and mumblings went by the wayside as I read *The Diary of Anne Frank* in between the sentence writing marathon. I became deeply thankful for the house that I lived in with my family—troublesome as they were sometime—and for food and my own bed to sleep in, much more my own room where I could pen my thoughts at my desk. I said to myself, if I can remember that in just four years, I will be free from here. I can handle anything.

Amidst all the chaos of emotions and my having to write a thousand sentences, Amber was far from my thoughts—until the first letter from her arrived in the mail. Feeling guilty as could be, I carefully opened the envelope. She had written several pages in cramped handwriting that was hard to read. And she had quite a story to tell, a tragic tale.

Amber had been the object of a lot of teasing and abuse by kids her age in the Missouri town to which her family had moved. I could barely make sense of what she had written, except that something awful had happened to her on a hayrack ride and when she woke up, she couldn't remember what had happened. She ended up in some kind of mental hospital. She started having visions, I read in her letter, and here her handwriting became more of a scrawl, as if she were filled with excitement as she wrote. Visions of Jesus at her side, she wrote. Him talking to her, holding her.

Placing the letter down on my desk, I went back to writing sentences while I thought about what she had written. I was scared and confused. I would have loved to have Jesus come to me, but honestly, frightened, too. Who wouldn't be? And why did she have visits from Him when neither Rita nor I did? Maybe it was a blessing? For Amber that she did have them, and for us that we did not.

It was just all too much, and I put the letter and all thoughts about Amber aside. It was enough that I made it through each day; what's more, my parents mystified me about their own relationship with Christ. Were they followers of Him? Were Rita and I that bad that they would lose their patience with us, erase all evidence of their salvation? This must be what the preacher talked about all the time, back-sliding, going so far back from God that people bring hell on themselves.

I didn't pray much myself, except for crying out for help to Jesus. Always looking at that picture of Him in the hallway between Rita's and my room knocking at the door. I heard him, did He hear me crying? Maybe not, because I was very angry at Him.

And yet. And yet. I still was so glad in an elemental way that Mom, at least, went to church and took us along. Dad often did not. His way with God was sporadic, sometimes strong—one year for a few evenings we even did a family devotional with us kneeling, reading the Bible, and praying—but most of the time, Dad's way with God was secretive. He'd go off to the garage at any hour of the night to pray for hours, Mom told me years later. Privately, I admired that. If you have something big on your heart with God, you need your own space with Him.

One Sunday when Dad did come with Mom and us girls to church, as usual, Pastor Leon gave the congregation an altar call. Pastor Leon, I remember, had been particularly emotional and pleading with his congregation—with us—to come forward and receive the gift of eternal life. The softly playing organ music was the signal for us to stand up and begin singing, "Just as I Am." My voice was quivering, my hands sweaty. Then I saw our father stagger down the side aisle, his face contorted, making his way to the altar. Something in me broke and I rushed to the altar. Rita followed me.

Kneeling at the altar, a wash of tears coursed down my face. Rita was right beside me. I glanced over at Dad who was kneeling down low, his hands over his face. An old guy came to my and Rita's side and asked if we wanted to receive Jesus as our Savior. I looked up at him and nodded through a sheet of tears.

"Do you want to give your life to the Lord?" he asked. I again nodded. Sobbing, Rita, did the same.

The old man, a deacon most likely, and who was probably only in his fifties, but he looked ancient to me, held his hands over us, praying, asking God for His blessing on us and to receive us as His children. Rita and I remained at the altar, crying, happy. I understood then at that moment, what the preacher was always talking about when he said that Jesus would remove our sins and make us white as snow. There was a lightness in my heart, a new purpose. I wanted to love God and my family—my parents and my sister—as fully as I possibly could with all of my twelve-year-old heart and soul. I looked over to where Dad had been kneeling at the altar, but he was already gone. Rita and I smiled at each other in our newness, got up, took the Kleenex the deacon offered us and went back to our seats. Feeling squeaky clean, I joined in with the rest of the church singing the last lines of the invitational, "O Lamb of God, I come, I come."

*****

My being reborn was a miracle, a holy moment. In the weeks and months following my Salvation Sunday, as I began to think of it, I savored the moment I gave my life to God, tried living up to my positon as a born-again girl. One Sunday when the preacher gave a sermon about being sanctified, I was confused. I thought it had been a done deal, this being born again. So I asked Mom one summer afternoon while I was having a peanut butter sandwich in the kitchen. She was busily styling one of her many wigs, the blank pallid face of the dummy head peering up at Mom while she took her rat-tail comb and teased up nests of hair from the curls.

"What does sanctification mean? How do you do it?" I asked her.

"I don't know," she said, vigorously teasing the wig with her brush.

"How do I find out?"

"Not sure," she said, pulling the bangs of the wig down onto the dummy head.

In all fairness to Mom, I think most people don't understand what sanctification is—that long journey of walking with Christ sharing in His sufferings. All I knew at the time was that I wanted to be a good girl down to my toes. But I can remember the horrid moment when I realized that I would indeed tell a lie—not only tell it but also plan it—when I knew that I was catching a cold or just getting sinusitis again. I knew what was coming: Mom would glare at me as if I'd done something bad, she'd stick the thermometer in my mouth, and I'd suck air into my mouth as much as possible to lower the temperature. Being sick at 2206 Sherman Street was like a jail sentence. I would be banished from going to the Wednesday night youth group at church, for one thing. Mostly, it was just the death-knell looks that Mom would shoot me, making me to go to bed even earlier than usual. I wanted to make sure I always finished my homework. My teachers' respect and encouragement I thrived on. Besides, a girl needs to dream and plan her life, she needs a little music from her transistor radio, but she can't always do that with the lights off and admonitions to not make a noise.

So I wasn't going to let that happen this time. Fighting the sniffles one evening as I picked out my clothes for school the next day, I plotted in my mind what I would tell Mom when she asked if I were coming down with a cold. And that's when I turned and stared out the window, mortified of the sin that I was planning to commit. But just as suddenly, I rationalized it. If you had a Mom like mine, you'd do it, too, I said to an imaginary friend.

Between not knowing what sanctification meant and desperate with the knowledge that I could never live up to being the born-again girl I wanted to be, my hope in Christ staggered. The ensuing years of teenagedom crushed my spirit. Adding to the mix of confusion, the congregation of the First Church of the Nazarene split in half when rumors had started after someone had seen Pastor Leon hug his secretary. In my diary I wrote, "I can't believe this. How can church people be so cruel?"

When I was thirteen years old, Mom ended up transferring her church membership to Heartland Community Church, a little chapel at the maple treed corner of Second and Main Street with beautiful stained glass windows. Andrew, a cute red-haired boy my and Rita's age, played the organ. His father, the Reverend Macy, was the preacher whose laugh I came to adore. Those four years that Mom and Rita and I attended the church—and not once did Dad—Mom would often be in tears as she ascended the stairs to the narthex, but when Reverend Macy reached for her hand, she breathed easily, staying to talk with him. He would listen to her, reaching out for other church members' hands and smile at them all while keeping his attention on my mother. When Mom's sobs began to subside, he would put his arms around her shoulders and guide her into the choir room.

Reverend Macy embodied the heart of a true Christian, I believed, though I couldn't articulate that at the time. His preaching was benevolent, wrapping everyone up in the warm arms of Christ. He always invited people to give their testimonials. To this day, I still remember Shirley, a jaw-dropping beautiful lady with luscious hair and a buxom figure, wearing high-heeled shoes and a pretty, slimming suit. She went to the pulpit and told her story of racy living and how she eventually caved in to the desperation from which she had been running. Tears coursed down my cheeks as I heard her tell the story of how the love of Christ transformed her into a woman with hope. I listened, rapt, not glancing once at Andrew to see if he was looking at me.

Sometimes Reverend Macy would invite Mom and me and Rita to sing as a trio for the special song during the offering. My memory of those times shine, in spite of the moments when Mom would glare with her big brown eyes at me and Rita when we would sing off-key. But when it came time for us to go up to the pulpit, we three sang "How Great Thou Art" like we meant it. I know I did. I felt the love of Christ even though there were confusing and conflicting messages everywhere in our house. In church, at the little stained-glass church, I felt safe and secure. Playing little sneak-a-look games with Andrew certainly didn't hurt, either. In the house of the Lord there, there was love.

During all the twists and turns of my early teen years, I was being pulled and pushed by so many loves and heartaches. I survived it all by looking ahead to when I could leave everything and everyone behind. Amber and I did write a few letters to each other. Her visions of Jesus increased with intensity; she was not even on a plane equal with me anymore. We were too far apart in miles and thoughts. I had to let go the only best friend I had up to that point.

Five years ago when I came out to Wheaton for my annual visit home, I found out that Amber was living with her brother Leroy. So I drove out to his house in Nickerson, a little town just fifteen miles south of where Rita and I grew up. I marveled in the beauty of the countryside, in the sunflowers arching their heads up as if they were singing to the maple and elm trees dotting the plains. A train lumbered by, wailing like a lone lover, giving me goosebumps.

By the time I found Leroy's house, I was breathing easy, not too nervous about seeing Amber for the first time in over twenty years. Leroy invited me in and walked me to the living room. There was Amber with that shy smile I would recognize anywhere, even though she had gained a lot of weight. She looked like a big loveable doll.

I went to hug her. She pulled me down onto the sofa next to her and a young girl—Amber's daughter Rachel. I fell in love with Rachel, whose eyes were warm brown just like her mother's.

Rachel watched me for a moment, looked down at my shoes. She smiled. "I hope you like the gift that my mother made you," she said.

Amber handed over a large circular potholder, similar to what she and I used to make at the summer vacation Bible school with the

Salvation Army. I took the potholder, touching and treasuring the bumps in the yarn; I knew all about mistakes from crocheting: the bumps and lumps are as meaningful as the perfectly stitched places. Maybe more.

"I love it," I told Amber and Rachel.

"Where are we going to go?" Rachel asked me.

"Sssshhh! She just got here," Amber said, stroking her daughter's wavy hair.

"Where do you want to go?" I said.

Rachel shrugged her shoulders.

"How about we just take a drive somewhere?"

The day ended up being a postcard-picture kind. I drove them out to Mushroom Rocks State Park near Kanopolis Lake. The strange rock formations—Dakota sandstone concretions, said the park brochure—really did resemble giant mushrooms clumped together under beautiful maple and oak trees.

"This one looks like a giant man's trousers," Rachel squealed and ran among the formations. I took photographs of her and Amber hugging each other by the rocks.

We also went to Pawnee Rock, a nearly 150-foot-high rock jutting up above the Kansas plains. The rock is where Comanche, Kiowa, Arapaho, and Cheyenne Indians would shoot at travelers and traders along the Santa Fe Trail. Amber and Rachel followed me up to the top. The view went for miles around.

Next stop was an antique shop in Pawnee Mission. Amber found a doll—she still liked them—and Rachel a swirled glass ball which she liked to turn around in her hand, gazing at its colors from all angles. But the best part of the day was as I was driving them home, we discovered a field of sunflowers.

"Haven't you seen sunflowers before?" Rachel asked me.

"Not this many in one place," I said, pulling over to the side of the road.

I got out of the car and danced over to the sunflowers. Some small birds were pecking the seeds out of the sunflower faces. "Oh, you guys, come over here, look at this. Oh, it's so beautiful!"

Amber and Rachel joined up with me.

Rachel snapped a picture of me and Amber, and then I took one of them together.

The rest of the drive to Leroy's house we all chattered and giggled, Amber caressing the doll's hair and Rachel holding her up her glass ball to admire it. I pulled into the driveway and we all got out of the car. The hugs we all shared were tender and long. I promised Amber I would see her again.

But in the ensuing years, Amber's visions and general health got dramatically worse. Leroy could no longer care for her. The assisted care living facility in Peabody was the best option for everyone.

– 5 –

THE TOWN OF PEABODY is beautiful, a small settlement gathered around a river. There are farms, a Main Street with buildings from the 1800s, Victorian-style houses, and a big beautiful park with old-fashioned flat swings. Even adults like me can sit on them and sail up into the sky.

As I turn now into the driveway of the hospital, my heart is racing. Leroy is going to meet me there. As soon as I walk into the lobby, I see several people who live at the place lolling around. I smile at them before I check in with the receptionist. She tells me that everyone will be right out to see me.

I start to sit down in one of the chairs, but a lady with an intense stare comes up next to me. I know she lives here. "Are you a Christian?" she asks me.

"Yes, I am," I say.

She nods. "I can tell." She begins to walk away.

I know that she means that as a compliment. I am always amazed by the power of the spoken word, how the few words from a person's mouth can create or destroy a moment, even a life. God bless the woman, for she has helped me sit up a little taller.

Leroy comes out to meet me, with Amber at his side.

Amber and I stare at each other for a moment. She is heavier than the last time I saw her. I reach out for her and we hug.

"We are keeping things really simple today," Leroy says. "We're going to have a picnic in the park."

I like that idea. And I'm very glad Leroy is here to accompany me on my visit with Amber. She walks slow and scrambles her words now.

Leroy drives us in his black SUV to the local market where we pick up sandwiches. Amber wants some red-hot Cheetos, so he gets those, too.

"What kind of pop do you want?" he asks me. His gaze disconcerts me, reminding me of my English prof at St. Thomas University in San Diego. I'd had a crush on him.

"Something orange," I say.

Leroy grabs a Coke for himself, root beer for Amber, and an Orange Fanta for me.

I help Leroy help Amber into the car.

"Hey, where's Rachel?" I ask.

Leroy shook his head. "With another relative."

I get into the passenger seat. Amber is already chattering a mile a minute. When Leroy glances at me, we smile at each other.

Our afternoon at the park is sweet and simple. We plop down at a picnic bench and eat our sandwiches and spicy cheese curls, drinking our pop fast to get the sting out of our mouths. Mourning doves and boat-tailed grackles rustle and fly over our heads in the towering trees above.

"Time to swing!" I say.

Leroy pushes Amber in her swing first, then me. Amber and I are already pumping high by the time Leroy gets into a swing. We sail for quite a while, whooping and laughing.

"I want off," Amber says suddenly, her face crumpling off like a baby's.

"Okay, me, too," I say, scuffing my feet in the dirt to slow down. "Leroy?"

"Wait, I got it." I half-jump out of my swing and come over to Amber along with Leroy. We gently pull on the swing to slow her down.

"Let's go on the merry-go-round now," Amber says.

I look at Leroy. Merry-go-round? I was scared of that contraption even when I was a little kid. Leroy shrugs and I get on the thing while Leroy helps Amber up.

"Get toward the center and hold on. It will be a better ride for you," he tells her.

Then he pushes the ride slowly, steadily. Amber grins slow and easy as the world spins around us. I hold on while Leroy jumps on. His weight throws the ride off a bit and we all rotate like a planet off its orbit. I am dizzy, though not so much from the ride as I am from what my heart is doing with Leroy so close. I had no idea that my heart had been so interested.

The merry-go-round bumps and grinds to a stop.

"Again," Amber says, still holding on to the center bar.

"No," Leroy and I both say.

We make our way to the jump-up animals. Amber gets on the back of a horse, I find a giraffe, Leroy a rhino. We spring up and down on our animals. Amber and I break out into one of our giggle spasms, and I can barely hold on to the neck of my giraffe. Through my tears, I watch Leroy watching us. He smiles, shakes his head.

I climb off the giraffe and go sit down at the picnic bench. Leroy walks over to my side, both of us watching Amber giggling and having fun.

"Is it hard for you?" I ask him.

"Easier than when she lived with me. I never knew what she was going to do. She'd be sad one moment, angry the next. Sometimes she'd take a knife from the kitchen and go after me. Or she'd hold it to her own wrists," he says.

The impulse to reach for his hand overtakes me, so I move a couple of inches from Leroy. "You've done the right thing, having her live here in Peabody."

"I don't know, just don't," Leroy says, looking up at the trees, then at me. I twist my wedding ring around on my finger.

"Please, I want off!" Amber says from her perch on the horse. She is sitting still, looking down at the ground.

Leroy sighs, then jumps up, runs to her side. I gather up the paper plates, napkins and empty cheese curl bag, crumpling them all up and throwing into a trash bin. The clouds are gathering close in. I watch Leroy take Amber's hand and lead her gingerly away from the playground. The lonely wail of a train just outside of town brings tears to my eyes.

*****

55

I called Mark last night to tell him about my day. His voice nearly put me to sleep, but not in a good way. We ended up talking in circles the way we always do, him wanting to give me suggestions as to what to do or say to this or that person and me pulling my hair and interrupting him. The pressure around my eyes and nose felt like old mold squeezing into my brain. I yawned, said I loved him but that I was tired, and I hung up.

For the next three hours, I downed several glasses of wine and watched an "Officer and a Gentleman" on HBO. At the scene on the beach where Richard Gere tells Debra Winger to leave him alone after he finds his buddy hanging from a self-made noose in the bathroom, I went through a half box of tissues. As I watched Gere carry Winger out of the paper mill, I sank into a resentment. If only, if only, I said, scowling, crossing my arms over my chest.

Now I am paying the price for my indulgence. The sun is streaming into the hotel room, baking the walls and my eyelids. I have to be at Aunt Sophia's in an hour and a half; slowly, I open my eyes.

*****

"Renee, are you okay?" Aunt Sophia doesn't miss a thing, never has.

I glance at her and Mom sitting in the porch swing. "Bad night last night."

Of course, they want to know all the details, but I tell them just another argument with Mark. They are used to that.

I get my tape recorder out of my big beach bag.

"Want some iced tea?"

"Thought you'd never ask," I say, taking the glass from Aunt Sophia. I punch the record button. Aunt Sophia settles into the porch next to Mom. "Where were we last time?"

I sip my tea. "Mom gets freed," I say.

"That's right. I got a job at the Holidome—"

"But that wasn't working out. It was a hectic job, and she was an emotional wreck anyway," Aunt Sophia says.

I look at Mom, silent listener to the tale of her own life. She strokes her fingernails.

"So I went over to talk to my friend at the Santa Fe Junction and asked if they would hire Margie as a hostess. So she started working there, and that's when Jim would come in to eat, because he was divorced."

"That's how I met Jim. *So* we…dated for several months. Then got married," Mom says almost shyly.

"I tried to talk her out of it, but it didn't work."

Mom giggles. "I should have listened to her."

"But you know, when you're alone?" Aunt Sophia looks at me. "And you're broke?"

I nod. Been there, done that.

"I know, it's scary," I say, shutting off the tape recorder. "Can we talk for a few minutes about something?"

"Sure," Mom and Aunt Sophia echo perfectly.

"Don't you think that the women's libbers really messed things up?" They both nod, but I go on, not wanting to be interrupted.

"I think all this baloney had its beginnings in the '70s with those T-shirts that said, 'A woman without a man is like a fish without a bicycle,'" I say.

Mom looks at Aunt Sophia.

"What? You've never seen that T-shirt?" I ask them.

"I have. And I thought they were funny," Aunt Sophia says.

"Well, I just got finished reading "Growing up Tough," an auto-biographical book by Taylor Caldwell. Ever heard of her?"

They both shake their heads. I go on.

"Okay, so Caldwell wrote this book in 1971, the same year when I began to first hear the idea of women's rights, that a woman can do all that a man does, and should do. From the start, I was politically incorrect."

I turn to look at Aunt Sophia. "In what way do you think I was politically incorrect?"

She swats at a fly and goes over to sit next to Mom. "Because you still liked guys," she says.

I laugh. "Good enough. But when I heard all the women's libbers talk about what women had the right to do, I secretly hoped that I would not have to go to war just as a man would. Anyway, this author Caldwell really echoed my own thoughts on the matter. She basically said that the ruin of a nation—maybe even our own—starts from the masculinization of its women and the feminization of its men. That's what Russia had done."

Aunt Sophia nods her head up and down, gives me a thumbs-up gesture. Mom's eyes widen, trying to see the big picture.

"Mom, what I'm saying is, I have always wanted to be the cherished one, the protected one. And I don't want to have to support a man. Financially, I mean."

Mom snaps to attention. "But of course not! What woman would want that?"

"I didn't. But that's what happened with Phil. Then with Kevin."

"And now, Mark?" Aunt Sophia asks me.

"No, no, he does go to work." I stop and look up to the sky for a minute, watching the trees swirl their hula skirts in the wind. I think of the way Mark goes to work every day, hauling his box of window-washing supplies. Who knows what he really does all day, though? And lately he's been so reluctant to give me cash when I ask for it.

"Anyway, Mom, the whole point of what I was trying to tell you, is I can understand why you would want to get married again."

Mom's eyes widen even more. "Oh, thank you, Renee. You're right."

"Jim had a steady income, fairly good. He was not a bad guy, just a physical wreck," Aunt Sophia says, stroking the hair at the back of her head. "And I thought, I don't want Margie to have to take care of him."

"But he was very appreciative of anything and everything," Mom says.

"Yes, like the time we took him up to see the memorial walls at Washington, DC. We bought a van and took turns driving. There were good days when he was fun. But it was ruining your mother's life. She was the chauffeur, the nurse, the cook, oh, brother!" Aunt Sophia says, stirring more sugar into her tea.

Mom shrugs. "And then he died in '90s on my dad's birthday. A blood clot killed him when he went in for surgery on his knees."

I move to sit next door to Mom. We hug, then push back with our feet, laughing when the swing pitches forward with a groan.

"You loved him, didn't you, Mom?"

She nods her head real fast to smooth over the emotion.

"Hey, you girls, whatcha up to?" It was Albert, suddenly appearing at the end of the street from the shed where he had been working. It was remodeled from Grandma and Grandpa Howell's chicken coop.

Albert hopped up onto the porch.

"Girl talk!" Aunt Sophia says. "Men aren't allowed." She and Albert kiss.

"Fine by me. I'm going in for a shower. Dinner out tonight?"

Mom, Aunt Sophia and I make a chorus of yes.

"We've made our husbands like each other," Mom says when Albert shuts the door behind him.

"And they're as different as night and day."

Mom's current husband Sam had known her and all our clan when she was still married to Dad. And he knew her during and after the divorce, during and after her marriage to Todd and then Jim. No matter what her age, Mom always managed to turn heads when she walked by. So one day shortly after Jim had died, Sam came over to Aunt Sophia's house to see if Albert could help him with something. Aunt Sophia, Albert and Sam were all standing out on the driveway talking when Sam noticed Mom out sweeping the porch of the little house next to Aunt Sophia. Mom always returned eventually to Sherman Street.

Sam asked Albert if he thought Mom would go out with him. Albert said to ask. In the meantime, Aunt Sophia had gotten her a date with a millionaire.

"He was filthy rich, and when his parents die, he is going to be unreal filthy rich," says Aunt Sophia. "The four of us actually went out on Mom's first date with this guy, but your Mom was bored to death. She couldn't relate to him at all and all she could think about was Sam."

"I had to eat raw oysters," Mom says, her whole face scrunching up into a grimace. "On a cracker. I just about gagged."

"We all just swallowed them whole and wished we could have crawled into a hole." Aunt Sophia laughs at her own rhyming.

I smile, thinking of how the two of them must have looked. I could imagine Mom daintily biting into the oyster, masking her horror over the hideous, slimy thing in her mouth. The way her eyes must have moved and changed would have been as comical as the late Lucille Ball's. Aunt Sophia would have made coughing sounds and gulped water. I myself wouldn't even have tried the oyster, no matter if my date was a millionaire.

*****

The friendship between Mom and Aunt Sophia made things more bearable for me growing up. I knew if the going got too bad, I could always run to Aunt Sophia or Grandma Howell. But I never did. I knew Aunt Sophia heard the wails in the house next to hers. I knew she gritted her teeth and shook her head. But I also had the common sense to know that if in fact I ever did go crying to Aunt Sophia or Grandma and demand that they do something for Rita and me, they might have called the police. And that would have torn us all apart. I didn't personally know any foster children, but my guts told me that a foster home was not a home at all. Actually, I had learned a lot from all the books I used to tote home from the library on summer vacations. Reading saved my sanity and gave me a look into the world outside, of other people's stories of their hopes and heartaches.

"But you've managed to stay friends through all of the ups and downs," I say as a summing up. I didn't know if Aunt Sophia had ever pondered over whether a friendship was sacred enough to withstand the unjust castigation of her own nieces.

Aunt Sophia doesn't miss a beat. "Because of unconditional love. When you have a friend, you love them totally for who they are."

My head is spinning. I can understand how and why they say this about each other. But at whose expense? I dare not think about that too much.

They have always been opposites of each other, Mom and Aunt Sophia. Mom is like a closed book while Aunt Sophia does not mind if she is the talk of the town. And I have a little bit of both of them in me.

I look down at the picture of the whole clan on a Halloween night. We look endearingly ridiculous in our costumes. Together, we all really did have a good time. Separately, we had our problems.

"Mom? Aunt Sophia? Remember when we all used to jump into the pickup truck for a jaunt somewhere?"

Mom smiles. "I don't want to go home," she says. It's the first line of a little ditty we had all made up to sing together on our way home after a spell out somewhere.

"Grandma Bell had to have been very old," Aunt Sophia says.

"Goodness, yes," Mom says, perched forward gazing at Aunt Sophia.

"When she hopped up into that truck," Aunt Sophia takes a sip of her tea, staring off into the distance and counting with her fingers. "In 1963, when we adopted Myra, my mother was in her fifties. Grandma Bell was twenty years older, so she must have been seventy-seven—no, no, she was eighty!"

"I don't know how she did that," Mom says.

*****

I never thought of Grandma Bell as old, even when I was very little. One of my earliest memories of her is an afternoon when I was about four years old. The sky was big and blue, and I was its beloved; I was running around giggling in Grandma's back yard chasing a butterfly, sure that it would become my friend when *baaam!* I fell down hard on one of the cobblestone steps. The sky was no longer my friend, neither the butterfly. I was mad at it, mad at the ground and the One who let me fall, the Someone up in the sky watching and waiting. When finally I caught my breath, I screamed and wailed. Grandma Bell scooped me up and carried me to the back steps. She rocked me, telling me I would be all right, giving me lemonade to drink. I clung to her, loving her smell, her sweet words.

"You just scraped your knee, that's all," she said.

But I was still angry, bellowing out at the God of the butterflies.

A few years later, Grandma Bell helped me get out of another scrape with God. She and Grandpa had taken me and Rita to church one morning as they sometimes did. I always loved how their car smelled on those mornings, the sun heating up the dust in the car so that it had an exotic light perfume, making me warm and lusciously sleepy.

One Sunday, Rita and I stayed for the entire day after church with Grandma and Grandpa. Toward evening, Grandma let me comb her long white hair after she unpinned it from the tight bun on her head. Grandpa silently sidled up to us, smiled, and then started walking around the house again. Now Grandpa I did think of as old. I watched him roam around the house, his hands behind his back. He was a gentle, quiet man, and I knew he loved Grandma very much, me and Rita, too, by the way he smiled at her and at us, never lifting his voice. When it came time for dinner, I asked Grandma what was wrong with the bread, for it was brown like it was old or something. Rita and I were both used to the white, fluffy, soft bread from the Rainbo Bakery.

Grandma said that her bread was whole wheat, "good for my constitution." I didn't know about any constitution, but I thought she might be a little loopy. She made sure that both Rita and I tasted it. I was scared to take a bite of it and was surprised by its sweet, nutty flavor. But my mouth was dry from worry over what the preacher had gone on about that morning in church.

Rita and I sat on the porch watching the lightning with Grandma and Grandpa after dinner. Each time the sky lit up with green crackling fingers, I shivered, the hair raising on my arms. I watched the wind toss the branches of the elm trees.

I snuggled up next to Grandma. "Why is the preacher so mad at us in church? He always yells," I said.

She took me in her arms. "He's not angry, just trying to get us to understand something important."

"Can't he do that without yelling?"

"I don't know. I'll ask him sometime."

I looked at her, still pretty even after age had walked across her face. I hoped she would ask the preacher. I don't doubt now that she did. She would have moved mountains for me. It seems to me that the preacher did, in fact, not yell as much after I had confided in Grandma.

*****

"She wanted you," Aunt Sophia says now. "Your grandma. If Margie would have given you to her, she would have been happy forever."

Mom clears her throat, smiles.

"Grandpa Bell always gave me Wrigley's gum."

"From his roll top desk, right? He did the same with your father and me, too," Aunt Sophia says.

Mom sits up. "Oh, is that right?" she asks. It makes me wonder where she had been half the time when Rita and I were kids. More than likely, her head had been full of dreams of requited love. Not so unlike mine.

"Yes, he was a good grandfather," Aunt Sophia says.

I tell her and Mom the story of my own roll top desk experience.

"One summer afternoon, after Grandpa had given me and Rita each a stick of gum, Grandma beckoned us to sit down beside her. She pulled the Bible out of the desk and read some verses. I didn't understand them at all," I say. Aunt Sophia smiles at this.

"Then she told Rita and me that when we were older, we would have a decision to make. She told us that she hoped we would decide to go with God and obey His will. She picked up the Bible—that enormous book!—and told us that in it we would find everything we would need. Read it every day, she said."

"Oh, I can't believe that she would have made you promise such a thing!" Mom says.

"It's okay, Mom. I knew she was just looking out for us. So Rita and I said we would. Read the Bible, I mean. We promised her."

But I remember that Rita could barely stand still. She wasn't scared of Grandma's command; she was just wanting to get out when there was still so much sun outside.

"Anyway, Grandma was real nice. She said we were good girls, and we could go out and play."

We did, with Rita running off to find bugs and creeping things and me snooping around the trees and hedges to see if I could find any bird nests. The sparrows were always up to shenanigans, chirping up a storm and I could watch them for hours.

"And we all know what happened after that," Aunt Sophia says now.

"What do you mean?"

"Well, you haven't really stuck with the Bible, have you?"

I can't believe how this conversation is going. "Um, well, yes, I do, I have. I mean to the best of my ability."

"But are you still with Truth Universal?"

Mom was silent, watching Aunt Sophia and me, her eyes wide.

"I…I…don't want to be. I am not happy with it. With the people. With Mark," I say. I feel like a guppy fish, my mouth opening and closing.

Aunt Sophia picks up her iced tea and sips it, looking at me over the rim, puts it down again. "Mm-hhmmm, that's what I thought," she says, smoothing her long black-and-white skirt over her legs.

"Hey, what's going on?" Mom is on the edge of her seat.

"Nothing, Mom. I just have to go. I'll finish up the interview tomorrow," I say, clicking off the tape recorder.

After I pile everything up into my arm, I run down the steps and over to my car where I throw everything onto the passenger seat. I wave goodbye, get behind the wheel, and drive away.

I don't know how she does it, my Aunt Sophia. She sees right through me, it seems. And out of the blue, she comes at me like a storm. Yet I know she does so because she loves me with an intensity that can't put up with a lie of any kind. I needed to finish up the interview anyway, I tell myself as I turn into Rita's driveway. Still, I felt bad that I left Aunt Sophia's on a sour note.

– 6 –

GEMMA, EVAN, CAMILLE, AND Derrick come running out of Rita's front door. I'm going to take them this afternoon to Exploration Place in Wichita. Heather wanted to hang out with a friend. The screen door opens again, and Rita saunters out, her long brown hair swaying in the wind. She has that slow smile I have secretly envied all my life. I even practice it in front of the mirror, but no luck.

"Hey!" Rita says, leaning into the passenger window.

"You sure you don't wanna come along with us? We can make room," I say, looking at the kids seated behind me. Well, it would be a squeeze.

"Nah. Zach and I are going to watch NASCAR."

"Okay, I'll have everyone back around seven o'clock. We'll probably get something to eat on the way home," I say.

Rita waves us goodbye, and off we go. The wind kicks up a stray plastic bag and carries it up into the sky.

*****

I have to practically run following the kids looking at all the science exhibits at Exploration Place. We all stand like giants looking down at the Kansas-in-miniature exhibit. Their favorite is the tornado machine. They each take turns standing in the tube. The kids laugh like crazy when Derrick gets in and his Afro balloons.

We head over to the exhibit that takes a photo of them and shows what they will look like when they are thirty, forty years older. They beg me to take my turn, but I say no. I'm feeling old as it is. At the reflecting pools outside mirroring the Arkansas River, I can feel my heartbeat slow down. I pat the stone slab next to me inviting the kids to sit with me for a while. I can't stop thinking about this afternoon, the way that Aunt Sophia had looked at me as if she knew I was in the middle of something not good. She knows that I have been in Truth Universal for ten years, starting the year I met Mark. I'd gone around with so many guys, going to live with them when my money ran out or I lost or just plain quit jobs. By the time I met Mark I was in a place where I just wanted to stop running. I subconsciously knew that I had been fleeing from God the first ten years after I graduated from high school. But I was so tired and confused, hurt and lonely. And when I walked into my first Truth Universal gathering, at the invitation of my roommate—I was living just like the sitcom *Three's Company*, with two other guys—when I walked into that first fellowship meeting, and heard Scripture read aloud, something shifted within me. I panted like a deer at the waters. So hungry and thirsty for meaning and purpose in God's words.

"Hey, Aunt Renee," Gemma interrupts my thoughts, "can we get pizza?"

I look down into her blue eyes. I am getting hungry, too. The other kids have started dipping their toes into the pools, even though there are signs all over the place telling them not to.

I stand up. "All right, everyone, I'm tired and hungry. Anyone for Pizza Hut?"

*****

The kids are all chattering as I back the car out of our spot in the parking lot. I notice a gigantic blue-black cloud looming behind us.

"Oh my! Do you guys see that?"

Gemma and Camille look behind them. "What?"

"The cloud!"

"Oh. That. Yeah, it's no big deal. It'll blow over," Derrick says.

"Or not." Evan laughs.

"Geez, I think there's a tornado in that thing," I say, leaning forward on the steering wheel to look up at the sky.

Derrick turns the radio on, almost jumps back when he hears the music. "What? Wait! You listen to classical music?"

Everyone laughs.

"Yep. Helps me think."

"Hey, can we get cokes with our pizza?" Gemma asks.

"Anything you want," I say, sailing along on the road, the tires making their high-pitched hum that only Kansas highways can make. I sing Vivaldi, using my arm to conduct the orchestra that only I can see. The kids are groaning and rolling their eyes.

"All right, all right," I say, turning the radio to a station I know they both like.

By the time we get to Wheaton, the sky is a massive bruise. My hair clings to my neck even though I have the air conditioner on. Derrick twirls the dials on the radio, making me crazy.

"*Shhh*, I can't see!" I tell Derrick.

"Haha, that's what my mom says sometimes," Gemma pipes up.

"Yeah, and our mom used to say the same thing. When something is too loud, I can't see," I say, turning onto Main Street in Wheaton. Creepy how there's so little traffic on a Saturday afternoon.

I roll down the windows to smell the air. At that moment, like a blast from heaven, the tornado sirens let out their wail right next to us. Camille and Evan clamp their hands over their ears, Gemma cowers down and Derrick leans out the window, whooping it up. And I scream.

And gun the engine. "I have to get you guys home! Now!"

"Aunt Renee, we'll be okay. It'll pass," Camille says, tapping me on the shoulder.

"How can you say that?" I say, hyperventilating, my shoulders hunched over the steering wheel.

"We've seen this a hundred times," Derrick says.

The stoplight turns red and I slam the brakes. The tornado sirens are still going. The kids are acting silly, singing and making faces at each other. Must be all those negative ions in the air.

Finally, I get us all to Rita's house. It's pelting rain by now, cold even on this summer late afternoon. Rita and Zach are glued to the TV, watching the red radar circle spin around on a green map of the three counties affected by the storms.

"Hey," Rita looks up at me. "Are you all right?"

"Well, now I am. I got these kids here as fast as I could," I say, breathless.

Rita grins, lifts back her hair with her hand. "Everything's going to be okay."

"Some guy died at Cheney Lake," Zach says. "He wanted to stay on his boat out on the lake."

Oh, well, now that was stupid. Poor guy. Didn't he know he would be electrocuted? I remember the time when Amber's cousin Nellie along with several of my friends from church were on a rare trip out to a lake one summer evening. As soon as that sky got dark and thunder boomed, the youth director yelled at everyone to get out of the water. Otherwise, it would be Fry City.

"Want a beer, Renee?" Zach gets up to go to the fridge.

No, thanks, I tell him.

Derrick goes to his room and comes out holding something in his hands.

"Hey, hey, hey! Are you really going to do that?" Rita says, half yelling, half laughing.

I follow Derrick out the door, his back turned toward me. The rain is coming down in sheets. A car coming down the street moves slightly with its headlights on, even though it is just seven o'clock in the evening—here the darkness does not descend until nearly two and a half hours later.

Derrick turns to me, grins, a firecracker lit in his hand. "Watch this." He waits till the car passes, then throws the firecracker out onto the street. We watch it snap, crackle and pop in the rain. Something about the sky crying, the tornado terror and Derrick's glee in doing boy stuff sets off a spasm of giggles in me.

One by one, Derrick lights the firecrackers then throws them out.

"Okay, that's enough," I say after several minutes. "I mean, really."

We both go back in the house.

"It's over," Zach says.

"Storm's passed," Derrick says, nodding, looking at the radar map on the TV.

Outside, the rain has let up already, like magic, with the sun poking through a giant hole in the clouds.

Half an hour later, I drove the kids to Pizza Hut, and now all of us are tugging pieces of the pie from the pan, vegetarian for my part, pepperoni for the kids. We all gnaw at the pizza and guzzle our sodas. The kids retell stories about my having been scared out of my wits from the tornado. Some things are worth being scared spitless over.

*****

It wasn't just the tornado itself that made me a complete paleface. With those kids in my car, I had had complete responsibility for their lives.

But there was something else. When I hear tornado sirens, or see a twister cloud drop into the horizon, no matter how far away, the sight tugs at my heartstrings. If only. If only I'd had my chance with Devon. The guy who I used to write poetry about in English Lit class when the teacher told us to write a pretend eulogy about someone. When she gave that assignment, I tried hard to ignore the other girls' talk behind me about Ryan O'Neal and Ali MacGraw in the *Love Story* movie over the weekend. The girls crooned, "Wasn't it just so sad?"

I twirled the pen around in my hand and looked out the window. Billowy white clouds moved in the sky. I got all moony about Devon again, about how he wouldn't look at me in the hallways at school. My diary was filled with the daily accounts of when and if I did see him, and what he did and said. My hours were filled with daydreaming and wondering what he did all day. I imagined that he would become a great scientist, studying the movement and ways of clouds and hail and ice. And that's how I wrote a eulogy about the boy I was in love with, that he somehow had died while doing a dangerous experiment involving the heavens and hail and ice.

I got an A for the assignment, even though the teacher marked all over the page: *How is this even possible?* She just didn't know Devon.

There is something powerful in the imagination of a sixteen-year-old. Because almost twenty years later, Devon didn't die. He did

69

one better. He received the Young Scientist's Award from President Bill Clinton for nothing less than his work in tornado research.

And that's why Dad wants me now to interview him. "Go on, kid, it'll be great," he told me after Rita and I watched the video featuring Devon and his team of storm chasers. I wanted to slug Dad, I wanted to hug him.

*****

I've always had a love-hate affair with Sundays, particularly the mornings. My body and soul ache with longing for the old days of going to church with not just my parents, but my Aunt Sophia, Grandma Howell and Grandma and Grandpa Ball. Sitting in church, I'd go through a minefield of emotions. The preacher would always screw up his face in anger or what looked like to me extreme sadness and he'd raise his fist and shake the pulpit. "When are you going to let God take you to the promised land?" he'd rage.

I had no idea there was a land promised for me. Where is it? I'd ask God silently, my head hurting from the little hat I wore that was too tight on my head. My stomach rumbled from hunger.

When we all sang together "Great Is Thy Faithfulness," my heart trembled. I looked at my parents standing side by side, my sister next to me, calm and good to me if only for those few moments, and at all the people around dressed in their best singing. I felt a peace similar to when I watched the fat, funny robins pulling up worms in our backyard. Maybe this feeling of family was the promised land.

*****

So here it is Sunday morning, and I'm all primped and prepped as I go to church with Aunt Sophia and Albert. First Church of the Nazarene has changed a lot since I was a little girl. It moved from the blond, bland building on Fourth Avenue to a gigantic roundhouse structure on North Monroe on the edge of town. I miss the smell of baking bread but there are fields of wildflowers and grasses surrounding the church as Albert parks the car.

"It's changed. Our church has changed," Aunt Sophia says. I nod, thinking she meant the locale. "The music is different now. All this hand-raising and clapping. None of the hymns anymore."

What? No hymns?

Albert grins, grumbles a little. "It's the young people. They've taken over."

I half laugh, half groan. Young people? Does that mean I'm old now? When did this all happen, my not being part of the new wave of people?

Maybe it's because I've been involved with Truth Universal ever since I married Mark. I haven't made many close friends within TU, and many people consider it to be a cult. Aunt Sophia sure does. I'll never forget the letter she wrote me when I told her that I had joined up with Truth Universal. She was furious with me.

TU taught things I'd never heard before, which should have sent sirens off in my heart, such as Jesus is not God. And that if we get sick, it's our own fault. But we have always sung hymns. Truth is, though, they feel flat when I sing along with the group, not the same way I was lifted up by the words and the emotions when I was under my parents' wings, torn and weak though they were.

*****

Aunt Sophia and Albert lead me now into the enormous sanctuary. I am as shy as a thirteen-year-old as I walk into the room full of people twenty, thirty years older than me. A lady about my age comes rushing up to me.

"Oh, Renee, how great to see you. How are you?"

Staring at her, I see a familiar face, kind of blowsy.

"Delores?"

"Yep. It's me."

"Well, well. How are you? You live here in Wheaton?"

"Oh, no. Texas. Visiting my mom. I've been married thirty years, got two boys. Whoooh, they are a handful. What about you?"

"Married, no kids. Working as a reporter in San Diego. I've got five nieces and nephews. Love them."

I'm not feeling very Christian right now, remembering all the stuff that Delores did and said to me. Sizing up her blond hair, big pear-shaped body, I hide a giggle behind my hand.

"What is it?"

"Ah, just remembering things. You know."

Delores smiles, evades my eyes. You see, Delores was jealous of me when I was a kid. Except that I didn't know that when I was ten years old. All I knew then was she hated my guts. She'd invite me to sleepovers at her house with the other girls from our Sunday school class and then she'd concoct all kinds of ways to tease and pester me. Delores was the boss among her circle of friends, so they did bizarre things when they had to. I grit my teeth now, remembering the time that she devised some sort of game in which they threw a blanket over me and then had everyone sit on me to see how long I could breathe. The next morning when all of us gathered in the kitchen, Mrs. Pine asked us if we all got a good night's sleep. Everyone all avoided looking at me, said yes, of course. I stuffed my mouth with pancakes and syrup.

Delores's contempt toward me exploded one Sunday afternoon when First Church of the Nazarene Church members stood around gabbing and gossiping in the parking lot. Out of the blue, Delores appeared at my side.

Her mouth turned upside down, she said, "You think you're so special." Then she took the bottom edge of my red-and-white-striped dress I was wearing and that my mother had made for me. I had promised my mother that I would keep the dress perfect, no matter what. It was a silly promise, really, because I loved wearing dresses and was never a tomboy. With the other kids standing around watching, Delores yanked hard on my dress, tearing it down from the waistline. In front of God and everybody, I stood in the parking lot with my dress hanging in tatters.

I wanted to claw her eyes out, but I just trembled in my torn dress, thinking of the terror my mother would unleash on me. Delores scoffed at me and pranced off.

I was still shaking in my shoes when Aunt Sophia approached me, her mouth gaping, eyes wide. "What in the world?"

"Delores. It was Delores. She just did it. For no reason."

"For no reason? Whatever do you mean? Did you say something to her?"

I shrugged. "I don't know why she hates me so much."

Aunt Sophia took me by the hand. "I'll explain it to your mother."

I could barely breathe on the drive home.

"I know you're worried about what your mother will say. But I'll take care of it," Aunt Sophia said.

While Aunt Sophia went up to the front porch and rang the doorbell, I stayed in the car. I watched Mom bang on the screen door with her fist as Aunt Sophia told her what had happened to my dress. Finally, Aunt Sophia beckoned for me to get out of the car. I did, hugging the torn dress to myself.

"Well, good grief, get up here," Mom said. I could see the anger flash in her eyes.

"Margie, now remember, it's not Renee's fault. It's Delores, all her fault."

By then I was crying. "Momma, I loved this dress, I did. And I know how much you worked on it, and how you don't like to sew, and I was so proud to wear this dress, and—"

"Renee, just come inside," Mom said, coldly.

I walked past Aunt Sophia, looking back up at her as I stepped into the house. Aunt Sophia blew me a kiss. I smiled but began shivering in the cold house. My parents were the first people in Wheaton to get an air conditioner. I was always chilled to the bone in the summer.

Mom closed the door and I turned around to face her. "Momma, I think she was jealous. Delores. I think she wished her mother had made her a dress like mine," I said.

Mom pursed her lips, nodded. "You're probably right," she said. "But I'm never sewing anything for anybody again. That's it."

So I'm remembering all this while Delores is blabbing about her boys and how great Texas is.

"Let's have lunch while you're in town," she says now.

"Mmmm, yeah, well, no. I don't think I'll have the time. But good to see you."

Secretly, I hope those boys of hers give her a lot of grief. I turn to find Aunt Sophia and Albert. They lead me to the back row where we all sit down. Somebody hits a drum, the band strikes up, and I nearly jump off the pew.

"Told you," Aunt Sophia whispers, winks at me.

For fifteen minutes, we have a series of stand-up, sit-down praise songs. Several people lift their hands while singing and praying. I wanted that yet did not.

Stifling a yawn, I sift through the bulletin to see when the real music would begin.

"Choir comes on in a few minutes," Aunt Sophia whispers, reading my mind.

The offering plate is passed, and that is when the choir files in. They sing "I Can Only Imagine," a song I've never heard before that does bring me to tears. Yes, what will I do when I see the face of Jesus? Cry, jump for joy, fall down on my knees, dance, go mute? Hug him? What would it be like to hug light?

*****

Not a lot of choices in Wheaton, Kansas, for lunch, although the city has had chain restaurants popping up all over like any other city. After church, Aunt Sophia and Albert opt for Great Steaks, a little joint that's been on Main Street for ages. Thankfully, it has menu options that don't involve red meat. I tell our waitress I'll have the chef's salad and a cup of coffee. Seems like I can never get enough of coffee on this visit home. I hide another yawn behind my hand.

We're sitting in a corner booth so that we can watch the people around us. It's one of Aunt Sophia's favorite activities. She knows practically everyone in town. I watch as she orders a sirloin steak with mashed potatoes and vegetable of the day—no broccoli, not ever, she tells the waitress. They laugh like it's an old joke. Albert orders the pot roast, cherry pie for dessert.

"I Am in Hog Heaven" says a sign on the wall behind the counter. I sip my coffee and watch the short-order chefs sweating over the hamburgers.

"So. What did you think about the sermon?" Aunt Sophia asks me, swirling several packets of sugar into her iced tea.

"I was wondering when you'd ask. I liked it. But I have a problem with the whole thing about God predestining people, you know, to be His people," I say.

Albert gives me a thumbs-up. "I am not a fan of that idea either. Don't worry about that too much. If you're chosen, you're chosen."

"But if you're not?"

"Wait," Aunt Sophia says, holding up a finger. "I know how to deal with this theory. It's not that God chooses us or doesn't. It's that we choose Him or not."

"Well, then, why isn't it just explained that way? Why did the pastor go on and on about being chosen?"

Our waitress comes now with our food.

Albert says we should pray.

He takes Aunt Sophia's hand, and she takes mine. "Lord, thank You for this sweet time together, for Your wonderful mercies and grace. May we never take them for granted. And we ask for Your blessing on this food. In Your Son's name, Amen."

We are all quiet for a minute while we dig in.

"But about this thing on being chosen," Albert says between mouthfuls of pot roast, "here's what I think. I think that the whole theory helps bring in money to the pastors."

Aunt Sophia and I laugh. "How is that possible?"

"Well, it's banking on fear, isn't it? Really?" Albert looks at me, winks.

I feel a renewed sense of respect for this man. He'd swept Aunt Sophia off her feet right into the bedroom. The same year that my mother and father were getting a divorce. The same year that I plotted and planned on going into the Navy to get away from the mess.

I dug into my salad. "Aunt Sophia."

She looks at me, dabbing her mouth with a napkin. "*Yes?*" She smiles.

"Remember the chef's salads you used to make for our Ground Hog Day get-togethers?"

She holds up a finger, takes a sip of her Coke, and sets it down. "Sure, I do. It's built into my DNA," she says.

"I loved those times," I say, aghast at my eyes getting watery.

"Well, so did I," Aunt Sophia says, grasping my hand.

"I miss everyone."

"Me, too. Especially my mother and grandparents. They taught me what's important in life. Because of them, I love the Lord and hope to walk in His ways the rest of my life."

I dab at my eyes. "I think I've failed."

"Oh, no, you haven't," Aunt Sophia says.

"We've all failed," Albert says.

"Not like me."

Aunt Sophia puts her fork down. "Renee Lynne, listen to me. You are a miracle of God. I mean it. You just have some work to do."

"I'll never live up to what Grandma Bell asked me to do. I think she thought I was a perfect little girl."

"But you were. To her. You could do no wrong in her eyes."

"But that's the problem. I *have* let her down. Let God down. And myself." I take a sip of lemonade to clear my thoughts for a while. "I feel so awful for not going to her funeral service. When Dad called to tell me Grandma Bell had died, I felt nothing. Just nothing."

Truth is, I was between two men at the time. I didn't want to be that way. But if I didn't move in with my boyfriends, I would have been on the streets. And that was when I didn't have a drop of wine, was hitting the Big Book of AA instead. I was surviving. Maybe if I'd prayed more? Read my Bible more?

"The past is past," Albert says.

"We all need reminders of that," Aunt Sophia agrees.

"But just do me one favor," Aunt Sophia says.

"What's that?

"Get out of TU."

"Huh?"

Aunt Sophia looks at me straight on. "You know what I said."

76

I nod, take another napkin and wipe my eyes. "You know what? I will."

*****

When Mark calls me that evening, I don't want to talk to him. He always digs around in any conversation with me, like he's playing psychoanalyst, so most of the time I don't tell him anything. I certainly am not going to tonight.

But then he hears something different in my voice. "Hey, what happened today?"

"Nothing. I just went to church with Aunt Sophia and lunch after. Then I went for a long drive by myself. You should have seen the beautiful big hawk that landed in a tree—"

"How was church?"

"A little boring. They don't sing hymns anymore."

"Oh, well, now, that's strange, don't you think?" he says and laughs in that squeaky voice he gets. I imagine him stroking his knees, up and down, up and down, sitting in his raised chair at his enormous desk, clicking off and on the tape recorder of some mealy-mouthed high-up guy in TU blabbing about the Passing of the Patriarch papers. I always think of bald old men sitting in a room papered with musty murals and discussing the intricacies of club rules.

I yawn. "Actually, it wasn't so bad. But, listen, I am very tired and I need to go to bed."

Thankfully, he doesn't try to play with me on this. After we talk for ten more minutes, I yawn some more and tell him good night.

"But wait—I just want you to be happy."

"Oh, Mark, I am. I am." Without you, most definitely.

"But I want to help you—"

"I don't need any help! Oh, my God, please! Good night already, okay?"

I hear him do one of his concerned sighs; I roll my eyes.

"Okay. Talk tomorrow?"

"Yes, of course. Good night now." I hang up the phone, despite the feeling of bugs chewing up my insides. It is going to be a long night.

From the balcony of my room at the Econo Lodge, a second-rate motel with sagging beds and peeling paint to which I always return for its smack-in-the-middle-of-town locale, I watch the traffic on Fourth Avenue. The sky looks yellow because of the streetlights. In the distance, I hear the train and my heart speeds up.

I'm out the door in two minutes, running toward Second Avenue. Just as I approach the intersection of Second and Main, my lungs bursting, I see the giant iron horse huffing and puffing. The train hollers and wails, a mighty surround-sound as I sit on the bench in front of Dairy Queen and watch and listen. And weep.

*****

When the last car of the train vanishes into the darkness, I stay seated, listening to the night music of insects. Moths are buzzing about around me; I can feel their wings brushing against my arms.

I've been way off the mark, I say out loud. Moths swarm around me, tickling my arms and legs. I look up at the moon, studying its craters for a moment. I just want to get close to you now, God.

I sit down on a nearby bench and stretch out my legs, listening to the whining of trains on the edge of town.

Then I hear a voice clear as day: *I've always been here for you.*

I stop and look up at the sky. "Was that you talking, God?"

A young couple walks by me, him hugging her close, eyeing me like I'm a lunatic. I laugh and they hurry on by. I'm embarrassed even more now.

Suddenly I want a glass of wine. *Need* a glass of wine. I run like the wind back to my motel room.

− 7 −

MONDAY MORNINGS ARE NEVER good to me. So I am really surprised that I feel as good as I do, in spite of the voice I heard last night and my fast guzzling of wine afterward. But I quit after just three glasses.

Today I plan to wrap up the interview of Mom and Aunt Sophia. I've put on extra mascara and even some lipstick and fluffed out my hair.

The hugs from Mom and Aunt Sophia feel extra special today.

"So let's see where we were last time." I start to rewind the tape recorder.

"I remember. We were talking about Grandma Bell," Mom says.

"Aha, that's right—"

"Actually, I wanted to bring up something," Aunt Sophia says.

I'm starting to sweat. "Yeah?"

"I know you always thought Grandma Bell was in such great shape, but she actually had quite a few health problems. I had to take care of her and my parents till their dying days," Aunt Sophia says.

That information isn't new. I remember the bloodied Kleenex lying around Grandma Bell's house and the furious whispers erupting between her and Aunt Sophia one year. The whole family was there spending Christmas at her house. I'd heard from my parents and Aunt Sophia that Grandma Bell had high blood pressure, but I had no idea at that time. They also said that Grandma Bell detested going to the doctor. I was all of nine years old, and I was completely on Grandma's side.

"I thought it was only after her stroke that she had to be looked after," I said.

"No, I had to watch over her since I was a teenager. And I was the only one in the family except for Grandpa Howell who drove, so it was up to me to go into town for medicine or anything. But I had no remorse because I was the only one around to do it," Aunt Sophia says.

And so?

Aunt Sophia takes a sip of her tea. "There's something else, though," she says.

Mom and I both look at each other, shrugging our shoulders.

"She had what I call religious sickness."

I sit there gaping, breathing through my mouth like a guppy.

"Sophia, whatever do you mean?" Mom implores her.

"She was always worried about her own salvation. Always doing things to try and make up for what she thought she had done wrong."

But what does this have to do with me? I wonder. As soon as I ask that question, I know exactly. I turn to watch some robins dart about the trees. If only I could fly away. Yet I need to hear this.

"Aunt Sophia? I thought Grandma was a Christian. I know she was!"

"Oh. Yes. No doubt." She puts her glass of tea down and waves away the flies starting to buzz about. "But she was obsessive about it. Like your dad, too."

At this, Mom plunks down her glass and wipes her mouth. "Sophia? Really! What on earth?"

"Now, Margie, you know what I mean. Those hours in the garage."

I shut off the tape recorder.

"Would you please tell me what in the world—"

"I think your dad has the same obsession that your grandma did. She never felt she got it right with God."

"But she loved God. She wanted me and Rita to be, to do—"

"I know. You're right. She really loved God. But with her she thought she had to earn that love. If she did enough things right, or not too many things wrong, that felt safe with her, that she had an *in* with God."

I picture Grandma Bell and the way she was, hugging and loving me, driving me and Rita to church, sitting next to us singing, "Great Is Thy Faithfulness."

Mom comes over to sit beside me in the porch swing. I put my arm around her.

"Well, tell me what you mean by this religious sickness. Give an example," I say, trying not to cry.

"She would have whole months of doubting she was going to heaven, of being saved." I shiver at this. "She used to call people up she knew from church and apologize to them for all the bad things she had thought of them. And of course, they didn't know what she was talking about."

"Sounds like what Grady had. OCD," Mom says.

"Sure enough. She actually ended up going to a mental institution."

"What! I never knew this before!"

I want to protect Grandma's reputation. There has always been a kind of secrecy or covering up of things in this family. Like the time that Rita and I went to Youth Group on a Sunday evening and the discussion for the evening was the evils of drug use. The youth pastor announced that Aunt Sophia was going to give a little talk on what happens with drug addiction. Rita and I had looked at each other wondering what she was going to say. Aunt Sophia got up calm as could be and talked to the kids as if they were her own. She said that her best friend, Margie—Mom!—had been addicted to prescription drugs from several different doctors and that she ended up in the hospital.

"She almost died from the withdrawal from them," Aunt Sophia said to the kids, to me and Rita, the first time we'd heard such a thing. I was shocked, ashamed, fuming mad. The other kids barely glanced back at Rita and me as they started peppering Aunt Sophia with questions. I wanted to stay. I wanted to leave.

And I never did find out the exact reason why Mom, too, ended up in a psych ward. Way back when Rita and I were so little that we could barely tie our own shoes, we went with Mom and Dad on a day trip. I had no idea where we were going or why. But when we stopped at this big building out in the middle of nowhere, Dad said that it was time for Mom to stay away for a little while, so we had to say goodbye, just for a little while. I still remember the agonizing pull in my heart of being torn apart from my mother. She was so exquisite then, big brown eyes under a short bob of auburn hair. Her voice was rich and low, consoling me as I clung to her. After a few minutes, she moved my arms from around her, said she had to go now. She walked up a huge flight of stairs, waving at me and Rita.

I hated Dad then, with all the passion a five-year-old could muster. Mom stayed away for at least a month, long enough that our cat Fluffy ran away and our parakeet Misty died. When I've asked Mom about it, she just said that Dad had her put away. That's all I ever knew.

"What is it about this family?" I lash out at Aunt Sophia now. She shrugs.

"Does God hate us?"

Mom looks at me. "Well, no, Renee..."

"Quite the opposite," Aunt Sophia says. She fills her glass with more tea from the pitcher.

"What do you mean, quite the opposite?" I ask.

"Well, the very fact that Grandma Bell and your dad and your mom, even you, Renee, turn to God, ask for His help in the middle of everything, well, that just proves we—you—are His."

"But this family, we—are filled with potholes. We're cracked. How do we know if we're onto the truth or not?"

Mom clears her throat, raises a finger. "Can I say something?"

"Please do, Mom."

"I think, I think that we're not to worry. If we don't know exactly what the preachers and pastors think we should know, that's not as important to God. What matters to him, I think," she clears her throat, "is that we want to love God, we want to know Him." Mom stops, looks at Aunt Sophia. "Isn't that about right?"

"Couldn't have said it any better."

A wash of relief overcomes me. Aunt Sophia sees the tears bubbling in my eyes. "You all right?"

I nod without speaking.

Aunt Sophia goes into the house and comes out with a box of tissues. "Just promise me one thing," she says to me.

"I know, Aunt Sophia. I promise."

*****

After the interview, Mom and Aunt Sophia asked me if I'd like to join them for lunch, but I excused myself, saying that I needed to have the time to wash my hair and catch up on some sleep. What I didn't tell them is that mostly I just needed to be alone. I wanted to go for a long drive. Oh, how I love driving in Kansas, especially in June during the wheat harvest. I never know what I'll see. After Mom and Aunt Sophia made plans to go with me to lunch in a couple of days, we said our goodbyes and I drove off with a tape of Enya playing.

Highway 17 takes me straight south to prairies and wheat fields. Blue and black clouds gather in the sky, making the wheat fields look even more golden. I get out of the car, keep Enya singing "Shepherd Moon," and get to work with taking photographs. Zooming in, I see a hundred starlings swirling in the sky about one hundred feet out. The Enya tape stops playing. The hair raises on my arms as I listen to the buzz and whirr of a thousand unseen insects.

Further south, I am singing "On My Way Home," one of my favorites of Enya's songs. The dirt road cuts straight by some wheat fields already plowed; the soil is a deep rich brown. After a bend in the road, the lay of the land changes with a slow-running curved stream dotted with trees. Off to my right is a farmer on a huge combine razing the wheat. The man is so close I can see the wrinkles in his sun-warmed face. We both wave to each other, smiling. One of the reasons I love driving in Kansas is that I'm often alone and can stop at any point to take a photograph. This is exactly such a moment, but I can barely see for the tears running down my face. I'm in heaven. And why do I live in California? Because I have a wedding ring on my finger.

*****

On my way back to the Econo Lodge last night, I had plenty of time to think about yesterday's interview with Mom and Aunt Sophia. As soon as I walked into the door of my motel, I got on the phone and called Mom. We made a date for this morning to go out to Lindsborg, a quaint Swedish town. We know without saying to dress up.

I drive out to her house and walk inside breathing in the aroma of freshly brewed coffee. Out the window are sparrows and doves splashing about in the birdbath. Mom's cat Star watches them from her throne of cushions, her eyes narrowed to slits.

"Is this okay?" Mom emerges from her tiny bedroom wearing a sky-blue dress. Today Mom wears a brunette wig.

"You look great, Mom." I look down at my own full white skirt. "And me?"

"Very nice. I have the perfect necklace to go with your top."

Mom is the best dresser, always has been. When she started selling Avon, her jewelry and accessories made her look like she was an heiress. So I am excited knowing I will wear one of her favorite pieces.

She returns now with a necklace of pearls and crystal red beads.

"This will go perfect with your outfit," Mom says, placing it around my neck. I lift up my auburn hair, the longest it's been in twenty years.

"There. That makes it," Mom says, her brown eyes just as huge close up as I remember when I was just five, ten, fifteen years old.

I look at us in the mirror together, she in her baby-blue dress, me in my white skirt and rose-print sleeveless top and necklace—and I get a shiver.

"Mom, I'm starved."

Since Mom likes to drive, too, I get into the passenger seat of her Buick; it still has that new-car smell. Even when she was bussing Rita and me to and from school, she had a brand-spanking shiny new car. Somehow Dad could afford it. Maybe it was because he literally brought home the bacon from his accountant job at the Winchester's Packing House. Bacon and ham and pot roast were the perks of a full-time job at the slaughter house. I shudder now, thinking of the time that Dad took Rita and me and Mom on a tour at the place. He was so proud, so happy. It was a real treat to see Dad that way since he was usually so serious and stern. Rita and I paraded through the place, mildly bored but secretly exchanging giggles and glances at each other for our parents' mooning over each other.

All the fun stopped, though, when we stepped into the green room. Rita and I saw the huge blade on the side of one wall of the cavernous space. "Daddy, what is that?"

Dad fidgeted with his hands. I'd never seen him do that before. It made me nervous.

"Well, girls, uh, Margot," he said, glancing at Mom, "this is where the animals, you know, they get made into meat."

Rita and I stared at him. My stomach dropped to my knees.

"And how do they do th—" I put my hand out to Rita to stop her.

"We know, we know. Can we see another room now?"

Dad cleared his throat and steered us all into the office where he plunked in numbers on an adding machine all day long.

I couldn't shake the awful thing I'd just seen. "Daddy, how do you work in here with, with all the noise…of the animals?"

Dad smiled. "Oh, I just turn up the music on my radio here."

After that night, I never looked at a strip of bacon or a piece of ham or a rump roast the same way. But what was I supposed to do? Tell Mom that I wouldn't eat meat anymore? We just didn't do things like that to mothers back then.

Dad went in every single day at a hard place to work—he rarely missed a day except for the times when his back gave out and I could hear the groans that he made and Mom getting on the phone to call the doctor. But Mom had to have her new car every few years. I never thought anything was odd about that, just figured it was like one of the pieces of clothing she bought at thrift stores. When she got tired of it, she'd throw it out and get another one.

I am reminded of all this as I slide into the passenger seat of her maroon-colored Buick, the air-conditioning already working. We both look good in this car, I am sure of it.

"What are you smiling about?" Mom backs the Buick out of the driveway.

"Remember when truck drivers would almost run right into us?"

"What! When?"

"Oh, you know. We'd be stopped at a traffic light and a big old truck would be making a turn and the driver could hardly keep his eyes off you. Rita and I would be scared he'd slam right into us." I laugh.

"Uh, no, I don't remember."

She doesn't remember a lot of things from the past. But that's okay.

"What happened?"

"Huh?"

"I mean, where was this guy?"

I burst out laughing. "Mom, it wasn't any particular guy. It was just that you would literally cause traffic jams."

"What on earth do you mean?"

"Okay, picture this. You're wearing your long wig with the big curls, and your face is all made up pretty. You've been selling Avon all afternoon, and then you come to pick Rita and me up from school on our way to Grandma's. So there we are at a traffic light on Fourth Avenue waiting for the light to change and all the trucks go lumbering by. And when the truck drivers need to turn and they see you behind the steering wheel, they just about slam into us because they're staring at you."

Truth is, Rita and I used to get so mad. I admit, even jealous. I mean, there we were, still in junior high school, starving for the kind of looks from guys that they threw at Mom. It just all seemed unfair. And weird.

"I don't remember that," Mom says, fiddling with the radio dial.

"Yeah, I think you were off in your own little world."

"Hey, what music do you like?"

"Anything today."

"What's that?"

"Mom, it's okay. Let's just enjoy the scenery."

And we do. Even as a little kid and later, a sullen teenager, I did like it when Mom and Dad took us out on a Sunday drive. The plains and prairies were dull to me, then, but I loved the rhythm of conversation that we had, all of us, even though Rita would try her best to pester me in the back seat next to me. We'd all say "Whooo" and "Wheeee" when we encountered a hilly road. On the plains, approaching a high road from a low one is akin to stepping heavenward. The wheat fields didn't make me want to sing harmonies like they do now, but the sight of the tall, green cornfields had us all want to get out of the car to get a closer look.

Just like now. Fifteen miles away from Lindsborg, Mom and I discovered a cornfield. We oooh and aaah and giggle while I try and snap a picture of us with my camera. The wide-angle lens takes in the scene of the cornfield behind us, as well as our image, too, shoulder to shoulder, smiling, heads touching. Out under the heat and sun, I can smell Mom's perfume, Candid by Avon. Always one of my favorites, I say, hugging her.

Back in the car, I offer Mom some trail mix of peanuts, almonds, and raisins mixed with M&M candies. Not wanting to set off a sweet tooth, I eat around the candies and hum and sing along with the Carpenters' "Top of the World" playing on an oldies station. Oldie. That's what I am now? I look at Mom. She is silent as a statue, staring straight ahead.

Mom turns to me, turns off the radio. "Renee, I have to tell you something."

I stop munching. "Okay?"

"Yes, yeah." She grips the steering wheel. "I have wanted to tell you this for a long time."

I put the baggie of trail mix aside. "What's wrong?"

"Nothing. Oh well, nothing now," she says, looking at me, half smiling, half frowning.

I look ahead. The road is clear.

"I-I…just want to tell you how bad I feel for how I treated you girls growing up. I mean, I don't even know why I acted that way half the time."

I'm frozen, my turn to be the statue.

"Renee, I am really so sorry. For how I was with you and Rita."

"Okay." I nod, as though my head were a puppet's.

Mom reaches her hand out to me. I don't know what to do with it. So I listen, still staring straight ahead.

"Whenever I see something on TV, like those Lifetime movies—Oh, boy, I can't handle it. I just am reminded by so many things. I don't know why I did what I did. To Rita and you."

A tear is running down Mom's face. I don't feel a thing except a strange sort of displacement. How do I wipe away eighteen years of terror and uncertainty in one morning? Yet I've already forgiven my mother, did years ago, although I can't place my finger on an exact day. Rita had a lot to do with that when she asked me to be her maid of honor, and I was catapulted into sudden family relations once again. That was just six years ago.

"Mom." I smile at her. I think of the Bible verse I've learned with Truth Universal. They may be screwed up in their theology, but I've sure learned a lot of Bible these past nine years. "It's okay now. Just remember that your sins—um, your mistakes are removed as far as the east is from the west." I couldn't bear to say aloud to Mom that she was sinning, had sinned. Something seemed weird, just wrong about that. That's God's business.

Another tear slides down Mom's face. She nods, smiles, and says thank you.

*****

As liberating as it was to have Mom tell me how sorry she was for how things had been for me at the house on Sherman Street, I was left feeling like a boat adrift on the open ocean, a homing pigeon without a home. In what direction would I take my life, now that Mom admitted that things had been bad between us, between me and Rita and Dad. What would I do with that? For decades, I'd swept my parents' misdeeds into the far corners of my mind. Why would I want anyone to know what had happened? She's a basket case, I imagined people would say, echoing how I'd thought about myself as a little girl, a mixed-up teenager, a crazy young lady, and a batty middle-aged woman.

With Mom's outright admittance of and apology for her and Dad's behavior, I could no longer pretend that I'd just had an overactive imagination. I had real scars, marring my outlook on life. Hopes. Dreams. Loves. Everything.

Suddenly I realized I had a new responsibility. I couldn't hide under the scars or the war stories. Though I'd forgiven Mom a long time ago, I continued to be stalemated in making any plans or do what I really wanted in life. Fact is, I didn't even know what I did want. Except for some vague notion of writing a book, maybe traveling some, and falling in love, I had no ambition, no pipedreams, nor any drive to undertake projects besides crocheting half a dozen rugs, purses, and pillows. I often fell into deep wells of despair. I would walk around in a daze at craft fairs, attend book-signings and author talks, listen to poetry readings, even walk on the beach looking for shells, but I'd still feel as if I'd been dropped off on an alien planet. What was the point of anything? A myriad of counselors I saw over the last twenty years always tried to get to the bottom of this. They would tell me that, of course, my childhood and adolescence were to blame for my confusion. I'd get so mad over that blanket statement. It was just too easy. But now, here, the truth I see as clear as day: I could never finish anything because I always had the background bickering voice knocking everything down. That voice was what I cowered under: Mom's. Sometimes Dad's. It made me sad, mad, too.

Yet with Mom's apology, won't I now have to have a clear vision in life? How does that even happen? I look around at my motel room. The cracks in the ceiling, rips in the carpet just add to my feeling of low self-worth. I pour myself more wine into a plastic cup and walk outside on the wrap-around balcony overlooking the street. Lightning is steaking across the sky.

Mom and I had a good time this afternoon in Lindsborg, a cute town known for its Swedish restaurants, festivals, history, and culture. To me, the food is rather odd and bland, heavy on the meat, with things like pickled herring and the proverbial Swedish meatballs. At the Swedish Crown Restaurant, Mom and I had pea soup and crispbread topped with cheese and cucumber slices, and of course, coffee. Afterward, we walked along Main Street and peered into the little shops. We watched a wood-worker carve Dala horses, got some

Swedish candy, went to a glass blowers' shop where Mom bought me two glass cardinals.

Afterward, Mom drove up to Coronado Heights, a sandstone bluff rising three hundred feet from the plains. The formation is named for Francisco Vasquez de Coronado, who visited central Kansas in 1541. Coronado was looking for the Native American community of Quivira, where he was told that trees hung with golden bells, and the pots and pans were beaten gold. The view from the top reveals the pretty patchwork of fields all around. I took a picture of Mom up there, then she took one of me. It was awkward, a little, having her do that. I mean, I felt kind of pretty, my auburn hair swept off to one side in a long ponytail. While she was taking the picture of me, Mom made little sounds of appreciation, and it was all I could do to shut out the old voices I used to hear from her: *get that hair out of your face, you look like a sheepdog, wipe that smirk off your face, what's wrong with you, you're so clumsy.* But as I smiled at Mom behind the camera, I took all those voices and put them on a shelf out of my reach, which is what I've been doing anyway for the last twenty years.

I smile now, thinking of the time we spent together today. A spackle of lightning crisscrosses the sky. And another one. The thunder makes me jump and toss wine onto myself. Giggling, I watch fat raindrops splat onto the balcony. They make a funny rhythmic sound plopping onto all the cars in the parking lot. Something hard and cold hits my finger. What sounds like miniature firecrackers erupts all around. Pea-sized hailstones are slamming everything; the building sounds as though it might come tumbling down. People from the neighboring rooms come out to take a look, barefoot, puffing on cigarettes. The hail sounds get louder and wilder.

"Whoa! Look at the size of those stones," the people from the next room said.

The hail is now golf ball size. The racket is unbearable. I look down at my rental car and die inside. Should have bought the insurance they always try to sell me at the rental agency.

Rita answers the phone when I dial her house. "Is it hailing there?"

"Sure is," she says with her drawl. "Fun, isn't it?"

"Rita, get Zach on the phone, please. Now."

"Okay, girl, what's going on?"

"My car is getting totaled with the hail."

"It'll be fine."

"Just, please, put Zach on the phone."

Zach has just as long as a drawl. "Hi, Renee, what's up?"

"Zach, I'm in so much trouble now. My car. It's going to be a wreck. The hail. I should have bought the insurance. But Mark always tells me not to bother. What do you think?"

"Oh, well, I wouldn't know about that. But I can tell you that your car will be just fine. It always sounds a lot worse that it is."

"Really?" The hail is still slamming down hard.

"Hey, Renee?"

"Yeah?"

"I can promise you the car won't get damaged. First thing in the morning, go down and take a look at it. And then call me."

"It's a deal. Thanks, Zach."

After I hang up, I sit for a while and watch the hail and lightning. My heart speeds up with an odd sort of excitement. I get on the phone to call Mark.

*****

When I got up this morning, I pretended I didn't have a care in the world as I slowly brushed my teeth, washed up, and got dressed. The sky was robin-egg blue, not a cloud in the sky. How does that even happen? A storm blows through, practically knocks the wind out of us, and blows our houses down, and next day it's clear as a bell. But this is Kansas. Anything can happen.

My heart was knocking around in my chest as I went down the rickety stairs of the motel. I kept my breathing even, pretending still that I couldn't care less about what happened to my rental car. Kept my head down and told myself I was really just going to the farmer's market down the street—which was true—but first, the car.

I walked around the Metro and looked for signs of hail. Nothing, not even a scratch. Zach was right.

At the farmer's market, I bought grapes and some cheesy bread, a bag of popcorn, some cinnamon almonds and a wooden carving of a woman with a bird on her finger. This good mood of mine is going to be around for a while, I told myself.

I swung by for Rita's kids. She was still asleep, would be until at least 11:00 a.m. Derrick answered my knock on the door. The kids had a smell like warm honey as they clambered into the car. We went to Crystal Park to eat our goodies, watch and feed the ducks and geese.

Now I am taking the kids around town, stopping in front of different houses.

"What are you looking at?" Evan finally asks when I stop in front of a house on Maple Street between Seventh and Eighth Avenue.

"Mmm, just checking out what houses on the market look like. Should we go in to this one?"

They all practically chomp at the bit at the idea. I am pretty sure they would all like to see what a nice house looks like, other than Mom's and Aunt Sophia's. At home, the kids all have to sleep in the basement, except for Heather, who gets the front bedroom adjacent to the living room. It's the same room where Rita and I bedded down one night when Todd had completely freaked me out while Mom was out selling Avon one night. He had been out drinking, and Rita and I were in the living room watching TV. When we heard Todd come into the house, Rita and I reacted the same way we always used to with Mom—we hurried to the TV to turn it off. It was hard getting out of that habit after years of watching *Star Trek* on summer afternoons, huddling down on the floor, eyes and heads craning up when we heard a car come down to our dead-end street. When Mom sailed into the driveway in her shiny cobalt blue Buick, Rita and I would scramble on our knees to turn off the TV and walk like twin hunchbacks to our separate rooms.

Todd's eyes were all red and goofy, his face flushed, and he coughed like crazy inhaling on his cigarette. He leered at us. "Whatcha girls doin'?"

I shook like a leaf on a tree, not so much out of fear but rage. I knew what that look meant on his face, and I wasn't having any of it.

"Rita, get beside me," I said. She did.

Todd hooked his fingers through his belt loop. "You girls been bad? You need to be punished?" He swaggered closer to us. I could smell his beery breath.

"Get the hell away from us!" I said.

Todd laughed and held out his hand to us. I dragged Rita by the arm and went to the phone, called Grandma Fraser. She was there within ten minutes and drove us out to her house for the night. I have no idea now why Mom wasn't yet home. She must have had some Avon customers who wanted to buy everything in the book.

Rita and I were oddly excited to be at Grandma's house. She never was a fuzzy-wuzzy warm grandmother-type; she always talked with us in a crisp and cool manner, but she was generous in other ways. The best part, she lived in town, not far away on a dead-end where the crickets were louder than our own breathing, but on a busy street where cars and trucks lumbered by every hour of the day and night.

That night Rita and I were on different vibes than normal. She was bouncing all around, pulling aside the curtains to stare out the window, sitting down only when Grandma Fraser told her to do so, but would be up again, half-dancing, making up a crazy lyric about a lost rabbit—we were in Wonderland!—and I sat down and started writing a long poem, which to this day I have never found. Grandma served us ice cream with cookies, which we lapped up like we were little kids. After we finished, she told us to get ready for bed.

The night indeed was deep black outside, the hour long past our normal bedtime, and we were still so jazzed—something was in the air!—but we climbed into our pajamas and crawled under the covers of the small bed in the front bedroom. Grandma came to the door to wish us good night, turning the lights off. Exhaustion ran through my blood like a heavy drug, but Rita was still amped. She tossed and turned and burrowed in close to me. That would have been okay, except she kept moving and giggling, shaking the bed, pinching me.

I sat up glaring at her in the dark. "Will you stop!"

"You're such a killjoy," she said, elbowing and pinching me.

I slapped her hands off me.

The lights snapped on. "What's going on in here?" Grandma stood in the doorway.

"Rita won't leave me alone," I said. Good grief, I'm a stupid tattletale.

"I'm just so excited," Rita said, her voice smaller under the glare of light.

Grandma stepped into the room. "I know you two got scared tonight at home. I'm glad to have you here. But you must settle down. Now. Got it?"

We both nodded, me glaring at Rita.

"Okay. Now go to sleep. I'll take you to school in the morning." Grandma closed the door behind her.

But Rita was still adrift in her bliss. She continued to rock the bed, while I just wanted to go to dreamland. It wasn't until decades later that Rita told me what was going on with her that night.

"I always felt so far away from everything at our house on our dead-end street. I loved being at Grandma's house that night. Loved the trucks and cars, the traffic. I felt so alive there," she said.

Trucks and trains and traffic excite me, too. Every time I fly home to Wheaton, I check into the Econo Lodge because it's on Fourth Avenue, nearly as busy as it is a couple of miles east at Grandma's house. Living in the suburbs in San Diego is pleasant, but far removed from the heartbeat of the city. So on my first couple of nights at the motel, I always do just what Rita did at Grandma's house: pull aside the drapes, look out the window, and open the door. But I always keep the chain lock on.

As far as Todd goes, Mom finally saw what Rita and I had: he was a total letch. He used to pat my behind when Mom wouldn't see. He had bad breath, a raspy cough, and his constant smoking burned my eyes and throat. I couldn't fathom what Mom saw in him, except that he was the antithesis of Dad. Where Dad wore white shirts and black pants, smelled of aftershave and hair gel, and he never drank a drop either of coffee or alcohol; Todd made noises with his mouth and stomach, had a cigarette always dangling from his lips, and he rode a Harley–Davidson. I think Mom liked how she felt on the back of that thing, free and easy. She and Todd went to taverns where they danced the night away. Polka dance is my favorite, she wrote once in a letter to me.

Dad wouldn't have dreamed of doing those things. Another thing Dad didn't do was look down the blouse of every woman he stood next to. Todd did all the time, often with Mom right by his side. That and his rough way with her eventually made Mom plan her escape, with Aunt Sophia's help.

Mom's had trouble with men all her life, with them leaving her, or she leaving them, or they just up and died. Married five times. I'm not far behind her. All we ever wanted, Mom and I, was love.

– 8 –

THE REAL ESTATE LADY opens the door to me, with the kids in tow. Her name tag says Corinne. At first, she grins at me, then steps back when she sees all the kids. "I'm here to see the house."

"It—uh, this, this is just a two-bedroom house," Corinne says.

I shake her hand and introduce myself. I tell her not to worry. "These are my nieces and nephews. I'm just looking for myself."

"Oooh, she's baking cookies!" Gemma says, sniffing the air.

I laugh. "They do that on purpose to make the house seem more like home."

"Can I have one?" Gemma persists. Corinne walks us to the kitchen and hands Gemma a plate of chocolate chip cookies. Heather and I take a cookie, too, and look around the kitchen and living room.

Heather, Gemma, and I wander over to the sliding glass door that looks out over a little lawn. I could plant vegetables here, if I wanted.

Derrick, Evan, and Camille have gone off to check out the bedrooms. I can hear them already claiming their make-believe spaces.

"So, what is it you're looking for?" Corinne breaks my reverie.

"I'm just doing some dream-shopping. I live in San Diego."

"Oh. Family there, too?"

"Um, no. I mean, yes. My husband. But everyone else is here."

"And you could have a dog, and a cat—and a bird over here in this corner," Gemma is saying.

The kids and I grab more cookies before we leave the house while Corinne talks to another client. I take one of her business cards from the table in the foyer. Who really has a table in the foyer, or for

96

that matter, a foyer? Shoving the cookie in my mouth while I unlock the car door, it occurs to me: I could. I could have a foyer.

*****

Evan asks why we looked at the house. "Are you moving here?"

I consider the question. I don't know the answer. "I can't. Mark wouldn't think of it."

"But why?" asks Gemma.

"Why what, I mean, which why?" I have them laughing by now.

"Why won't he move here, too?"

"Because this—I mean, you guys—are not his family. His is up in New York."

In the rearview mirror, I see Heather and Camille whispering to each other.

"Hey, you! Heather, what are you thinking?"

"Nothin'."

"Huh, not true. I so want a room like the one at that house," Camille pipes in.

"So do I," Evan says.

Rita and Zach have had it tough, raising five kids on Zach's meager income as a printer. The little house they live in now used to be where Grandpa and Grandma Fraser lived. After Grandpa died, Aunt Shirley and Uncle Charles invited her to live with them out in Florida, so Grandma had to put her house up for sale. Rather than go through a real estate agent, Grandma offered a good price for Rita and Zach and their kids to move into. Good deal, except it was a two-bedroom house, barely big enough to hold a family of seven. All of them squeezed together like that reminds me of the poem of the woman living with all her kids in a shoe. The kids have had to sleep in the basement all these years. My stomach turned, my skin crawled when I happened to glance down the stairs into that black hole. Curtains hanging on a clothesline separated the boys from the girls. The musty odor of something bad—rats? mold?—surely gave them the sniffles. The kids always seemed somewhat wan, lethargic.

But I've always admired Rita. She brought five kids into this world, albeit by different guys. Still, she chose life for those kids rather than abortion—unlike me. Everyone in my family thought Rita would be the one to play it crazy and I'd be the mothering kind. Just goes to show that nobody in my family really knew either of us very well. The irony depresses me. By the time I was thirteen years old, I knew with as much certainty that the sun would rise the next day that I would never have any kids. When I turned sixteen, I promised myself that I would get away, get out from under the blaring silence, crushing pressure of trying to live by a double standard. My parents went to church most Sundays, my dad tried nightly devotions for a few weeks to no avail (I did hold dear to my heart that my father was trying to draw us in, but my sister's and mother's eyes darted nervously about, glaring at me, too), we did say grace every night before dinner, but that is all the evidence I could see of having any salvation that I learned about in Sunday school and the preacher yelled at us about. But when Rita and I went down to the altar that one Sunday—sobbing alongside Dad—I know, I believe that something shifted in us permanently, though we never spoke of it.

So Rita likes her beer now. I understand that. I have my wine. I don't like that. I am trapped between two worlds, the shell of my skin and the seeking of my spirit. Perhaps Rita is, too.

Aren't we all

*****

Rita is all ready to go when I drop off the kids. She and I are going for one of our "drives to wherever-we-end-up." The cool thing about Kansas is you can go forever in a straight line, turn the corner to go north or south or whatever direction, and you can't get lost. If you do get lost, a passing car or a farmer out in the field will point you in the right direction.

I am caught off guard that Rita is up and raring to go. She usually takes a long time to get moving in the morning, longer even than me. I watch her walk out of the house and toward my car. She has on blue jeans and a long lacy top.

"Oh, pretty!" I tell her as she gets in, her long brown hair moving over her shoulders.

She grins, looks me up and down. "Not bad yourself."

We are both hippies at heart, still listening to '70s music. I turn the radio dial to a station playing oldies.

"So, I'm thinking of Sterling, grabbing some eats at the Snack Shack by the lake, and then heading over to the Great Bend area."

"Sounds good to me," Rita says, putting her purse on the floor.

We head out of town, cruising down Fifth Avenue, both of us looking toward Sherman Street, our childhood neighborhood, as we pass it. I love Sherman Street, Rita doesn't.

We both sing along to that old Fleetwood Mac song on the radio about walking in dreams. As I drive us into Nickerson, Rita tells me she has looked forward to this afternoon out. We stop at the railroad track, waiting for the train to pass, making me think of where Rita and Zach lived in their early marriage. The train would pass by day and night, rattling and shaking the very foundation of the two-story yellow house. Rita was living there with her kids the year she married Zach; I'd flown out to be her maid of honor. We'd spent hours talking, crimping her hair, planning wedding details, going out for dinner with her and Zach's friends. And I met her kids for the very first time. Gemma wouldn't arrive yet until the next year—whom Rita referred to as Zach's wedding gift.

"I sure miss that old house where you were on Third Street."

Rita groans. "Ugh, no, I don't. I know the kids liked it. But the place was falling apart."

Rita and I look at each other, remembering what we call "the night."

"Oh my god, wasn't that scary?"

"Well, um, no, it wasn't for me," Rita says, laughing.

The road in front of us curves and bends as we wind into Sterling.

"I'll always remember that night as 'the storm.'"

"It was just another day in July for us, but I knew, I tell ya, I knew you needed to get back to Aunt Sophia's," Rita says.

The breeze is blowing our hair all around, and I round the bend in the road to the city limits of Sterling. The Eagles are on the radio and Rita and I are feeling good.

And that's when I hear the siren. My rearview mirror shows the flashing lights of a police car. "Oh-oh, just be cool," Rita says.

I'm the furthest thing from cool, my hands shaking as I get my registration to the rental car out of the glove compartment and reach for my license. I see the cop tip his big police hat and saunter over toward my car. He leans in and asks what's up.

"We are sisters," I say, my voice trembling, "and I'm visiting from California."

"We're just going for a drive," Rita says, smiling, all coolness.

"Well, let me see your license and registration," the cop says, inches from my face. His breath smells oniony.

I hand him the documents and then turn to Rita. She whispers it's okay.

"Well, now," he says, giving me back the license and registration, "I really should give you a ticket, but I'm just giving you a warning." He writes on his pad, tears off a piece of paper and gives it to me.

"No need to show up in court anywhere. But slow down. You were driving forty in a 25 mph zone. Have a good day."

"Thanks, Officer." Should I have said "sir"?

Rita and I sit waiting for the cop to drive off first. I sit, still shaking. "Sorry, sis. I should have told you this is a cop hot spot," Rita says.

Something between sobs and rage quiver up inside me, my hands quivering, and my breath ragged. I take in great gulps of air trying to calm down.

"Hey, girl, he just gave you a warning, that's all."

"I know. I know. Crap, I get so mad when I get scared like this."

Rita laughs. "You'll be fine. Don't you remember that the same thing happened a couple of years ago?"

I get some Kleenex from my purse and dot the tears from my eyes. "What do you mean?"

"What, you don't remember?" Rita bellows. She laughs hard, her face scrunching up. Finally, she turns to me. "Girl, I can't believe you can't remember that. Man, oh man, a cop pulled us over almost at the exact same location. For us doing the same thing, dancing in our seats and you driving too fast." She bursts out laughing again.

I can hardly remember that, which freaks me out. "Okay, okay. Know what? I'm hungry and I need to pull off the road for a while."

"Okay. Where we goin'?"

"Right up here to the Snack Shack. They have the best fried mozzarella cheese sticks."

As usual, Rita isn't much hungry, but I order the cheese sticks, some fried okra, and cherry lime slushies. We take our loot to the lakeshore and plunk down on a picnic table.

"Girl, you are still shaking."

"I know." The fried mozzarella sticks and okra are hot as blazes in their little paper sacks. "Have some. I can't eat it all."

We sit and crunch and munch for a few minutes, watching the wind make ripples in the water. Rita and I swam here a couple of summers when we were in our early teens. It was fun enough, but I remember wanting to stay far away from the raucous boys splashing and crashing into me. I would always climb up on the buoy to get away from their animalistic grabbing and growls.

"The thing that the cop set off for me is that I remember being pulled over when I was—what, twelve years old?—for running a stop sign on my bike."

Rita laughs. "Wow. That's an accomplishment."

"Don't they have anything else to do around here other than pull people over?"

"Hey, what's the big deal? It's just one cop bored with his job."

"You know something? Cops around here play God. They do. And sometimes I think God plays cop."

"I never thought of it that way," Rita says, her right eyebrow raising up as she sips her limeade.

"But I think I'm wrong in how I think about God."

Rita takes a fried mozzarella stick and pulls it apart slowly, watching the cheese ooze out. "You know what I think you should do?"

"Chill?"

"Well, that. But not what I was going to say. I think," she pops half the mozzarella cheese stick in her mouth, chewing, watching me, "I think you should call Devon."

"What! Why in the world would I want to do that?"

"Because you've wanted to ever since Dad showed that video."

"That doesn't make it right."

"Aha, see you admit it." My sister can swivel my head, I swear.

"I really don't want to talk about this anymore."

"Okay. Suit yourself. But let's go for a drive," she says, wadding up the paper bags. We take our slushies with us to the car.

As flabbergasted as I am at Rita's suggestion for me to call Devon, I determine to make the best of the afternoon. After all, I was the one driving. And I had questions to ask her.

We head out toward Lyons where the water tower stands high and proud above Cow Creek. Like it was yesterday, I remember the time when the family piled into the pickup truck for a fishing trip out here. Grandpa Howell loaded his fishing pole with bait, motioning for Rita and me to join him at his side. I felt confused for a number of reasons. Grandpa Howell could hardly see, something called glaucoma in his eyes. Rita and I had looked forward to playing on the swings and teeter-totter and having the picnic lunch that Grandma Howell, Aunt Sophia, and Mom were spreading out on the picnic tables. But Grandpa insisted that we take a fishing lesson from him. Rita plunked down onto the bridge overlooking the water and watched Grandpa catch a fish. I drummed my fingers on the railing overlooking the creek, hemming and hawing as he pulled up a catfish. I could see the whiskers of the catfish quiver as Grandpa reeled it in. Rita squealed, and I ran away when I saw the fish gasping.

I asked Rita if she remembered that day.

"Grandpa took us fishing?"

"Well, no, but he wanted us to give it a try. Over there," I point to the creek as I drive by.

Rita shakes her head. So I retell the fish-out-of-the-water story.

"I feel like that fish sometimes," I say.

Rita laughs loud. "What do you mean?"

"Like I'm trying to breathe through cotton. My heart starts racing and my breathing gets really shallow."

"Oh, boy, do I know that feeling."

"Yeah, well, I think it's the number one reason why I continue to drink." There, I said it.

"That doesn't make any sense," Rita says, sloshing the rest of her slushie in her cup.

"But you just said that you get those feelings, too. It's an anxiety attack."

"Who wouldn't have them after what we've been through?" Rita says. It's her favorite line.

"That was thirty years ago. Aren't you—we—past all that by now?"

"How can you get past it? It ruined me."

My stomach tightens. "Rita. Really? Ruined you? That's what a 'counselor'"—I raise my hand in making quotes—"would call a defeatist statement. You're letting our mother run your life in your head even though you won't even talk to her."

Rita glares at me.

"You believe in God, in Christ, don't you?" My voice is a little softer now.

"Of course. I went up with the altar call way back when, right beside you."

I nod. "But has that been enough?"

"Whaddya mean?"

We both look at the pastures and wheat fields rolling by us on West 56.

"Well, for me, I just know that day is like a wonderful memory to me. It was very real the things I felt and the prayers I said about giving my life to Him. But I've been sidetracked a whole lot."

Rita picks up her slushie and swirls the straw. "By what?"

"Life. Love. Jealousy. I mean you name it."

"Your point is?"

"I find myself doubting my own faith all the time. I mean, how can I really be a Christian if I continue to do the things that I don't want to do? And I don't mean what Paul the Apostle talked about in Romans."

"Girl, you are giving me a headache. What in the world are you talking about?"

"Don't you ever think about not drinking anymore? I know I sure do."

Rita rubs her temples. "No. I don't. It's Mom's fault for getting me hooked in the first place. She gave me my very first beer. I was seventeen years old."

Oh. My. God. "When did that happen?"

"You know, when I had to live with Mom and Todd before I went into the Navy? Well, they used to bring me along with them when they went out drinking and dancing at this bar in Burton."

Brought her along? "Why?"

"Hah. Guess Mom didn't trust me to leave me alone at the house."

"That is just bizarre."

"Yep. So anyway, one night I started asking Mom what beer tasted like. And she let me have one."

"Did you like it?"

"I spit it out on my first sip."

We laughed. "I did, too, first time I tried it. Said it smelled and tasted like skunk juice."

"Eeewww. But the rest is history. I liked beer after that."

By this time in our conversation, I've driven far enough to Cheyenne Bottoms, the largest marsh wetlands in the center of the United States. Rita and I get out of the car to stretch our legs. An icy wind almost knocks us over.

"Will you look at that?" Rita points up to an alien-looking cloud with white bosomy bumps on its underside.

"Are we in trouble?"

"Haha, girl, you're always in trouble in Kansas. You know that."

She means it in jest, but it is something to ponder. My hometown and all its memories get me walking on a narrow balance beam. My knees are shaking. "Seriously. Is it going to hail?"

"Maybe. Let's drive to the end of the road here."

Why not? The bosomy cloud is getting wider and darker as I drive us out to the end of the road. The water is churning up dark and frothy. "Rita, I'm not liking the looks of this."

Lightning strikes across the water.

"Oh, shit!" We echo each other.

The car kicks up dust as I back out maniacally. Rain splats across the car like a thousand insects dying on impact. The alien tit-cloud has exploded.

"Let's go!" Rita screams.

*****

I got us safely home, both of us watching the cloud melting behind us as we scrammed like there was no tomorrow. We stopped only to get food back in Lyons at McDonald's. While we munched on fries and me a fish sandwich—"Really?" Rita said with raised eyebrows when we ordered at the drive-up—and she a quarter pounder. "Oh, really, huh?" I teased her. I've never seen her eat more than half of anything, anytime, anywhere.

It was nearly dark going back home and I didn't care that I was driving fast. Rita had the chatter bug big-time, laughing and carrying on like she used to do when she was a kid even after Mom had just about knocked her down on the floor for some infraction.

By the time I dropped Rita off, we were both bleary-eyed and happy in a weird way, hugging each other tight.

Now in my darkened room at the Econo Lodge, the TV throws blue light onto the wall. I'm waiting for the train to make its stop in town. Funny how I depend on that. I depend on a lot of things, really. This glass of wine, for instance. I look forward to the slippery, easy way that my muscles and mind feel after I've swallowed a few sips. Which isn't good. No. But I don't know which way to go. And here comes again that feeling that I'm losing something. Or somebody. Soon. I put down my glass and get down on my knees. I don't know what to say, except "Help me, Lord."

*****

It's been pleasant here in my hometown, but now I've got to think about heading back to where I live. All the open space, the winds and storms, the memories and mind-sets of people out here have me feeling on edge. I am craving the mountains and desert, the smell and swell of the ocean, and something to do in the evenings other than listen to and watch the trains go by or lightning spackle across the sky. Besides, I really need to get back to Mark. When I called him last night, he sounded downright perturbed. I can't risk that.

I need to see Dad before I leave town. And I'm going to break one of his cardinal rules during my childhood and teen years: Never call or talk to, or heavens be, visit him at work.

So here I am swinging open the door to Wagoner's Auto Repair. When Dad found himself laid off suddenly from Winchester's, he was fifty years old. The meat packing company was cleaning up its image and sweeping out old ideas, along with people. Dad pounded the streets for months looking for work. I remember a rare time when I had called him. I'm too old for this, Renee, he'd told me. No, I said, you're not, remembering how Dad's hair looked that of a swanky billionaire.

My dad was never too old. I told him that. "Yes, I am. Nobody wants to hire a fifty-year-old man."

Bill Wagoner finally did, welcoming Dad like an old friend into the small business. While an auto repair shop hardly seemed the kind of place where Dad would work, neither was the meat-packing company. But Dad fit in wherever he was. Dad told me that Wagoner's business practically doubled ever since he started working there. Bill could not praise Dad enough for his friendliness and making customers feel at ease. I wished I could have seen more of that side of Dad at home, instead of the silent, sullen way he was around the house, dodging our words and glances.

Forget all that for right now. I straighten my shoulders, throw open the door and walk into the dimness. There Dad is sitting at his desk, his long arms and legs all akimbo in the short swivel chair. He turns to see me approaching, and his face crinkles into a big smile. He still has that billionaire hair.

"Hi, kid!" he says, standing up.

"Hi, Dad."

"What brings you here?"

"Just wanted to see where you worked. I'll be leaving day after tomorrow."

Dad wheels over a chair for me. "Well, sit down. And talk to me."

My heart is bumping around all weird and funny, as if I'm on a date, for crying out loud.

"Actually, I just wanted to see you in action here, on the job."

"Oh, in action here, huh?" Dad does his funny swagger of the head, winking at me.

I laugh. "So what are you doing today?"

He bends over some notepads on his desk. "Figuring out some customer invoices. But I'm going to take a few minutes just to talk with you." The phone rings.

"Go ahead," I tell him.

I snap a picture of him talking on the phone and smiling. He talks for a few minutes, then hangs up.

"Where were we?" He laughs, tapping his foot on the floor. Even now, when he does that, I get a monstrous craving for Mom's double chocolate chip cookies. He used to look up at the sky through the window and tap his foot while eating one of those warm, melty wonders. I would dream and eat right along with him.

"You said you had something to tell me?"

"Oh, yes." He wheels my chair around so that I can face him directly. I snap another picture of him, feeling an odd mix of guilt and glee.

"Kid?" He clears his throat. "Renee. You're good at what you do. Writing and interviewing people. And taking pictures. Aren't you?"

I nod, wondering where this is going.

"Well, I want you to know that I believe that you will be successful in whatever you do. Whatever you decide to do. I believe in you."

It's another one of those gaping guppy moments for me. Why is Dad telling this to me now? What did I do to deserve this, this—blessing, so to speak?

"I should have told you a long time ago. I'm proud of you."

I haven't realized how long I've been wanting and waiting to hear those words. Tears are streaming down my face.

Dad plucks a tissue out of the box he has on his desk and gives it to me.

I blot my eyes, my hands shaking. I ask Dad if he remembers the time he gave me that little red diary.

"What was that?" He bends his ear toward me.

"You've got to remember. One evening when I was about thirteen years old you got home from work kind of late, and it was snowing outside, I remember that, and you kissed Mom like you always did. But you were holding something behind your back. Mom asked what it was, and you said it was for me. And then you walked over to where I was standing watching Mom cook and handed me a diary with a key and gilded pages. And you told me to write my dreams in it."

Dad nods. "I do remember."

"And I wanted to. Write my dreams. I did. But I also wrote about all the frustration I felt about, uh, mmmm, about Mom. About things with her. And about Devon."

"Oh, kid, I'm sorry about all that. It's been heavy on my mind all these years. And I still think you should call Devon."

"But, Dad, I'm married."

"So? You can still talk to him. Interview him."

I am incredulous, not sure over what more, the fact that he has given me a blanket-blessing or the go-ahead to call the man I still love. Oh, no. I've admitted it. Yet he is a man I hardly know. It was the boy I fell for.

"Kid, you're blushing," Dad says laughing, holding his arms against him in his typical tickled-to-pieces pose.

I straighten up and look at him. "Dad, stop it. I'll think about what you've told me."

"Good. Interview Devon about tornadoes. In California," he says matter-of-factly. Dad swivels over to his desk to study an invoice.

"Dad, you know we don't have tornadoes in California."

He turns to me, with one of his big grins. "Maybe not yet."

I don't get this, just don't. But I am going to go with it. Because Dad is in rare form.

*****

Nearly two hours I spent there with Dad talking, teasing and taking his picture. His boss came over to greet me and shake my hand. Bill Wagoner said I was a real looker. Dad tapped his foot, held his sides and laughed and nodded at that. "She is," Dad said.

If only he could have paid that kind of attention to me when I was a teenager in love and lost in a world of my own. But I dared not bank on "if only." So I just smiled at Mr. Wagoner and thanked him.

And then it was time to go. Dad was starting to get that restless look in his face, pursed lips, set brows. So I stood up, my arms wide to indicate a hug. Hugging him is difficult to do, seeing as how he is six feet, six inches tall, me five feet six inches. Besides, Dad has never been a hugger. But he pushed himself up and stood, bending forward to envelop me in a loose grasp. I breathed in his clean, soapy smell and the Old Spice cologne he's worn ever since I can remember.

"Just remember, kid, you can do whatever you set your mind to," he said when we let go of each other.

Looking back on that now and thinking on what he said, I take comfort in his words, but I find myself going deeper with that thought. Whatever I set my mind to do sounds wonderful, like a door opening into a secret garden, but if I am the only one who sees the garden, what is the point? Without God, I am a vapor, can do absolutely nothing that will last beyond this earth-time. Yet with Him, I can do everything in His name, His purposes. I've been meditating quite a bit on one of my favorite Bible verses, Philippians 4:13: I can do all things through Christ who strengthens me.

Change

– 9 –

My last visit with Dad was also my last day in Kansas for this trip home. I had to leave the land of the south wind and get back to my daily busy, loud world. On my way out of Wheaton driving to the Wichita airport, as I passed by Wagoner's Auto Repair, my heart swelled, tears jumping to my eyes. I wanted to stop, just one more time, to see Dad. Yet it was more important that I left with his blessing on my mind, as much as it still mystified me.

On the plane ride to San Diego, I stared out at the marshmallow cloud mountains, meditating on everything I learned about my family this trip. The call of Kansas was strong, yet so much kept me in San Diego. Mark, for one. But, well, he really was just the one. I could count on one hand the number of friends that I would maybe stay for. My work as a freelance reporter kept me busy and bouncing from one newspaper to another, but I had no family strings, or friend-strings, for that matter.

I was still thinking about all this as I pulled my carry-on bag behind me and walked the ramp from the plane into the gate. There was Mark waving at me. He stood with his feet wide apart, left hand on his hip, his Gumby ears sticking out under wispy hair, lips in a thin pretend-smile. My heart sank. No chemistry between us whatsoever. We kissed perfunctorily. He started to put his arm around me and I waved it away. Can't do that while dragging this thing, I said.

I was surprised when he took the bag into his own hands and grasped my left hand with his. We waited for an eternity at baggage claim for my Samsonite black luggage to come down the chute. Finally, Mark and I walked to the baggage office to file a form. The guy was as bored with his job as I was with myself. It'll be here in the morning, I'm sure, the baggage guy said.

Mark opened the passenger seat to his hatchback Hyundai loaded with every piece of his window-washing equipment. The smell of Dawn detergent suffused through the car. It was still early evening and Mark suggested we grab a bite to eat at Denny's. He loved Denny's, I didn't. But I was hungry. So we went.

The traffic, the noise, the cars, all those cars like brassy stinging beetles, and the packed-in buildings, got under my skin. So many cars, I said, stunned. Mark glanced at me, laughed.

And it's so big and crowded, I said.

Mark said, compared to Kansas, sure.

I hated it. I hated it. But what was I to do except get back into the swing of things? I was going to change a few things, though. Starting tomorrow.

*****

Mark is on the rampage again. I pour my third cup of coffee and he yells at me to get back into the living room and sit down and listen to what he has to say. He just about spilled his own coffee when I told him just now that I didn't plan on going to Truth Universal's fellowships today or anytime ever again.

It's taken me a long time to admit to myself that Truth Universal is far from being "the way." If I had to explain to a stranger what the organization was, I'd honestly say a cult. But not in the way you'd normally think of a cult, with people living together on a farm or commune. The first time I ever heard a guy teach at one of their fellowships, I thought I'd heard the freshest exposition on the nature of God. He talked about the Holy Spirit being a gift, something to be received. I'd never understood the Holy Spirit when I was a kid and teenager trying to wade through the preachers' goings on about the ways and wrath of God. As a kid, I'd sit in church with my Easter hat pinching my head, my shoes squeezing my feet so hard so bad I wanted to stand up and scream. But I didn't. So I sat through the sermons and hardly heard a word the preachers said except, "Don't you want to go to the promised land, to Canaan?"

Yes, I did. Hadn't I paid the fare already?

I really didn't know anything about the nature of God except that He had allowed me to be born, which made my parents perpetually mad at each other, at me and Rita and apparently, God. I also knew by way of Sunday school and memorizing Bible verses that God had sent His Son to die for us so that we could have eternal life. And then we were supposed to take up our cross and daily die for Him. Um, I was dying every day at home under my parents' hands and words. I prayed for help every day in some way, but it never came. That's what I thought at the time. Later, I would realize that my Aunt Sophia next door, as well as my Grandma and Grandpa Howell and their parents, my Great-grandma and Great-grandpa Bell living across the street, were saviors leading me in the path of my Savior.

By the time I left home, I had abandoned thoughts of a just God, much more Bible reading, praying and attending church. Rita and I had watched our parents split up and marry different people. Something shifted between Rita and me; we lost what trust we did have in each other. All boundaries were broken, and I was laid out tossing in the wind. When forced to live with Mom and Todd, who were not even married yet, I ran away from home, stealing peanut butter and bread and a big bag of M&M's from a store down the street where I found a room for $80—the same price that Dad made me pay for living at home when I got my first job at sixteen years old. My room was up on the second floor of a rickety old apartment building. From the lumpy bed in my tiny room, I looked down on the world of the simpering souls walking on the sidewalk and chomped on M&M's. Goals? Only to avoid pain and plot a better, longer escape.

But I never got a chance, for on the very next day, I got a knock on my door from my landlord. You got company downstairs, he said.

It was Mom. And my supposedly good friend Jackie Ryan. I'll never forget her because every time I hear that song on the radio "Jackie Blue," I always think of her, and what I wish I could say to her now. Jackie was standing behind Mom looking to the right, to the left, fidgety while Mom blared at me with her big brown eyes and jabbed her fingers in front of my nose.

You could have died in a fire here at this place, it's so run-down, she went on and on. Then she took me by the arm and pulled me over to her car. Truth be? I don't think she was all that concerned about whether I would have died if the place had caught fire. Looking longingly up at the little window where I'd eaten my peanut butter sandwich and M&Ms just an hour before, I squeezed my eyes shut and tried to block out Jackie's apologies and Mom's rantings. It was a wicked cacophony.

What I wish I could say to Jackie now is this: If only you had known what was really happening at home. But there it is again, if only. There's never any time for remorse.

*****

Abuse has a way of spreading its dark wings and carrying you off to even darker places. That's what it has been like with Mark. I married this man because I was sick and tired of my roller coaster of relationships with guys. Nearly four years in Alcoholics Anonymous back in the '80s had me on a dizzying ride of moving from one place to another, sometimes living only three months at a time in the same place. Homelessness was just a step away in those days, had it not been for whatever guy I was in love with. Even now, Phil Collins' song "Just Another Day in Paradise" gives me the chills. Guardian angels I could believe in. God? He was just too big, too bossy and too mad.

Still, I married Mark because I was homesick for God. Because of Mark, I heard and read the Scriptures for the first time in twelve years. He took me to seminars and regional gatherings of Truth Universal. When I sang the old classic hymns, I thought my heart would break with simultaneous glee and guilt. I fell in love with God again, though I was hearing a different sort of story about Him. The TU people talked about how we could bring prosperity or poverty on ourselves, depending on how much we blamed God for it. They also taught that Jesus was the Son of God, yes, but a mere man.

And there was the Trinity issue. Oh, the Trinity. Growing up in church, I could never rest with the concept of God being three in one: the Father, the Son, and the Holy Spirit. I almost felt like God was being, um, three-faced. To make matters worse, I had begun again the love affair with wine, guzzling up to eight glasses of wine at night, drowning and shouting out a passionless marriage. Mark lit up in his big boy office high chair, twirling knobs and flipping switches of his audio-computer set up. He'd come out glazed-eyed from Mary Jane and I'd be boozy and crying as I pounded out my story on an itsy-bitsy word-processor. Words between Mark and me quickly became weapons nearly every night.

I might have stayed forever with him, though, because I didn't want to disappoint God any more than I believed I already had. I would have stayed, slamming down the wine and oozing boozy prayers every night to God until Mark betrayed me in the most bizarre manner I could imagine. And it had nothing to do with sex. Now I was just biding for time.

*****

My dad's near-plea for me to call Devon infuses my days and nights. My palms get sweaty and my mouth dry just thinking about it. But Dad's right. I need to think like the journalist that I am. I found out that Devon works at the Norman, Oklahoma Center for Atmospheric Research. He is doing exactly the kind of work that I imagined when I was assigned to write a eulogy in my high school English class.

My hand is shaking now as I pick up the phone. I half hope he won't be there so that I can forget about it. But on the third ring he picks up. My heart pounds like drums at a pow-wow.

"Devon? Is this Devon Rawlings?"

"It is. Who's calling?"

"Well, you could say this is a voice from the past." I laugh, rub my temples, shaking my head at disbelief in myself. "I'm, uh, my name is Renee. My last name was Howell. I don't know if that rings a bell with you."

Silence. I stand up and twirl the phone cord in my fingers, sit back down. "We were in the same English and social studies class together. You know, we used to finish our work before everyone else and then make car racing noises in the back of the room. The teacher made us move apart from each other after that."

Really? I'm telling this to him now?

"Oh yes. Yes, I remember. How are you?"

Oh. My. Goodness. "I'm doing well, thank you. This is not really a social call, though. I wanted to know if I could interview you."

Devon laughs. I wonder if his Adam's apple moves when he laughs. I wonder if his eyes are still as blue as they ever were. "What would this be for?"

I stagger around in my mind for an answer. I write for several little community newspapers around San Diego, but not for the *Union-Tribune*. Well, maybe it was about time.

"It's for the newspaper out here. Did you see the movie that came out just a couple of months ago? Twister?"

Again, Devon laughs, a little snuffing sound. "Actually, I went just last weekend with my son. Eight years old, and when the cow got caught up by the tornado, he said, 'There goes a moo-cow.'"

"And when the second cow went flying by, he was upset by that. But I told him the likelihood of that happening was very rare."

It's my turn to laugh, if only to calm my knocking knees. "So what about when the two tornado chasers strapped themselves to a pipe in the barn and held on while the tornado took out everything around them? Would that even work?"

"Only in the movies," Devon said.

I stand up, twirl the phone cord. "So, Devon, can we continue talking for a little bit now? I mean, can you do this interview now?"

"Sure. But let me ask you something first."

"Go for it." I sound just too cheery.

"What are you doing with your life?"

"Wow. That's an interview-breaker. Or maker." I laugh. "Well, I got a B.A. in Spanish at San Diego State and—"

"Spanish? I thought you would major in English."

"It's a long story. I loved English and writing and reading, but studying it in college seemed to ruin it. I didn't want to dissect it, just read and enjoy it."

"Makes sense to me. But why Spanish?"

Part of me wishes I could crawl into a mole hole, but talking with Devon has always been on my to-live-for list. So here goes.

"Spanish was the most difficult thing I ever learned except for math, I'm ashamed to say".

"Oh, but why would you feel that? Math is a difficult subject for most people."

"I didn't want to be most people," I said. "I wanted to be different."

"Sounds like you are on your way."

"Hhmmm, I like how you put that," I say, laughing like a schoolgirl. I catch a glimpse of myself in the hallway mirror and straighten my shoulders. "Anyway, I just went for it, tutoring Spanish at the community college, then later at the university, I wrote papers—and even poems—in all kinds of classes and I, um, well, I graduated with honors at San Diego State University."

Devon clears his throat, pauses, as if he's been off doing something else.

"But I know that my life story pales in comparison to what you've done," I say.

"Don't say that," Devon says. "I'm a scientist, you're a writer, everybody is important, all of us."

I pull and twist my hair, fighting the tears in my eyes. "Hey, so can I interview you now?"

"Go for it."

Devon tells me all about his chasing twisters with a team of tornado scientists. I never knew what my eyeteeth were, but as I listen to him tell his adventures, I would have given them up, as they say, to have gone on a journalistic adventure, riding in the storm chasers' van with him, taking pictures of him at work, in repose, maybe of him stealing a glance and smile at me.

"We study tornados so that we can better predict them," he says.

"And how has it been going?"

"It's been slow. It's almost impossible to predict tornadoes, so we mostly concentrate on getting the word out early about a tornado coming through town."

I ask if tornadoes can occur anywhere. "Even in California?"

"Oh, most definitely. They may not be of the same caliber as our Kansas tornados. If they do happen in California, it's more in the form of water spouts over the ocean."

"But should we expect doom and gloom from a water spout over the ocean the same way that a tornado can bring destruction to Kansas?"

He laughs. "No, not really, because most water spouts are far away from shore."

I stand up again, wrapping the phone cord around my hand. "Devon, what I really would like to know is…"

"Yes?" His voice sounds like it used to in seventh grade.

"What is the scariest situation you've been in?"

He sighs. "Whew, that's a good question." He pauses for a moment. "To tell you the truth, I kind of felt like I was always testing God. I don't mean in the sense of trying to prove that He really exists, but in that I was always daring to drive up closer to catch that perfect freeze-frame of a tornado funnel just to get more information we wanted. It was…it was stupid, a lot of times how close I got…and made my team members get."

"So you still believe in God?"

"Oh, absolutely. If anything, my reliance on God has grown," he says, his voice confident and warm.

I look at my watch, ask if he has time for one more question.

"Fire away."

I think of my dad and wonder what he'd like for me to ask Devon.

"When did you decide that you wanted to study the weather? I remember your winning an award for your experiment with the effect of aspirin on rats, but I don't remember anything you did about the weather."

"No. You're right," he says right away, as if expecting the question. "It's hard to do experiments on weather. But the truth is, it was the sky I always had my eye on. I'd always chase clouds running around with my head craned up, looking at the sky. I'm surprised I didn't walk into any holes or get hurt."

I hear him take a drink of something. Coffee? "But why the weather?"

"Well, this is going to sound really corny, really 'Kansas,' so to speak, but I see God in the weather. I mean, the evidence of Him is everywhere in His creation, of course, but the weather is so *on us*, you know? We are at its beck and call. So much of our lives hinges on what the weather is like. When we see angry black clouds, we tend to think God is angry; when we go walking on a beautiful spring day, we think He must be pleased with us. And when the sky opens up and the winds blow and the rain comes down, people get happy. As if God's talking to them." Devon clears his throat and laughs. "Does that even make sense?'

Oh. Yes. I have goosebumps all over my legs and arms and places I didn't know I could get goosebumps. "It certainly does. I love how you talk about it. Do you think most weather scientists feel like that?"

"Sadly, no. Most scientists are still agnostic when it comes to God. But every time I look a tornado in the eye—sorry, couldn't resist that," he says laughing along with me, "It's just more confirmation for me. I don't understand why He allows tornadoes to do the damage or why others just kind of float off, but then He's God, you know?"

"I know." I want to throw away everything in my life that is ugly and throw myself at Devon. In my dreams. I have some praying to do.

He tells me about the day that President Clinton presented him with the Young Scientist's Award for his work in tornado science. "That was unexpected. Pretty cool," he tells me.

We chit-chat for a while longer; he wants to know if I have children and I try to sound casual when I tell him it's never in my DNA to have any.

"Oh, I'm sorry," he says, sounding genuinely sorrowed.

"No need to be. My sister has five kids, so I am a very happy aunt. Well, I think this interview is over. Thanks so much for your time, and I'll let you know when it gets into print."

"That would be great. Come look me up if you ever get out here."

He hangs up before I do, and I stare out in space as if there's no tomorrow.

*****

I don't know why my parents hated the idea of me liking Devon, why I was tortured so much by them. Rita and I had enough trouble being bullied by the other kids at school, with them coming up to us and making hog noises, taunting us about our appearances.

"Flat face, fat face," they always teased me.

"Stringy beany," they called my sister.

Between the torture at home and the teases and taunts everywhere else, you'd think that Rita and I would have buddied up more. But that was never the case. So when Mom, Dad, Rita—even Aunt Sophia—found out that I had my eye on the smartest boy in high school, they never let up. They all gave me moon-eyes and winked at each other. Mom accused me all the time of sulking when all I really wanted to do was gladly do my chore of washing the dishes in warm sudsy water. Sometimes peace can come in a pan of dishwater, but Mom and Rita wouldn't even let me have that. Dad would chuckle, tapping his foot on the floor while he smooshed the last of Mom's chocolate chip cookies into his mouth.

"He got a moustache yet?" Dad would ask me, making Devon a joke.

Neither Rita nor I were allowed to date until we were sixteen years old, which seemed barbaric to us at the time, but I really wasn't interested in any boy except Devon, anyway. Yet hormones won out, and I ended up with Bobby. He wooed me with his '50s music and that motorcycle of his. I needed to feel a little racy, what with all the thou-shalt-nots and frowns and scowls from my parents. How and why they even allowed me that wild and crazy time with Bobby is beyond me. Bobby saved me from complete boredom and frustration, and, truth is, he was a great kisser.

Yet in the back of my mind was the image of Devon, his brilliance, his staying on course. I broke it off with Bobby after we'd been dating for a year. He'd croon '50s music, singing to me I was his angel, and then strumming his guitar while he sang "Why Do Fools Fall in Love?" After about a year of this, I told him I couldn't go with him anymore.

"You're too serious for me," I said, standing at the front door when he rang our doorbell.

Immediately, he got that hangdog look in his face and shuffled off. I felt bad but would have felt worse by leading him on when my heart wasn't with him. Love and its tricks are cruel.

Miraculously, just before my seventeenth birthday, I did get a chance to hang out with Devon. Quite literally. It was at the high school picnic in Crystal Park. Bored with the gadabout gossips, I went to the swings and sat down in one, half-heartedly twirling around in it, pawing the sand with my foot.

"Hi," said a voice beside me.

It was Devon—in the swing next to me.

I smiled, said "hi" back, my heart thumping like a jet plane taking off.

"You don't like picnics?"

"I do. Just not all the chit-chat. What about you?"

"The same." He stopped twirling in his swing and turned to me. "How have you been?"

I laughed. "You really want to know?"

"Yes, I do."

I could hardly believe my luck. I looked into his blue eyes dazzling like sapphires. "Well, I'm happy about graduating, but unsure where I am going. And disappointed in how things have been…with my parents." I say.

"What's wrong with your parents?

"Getting divorced."

"Oh. I am sorry about that."

"Don't be. In some ways, it should have happened a long time ago. They were not nice to me and my sister. They were so strict, abusive, really, wouldn't let us do anything." Telling the truth suddenly gave me more courage. "My sister and I never went to any school activities, to speak of, and we always had to go to bed really early. Embarrassing. In the summertime, the sun would still be up when we went to bed." I looked down at the sand, then up at Devon. He had not turned away or smirked; he was nodding.

"Same thing with me. I mean, not my parents getting divorced. I'm sorry about that. But my parents have always been very strict. And guess what? They made me to go to bed early, too."

I stared at him in the waning light. "But, but, why? Devon, I always thought you had it so good. You won all those science awards, you played violin, you—"

"And that is because my parents were very strict with me, too. They didn't want me getting caught up in other things that would take my time away from scholarly activities."

Scholarly? Who says scholarly these days? I smiled at him. "And you didn't mind this…this way your parents were?"

"Well, sure, I did. I resented it a lot. I never dated." Devon twisted his swing again, then let it unroll gradually.

"You never dated? But what about that girl that always walked alongside you at school?"

"Uh, there's never been any girl."

"Didn't you ever see me or hear me when I called out to you?"

Devon turned to face me. "Called out to me? Where were you?"

My face burned with shame. "Just walking down the hall. I used to call out your name, but you would just burrow on down the hall."

"I never knew that. I would have said hello back," he said, untwisting himself on the swing. He put his foot down. "Well, maybe not. I was—I am pretty shy."

"You?" I was incredulous. But it made sense, really, that he was shy. If he'd been brought up by strict parents, that's a natural.

"You know what?" he turned to face me again. "Our parents, well, I should say my parents because I don't know about yours—but my parents did the best they could. I have not had the best time of it. But because I listened to them and did my studies like they told me to, I will have a better future. And, maybe, just maybe I will reach for my dreams."

I liked what Devon said, but I knew that my parents were way over the line in how they punished me and Rita. For now, I just want to keep these sweet moments between me and Devon forever.

"You're right. I guess we should go get a hot dog now?"

We walked together for a few yards, then in unspoken agreement, we drifted apart going to our own clump of friends waiting for us to return.

It's too easy to remain bitter about the fact that Devon and I never crossed paths again. Except through letters, which I wrote first to him. I gobbled up his letter back to me, going to my little sun nook and laying out the pages on my desk. His handwriting was exquisite, a work of art; his words, poetry to my soul. "I live my life every day with thanks to God for His saving me. I live my life for Christ, and I try to keep that in mind in whatever I do."

I paused for a moment and put the letter to my chest, just like some older lady in the movies would do. I was older, but this was no dress rehearsal. Picking up the letter again, I read what he wrote about himself.

I am busy, I am happy, I try to keep my life simple. I don't have any vices, but I must admit that I do love to smoke a cigar once in a while. I know that it is a nasty smelling habit, and I really shouldn't but since I have it maybe once a month or so, I figured that it is okay. But I probably shouldn't. Especially because I would like to settle down soon with someone special. I could fall in love at the drop of a hat.

The rest of the words flew into thin air as I sat, smitten, wondering how I could just take off and drive 1,800 miles without a care in the world toward Oklahoma. Toward him. But I was hitched at the time, with a wedding ring on my finger and a gallon of wine in the fridge.

And maybe the worst part of it was that Devon had a true love of Christ, while I'd been backsliding.

When Devon got married, Aunt Sophia made sure I knew. She sent me a letter with a newspaper photo of him and his bride, a long-haired blond. She was a pharmacist, the wedding announcement said.

All right. So I couldn't have Devon then, and I can't have Devon now. I probably don't even want him. I am married, for heaven's sake. But I am curious to hear what Dad will have to say about my interviewing Devon.

*****

Dad answers on the second ring, surprising me. I look at my watch: four thirty here, so it's six thirty there, dinner over. I picture him digging into a mountain of ice cream in the dining room, right next to the phone.

"Dad?"

"Oh, yes, kid," he says, with that mock self-important tone he uses. It's his silly way of showing I'm special. I can picture him tapping his shiny-shoed foot under the table, just like he used to.

"Guess what I did."

"Hmmm, well, can you give me a hint?"

"Yeah, it's something you told me I should do when I get back to San Diego."

He laughs. "What, go to the beach and send me some sand?"

"Dad. I called Devon."

A pause. "You did?"

"Yes, I interviewed him. I talked to him about tornados and about weather and about life…and everything."

"Oh, my, oh my. I would have loved to have been a fly on the wall."

I laugh, but with an edge of something bothering me. "Dad. I've got to ask you something. Do you have a minute?"

"Sure. Make it short, though. I've got to read the paper and other things before I head to bed."

Very glad that he cannot see me rolling my eyes. "Okay. Here it is: why did you want me to call Devon? And interview him? I mean, after all these years when you knew that I died many times over as a teenager just because he wouldn't even look at me. Now he's married, I'm married, so what's the point? What were you thinking?" Hoo, boy, my heart is racing. I feel as though I were yelling—at my dad. Who does that, unless they want to die?

"You're a reporter. You have the perfect reason to talk to anybody any time," Dad says, then clears his throat. "Renee, to be honest, when I found that tape about Devon's storm and tornado research and remembered how you used to like him—"

"And you and Mom and Rita all teased me about it."

"Yes, we did. And I'm very sorry about that. We should have taken you seriously."

Tears jump to my eyes. "He was a good guy, Dad. He still is a good guy."

I hear Dad moving the phone. "I know. So was the interview good?"

"It was great. Now what do I do?"

– 10 –

MARK IS IN ONE of his moods this morning over my declaration last night that I wouldn't go to TU fellowships anymore, not even to Alex and Maureen Landry's. They are my favorite people here in the San Diego region of Truth Universal. In truth, they are the only people I have really cared for within the fellowship.

I brush aside this thought and try to ignore Mark as I bustle about getting coffee in the kitchen, then retreating to the bathroom. I put on mascara and smooth lotion onto my hands. Can't have another one of the students I tutor tell me I have old-looking hands. Mark comes to the bathroom and tells me to come into the living room and sit down so he can talk to me. This absolutely twists my gut. I make noises in the kitchen getting a second cup of coffee, then skulk into the living room. The trolley rumbles on by outside, giving me a kind of comfort.

"I have ten minutes before I need to leave for work," I say, sagging into a chair.

"Just listen to me," Mark says, closing one eye to focus his other on a spot on the coffee table. When he does that, I know he's in this diatribe for the long haul.

"Now tell me why you would want to leave Alex and Maureen's fellowship. It doesn't make any sense. I know you much you love them, love their fellowship." He opens both his eyes and turns to me. "Don't you?"

"This has nothing to do with how much I love them."

"Well, then, what is it?"

"You've put them against me."

"Where do you get ideas like that?"

I let him figure it out while I get my jacket and my tutors' notebook. I ignore his "Where you going?" as I calmly shut the door behind me.

Alex and Maureen Landry are the only ones who ever made us feel like we were family. Mark and I would stay sometimes all day Sundays at their house in Del Mar, watching movies on TV like *The Lion King* with their daughters Jeanne and Leanne. I'd cuddle up with the girls and their floppy-eared cocker spaniel Waggy.

Sometimes Maureen and the girls and I would go off on our own and do things together. One afternoon, I brought my camera along and told the girls to bring some pretty floaty scarves and Maureen drove us out to the beach. I told the girls to scarf dance.

"What's that?" Jeanne asked.

"Make it anything you want. Just dance around with the scarves."

Leanne started spinning around, her long blond hair moving along with the lavender sheer scarf. I started taking pictures of her, with Maureen smiling and encouraging her.

Jeanne began to imitate her sister, and soon the two of them looked like they were in a world of their own. The birds sang, my camera snapped, Maureen watched. The sun shone like gold in the girls' hair. I was walking on light, capturing the images of their faces, the breeze in the scarves and their hair.

The afternoon was beautiful, a time with angels. I thought we would all be together forever as friends, as family, reading the Bible together, singing hymns, thanking God for what we had.

One of the things that Alex and Maureen liked to do was order out for the white pizza at a local Italian restaurant. The girls would grab a couple of pieces for themselves and then trot off to their bedrooms. It was time for us adults to hang out, relax, and jive. Alex is a musician, used to play jazz in New Orleans, and he had a full set of drums in the house.

Alex would open a bottle of wine, usually red, to drink with the pizza.

"Everyone want a glass?" We all said yes.

We'd eat and drink and listen to Alex tell stories of his playing music with the jazz greats. He even had a gig for a while with the band Starship.

"But I turned it down when I realized that I wanted to spend my life teaching and preaching God's Word. You can't live in two worlds at the same time," he said.

Maureen would slip her arms around him, and we'd all sip our wine dreamy-eyed. Then Alex would put on some music and play his drums. The long day of hanging out, being in the sun, and now having the food, wine, and good vibes—and dancing to the beat of Alex's drums—made me dizzy with happiness.

The one bad note was always Mark. He'd rag on me when we got home, wondering why I wasn't as happy alone with him as it appeared I was with the Landrys. I sweet-talked him until I was sick to my stomach.

Looking back on those three short but nearly perfect years, I understand now what happened and why. But then, I had no idea what storm was brewing under the surface.

*****

I suppose that I adored the Landrys like God says you shouldn't. Don't put anybody or anything, for example, on a pedestal. But I didn't realize that I had. All I'd ever wanted was a family of friends, and I had them in the Landrys. That verse in the Bible about people laying down their lives for their friends? I might have done that. Awful thing is, I doubt I would have done so for Mark.

The downward spiral of our friendship with the Landrys coincided with the breakdown of our marriage. Mark was constantly harping on me at night for hitting the wine in the fridge, and I eyed him suspiciously at his blood-shot eyes and stumbling. At the same time, I'd just been hired for my kind of dream-job as a newsletter writer for the Mid-City Business Association of a blight-troubled neighborhood in San Diego. My days were jam-packed with meetings and interviews and lunch dates, and Byron—my boss—was better than any I could have ever dreamed up.

Byron was gay. It did not matter to me; I still fell heels over head in love with him. I breathed, lived, ate, and chose the clothes I was going to wear all for him. This crazy crush I had on Byron gave me a reason to get up, get going, and get busy with community. His being gay kept me from trying to walk over the boundary of wedded commitment to romance outside of marriage. Can't say I didn't have my daydreams, though.

My job, Byron, and the final blowout with the Landrys helped me get on my feet. But learning when friends are not really friends was a hard lesson. Not even Mark was a friend, I suspected, but found out for sure soon enough.

His own love affair with Mary Jane kept us up at nights arguing and blowing to bits any conversations we tried to have. Top that with no degree of physical intimacy, and a divorce would soon be born. But first, there was a confession that Mark made to Alex; one afternoon, he laid it all out that I had a drinking problem. She drinks so much, Mark told Alex, and I don't know what to do. Alex and Mark discussed the fine points of the art of drinking—because the Bible does not say drinking is bad; after all, Jesus made wine from water at his first miracle, and he sat and supped with drinkers, for heaven's sake. I stood in front of the fridge, door open, mid-pour of my second glass of wine, frozen with disbelief when Mark told me this.

I could have lived with that betrayal of disclosure of our "family secret" if it hadn't gone any further. Little did I know that Alex and Maureen had discussed it among themselves, then took it to the head honcho of the whole TU branch. So the next Sunday when I went to the Landrys for fellowship, Alex taught on the evils of drinking too much.

"Everyone here knows I love a glass of good red wine," he said, looking around the room, then stopping to gaze directly at me. "But there's a difference between drinking to enjoy the fruit of the vine than to let the vine strangle you. It is absolutely wrong for a believer to drink to the point of intoxication."

Alex continued his teaching, turning several times to look pointedly at me. Maureen cleared her throat and pretended to be busy with her Bible; Jeanne and Leanne watched open-mouthed, confused. Mark reached for my hand, but I jerked it away. The dozen or so other people present, including friends I'd invited, seemed oblivious to what was going on.

As we sang the closing hymn, I went out to the car and sat in the passenger seat for half an hour. It's all over, I kept saying to myself. Our friendship is all over. They hate me. When I heard knocking on the window, I nearly jumped out of my seat. It was Alex, Maureen, and Mark. I rolled down the window.

"Hey, we are all going to get Mexican food for lunch. You ready to go?"

And of course, I went. That's what victims of abuse of any kind do. They go along. And they buy everything hook, line, and sinker.

The day stretched out sweet and warm as they always did with the Landrys, sitting around and talking, playing music, lying on the couch. We watched *Fly Away Home* on TV, with me tearing up at the girl-flies-with-the-geese scenes, and then came time for dinner. Alex ordered one of our favorite pizzas, a white pie with chicken, artichokes, garlic and Alfredo sauce and we sat around the breakfast nook waiting for the pizza man to come.

I was getting that squirrely feeling in my stomach, wondering about what we would drink, since, after all, wine would be out of the question. Alex got up and walked down the hall. I held my breath when I heard the familiar chink of glass against glass.

"I'm opening a nice bottle of Pinot Noir. Anyone want a glass with me?" Alex said from the hallway.

"Sure," Mark and Maureen said, not looking at me.

"Renee? Don't you want a glass?"

I got up and went to the hall where Alex was standing, bottle in hand.

"It's okay. It's good to enjoy it," he said. He put down the bottle and pulled me in for a hug. As stiff as a board I was in his embrace. When he let go, he put his hands on my shoulders and looked at me, a little smile on his lips. "It's okay."

"Sure, I'll have one," I said.

The pizza came, we ate and laughed and played music, and the wine flowed among us all.

"Let's go into the living room," Alex said.

"Is it going to be a drum night?" Maureen asked.

"Oh, yes," Alex said.

Maureen put a Fleetwood Mac album on, and Alex went over to the drum set up in a corner of the living room. He straddled the seat like a bar room stool and started a hypnotic rhythm. Maureen, the girls, and I began moving to the music and the beat of the drums and our hearts.

The door burst open and in walked James, one of the regional TU regional leaders.

Alex stopped playing; we stopped dancing. Alex shook hands with James and walked away from the drums.

"Oh, don't stop on account of me! I want to join in. You guys got a good thing going here," James said.

Mark joined in with the revelry, too, this time. James started a Conga line and the rest of us followed, with Alex slamming the living daylights out of the drums and our heads. Mark was all grin and goofy in the fun; my head was fuzzy. A part of me stepped apart from all that was going on and looked at it from above. Is this the right way to live? For a Christian?

I realized that if I ever brought anyone to these TU meetings, I would feel terrible, a wolf in sheep's clothing. Because that's how the Bible was presented by the TU masters. Never mind that the Landrys were my best friends. Some friends they were. I needed to hang them up, with the whole TU shebang.

It always takes a while for me to get convinced of anything. Letting go of the Landrys, of our memories and times together, didn't happen overnight. In spite of my declaration that I wouldn't have anything to do with TU ever again, I went with Mark for several months to Alex and Maureen's house. There were always the wine wars within my soul on Sunday nights after we'd spent magical hours together, singing in fellowship, eating Mexican food or going for a picnic in the park, watching TV back at the house, playing with Waggy, and then ordering dinner. Sometimes Alex would turn on the jets of their Jacuzzi. While we waited for the water to warm up and the pizza man to arrive, Alex or Maureen would pop a cork of a bottle of wine, pouring glasses for Mark first, then themselves, waiting for my "yay" or "nay" on glass for me. "Of course," I'd say, my high voice covering up the confusion and despair. But when we'd all slide into the Jacuzzi under a sky of stars and raise our glasses, I let slide off the coat of armor dragging me down. Alex and Maureen and Mark were all smiles and singing the praises of good wine and the God who made it. Yet I'd always make sure that my legs or arms never got too close to Alex.

The courage to say goodbye came closer on a sunny Sunday afternoon. Alex invited me to go on a motorcycle ride with him, "Just a spin," he said, like a challenge. Maureen nodded at me, said, "Go ahead."

I went out under the glaring sun, following Alex to his motorcycle. He handed me a helmet. Hated how it felt on my head, as if I were a Martian on a moon. I'd once been a carefree girl on the back of a motorcycle, my hair flowing in the wind, arms wrapped around my boyfriend when I was sixteen years old. The thought of encircling Alex's waist now sent jangly waves of nervousness through me. He must have sensed it because after I threw my legs up over on the seat behind him, he looked back at me before he put on his own helmet.

"You need to put fear away, Renee. You can't let it rule your life," he said.

"Got it," I said, but he could only see my mouth moving behind the helmet-cage I was wearing.

As he turned the ignition on, I had a flashback of being with Bobby. I giggled in my helmet-cage. Here I am with Alex and I am dreaming of Bobby, my love at sweet sixteen. He, too, had a motorcycle, but we owned the wind when he rode. My first days of riding with him were tremulous, like our falling in love. He told me to lean into it, don't fight it, when he felt me trying to right myself on the motorcycle.

"Don't try to sit up straight on corners. It's dangerous," Bobby said one afternoon on my first time out with him on the motorcycle. He kissed me on the cheek. "Want to try again?"

He clasped his hand over mine holding onto him. We weaved in and out the tree-lined streets and out toward the edge of town.

I was still daydreaming about this when I realized Alex was slowing down to a stop. Pulling over, he flipped up the front of his helmet and motioned for me to do the same.

"You're riding wrong," he said.

"What do you mean?"

"You're sitting up straight when I turn corners. Now let's try this again. And trust me, trust God."

To trust him was to trust God? I didn't like that, but I didn't say anything, just strapped on the ridiculous helmet again.

Alex took off again and I started praying aloud. Alex pulled over again. This time, he didn't even bother with flipping up the front of his helmet.

"What are you doing? Who are you talking to?"

A rage was doing a slow burn in my heart. I moved off the cycle, took off the helmet, and stood right next to Alex, looking up at his face. "I was praying."

"For what?"

"I was thanking God. Is that okay?"

"It is if that's what you were doing." He was so close to me I could smell the onions in the salsa he'd eaten earlier

"Why do you question what I was doing? Why is it even important to you?"

His demeanor instantly changed, breaking into a smile, and squeezing my shoulder. "Renee, you're a great lady. I just wanted to make sure you were okay. You kind of freaked me out. I thought you were talking to yourself or talking behind my back," he said, laughing suddenly, slapping his leg.

I just stared at him.

"I guess I was kind of hard on you about this fear stuff. You just always seem so stuck on issues. Remember, you're a daughter of God!"

If I was a daughter of the Most High, why did this man who I thought was a friend treat me as if I were all wrong?

"What issues? Come on, say it!" I stamped my foot.

"Oh, there's no reason to get into it. You know that Mark is just concerned."

"I don't care what Mark thinks. He's a pothead. You got it?"

"You don't know that!"

"You don't live with him!"

"Oh, Renee, you take things too seriously," Alex said, pawing the concrete.

"Alex, you are a total fake."

"And you're a freakin' wino!"

A couple who were out walking in the neighborhood stopped to stare.

"Alex, take me back now. And no more talk," I said, wishing my body would stop shaking with fury. Neither Alex nor I bothered putting on our helmets. Alex gunned the engine, and we took off. I didn't know what Alex was thinking, but I was praying, nonetheless. This time, silent.

Maureen and Mark barely even knew anything was wrong when Alex and I walked into the house. We loved up Waggy when he stood on his hind legs and put his paws up on our legs. His eyes got big and his tongue hung out with pleasure as I rubbed his ears. I will miss Waggy, I thought to myself. Even more, I will miss Maureen and the girls.

After our Sunday night pizza, which tasted like cardboard, I listened to Mark and Alex sharing memories of the old days in Truth Universal. They were always going on about that.

Maureen turned to me. "Are you okay? You're awfully quiet," she said.

"Just tired. I have to go home soon to study for my Spanish exam."

Maureen touched her hand on mine. The gesture nearly made me cry.

"I'll tell Alex we need to break it up."

Another half hour passed before Alex and Maureen finally stood at the door, bidding us good night. I hugged Maureen, hiding the tears in my eyes. When we let go of each other, Alex was standing right next to me.

"Hug?" he said, arms outstretched.

I did a quick embrace, slapping him on the back, pulling away from him right away.

"Thanks for a great day," Mark said, his thin hair standing straight up in a sudden breeze, revealing pink spots of his scalp.

Mark and I finally walked away. In the car, I cried silently to the radio playing Seal's "Kiss from a Rose," realizing that I would never again scarf dance or eat pizza with Maureen and the girls.

– 11 –

WHEN YOU LEAVE YOUR so-called friends in a so-called church, you end up leaving everything behind, even your husband. It's been a month and a half since I walked out on Mark. My home now is in Park Manor, a hotel close to downtown San Diego. I got my job back at the Improvement Association where I interview the merchants on Gateway Boulevard, attend design and economic improvement meetings. My old boss-love is not around. Wendy, a woman about ten years older than I, stepped up for the job. She has me chained to the desk half the time, but in some ways, I don't mind. I also like that I'm not rummaging in my closet every morning for the perfect thing to wear to impress a man. I don't need another man-love.

So Wendy and I have been talking and having lunch together. I have to say, she is beautiful. Her face is always perfectly made-up, and she wears high heels and business suits every day. Every time a man walks into our office, he gravitates to where she is sitting in the corner hunched over her laptop. As I sit at my own computer, feeling inconsequential in my skirt and print blouse, my insanely wavy hair tucked up with a barrette in a half-ponytail, I burn with jealousy watching Wendy bat her eyelashes at the man. Funny thing is, I don't think she even knows she's doing it. She's just one of those natural beauties, Italian, with deep-set dramatic eyes, long not-too-thick hair, and a good figure. She could have any man she wanted. But Wendy has confided in me the great desolation she feels with Tim, her live-in boyfriend of many years who won't commit to marry her.

"Why do you put up with this?" I asked her the other day at lunch.

She shook her head and stabbed at her Caesar salad. "I keep hoping," she said.

I understand, I told her.

Wendy has banked on her beauty to bring her happiness, she confided in me once. I admitted I probably have done the same. I'll never forget what I heard someone tell me once, though I can't remember who said it. "When being cute and young dries up, you have to have a personality."

"Don't you ever dream of having a life of your own?" I asked Wendy.

"Well, I have my dogs. And horses. Of course, my friends. Got my own bank accounts, too. I could leave anytime, but I don't want to. I want Tim," she said, stirring sugar into her coffee.

I don't want too many more lunches with Wendy and I can't sit on the fence anymore about Mark. I've got to face the facts. I understand the kind of hope that Wendy has. But for me, for right now, there are so many better and higher things to reach for. Like God.

*****

I'm going out on a date. With Mark. It's a last-ditch date that both of us are hoping will bring some romance to outdo all the hurts and crazies of the last ten years. We are going to Top of the Hill, a fancy-schmancy restaurant in downtown San Diego that I used to dream about guys taking me to.

Life is crazy mixed up. Here I am swabbing mascara for the second time on my eyelashes after stroking blush powder on my cheeks—and I never normally wear the stuff. I'm actually feeling nervous as if I'm going out on a first or second date. I've always wanted a redo on the first time that I met Mark. Pauline, a friend of mine from Truth Universal had invited me over for Eggplant Parmesan, so I was looking forward to us hanging out and talking—a lot about the Bible, actually, albeit TU's version of it. But I didn't realize how wicked it really was at the time, so I went along with Pauline, especially since she always spoke about God's love. Growing up at home had never really been an experience of His love, except for my sweet Grandma Bell and Grandma Howell.

But when I rang the doorbell to Pauline's place in the East San Diego neighborhood, an area crammed with apartment buildings and aging homes, this goofy-looking guy came up the sidewalk and opened the security door for me. "Ooh, you didn't have to bring me flowers," he said, taking them from me. I stood there, grossed out by the pink scalp under his thinning hair and his gangly arms, groping fingers. From the very start, Mark gave me the creeps. I don't know why I didn't listen to my innermost gut feelings.

"I see you've met each other," Pauline said, as we walked into her apartment. "We will have a really great time talking. Mark is a Bible scholar."

I could have won an Academy Award for how well I feigned interest in what Mark had to say at dinnertime. He was smart, like Pauline had said, but I thought of him as nothing but a Bible spout. He cranked out verses for anything and everything we talked about. The food was good, though. I was very glad about that.

But after dinner was over and we had a couple of glasses of wine in the living room, I was getting tired of constantly evading Mark's glances at me, so I yawned and said I had to get home. As we all said our good-byes, I had a feeling that Mark would be in the picture for a while.

Sure enough. He called me just a week later, asked if I'd like to go to dinner. I hadn't had a real date since I left my on-again, off-again boyfriend who used to growl at me if he had to pay for my movie ticket, calling me a gold digger. Somewhere between my first date with him at TJI Friday's and going to Truth Universal meetings and, in spite of myself, becoming impressed with Mark's seemingly fathomless knowledge of the Bible, I fell for his big blue eyes and deep thoughts. When he took me out, I easily swooned by Mark's generosity, his never blinking an eye if I ordered anything over ten dollars. It had been a long, long time since I'd been on a real date—I always paid my own check when I was out with the R-man, as I used to call him, when we had cheese omelets and coffee at the Village Townhouse in Ocean Beach, or when we went to the movies and had popcorn. With Mark, I began to realize how much I had wanted to be cared for, loved and cherished, whatever the cost may be.

But that was the rub. Within months after we celebrated our first anniversary, he had me running ragged under his questions and his accusations. The worst thing about our coupling is that it scarcely was consummated. Though Mark never made my heart bump in crazy love, I did have a normal healthy appetite for intimacy. But Mark went soft on me all the time, blaming me, claiming that I did not know how to touch him and his private parts to get things going.

Right now, I feel nauseous thinking about all that. What are you doing going on a date with this man now? I ask myself. I lean over the sink toward the mirror and stare into my eyes, hairbrush in my hand like a weapon.

The doorbell rings. This is it. I'm going to let Mark let me order whatever I want on the menu, but I'm not even going to think about kissing him.

*****

It's quiet in Top of the Hill except for the chink of knives and forks against plates and the rush of water and ice being poured into glasses. Every once in a while, I hear the popping sound of a champagne bottle opened. I am impressed that Mark got us a table next to the window. The city's skyline sparkles like jewelry against the black silk of night. Mark and I both watch a jet plane come gliding in and land like an exotic bird onto the runway.

"Want some wine?" Mark asks.

I turn to see the waiter standing next to Mark, poised with a bottle of wine, a towel draped over his arm, just like in the movies. Who could say no? I ignore all the images from our past.

We both sip and watch the lights of the city twinkle.

"We should order," Mark says. I look at him all spiffed up in a dark-blue suit I've never seen before. I could live like this, having dinner at a beautiful restaurant with beautiful people, my date staring at me like I'm the prettiest girl around.

"You know? I have always wondered what Steak Tartar is," I say.

"It's blood-red raw."

"Eeewww, oh, how awful." I giggle, looking up at him. His deep frown lines are nearly erased under his smile. "What will you be having?"

"Oh, probably the fish of the day. Trying to eat healthy so we can have dessert."

I'd already glanced at the menu when we first came in, and I didn't like what I saw—things I can't pronounce—and clams and lamb, things I don't eat. I remember what my mother said about the first time she ate oysters, and nearly laugh out loud.

"You want more giggle juice?" Mark has the wine bottle poised over my glass. I put my hand up.

"No, no, not yet," I say, looking at him. "I'll have the Chicken Marsala."

"You could have that anyplace. Get something exotic."

"I usually order omelets and sandwiches and spaghetti or salads. This is exotic for me." I reach for my glass of wine.

The waiter comes back, as if on cue. He takes our order and I ask for some bread. He gives us a fusty look, his mouth all pursed.

"What was that all about? Don't they have bread?" I giggle, swirling the wine in my glass.

Mark whispers, his eyes blue as blazes. "This is a nice place. Don't make a scene."

What I really want to do is just ignore him and everything about us and walk out onto the patio, soak in the night air—my arms lifted—and pretend to soar in over the city just like the planes roaring in. Instead, I roll my eyes and motion to Mark for more wine.

"Now be careful with this stuff," he says, all holier than thou.

Slamming my hand down on the table, I make him jump, the wine sloshing over the glass.

"Will you stop already? Who do you think you are?" I say, my voice a loud whisper. I see the diners at the table in back of us lift their eyes toward us.

"Don't start this again," Mark says, whispering. "Here, have a glass with me. I just want to be with you."

Honestly, I want to be here in this beautiful place. For just once in my life. And I do want to keep peace. So I lift my glass to his.

The chicken marsala is so tender that it melts in my mouth. Mark keeps offering me bites of his steak tartare, and I just giggle, waving his fork away. It's fun being like this. We feed each other alternate bites of potatoes, rice, roasted vegetables, and bread. The waiter had finally brought us a basket of warm sourdough bread with soft butter. The wine is putting a fine finish on the mood. I am thinking maybe we could start over, Mark and I. A lady likes to be taken care of. I don't care what the gurus of the '70s said.

"There's something I want to talk to you about," Mark says.

"Yeah?" Maybe he's going to do a redo on a proposal?

I watch while Mark tucks his hands under his chin. "I want to say to you how sorry I am that I wasn't there for you when you needed me. All I ever wanted was to give you the same kind of wonderful experience in Truth Universal that I had."

Oh, no. No, no, no. Not this again. When is that heavenly chocolate cheesecake coming? I take a sip of my water. "Let's go outside."

"Renee!"

"Let's just do it. There's a lounge outside on the patio. I don't want to talk in here."

Our waiter leads us outside. The burst of fresh air blows clear through my thoughts. I take Mark's hand as we walk to the railing to watch a 747 come in for a landing.

"I just wanted us out of the stale air for a while," I tell Mark, remembering a vacation we'd had in Santa Barbara nearly ten years ago. We'd gone to a restaurant that was poorly lit, crowded and the chairs were uncomfortable. I'd asked to move to the next table over. As we ate, Mark sent me daggers through his eyes. But that was the easy part. When we returned to our hotel room, he literally sat me down and yelled at me for five hours about how I was selfish and had no self-control. At first, I thought Mark just wanted me to say I was sorry. So I did say I was sorry, anything to shut him up. But then his monologue changed to accusations of my being unwilling to follow along with him, to go all-out for God.

"Don't you want to know God? To hear what he has to say?"

"Yes, I do, but not your god," I said.

That remark turned on more the faucet of his accusations and tirades against me. Sometime around 3:00 a.m. and my umpteenth cigarette, I begged him to stop.

"Let's just sleep on it, I said. I'll think about what you have said. I just need some rest now, okay?"

That whole night long I laid on my side turned away from him. Marital love we did not have.

Next morning, when I heard the birds singing in the motel's courtyard (so there *was* life after a night of hellish haranguing), Mark was gone. I rubbed my eyes, limped around the room, furious at myself for worrying about where he was. By the time I finished getting dressed, he walked into the door, carrying a big bouquet of flowers.

He placed the flowers in my arms. "I'm sorry. I hope we can start over," he said.

Flowers won't get you far, I said to myself. "I need some food. Can we get some breakfast somewhere and then just head home?"

On the drive back to San Diego a couple hours later, we were both silent, me fidgeting, Mark twirling the dial on the radio. I was willing to just wait things out and keep quiet. But then he slipped in a cassette tape of some fusty speaker from Truth Universal. "Can we please just not listen to that right now? Maye some music instead?" I said, pasting a smile on my face.

Mark slapped the steering wheel hard, glaring at me. Uh-oh.

We were stuck in the middle of LA's hell-on-earth traffic. I began to think that I had died and gone to the worst part of hell because Mark used that time to remind me of everything I did and said wrong.

"You never like anything I do or follow through with anything that we talk about. Like that time we...just like that time you'd promised me that you would bake cookies for the fellowship. But you never did, haven't yet. Don't you know that as a wife, you need to go along with what I want? You never are into anything I do. You don't like listening to any of the music or the people I like—"

"And I told you on that night that I didn't like being coerced into doing it," I said.

"As my wife, you have a responsibility to at least pretend to pay attention to and like the things that I like. I certainly do for you. We've gone to every place you ever wanted on vacation time—"

"And I paid dearly for it, didn't I? You remind me all the time of how I am not a good Christian wife."

"I never say that, and you know it."

"Mark, you've never actually said those words, but you know damn well that is what you are trying to tell me. Don't play all innocent with me."

And off we went. After fifteen more minutes of us ranting at each other in the middle of traffic that wasn't going anywhere, I told him to pull over to the next exit.

"Whatever for?"

"Because I don't want to be in this car with you. I'll take a bus home if I have to."

I would have, too, but Mark drove me to the nearest airport. It cost him a pretty penny to get me on the next flight home in a small aircraft. I love flying normally, but that afternoon, I barely saw the cloud towers as I gazed out the tiny plane window trying to figure out where God wanted me to go.

I didn't want to have a failed marriage. I just didn't. So I kept thinking ahead in just five-minute windows of time. When I got to San Diego, I called a friend and she picked me up, took me to her apartment, and we sat and talked, and I cried and pounded the table. And when Mark called to apologize, I relented, giving him the best ten years of my youth and health and beauty to him. All for none.

*****

I try not to think of all that while Mark and I stand at the balcony watching the jets throwing their crystalline lights over the jeweled city.

"Let's sit down," Mark says, leading me to the lounge chairs.

Our waiter finally arrives with a big slice of heavenly cheesecake. Mark and I pick up our forks. One thing we've always known how to do is eat and enjoy delectable desserts. We like to take turns taking tiny bites and relishing the taste in our mouths for a long time.

I watch Mark take a bite of the cheesecake's chocolatey velvet and savor it for a moment before he speaks.

"I have wanted to tell you for a long time that I am very sorry for how things have turned out between us. All I wanted is to make you happy, to give you what I had," he says.

I put my fork down. "Mark. You keep forgetting that I never wanted what you had in the past. It's impossible to bring back what you had, and even if we could, I don't want it."

"But you don't know what you are missing."

"I don't care," I say, cutting a large chunk from the cheesecake.

"Hey." Mark looks at me as if I'm a criminal.

I smile. "Can we just talk about something else?" I ask in my sweetest voice.

*****

We never did. Talk about something else, that is. He wouldn't let up about my having missed out on the best thing that could happen to anyone, life in the fellowship. Old TU talk that curiously makes me want to sneeze as much as it causes me to shiver. I am so over all that.

The date with Mark was a complete faux paus, but I am glad that I gave it a try; sad, too, a little. My days, my years with him, the good memories that we did have are for sure a thing of the past.

I need to call Aunt Sophia. And Mom. Soon.

It's been a fussing-with-my-hair day, the humidity cloying around my face and neck. I don't know which is worse: the stickiness of San Diego's summer monsoon or the dry brittle heat of the Santa Ana winds in September. If I am this miserable in San Diego's nearly perfect weather, I hate to think what would happen if I ever did move back to Kansas out of homesickness.

My parakeet Spunky eyes me warily from his cage. I got Spunky from the local pet store when I moved into this hotel. He hasn't really hit it off with me yet.

I go to the refrigerator and pour myself a cold glass of chardonnay, then walk to the window and watch a giant jet plane disappear among the buildings on its way to the runway.

"I don't know how they do that, Spunky. Seems like the planes would just crash into the buildings all the time."

Spunky bursts into a chirping song, doing a side-to-side dance on his perch. I go to the cage, set my glass down, and carefully slide open the door. Spunky peers up at me, bobbing his head up and down.

"Are you ready?"

My finger must look like a weapon to Spunky, but I keep it steady as I nudge it up just under his tummy.

"Up you go, up, up, up." That's what the pet shop girl told me to say and do.

Spunky steps up onto my finger and I grin like a lottery winner. "Okay, slow, slow now, cutie pie," I say, trying to control my shaking finger as I bring close to the open cage door. At the last moment, Spunky grabs with his beak one of the wires of the cage and holds on.

"What, do I have bad breath?"

I need a friend. I need my mother.

It's only four o'clock here, just past dinnertime for Mom and Aunt Sophia. I'm sure they're out having dinner together. They are all joined at the hip.

A little laugh comes from behind me, and I jump out of my seat. What in the world?

Once again, it happens. It's Spunky. He is imitating me. I sputter into giggles and reward Spunky with some treat bird seed. He hops down on his lowest perch and starts eating right away. "Love you, Spunky," I say.

I watch my little lavender and gray parakeet—I chose him out of his twenty other feathered friends for how he sat on the perch, one foot tucked into his tummy feathers, and singing like there was no tomorrow. Spunky makes me smile now, as the sky darkens and that eerie time between day and night overtakes me. It's the saddest time in some ways, but also the most exquisite of hours. So much room for repentance exists in that thin line between day and night, so many promises, too. Out of the blue, I remember a Bible verse I had memorized as a child in church. *Trust in the Lord with all your heart and lean not on your own understanding; in all your ways acknowledge Him, and He shall direct your paths.*

Unfortunately, I haven't been acknowledging God. Not the way that my grandparents had shown me. Or even my own parents. But how do I do that? How do I reconcile what my parents believed with the manner in how they talked to and treated me and Rita?

And TU really messed things up with their message of prosperity, that if I was living right, God would reward me with good health, wealth, and all things good. Actually, I should be one big mess, according to that train of thought. But I'm not. Then again, I am not the prime mover of my life. It's a miracle every single day that I don't get run over or get pneumonia or die from tetanus from that rusty nail I stepped on when I ran up to the roof of this place on the Fourth of July to see the fireworks over the city. Take the daily miracles a little more out, and there I am getting the tetanus shot by a doctor who was in a good mood and gave me a sweet smile of encouragement. So many things go right in this crazy world. My car still runs, I can walk and talk, people tell me I look good, I have a job, a handful of friends, my health, but it's certainly not because of my greatness or anything that I do. That much I know. Most of the time I don't even remember to pray unless it's little breath-prayers as I'm driving or eating breakfast or typing the minutes from the business meeting: *Oh, God, help my heart to stop hurting. Show me what to do.*

I plunk my glass down on the plywood coffee table. "Spunky? I'm ready to make a change."

He laughs.

*****

Wendy kept trying to pry out of me all morning what was my problem. I turned down her offer of lunch so that I could stay in the office. I need to catch up on work, I told her. When she finally walked out and went down the street to the Italian restaurant for the lunch special, I waited for a few minutes. Then I heated up the three pieces of falafel left over from the promotions meeting the other day.

The falafel is steaming hot now as I sit at my desk making a list of the things I want do before I leave San Diego. Yes, leave. When I'm leaving is immaterial; what I do in the next few weeks could be life changing. And I have no idea why, except that I woke up with this notion as bright and focused as the summer sun.

Call Mom. Dad. Aunt Sophia. Rita.

Take pictures—

At the tide pools at Ocean Beach.

At Torrey Pines Nature Preserve.

I run into a blank here and bite into the falafel. This neighborhood has so much ethnic food that I love, from Egyptian to Lebanese to Thai. I'd never find any of this kind of food in Kansas. The closest thing they have to ethnic is China Star, a gigantic buffet offering everything from egg rolls to chicken chow mein to that awful green gelatin salad. It's just not authentic enough for me; I've been Californianized.

The traffic is racing by outside on Gateway Boulevard, one of San Diego's first thoroughfares from New Town San Diego in the 1800s to out here on Thirty-Fifth Street when it was still countryside with chickens pecking in the dirt. Come to think of it, I really want to be in the country right now. I add *Drive to the Cuyamacas and hike the trails* to the list.

But there's something else tugging at me. Going for a walk out among trees and birds is a step in the right direction, but my spirit is needing something more. I add *Go to a real church* to the list. My heart thumping hard, I get the Yellow Pages and skim through to the large classified ads in the churches section. *San Diego United Methodist Church, Open Hearts, Open Minds, Open Doors.* I shiver a little. I don't want too much openness; that's how I got into trouble in the first place. But I've heard that the Methodist church has liturgical services, which I've never been to. I write down the address of the Methodist church. I've always wanted to see what a Baptist church in San Diego as well is like, so I circle the ad for one.

*****

149

At 9:00 a.m. sharp, I hear the clip-clop of Wendy's shoes on the back stairs of this old building, Bekin's Moving. The big metal door clanks open and she walks in, practically glaring at me. "What are you humming about," she asks, as I pour her a cup of coffee.

"Just made a to-do list that will change my life." I give her the cup of coffee. I've never minded doing that—making and serving coffee. Call me a feminist's wimp. I can think of worse things to be called.

"Can you make my to-do list?" Wendy says, her big eyes peering over the cup.

I laugh. "Well, do you want to come to church with me?"

"Ugh. No. Why?"

"Because it's something I've neglected to do for a long time and I want to get back on track."

"Hey, wait a minute." Wendy puts her coffee cup down. "I thought you already went to church."

"Not the real kind."

"Okay. My head is spinning. Enough of the chit-chat. Can you type up the minutes from yesterday's promotions committee?"

I walk over to my desk, pick up the stapled copy, and walk back to her desk. "Here you go. Did it yesterday. You want to come to church with me on Sunday?"

*****

I've never ever seen a sanctuary so beautiful. Where have I been all the last twenty years of my life? The sanctuary, already filled with hundreds of people in the elegant white pews, smells of perfume the minute Wendy and I walk in, light pouring in from the window behind the high altar. I see trees waving in the breeze and birds flitting about the branches. A part of me worries about the birds flying into the window.

Wendy clops along beside me in her high heels; she's wearing a black dress. I have on flats, a black skirt and a short-sleeved white blouse. I wish I had newer, better clothes. There's just something about Sunday mornings in church that make me want to look my best so that I can put all my body, soul, and heart into worship.

The choir is already singing when Wendy and I sit down in a pew about ten rows from the front. We turn to look back at the choir singing an angelic song I'd not heard before. The choir members in their white robes, hymn books open, and mouths formed in a perfect *O* shape look like angels sent from on high.

The liturgy has me fumbling with the bulletin, the hymn book and the Bible. Wendy knows her way around a little. "Catholic, remember?" she whispers, pointing to herself, smiling.

We read the Nicene Creed aloud together with the hundreds of other people in the sanctuary. All our mingled voices reverberate around the sanctuary and back around to Wendy and me, us both sounding like young children. A sweet memory of innocence and of praying and singing with my Grandma and Grandpa Ball seize my heart, nearly choking the words out of me. Wendy looks at me, her brown eyes big and concerned. I smile, nod my head, blink my eyes.

"It's beautiful," I say.

After all the singing and standing and praying and sitting and listening to angelic music, Pastor Moore walks to the podium, motioning with his hands for us to sit down. His silver hair gleams in the sunlight streaming through the high windows.

"In what ways do you truly love people?" he asks the congregation.

He smiles, nods. "Good, I'm glad you can't answer that question." Quiet laughter ripples through the sanctuary. "If you do or think you can answer it, you probably don't know how to truly love people.

"It's a contradiction in terms, almost. If you think you love people, then you are fooling yourself. We all do that. Me, included."

Pastor Moore clears his throat. "Let me tell you a story. Before I met my wife, and when I lived in an apartment by myself, I had a hobby of cooking Chinese food. Why? Because my days were long as a seminary student and it was one way I destressed. But I always had too much food. So I'd take pots of my extra wonton soup and orange chicken to the neighbor in the apartment next to me. Now, this guy really bothered me because he would play his music really loud late at night. I mean, really late, like midnight and beyond. I would bury myself under my pillows to drown out the noise.

"And he did take my pots of soup and anything else I brought him. I felt good," Pastor Moore says.

"But I had an ulterior motive. I wanted him to be good to me, I wanted him to like me. Is that so bad?

"Well, can anyone guess what happened?"

Wendy and I look at each other, shrug our shoulders.

"He never stopped playing that loud music. And me? I never stopped being resentful of him. I hate to admit it, but I wished I could have dumped a whole pot of soup on him."

Wendy's and my laughter join in with the others.

"But I was convicted on the spot, there lying on my mattress with pillows over my head. I thought the most wicked things about the guy. That's bad enough, right? Nope. The worst is that when I had given the soup to him, I hoped he would like me. Not so bad, right? Wrong again.

"You see, I didn't have the right attitude in my heart. I didn't want to listen to him or take the time to get to know him. I just wanted to shut him up. Is that any way to be a neighbor? Is that how a Christian should act or think?"

Pastor Moore stands at the pulpit for a throbbing-quiet second, then steps down. The angelic-sounding choir starts up again.

I have goosebumps, I mouth to Wendy, rubbing my arms. She nods her head, stands up with me as the choir director motions for us to rise and sing "It Is Well with My Soul."

I am not familiar at all with this song. Being in TU for twelve years has knocked me out of the Christian loop. I love this song, I whisper to Wendy wiping tears from my eyes. She smiles, shakes her head, and ends with me the last "soul" in a perfect sound.

After Pastor Moore closes with a benediction—I meditate on what that word means, never having reflected on it before; bene dice in Spanish means good word or speak—all of us in the congregation sit down again to listen to the organist play a selection from Beethoven's Symphony No. 7. Wendy and I stare out the window behind the high altar at the birds flying around in the trees. It's just so wow. I feel like I've died and gone to heaven already. But there's something missing, can't put my finger on it.

For lunch, Wendy drives us over to Bully's East, a place that's been around since 1971. It's dark and smells of booze and the TV is on in the sports bar. Antithesis of where we've just been. But I figure I owe Wendy one for dragging her to church, and she really wants the prime rib they have here.

"Okay, so lay it on me," I say, as we both dig into our salads.

"Lay what?"

"Tell me what you really thought of the service this morning."

Wendy shrugs her shoulders. "It was all right. Not my cup of tea."

"But I thought you were enjoying the music."

"It was nice," Wendy says, stabbing her fork into pieces of Romaine lettuce. "But I guess once a Catholic, always a Catholic. I was surprised at the liturgy, though. I did like that." She looks up at me. "Are you going to go again?"

"Maybe. But I want to check out another church next time. It's called Ridgeview Baptist Church."

Our server arrives with our entrees. Wendy gets her prime rib and french fried onions; I get grilled chicken with loaded mashed potatoes and vegetable medley.

I gaze down at my food and take a deep breath. "Lord, thank You for this food. And for friends. And a good boss. Amen."

Wendy smiles. "I never knew you were so…religious."

"Neither did I." I cut into my chicken and scoop up a bite with the potatoes.

"What changed for you?" Wendy asks,

"Everything," I say. "In the course of about a year."

I tell Wendy all about being in Truth Universal and how I felt trapped, cursed, and confused. Throw in a peg-leg past along with an embroiled childhood and you have the makings of a neurotic.

"But I am going to change all that," I say now.

"How are you going to do that? I mean, what makes you think you can change your own life?"

I consider her question. It's a good one. Suddenly, I think of Dad, and my talk with Devon on the phone. Dad had his own religious convictions, and so did Mom for that matter. Devon, too.

How did they know, how does anyone know to where their lives are leading?

"Who else is going to change it? Change my life?" I say finally.

– 12 –

Turned out, there was no need for me to change my life. Mark did it for me. The very next day after Wendy and I went to church and lunch together, I was sitting having coffee at my desk, perusing through the morning mail. The office door burst open and a guy in dark sunglasses walked through straight toward me. He handed me a thick envelope. Befuddled, I smiled, said "hi," but he turned on his heel and walked out again.

"That was rude," Wendy said, laughing from behind me.

"Tell me about it," I said, turning the envelope around to look at the return address "Law Offices of Dean Paxton." I ripped it open and yanked out thick papers. "Oh, God, oh, God. Wendy, it's a summons from Mark. He's suing me for spousal support."

Wendy laughed, holding her sides.

"How can you laugh? This is the end of the world for me! I'm getting sued! Oh. My. God. Oh, I hate Mark! I hate him." I headed toward the door, wanting to hurl myself in front of the traffic on Gateway Boulevard.

Wendy ran toward me. "Come back. Sit down. It's going to be all right. Mark has nothing on you. I promise. That's why I'm laughing."

While I sat and rocked in my chair, chewing my knuckles, Wendy called around to half a dozen people she knew. After what seemed an eternity, she said she found someone.

"He's a friend of mine, got his degree in law, so he can explain everything. He's coming over in ten minutes," she said. "Want a piece of leftover pizza?"

"No. Oh, Wendy, what am I going to do? I didn't want trouble with Mark. I just wanted to get away from him. So I could think. And breathe. And now this." I returned to chewing on my knuckles.

Wendy plunked down on my desk a microwaved piece of pizza on a paper plate. "Eat this, not your hand."

I watched her walk away in her black pumps, exuding confidence and a cloud of Italian perfume. If only I'd been like her...but if I had been, then I wouldn't have given Mark a second look. Ugh.

So I didn't need to worry about how I was going to charge of my life. But I wasn't about to admit that Mark had me by the reins. Hold on, I heard myself say.

It's God in the big picture. I picked up the piece of warmed up pizza and took a bite. Bad pizza. So what.

I sat up straight and took the summons paper in my hands. "God? This is yours," I whispered.

*****

Wendy's friend Neil is about our age, plain-looking, short with glasses, and balding. But I trust him. He comes across straightforward, sweet if a lawyer-type person can be called such a thing. Turns out he's Jewish, too, very devout. His mother just died. He told us when he arrived. He couldn't bury her right away because of the high holy days, so he was feeling fortunate to be able to keep busy.

"So sorry about your mother," I say. Feeling like a fool, I ask him what Rosh Hashanah is.

"Rosh Hashanah is Hebrew for Head of the Year, or the New Year."

"New Year? On what calendar?"

"The Jewish calendar."

I am falling into a hole just like Alice in Wonderland. "The Jews have their own calendar?"

Neil laughs, but not unkindly. "Well, the Jewish calendar revolves around when God created man and woman. So Rosh Hashanah is the celebration of the birth of the world and the beginning of the year, of marking time."

I take this all in while Neil sips the orange herbal tea that Wendy offered him. He looks through the summons and complaint papers from Mark. Wendy comes down to sit down beside me.

Neil takes off his glasses, twirls them in his hand, and looks at me. "Okay, I'm trying my best to hold all this in," he says, then doubles over, laughing. "I'm sorry, so sorry, but there is just no way that you need to worry about this, this Mark, is it? No judge would ever accept what he's asking. There's no way that your ex-husband-to-be will be able to get a penny out of you. You make less than half of what he does, you're making payments on your pickup truck and he's demanding that he take the truck? That's laughable. Okay?"

I burst into tears and run for the Kleenex box on my desk.

"Hey, that's supposed to be good news," Wendy says.

"It is. It is. But I can hardly believe it. You don't know Mark. He will try anything."

Neil comes up to me. "Not a thing to worry about. All you have to do is get your own lawyer."

I nearly buckle over. "A lawyer? I have to get a lawyer? Why can't I just do this on my own?"

"You have no choice. You have to get a lawyer to represent yourself," Neil tells me.

"He's right," Wendy says. "I've been involved in a few lawsuits. You'll never be able to stand on your own."

*****

Never able to stand on your own. Can't get that out of my head. It reminds me of something that I can barely put my finger on. I went ahead and hired a lawyer like Neil recommended, a Mr. Chris Pritchard. He tried to get me to reverse the charges.

"You could get thousands from Mark if you sue him for spousal support. Imagine that," Mr. Pritchard had said, revolving his pen like a tiny baton between his fingers.

I looked out the window. His office is just down the street from the Park Manor and has a far better view than I do of the planes coming in. I watch one now, the landing wheels down as it careens between the buildings. I keep expecting an explosion to go off at any minute from the plane crash.

"No. You see, I don't want to get money from Mark. Ever again."

Mr. Pritchard laughed. "You don't get the picture, do you? I'm telling you, the judge will rule in your favor to get money from Mark. Forever. That is, until you marry again."

I shook my head. "No. I don't want support from Mark. That's why I'm leaving him in the first place. He believes that I would never be able to live apart from his support. I don't want a penny from him."

Mr. Pritchard shook his head and waved me away. "Okay, so be it. I'll get the papers rolling."

A lot of people will tell me that I made the wrong decision about this. I do admit I like money as much as anyone else. And the idea of getting money for an interminably long time does thrill me down to my toes. But it just seems wrong, feels wrong.

Now back in my room at Park Manor, I sip from a glass of chardonnay, contemplating if God has it in for me or vice versa. I mean, really, whoever turns down her ex-husband's spousal support? Is this self-sabotage?

Spunky chirps at me. I walk over to his cage and stare in at him. "You know somethin'? We're good."

I wish Mom were here. Or Aunt Sophia. Or anybody from my family, for that matter. I think back on last summer—eons ago, already—and tears spring to my eyes. Spunky cheeps again at me.

Slow, careful, I put my finger into the cage and nudge it up just below Spunky's chest like the girl in the pet shop said to do. He does it. Spunky gets up on my finger. Feeling like the Green Giant, I keep my finger still as possible while bringing Spunky through the cage door, and finally in front of my face.

Spunky chirps so loud my ears hurt. I try not to laugh or giggle because I don't want him to fall off. He climbs from my finger up to my arm and then up my shoulder. He does his little parakeet dance, the feathers on his little head puffing up as he bobs up and down, chirping sweet nothings at me.

I can't help it now. I am giggling. Even funnier, so is he.

*****

Sunday morning, I slowly wake up in my odd bed, a circular king-size thing that swamps me. But I like that it is so far removed from anything that used to be normal in my life. Everything about this living space is a bit off-the-wall: red carpeting, oddly sized shelves up against the walls, a rocking chair here, a stuffed ottoman there. The ceiling beams raise dramatically up to an inverted *V* shape, and the best thing of all, the windows are tall and wide, allowing me a view of life outside.

I smile and stretch and yawn. Not until I pad over to the sink to make coffee do I remember the whole Neil-spousal support-Pritchard-lawyer ordeal.

"You're so cute!"

My eyes fly open and I just about drop the coffee pot.

"Spunky!" I bend over to look at the little guy, who is doing his parakeet dance. "You're so cute, too!"

Spunky bobs his head up and down, all happy, when I put in his cage some bird seed treats. I sit down to watch him and drink my coffee and eat a granola bar. Out the window the sky is blue, a cool breeze wafting in. I don't want to think about Neil or the lawyer or anything related to work.

"Wish you could go to OB with me today, Spunky." I shut the door before he chirps at me. I'm feeling guilty enough. Lord knows why.

*****

The jet planes roaring above Ocean Beach take me instantly back to the '80s when I was young and in love, foolish, but too full of energy and hope to care. I had thrown my cares to the wind, to the world, really, because I did not know God back then. I may have gone to the altar when I was a kid back in Kansas, but growing up on Sherman Street made me forget what kind of commitment I'd made to God. I was too worried about my parents wondering what they'd do to me and my sister to remember that God had made a commitment to me, too, when I'd given my life to Christ. TU simply threw another wrench into my personal relationship with Him. When you're told over and over that any problems you have are due to your own lack of faith, you take it to heart, find yourself steered away from the captain of your soul.

I walk along the beach remembering, thanking God, asking for forgiveness, for help. The beach just south of the pier is like a painting, the water way out in low tide, the rocky pools in front of me, exposing miniature ecosystems of life.

An old man is tossing up bread to a scolding flock of seagulls flying low over the sand; their reflection glimmers in the thin sheet of sea water shifting over the rocks.

I look down into the tide pool closest to me. There is a small fish with bands of brown and pink. He darts over to the nearest clump of algae, hiding. Blissed beyond words with this simple pleasure, I close my eyes, lift my face to the sun, smiling.

When I open my eyes, I see a man motioning for me to come over.

"You should get a picture of this octopus here," he tells me.

"An octopus, for real?"

"You've never seen one?"

I feel like a little kid, shaking my head.

"Then you gotta see this. Be careful, it's a little slippery," he says, taking my hand as we step over the shiny green algae draping over the rocks

"Right over there," he says.

I stand balancing myself on the rocks, aiming my camera at the water. And there I see it. A shadowy creature, hiding under the rock. I take a dozen pictures, not wanting to miss a second. Suddenly, the octopus pushes out from underneath the rock, its tentacles reaching out in the water.

"So cool," I say.

"It is, isn't it?" the guy says, looking at me intense, too intense.

"Thanks so much for showing me," I say, turning to leave.

"Need help?"

No, thanks, I tell him. I can do this. Though I am scared I'm going to slip and fall on all this slippery algae, I do need to get back to my own moments with God.

Slow, careful, I move like a wounded ballet dancer across the rocks, kneeling down to peer into the tide pools. In them are clumps of shells—tiny homes that have been abandoned by their occupants. All around me, hundreds of miniature cliff-homes—mounds of rock about two feet high, pock-marked—are filled with chitons, those green skeleton-like creatures.

I crouch down and look at all the flower-like sea anemones with shell fragments stuck all over them. I can't resist the urge; I gently poke the top of one anemone and watch it double up on itself to get away from me, the intruder.

In another serene pool of clear water, I see a multitude of hermit crabs, their shell-houses on their backs as they move around in purple and red algae. Drops of water are running down my face. I look around to see who is splashing, but there is no one. I wipe my eyes, realize that I am crying, happy.

The cliff wall is warm against my back, my muscles relaxing. The afternoon is so beautiful, a postcard from heaven. I turn to look at what's lodged in the wall and find a hard and crusty shell that seems lifeless. When I turn the shell over, I see a tiny hand-like part of the animal.

I don't know much about what all the different sea creatures need for survival, but I figure this little guy needs to be in water. Gingerly, I place the creature over a clump of the green algae. Within seconds, the hand of the animal appears as it moves over the algae. Wondering if I had done the right thing, I look to see where the shelled creatures are hanging out in the other tide pools and see that many of them are maneuvering around in the same way.

And then I see a little jewel of a shell clinging to the rock a few inches under the surface of the tide pool closest to me. Now I've seen shells that were red and pink, purple, blue, gray, and white, but I've never before seen a bright yellow and green one like this.

The mystery of the moment surrounds me like a cloak of comfort. I thank God for His creation. The seagulls soar above; a sense of peace warms me, tingling up my back. I don't want to leave, but it is three thirty in the afternoon—rush hour on the freeway.

Back at the pier, I watch the sea gulls screaming at each other until they barely have voices left. They are completely at home in the low tide, perched on the slippery rocks waiting for the incoming tides to bring in feasts. One of the gulls snatches up a crab, its legs thrashing about. The gull shakes the crab to unconsciousness. I remember reading somewhere that gulls have to resort to this kind of slow killing because they are not really great carnivores. The gull flies over to the next rock to dash his prey against the rock; the other gulls try to snatch it from him. The crab-owner gull at last swallows his meal.

*****

Spunky and I whistle at each other as I sit in the little kitchenette area eating yogurt with granola, thinking of the ocean. My sleep was sweet last night, best I've had in months. There's just something about going to see the ocean, pondering its vastness, its power. I woke up this morning singing "He's Got the Whole World in His Hands."

Spunky whistles again at me. I return the compliment and pick up the newspaper to look through the classified ads. It is time for me to look for a real place of my own.

I circle several places, calling them one by one, crumpling when I heard how much they wanted for rent. Then I see a tiny ad for an apartment-turned-condo with option to buy—just within a few blocks of where I work. Hard to believe, but the monthly payment would be a little less than what I am paying now week-to-week to stay here at Park Manor.

When I dial the number listed for the place, I think I've called the wrong number because a woman with a rich, bubbly voice answers, "Vivian Hansen, real estate."

I apologize and start to hang up. But Vivian asks if I am calling about a house or apartment. I tell her, yes, the condo on Williams Street. She asks me what caught my attention from the ad.

Just blocks from where I work and with option to buy, I answer.

Vivian breathes a sigh of relief. "Oh, good, then you know the neighborhood?"

I say yes, I do. "Um, who are you?"

"Oh, goodness gracious, sweet girl, I'm so sorry. I should have explained right from the top. I am a real estate agent, specializing mostly in residential and home sales. This is an unusual situation—the place you're interested in—because the lady who is selling the condo had to leave quickly for personal reasons. She will rent out the condo, but really would be interested in selling it eventually. Would you like to see it?"

Something about this lady, her voice, her *mothering* puts me at instant ease.

I say, yes, I want to see the place. She asks me a few questions about my situation, and I state the basic facts: I'm staying at a week-to-week place, going through a divorce, needing to find a more permanent place to live.

"I have a secret dream of one day buying my own place," I say.

Who said that? I stop and stare out the window at the people walking by. It's true: I want my own place. And I could do it. Why not?

*****

Vivian picks me up in an hour. As soon as she steps out of her car to greet me, I think of two words together: calm joy. Those two words don't belong together, but in Vivian, they do. She is in her fifties, has short red hair cropped close to her head, crinkly blue eyes, and a quick smile. Plus she drives a classy creamy-white car. I have no idea what it is. She takes my hand in hers.

"Nice to meet you, Renee," she says, opening the door for me.

She gets into the driver's seat and starts up the car. "You and I are going to be friends. I could tell from our conversation on the phone," she says.

"What makes you say that?"

"I've just got a feeling," Vivian says, flashing a beautiful smile at me. She is wearing some kind of floral perfume that floats around me, lifting me up. Everything about her I wish I was.

Wilson Street is in the City Heights neighborhood, just three miles from where I am staying at the Park Manor, so we get to the condo complex within ten minutes.

My stomach goes topsy-turvy when I see the building. Built in the '70s, it has the old-style shake shingles on the roof. The units that Vivian and I see from the street have oval-shaped windows. The building is exactly the style of place where I first met Mark at Pauline's place. I want to groan, I am so let down by its outside appearance. Instead, I follow Vivian and watch as she unlocks the gate to the complex. In the courtyard is a lantana bush, a favorite plant of mine I've nicknamed "Candy Bush" for its miniature orange and pink blossoms that smell and look like exotic sweets. Good sign for this place. But still.

"Number 11 is up these stairs," Vivian says. "Are you okay with that? A second-floor unit?"

"Actually, I prefer it. The view is always better up higher."

"Good." Vivian smiles at me. I find myself wanting to like this place just so that I can see her again. I want her to be my real estate agent. Besides, I like the sound of it: *Hello, I'd like you to meet my realtor.*

I follow Vivian up the stairs, my heart doing its pound-pause thing I've felt a lot lately.

At the door, Vivian stops to look at me. "You okay?"

"Oh, yeah, just nervous." I clasp my hand to my heart, catching my breath. Vivian takes my hand and looks into my eyes for a moment. "No need to be nervous at all. You're not committing to anything. Just to let you know, the lady who owns the place now, her name is Phoebe. And she's here now. She can answer any questions you have about the place."

Phoebe, a little old lady probably in her eighties, opens the door and lets us in. Vivian introduces us to each other and Phoebe invites us in.

The place is small, 525 square feet, as Vivian had told me. But I like the layout, the living room with two wide windows so that I can see out over the courtyard. The view isn't awe-inspiring, but I do like that I can see what's going on downstairs and the sky above. The built-in bookcase in the wall is a definite selling point.

The kitchen looks good, bathroom roomy, and the bedroom is bathed in a golden light, magnified by the mirrored closet. I linger here, day dreaming for a moment. There is just something about the idea of sleeping in my own bed in a pretty bedroom. I will put my cute daybed right next to the window so that I can wake to the day's first light.

I come back out to the dining alcove, stand and listen, ignoring Phoebe's and Vivian's glances at each other. The hum of traffic is just a quarter-block up the street on Gateway Boulevard. If I decided to make this my place, I could walk anytime to the Italian restaurant two blocks away. I would be able to hop on the bus and go anywhere, anywhere. I could write poetry on the bus if I wanted. I could—

"So, Renee, what do you think?" Vivian comes up next to me.

"Oh, I'm taking it."

Phoebe clasps her hands together. "You will love it here."

"But why are you leaving?" I ask her.

"Can't climb those stairs anymore. I'm just too old for that."

Fair enough. "Any problems that you know of?"

Phoebe shakes her head vehemently, reminding me of a five-year-old child who's just been caught red-handed. "Oh, no. It's so quiet here."

Vivian clears her throat. "Okay, Phoebe, can you talk a little about what the HOA requests are for the renter?"

Phoebe says just to pay the fees, which are included in the rental payment of $470.

That is what I pay for just two weeks at Park Manor. I look at Vivian.

"What is it, Renee?"

"Just wondering what it would be, how much it would cost to buy this place," I say.

Phoebe clasps her hands together again. "Oh, well, I am asking $39,000. And that would include this beautiful china cabinet over here," she says pointing to the oak and glass cabinet standing nearly eight feet tall. "I certainly don't need it where I'm going."

I sit down in one of Phoebe's rocking chairs—$39,000? That's right in the price line of a home I could buy in Kansas. Of course, back there, I would have an entire front and backyard and all the squirrels and cardinals that would come with the property. And the kids just a couple of miles away.

But I'm here now. Here is this cute little upstairs condo three blocks from where I work.

I look up at Vivian, my heart pounding. "Can we talk privately for a few minutes?" I ask her.

Vivian and I clomp down the stairs, and we go sit down in the wrought iron chairs in the courtyard. I feel eyes on us all around, so I whisper. "Vivian, why is this place $39,000? I thought this building was considered to be in North Park."

Vivian's floral fragrance wafts up as she leans forward and looks at me. "You're right, it is a North Park zip code. But it's not the North Park most San Diegans would think of. You know this neighborhood, right?"

I nod yes.

"And you are comfortable here?"

"Well, I don't think I would have ever considered living here before, but I do work in and know this area and I love the idea of everything being so close." I sit up straighter, suddenly giddy. "I can be a city girl pretty easily. So how much would my mortgage payment be for this place?"

Vivian does some quick calculating on her realtor's note pad. I shade my eyes from the September sun. I wonder how hot it would be at this place. Vivian finishes up with the numbers.

"I can't guarantee you this will be the payment, but I would imagine you'd be looking at something around $480," she says.

I sit back, looking up at the achingly blue sky, and doing some quick calculating in my head. The same amount of $480 is what I pay to live for just two weeks at the Park Manor. It's been doable, but it's not home. I can easily pay $480 per month, especially now that I've gotten a raise.

"Let's go talk to Phoebe," I say.

– 13 –

JUST ONE AND A half month later, I am the proud possessor of my own cute little condo. My mortgage payments of $470 are less than what I would be paying for rent at most apartments in the Mid-City area of San Diego. Wendy is impressed with what I've done. Okay, *I* am impressed with myself. Not until I had said aloud to Vivian and Phoebe that, yes, absolutely, I wanted to buy the condo, did I realize that owning my home was the hugest desire I had, other than falling in love with the right man.

It's been heaven here—as close to heaven as a poorer city section can be. I actually eat at home, buying heirloom tomatoes, arugula, garlic-stuffed olives, feta cheese, salsa, crackers and cookies and bread at Mid-City Market right across the street. As I sit eating in my dining room alcove, I watch the people walking by, groups of women in their native dress from Ethiopia and Somalia, young families holding the hands of their toddlers and older people inching by with their canes.

Enya sings softly from my tape player as I sit and watch the global parade outdoors. A sense of peace like I have never known lifts me up. Sometimes I think of Mark and wonder what he is doing. But I don't call him. I have no reason to. At long last, the divorce is final, made official on my birthday. Wendy took me to lunch to Casa de Bandini in Old Town to celebrate. She ordered margaritas for both of us as we noshed on chips and salsa and watched the sparrows bathe and flirt with each other in the fountain.

"I feel delicious," I told Wendy.

Wendy nearly spewed a mouthful of margarita. "How does delicious feel?" she asked me, dabbing margarita off the tablecloth.

"Relaxed. Wonderful. Full of hope. I didn't know I had it in me."

"You're not nervous about making such a huge commitment—a mortgage?"

I sip, thinking. "Yes and no. I remember my parents talking about mortgage payments when I was little. I always thought it sounded a lot like mortuary. When I looked up the word in the dictionary a few years later, I found that it was sort of related to mortuary—mort being death. Having a mortgage meant that you were tied until death to a house.

"I sort of have already been tied to a house in one way or another. With my parents. With Mark. But I've never had a chance to live on my own. I've always been a daughter or paid rent to someone or been a roommate or living with a man I didn't really want to be with. Miserable. Now I can decide to be happy or miserable on my own."

"Decide to be miserable?" Wendy asked.

"Yes. I can tell when I get up in the morning which way I'm heading. At least if I have my own place I have only me to blame if I'm miserable. I can't say Mark made me mad."

Wendy put down her margarita. "You know? I like the way you put that. I'm going to have to think about that."

Now, Spunky is doing his little tap dance on the perch. He wants me to let him out. I go and open his cage door slow, easy. He eyes me, eyes my fingers on the door, then hops down, one, two, three from each of his perches and then onto my finger. He runs back and forth across my finger, and I giggle from the tickling of his feet. I've got to go soon, I tell Spunky. He stops mid-tap-dance and bee-bops my finger in a parakeet passion play. After kissing Spunky lightly on his back—his feathers emanate a sweet, fennel-type fragrance—I place him gently on a perch. He looks so forlorn in his giant cage all alone. Fighting off the guilt, I head downtown to join up with my friends from Walk San Diego for a stroll along the Embarcadero and a bite to eat.

*****

I awake at 7:00 a.m. with the roar of the produce truck pulling in across the street and men unloading its contents. I get up and drink my first cup of coffee, standing and looking out the window, contemplating going to church. All this new freedom of going where I want to go to worship throws opens so many doors and windows. A little intimidating, but if I get into the right mood, I can consider it an adventure. Maybe I'll go to Catholic Mass again with my neighbor friend Alicia Gonzales, a sweet old lady. First time I went with her a few weeks ago at the chapel in Old Town San Diego, I was intrigued with the Latin liturgy, the incense and the ornate interior of the sanctuary. It's church on steroids, I whispered to Alicia, and she turned her big brown eyes on me, questioning. I shrugged and studied the bulletin. Bible study class Tuesday nights. Women's Ministry meeting and breakfast, Saturday mornings. Fall festival and craft sale in two weeks.

I remember thinking after I read through that bulletin: *I love real church. It's where I find life now and after.*

The priest gave a sermon about loving other people before yourself. "It's God's biggest command," he said.

But the practicality of it can be confusing. Jesus says to turn the other cheek if someone strikes you. And yet He tells his disciples that He had come to divide the world, even parent from child.

"So how do you reconcile the two?"

I lean forward a little, waiting for the answer. But the priest does not give us one. He tells us that we have to figure it out for ourselves. "Work out your salvation with trembling," he says.

Thinking about that sermon now, I find myself wanting to go beyond my baby-steps faith in Christ. All those years of being in TU and listening to its easy gospel of expecting God to accommodate me, and not the other way around, left me high and dry.

The phone rings; the sound startles me and I spill lukewarm coffee all over my hands. Spunky stops mid-preen, stands like a fluff ball on his perch, curious about the high-pitched ringing. The phone does have a witchy scream to it. I find the phone under a pile of towels I'd put over it in case Mark found where I was and called me in the middle of the night. He's been doing that lately.

It's nine o'clock in the morning. Would he call now? Probably not. I grab a towel to dry myself off and answer the phone.

"Renee?"

"Mom! I was just thinking of you. You'll never guess—"

"Renee, wait. Before you go on, I have to tell you something." Mom's voice is grave.

"Your dad. He's had a heart attack. I think. I don't know. Your Aunt Sophia told me. He—oh, Renee, he just up and collapsed."

My head hurts from pulling my hair. I look out the window at the traffic, look at Spunky. "When did this happen?"

"Earlier today. He's in a coma now."

"A coma?" I stagger, look for a chair.

"Yes. Oh, I feel terrible," Mom says.

"Mom, I'm going to fly out there."

"Oh, Renee, you don't have to. You were just here."

"He's my dad. I have to. I want to."

I hear her sniffling. She's always said that she wished she could have just been more patient with Dad's ways. I do hope I have learned some lessons from Mom. On what not to do.

I call Alicia and ask her to look after Spunky while I'm gone, and then I burst into tears.

*****

Thirty thousand feet high in the sky, I look down at the Grand Canyon. As sad as I am, wistful, and in odd ways, thankful, I understand what the strange premonition of my losing something was all about last summer. Already, I'm calling it last summer.

It's just so unreal. My dad in a coma. What a horrible thing to say. He is just sixty-one years old. The man sitting next to me is looking at me strange because I'm tearing my Kleenex to shreds. Thankfully, the stewardess—do they even say that anymore?—comes by with her cart of drinks and snacks.

"Rum and coke," the man next to me says.

"I'll have a Sprite, no ice," I say.

Having an alcoholic drink while flying has never been a temptation for me. I always want to stay awake and alert to see the cloud displays just out my little window and see the lay of the land. That old bug-a-boo of wondering if I have a problem with drinking grows while I watch Mr. Rum and Coke down his drink in three gulps, then signal for another.

In between eating my bag of peanuts, sobbing about Dad and hiccupping from the Sprite, I think about my love affair with wine. It really has been like a secret lover because most people don't even know I drink. Years ago, I did drink all day and all night, one day calling a taxi driver to come pick me up and drive me to the nearest liquor store. I was so cloudy-minded that I got into the passenger seat next to the driver, thinking I didn't want to be rude. Cringing with embarrassment even now, I remember that the taxi driver smiled at me, sideways-like, when I slid into the passenger seat. He tried to make conversation with me, I remember that. But I just smiled and pretended everything was just wonderful on my way to buy another jug of cheap wine.

But now, for the last fifteen years or so, most people never know that I drink, except Mark and the Landrys. Lately, I have cut down to two glasses of wine at night. Okay, three glasses. That's still a lot better than eight or more glasses, which I was used to consuming around Mark.

The stewardess comes around and collects our trash. I hand her my empty plastic cup, as does Mr. Rum and Coke. His eyes are all red. I feel sorry for him, somehow, sad for me, too. But I'm supposed to be sad. For my dad. I blow into my Kleenex, and Mr. Rum and Coke looks at me, compassion in his red eyes.

I smile. That's all I do, who I am, is smile. Even though a part of me, deep inside, knows better. "For we are God's handiwork, created in Christ Jesus to do good works, which God prepared in advance for us to do."

We shall see.

*****

When Mom and Aunt Sophia picked me up at the Wichita airport, they hugged me silent, tearful. That silence still hangs heavy around us in the car as Mom drives looking dead-on, not even noticing the pair of cardinals that fly in front of the car, as if they are trying to get attention. I look at Aunt Sophia sitting in the passenger seat. Even she does not speak much. It is her brother, after all, who is in a coma.

I sit silent in the backseat, not sure what to do with my hands or what to say. Thankfully, Aunt Sophia breaks the silence.

"You'll be staying with me, Renee," she says, twisting in her seat to look at me. "I know you have a motel reservation, but we all need to be together. And I have the extra room."

I am torn between gratitude and a free-floating anxiety because I never do well sleeping in someone else's house. And I'm mortified that I wonder where and how and when I can buy some wine. Aunt Sophia has never had a drop in her life and isn't about to now.

We arrive at Aunt Sophia's house. I hug Mom, rocking her slowly from side to side before I let go. Albert picks up my suitcases; Aunt Sophia and Albert walk me into the house toward the garage-turned-room, my room.

*****

I got maybe four hours sleep last night, but I don't mind. I feel clean and whole and close to God, even though I am sad about my dad. My dad, almost dead. But not a drop of wine did I have, not a drop.

The bag of M&M's I'd brought with me helped stave off the craving. Aunt Sophia had prepared ahead of time a scrumptious chicken and vegetable soup. Last evening, I sat and ate with her and Albert in the dining room and made small talk with them, thinking of the countless meals with the whole clan for Christmas, Easter, and birthdays. I struggled to maintain a balance between the memories and the realization that my father was lying cold to the world in a hospital bed. When I was done eating, I washed my bowl and spoon and gave Aunt Sophia a gentle hug. She wasn't in a mood to talk, so I just went to my pretty little room. Feeling all twitchy in my guts, I got on my knees and asked God to help me get through the night.

I had dim dreams moving in and out of sleep, pushing my hands under the pillows, continually murmuring little breath-prayers to God. By the time I woke up, the autumn shadows were skittering across the fence outside the window. At first, I thought there was a fire for all the bright orange and red on the elm tree leaves. *Fall in Kansas. How could I forget? How can I go back to San Diego?*

Now the aroma of breakfast is beckoning me out to the kitchen. Aunt Sophia is at the stove scrambling eggs. She turns to me, says, "Hi, sweetie," and I throw my arms around her, breathing in her Desert Rose perfume.

Aunt Sophia pretends to object, smiles. "Orange juice over there," she says, waving her spatula towards the counter. Funny how everything seems so much smaller than when I was nine years old and would watch Mom and Aunt Sophia carve a turkey in a giant pan on this same counter.

"Sleep okay?" Aunt Sophia asks.

"Not bad, actually, considering everything. And you?"

All the acts of politeness break down and we go to each other's arms, crying quietly. Albert comes in and embraces us both, quietly, then says a prayer for us, for Dad. We eat quietly, get dressed in a hurry, then Albert drives us to the hospital.

*****

I've never seen anyone so ashen as my father. Aunt Sophia, Mom, and I are all holding on to each other, quavering as if we're standing in front of the great Wizard of Oz waiting for his proclamation. But Dad looks nothing like a larger-than-life master. His six-feet-six-inches frame has shrunk beneath the sheets. The tubes and wires coming from his mouth, nose, and arms make him look like a failed Frankenstein robot. I could just die.

"Wha—what, what do we do?" I ask the air.

"Just sit by him." All of us jump at the voice and look around. A nurse emerges from behind the massive machine that is helping my dad breathe.

"Can he hear us?" Aunt Sophia asks.

"You never know."

Mom clears her throat. "How long has he, um, has he been like this?" Her eyes are huge in her face, gaunt-like.

"Four days now," the nurse says, then walks by us, her legs rubbing together making a crispy sound under her uniform. She stops at the door, turns around, and gives us a little smile. "The doctor will be in to check on him in a few minutes."

Why don't they put more chairs in hospital rooms? None of us is strong enough to stand. I point to the one chair for Aunt Sophia. She shakes her head, no, thanks.

"Sophia, go ahead," Mom says. I hold her hand in mine while Aunt Sophia pulls up the chair close to the bed where her brother lies cold as stone.

The door opens suddenly. We turn to see the doctor enter the room. His lapel pin says Dr. Stanley. Aunt Sophia stands up.

"Oh, doctor, please tell us what the situation is with my brother," she says, tears running down her face. I've never seen her cry before, ever.

In the space of a few minutes stretching like an eon, Dr. Stanley tells us that Dad is terminal. Terminal what? I ask.

He has maybe a couple of days. It's his heart. Weakened by the virus that he had. Didn't take care of himself.

"But he always took those Shaklee vitamins," Aunt Sophia said. "He swore on them."

"Yes, well, it might have even been good for someone in better health. But the thing is, your brother should never have lived beyond the age of forty. He is a miracle."

I look at Mom, and then the doctor. "What do you mean by that?"

"He had a virus and his heart was already scarred by the rheumatic fever he had as a child," the doctor tells me now, bored-looking.

"He's always been worried about catching colds," Mom says, staring with glazed eyes at the mustard-yellow wall. Everything is rushing at me fast: Me and Rita trying to hide any cold we ever got from Mom, me rushing to my bedroom so that I could kneel down beside the bed, bury my face deep into the mattress and cough while

I piled pillows over my head to muffle the sound. The daggers from Mom's eyes when she knew that Rita and I had the sniffles. And always, always the admonition to be quiet, to keep out of sight, to be invisible.

Mom seems to know what I'm thinking. She shrugs her shoulders. "Renee, his heart was weak. I always tried to keep the house quiet for him and free of germs," she says, shaking her head, remembering. "He about drove me crazy with all that washing of his hands, but…" She turns to Aunt Sophia.

"I feel so bad now," Mom whispers.

I think back to when I visited Dad in his office last summer. He seemed so happy and carefree, a little pale, but Dad never spent any time in the sun, so I didn't think too much about it. Still, he seemed subdued, somehow, even as he had leaned forward in that chair, looked into my eyes and given me his blessing.

In visiting him, did I unwittingly nearly kill the very man who hadn't wanted me and Rita in the first place?

The room goes white.

*****

Mom and Aunt Sophia told me that they caught me as I started to fall to the floor.

I never did get to talk to Dad again. By the time Rita came stumbling into the IRC room where Dad was lying, just minutes after Merilee walked in, seemingly shrunken by a foot in height and her eyes red and swollen, the machine with all the tubes running into Dad's body was screaming. So this is what flatlining means, I thought, my heart pounding.

The doctor rushed in, fooled around with some knobs on the machine, and took Dad's pulse. He turned to us, shaking his head. "I'm sorry," he said.

"No! No, you just can't do this. You can't just say you're sorry. What have you done?" The crazy woman screaming was me.

I hated this doctor, hated myself for hating him, for holding anger toward my father all these years, against Merilee, too.

"Renee, it'll be okay," Mom says now, reaching out for me.

"How can you say that? I lost my dad! Why did you keep so much from me and Rita?"

By now, Rita is doubling over as if she is suffering from labor pains. "Renee, please stop," she moans.

"What do you care, Rita? Huh? You sit there in your house and drink all day. What do you care?"

Aunt Sophia takes me by the arm and leads me outside the room. I kick and scream at her, lashing out, pummeling her stomach. And then I crumble, crying, crash-landing onto her shoulders.

– 14 –

PEOPLE SAY THE SMELL of death is terrible. It is not so much terrible as it is sickeningly sweet, here at the memorial service. Dressed in varying shades of black, all these people are wearing perfume and cologne, and I am about ready to gag from the scent. The fragrance of my own Avon's Candid perfume keeps rising to my nostrils in overpowering waves.

Mom and Aunt Sophia have drenched themselves in perfume, too—Aunt Sophia has spritzed half a bottle of her Desert Rose perfume on herself, and I recognize the scent of Avon's Moonlight on Mom. Both my mother and aunt look ten years older than they did just a week ago. I don't even want to know how I look. My reflection in the mirror only shows me what I look like when I smile, not when I am caught in a down-mouthed expression.

I glance over at Rita, dressed in black like everyone else. She is reading the program for the memorial service—about our dad, the man who did not want us, but I wanted him. Always have.

A memory stirs within me. I remember that one evening when I was thirteen years old; it had been snowing and sleeting outside. The sky was as dark as velvet already. Mom was cooking chili con carne, one of my favorite meals. The little kitchen was steamy warm, light from the overhead fixtures pooled around us, our own little campfire in a wild scary world. I was chit-chatting with Mom, a rare time when she let me hang around the kitchen, setting the table for dinner. We were both worried, wondering, though we never said a word—Dad was late for dinner. He was never late for anything, despite his slow-as-a-turtle ways that drove Mom crazy.

Finally, the door burst open. The snow and sleet was swirling behind Dad as he walked in, stomping his feet dry on the welcome mat. I watched and tried not to watch him go over to kiss Mom. He wrapped his arms around her for a minute—she still holding the wooden spoon stained red from the chili—and held her while they kissed. Honestly, I wanted that kiss to last forever. I wanted my parents to be happy with each other always. Blushing, I busied myself with straightening the tablecloth.

And then he walked right over to me, smiling. "I've got something for you, kiddo," he said, rustling a brown paper bag he'd been hiding behind his back. He took out something from the bag and handed it to me: a little red diary with its own key.

I took the little book from his hands, torn between smiling and crying. "Oh, Daddy, thank you. But, why?"

"You're a good writer. I've been admiring your schoolwork, Renee. I hope this diary motivates you to keep writing," he said.

Only one thing was wrong with that magical, mystical snowy evening: I wanted to hug Dad, but I knew I couldn't and he wouldn't. He was bigger than God to me at that moment.

But Dad had truly cared about me, in his own way. And now I think again of the blessing he gave me just a few months ago when the sun was hot and the elm trees burly with summer. My tissue is getting very wet. Rita gets me a box of them from under the pew.

Mom and Aunt Sophia reach for my hands. I take and squeeze theirs lightly, looking around the First Baptist Church: a low-lying, rather squat building saved by the A-frame shape of the ceiling and small squares of stained glass. People are standing in the back and on the aisles. Good heavens, Dad was popular. I'd heard that nearly two hundred customers from Wagoner's Auto Repair would be attending. I feel lost and confused. Dad always seemed to have a secret life, even when married to Mom. He emotionally distanced himself from her and me and Rita so well that I thought it was the norm. And in some ways, it was for that era. Dad knows best, right? I release my hands from Mom and Aunt Sophia's to get another tissue.

"This is a time I really wish my mother and grandma were here," Aunt Sophia says. I nod, thinking of Grandma Howell and Grandma Bell. If it hadn't been for them—and Aunt Sophia—I would have walked away from church forever. I can't help but smile from the irony as I consider the pew I am sitting in now.

Gemma leans over beside her mother to peer over at me. I reach my hand over Rita and squeeze her hand. The other kids are in various states of boredom, swinging their legs, running their hands through their hair, jabbing each other in private jokes. God, how I love them. I wish they had known Dad more.

But Rita had not even wanted any of them to come along. She herself hadn't wanted to come. I don't even think of him as Dad, she told me.

"Are you still going to punish Dad even though he's dead and gone?" I was incredulous.

Now we all sit and sweat and tear up and cough and shift in the pews. It's just all a nightmare. Still, I am in awe of something that I can't tell anyone else now: I got through the night before without a drink, and without the attendant free-floating panic. Thinking of this, I smile, until Mom turns to me with a wild, worried look in her eyes.

We are all sitting in the second row right in back of Merilee, her daughter Lara and son Thomas. Lara still has the same gorgeous blond hair she had in high school. A part of me keeps wanting to tap Lara on the shoulder and hug her as if we were meeting up with each other after a long absence. And the other part of me wants to tear her hair out. Dad always adored her, talked about her as if she were his very own. Merilee always liked to talk about how he fixed Lara up with her brand-new husband, who's sitting with her now, some guy named Pierce. What kind of guy is named Pierce? And why was my dad so enchanted with Lara? And with Pierce? Were my sister and I that abhorrent?

I know I am thinking nonsense, all selfish like a nine-year-old girl, but it is my dad's memorial service and I can pout if I want to. Can't I?

Just then Pastor Greeley comes up before us and begins talking about how wonderful Dad was, how he had always donated boxes of donuts and other treats to the office.

"He always knew the right thing to say to people and those donuts always lit up their eyes," Pastor Greeley says, fussing with a box of tissues. Merilee gets up, and like a meek kitten, talks into the microphone about how tall Dad stood in her eyes. Everyone laughs at that—Merilee stood only four feet, eight inches next to Dad. Rita and I look at each other. I roll my eyes, hard to do because my eyes are so sticky with tears.

For the next half hour, we sing songs, get up, sit down, and listen to people's tales about how great Dad was, most of them people from Wagoner's and from church. Mom and Aunt Sophia remain silent until Pastor Greely asks Aunt Sophia to come up to the podium to speak. Mom nudges her to get up.

It seems like forever until Aunt Sophia reaches the podium. She looks regal up there—as if she could herself be a pastor. She would laugh at that idea, I think as I hold Mom's hand. I look at Rita, who is sitting silent, smug, pumping her leg. She's never thought much of Aunt Sophia.

"My brother was the most guilt-free man I've ever known. What I mean by that is I've never known him to indulge in anything. Never taken a drink, never had a drop of coffee, never smoked, never chased after skirts."

But I remember that wandering eye Dad had. Saw it all the time in him, even as he was driving us all to church. He'd see a pretty girl walk down the sidewalk, and I in the back seat would catch his sly little grin and his peeking in the rearview mirror. I was furious at him at the time, and he'd see my reflection, turn back his gaze to the street. But I understand now that every grown man with an ounce of healthy sex drive in him does have a wandering eye. I've seen it in Mark. Still, there's a part of me that just wants to kick guys, especially after Mom's marrying Todd the Letch.

"But there's a side of him that you probably didn't know," Aunt Sophia is saying now. "He was a cloud-watcher. He used to run around the house looking at the sky. He always told me that if anyone ever doubted God existed, all they had to do was look up. These days, I know everybody is so sophisticated and science gets even deeper into galaxies we don't know about, but my brother said he could talk to God better if he looked up into the sky and considered God's marvelous creation."

Aunt Sophia chokes up. I have been holding up pretty well at this funeral, but listening to her has caused me to cave in. Rita gets the box of tissue, plucks one up for herself, and hands me the box.

As Aunt Sophia comes back to sit by us again, I am feeling so much angst. I can remember when Dad charged me rent when I got my first job, a piddly office job at school making copies of tests on the duplicating machine. My boss happened to also be my office skills instructor. I could barely stomach her smoker's breath, and the job bored me to tears. But it was a job, my first one, and I was elated about that. Until the day that Dad said I was to pay $80 a month.

I look at Mom, who's dabbing her eyes, too. This strange mix of compassion, empathy, and anger keeps pressing into my chest. I am remembering, suddenly now, against my will, that my mother had also been money-hungry—for my own earnings. I had come home for leave during Christmas break in my first year of the Navy. She and Todd cornered me one day, upset about something, explaining they needed to talk to me about my financial situation.

"What financial situation?"

Mom looked at Todd, then said, "You need a safe place to keep your money."

"Uh, yes, I do. And I have. The bank."

"Oh, no, that's not good. Because you're going to be gone all the time and you need a place to keep your money growing. So give it to us and we'll invest it for you," Mom said.

"That's right," Todd said between inhales on his cigarette.

"Are you kidding me?" I started laughing.

"No, we're not kidding! You are going to need help with your money. Why don't you trust us?" Mom was livid.

"I wouldn't trust the president of the United States with my money. And that's that. Leave me alone," I'd said.

Even now through all my bleary tears, I still want to laugh at the memory of my mother and Todd just standing there glaring at me. But I don't laugh; I blot my eyes with a tissue and look over at Rita who is still glum and gloomy, but not shedding a tear. She's creasing and re-creasing the funeral bulletin, giving Dad's face wrinkles he never had.

Rita must feel me studying her because she turns to look at me. "What's with you?" she says, her eyes flashing. Then she does that quick, disarming smile. What is she devising in her mind half the time? Often I do feel guilty about being the "good" big sister. Rita and I had had our share of corporal punishment. The anger, the rage, the turn on a dime that our parents, particularly Mom, would do, had raised up a sort of hypervigilance in us both. One Saturday I remember when it seemed things were going well, the spring afternoon sweet and warm. Rita and I had just finished having lunch, and I went off to my bedroom to do my homework or read, plan on going for a bicycle ride later. Then I heard strange noises coming from the bathroom, muffled whimpering, and the raised voice of Mom.

I got up and stood in the hallway between my and Rita's bedroom to listen. Mom was yelling at Rita to spit up what she had in her mouth. Food. It was food she'd hid in her mouth, food she hadn't been able to eat. Often when Rita could not eat properly without gagging in front of me, Mom would send her off to her room and Rita would pretend to eat but hide a lot of it in the book space under her old-fashioned schoolroom chair. But Rita did not have that kind of luck on that afternoon, and now I could hear Mom telling Rita to spit out the food she'd stuffed into the corners of her mouth like a squirrel. "Do it, Rita, do it, spit it out! Now!" Mom was saying. I could hear choking sounds. My heart sped up like a train. I heard coughing and muffled sounds, then a noise like something thumping on the floor.

"Do it, Rita, you stupid kid!" Another clunk, clunk against the hard floor—or the toilet?

"Momma? My head hurts." Rita's voice was thick with saliva, maybe blood, I didn't know. I stepped back into my bedroom and glanced out the window toward Aunt Sophia's house. What should I do?

I waited, like I always did, for Mom's anger to subside.

Five minutes later, I heard a scrambling about and steps on the bathroom floor. I scurried back to my bedroom, my heart banging so loud I was worried that Mom would hear.

I never mentioned the incident to Mom. Doing so would have been certain death for me. And Rita. There was always a monster at home, but nobody was allowed to talk about it.

*****

Somehow Rita and her kids and I and Mom and Aunt Sophia got through the whole funeral ordeal and the reception afterward. The spread of food was enormous, and I felt sick from the sight of it. How can I eat knowing that Dad is dead and gone? Where has he gone, as a matter of fact? Heaven? Of course. He never did anything wrong. Just like Aunt Sophia said.

Both Rita and I were more than a little miffed that Merilee and Lara almost completely avoided us at the funeral. I tried to reason with Rita that Merilee was just grieving. "Well, heck, so are we," Rita had said. Right she was. Still, we needed to comfort her, I reminded Rita. It's her husband who died.

"And our dad," Rita countered.

"Come on, let's go," I said, gently tugging at Rita's hand. I felt like we were eight and nine years old again.

With our heads down and anxiety chewing our insides, Rita and I walked over to Merilee who was weeping in the arms of one of Dad's friends from Wagoner's Auto Repair. Good heavens, the man must have truly been a saint, I thought, not kindly. Lara noticed Rita and me before Merilee did. Her eyes were red, but beauty still haloed all around her. Somehow I managed to walk up to her, tell her that I hurt, too, and we embraced, with her crying on my shoulder, me rocking her. "I loved Jerry so much," she said, pulling away. Something about that comforted me. She did not call my dad her dad.

"I know, Lara. He loved you, too. And your mom," I said.

"But…you and Rita were all he talked about," Lara said.

I looked over at Rita who had heard this, too.

"You're kidding, right?" Rita said. For once, I'm glad that Rita has never been one to play social niceties.

"Hi, Rita," Lara says, stretching out her arms. Rita stands silent and wooden. "No, Rita, I am not making it up. Your dad loved you and Renee. He was always talking about how he wished he could make it up to us."

Rita stood her ground. "Make what up to us?"

Merilee stepped up to us just then. "Oh, girls, I'm so glad to see you," she said, flurrying around Rita and me. She took my hand and looked into my eyes. "Renee, I can't tell you how happy—no, I don't mean happy, that's the wrong word, nobody's happy." Lara handed her a tissue and Merilee let go of my hand to blot her eyes. "I mean, I'm thankful that you came to your dad's funeral. Your dad couldn't stop talking about you after you left a month ago." I looked to Rita for help. She just smirked at me. I'd had enough of all this. I just wanted to go back to Aunt Sophia's garage-turned room so that I could eat a lot of chocolate, in secret, all by myself. But I'd have to wait a while, because of what Merilee said next.

"I want you kids—you and Rita—to come over to my house on Monday morning. Sophia, too. Your dad made a will and I want to get that taken care of right away."

"But, Merilee, you're still grieving," I said, reaching out for her hand.

She dotted her eyes with the other hand, nodding. "Yes, but if I get this taken care of, then I can rest and savor the memories of your dad." She looked up at me and Rita, who had her arms crossed over her chest. In some ways, I admired Rita for her stony coldness. Here we were the rest of us, all sloppy and slogging through tears and snot and awkward touches and words, but Rita held it all in.

Mom came up just then. "Merilee?"

The two embraced, crying. Rita walked away; I hung around by the two women who had loved my father. When they broke apart, I handed Mom some tissues. Her eyes were so red, her face so contorted by sorrow that I could barely hold it in myself. After another hour of sniffling, smiling through my tears at people who came to tell me how wonderful my dad was, that I was so lucky to have him as a father, Aunt Sophia could see that I was drained and dizzy trying to hold it all together. I told Rita that we were leaving; she hugged me, which completely took me by surprise. "I guess I'll see you Monday at Merilee's, eh? Could be interesting," Rita said.

I stared at her, nodding. "Yes, I suppose so." I went over to give Mom a hug. "Mom? Can we make a date in about a week to have lunch and talk?"

"I'd love that. But why wait a week? You free tomorrow?"

I started to say no, then thought I'd appreciate the time with her after church in the morning. Sundays can be so blue for me, a hangover from my childhood when heaviness seemed to hang in the air once we came home from church, as if some kind of need had not been met. Mother would often cook a simple but scrumptious-to-me dinner of minute steaks with mashed potatoes and succotash. Dad would carry his dinner off on a TV tray to watch a football game. Mom fussed around in the kitchen for a while and then went in to sit with Dad in the living room. That left Rita and me able to take our time with our food and watch our parakeet Twinkle play games with the mirrors in his cage. We would laugh and play with our peas and carrots. Sometimes Rita wanted to get into a food fight, so she'd flick her peas at me. I'd ignore her and drink my milk, and she'd keep throwing peas in my hair. Finally, I'd glare her down and threaten to tell Mom that she wasn't eating. I hated doing that, but I hated more the idea of getting a whipping on a perfectly lovely October afternoon.

For some reason, wanting to make Mom feel better tomorrow, on possibly the worst Sunday afternoon of her life, seemed like a direct mission from God. So I told Mom that I would love to have lunch with her after church.

As soon as Aunt Sophia, Albert and I left the memorial service and stepped outside to walk to the truck, the late afternoon heat slapped me in the face. Though the sun would not set for another four hours, I was ready to call it a day. I asked Aunt Sophia and Albert if we could make a stop at the local grocery store so I could pick up some chocolate.

"I think Sophia could go for a big bag of Guy's Potato Chips," Albert said, winking at me.

"Got that right," Aunt Sophia said. As soon as we got to the house, Aunt Sophia went to the kitchen to pour herself some Coca-Cola. She asked if I wanted any.

"No. I'm not drinking," I said, laughing. Aunt Sophia looked at me quizzically. "Um, I bought some sparkling water while I was there at the store. I can't have a Coke right now because the caffeine would keep me up all night."

The three of us went to the family room where all the Thanksgivings and Christmases, birthday parties and Groundhog Days from those days long ago were celebrated around the long table. Now everything looked so shrunken and small. We plunked down into easy chairs and munched, me with my chocolate and Aunt Sophia her potato chips. Albert tossed peanuts into his mouth while we sat and talked about going over to Merilee's in the morning.

I never dreamed that Dad would have a will, much less include me and Rita. I wanted to ask the unaskable question. But Aunt Sophia beat me to it. "I'm wondering if your dad left any money for you and Rita. Although I think it's highly improbable. Gave most of what he had to Merilee and her kids." Aunt Sophia was talking to the walls, not looking at me. "I doubt it. He's never been very generous with Rita and me," I said, remembering the whole pay-rent-to-live-at-home fiasco.

"Okay, enough of that," Albert said, good-naturedly. "Your dad really did not have a penny to his name when he died. And he loved you, Renee. I know he did. He told me so."

I stop mid chocolate-covered-blueberry and stared at him. "Why, when…did he tell you that?"

"Oh, he came over here one afternoon. You kids were both in school. Sophia was at work. Your dad had been out looking for work—after he was let go at the meat-packing place—and he just got so tired one day, he just drove out here. I just happened to be here at the house, having a sandwich and watching the news at noon before I got back with my crew.

"It was a hot day. He knocked at the door and I let him in. He was sweating bad. You know how your dad always seemed to look so put-together?" I nod. "He wasn't that day. His hair was all disheveled, shirt wrinkled and stuck to his back…"

"Wait a minute. Why didn't he just go to his own house?"

Albert held up his hand. "Just listen. He wanted to stop by and apologize to me." This time, Aunt Sophia sat up. "For what?"

"For being so hard on me when you and I were first married, Sophia. Actually, when you and I had first gotten together. He told me that he had held me in contempt. That he was sorry for doing only what God should do—judge people."

As Albert's eyes teared up, I wasn't sure what to feel: shock or sympathy. I couldn't handle any more emotions as it was, with my dad lying in a coffin, arms crossed over his chest, looking like he was just in a long, peaceful sleep. "Anyway, we sat down together and prayed and talked and then he went on this sort of confessional binge with me. Told me that he wished he had been a better dad to you and Rita." Albert turned to look at me directly. "Renee, he had wanted to leave your mother long before he actually did because he knew all the stuff she was doing to you and your sister, but he felt like it would have been worse for you two to be alone with her. He did not know what to do. He was a disciplinarian, and he wouldn't change that part—he told me this that afternoon—but he was sick to his stomach the things that your mother said and did to you girls."

"Albert, why in the world are you telling us this now?" Aunt Sophia said, rolling up her bag of potato chips. "Well, honey, I think it's good for Renee to know. And you, too, about what your brother said."

Aunt Sophia leaned forward in her chair. "Don't you see that Renee is already upset about losing her dad? I love you, Albert, but you sure make me furious sometimes, and this just about tops everything!"

"Aunt Sophia, it's really okay," I said, sounding like a pipsqueak. My voice is so high and timid.

"No, it's not Renee. I've had enough of this. I'm going to bed. Renee, I'll see you in the morning before church, breakfast at eight. Albert?" He looks up at her, reaches out for her hand. "Yes, honey?"

"I love you. Don't stay up too late," Aunt Sophia said, picking up her bag of potato chips, looking back at me. "Good night."

Albert looked at me sheepishly while she retreated to their bedroom.

"She'll be all right. She's just as upset as you. It's her brother, after all," Albert said.

He and I stayed up for another half hour, talking about my Dad. I cried some and ate more chocolate and then we both said good night. I watched Albert as he walked to the bedroom in the back of the house, listened for any sounds. I was sure that Aunt Sophia had long ago said her prayers asking for God's forgiveness and then fallen asleep. I was thirsty. Bad thirsty. Glad that there was no wine in the house, I went to the refrigerator to get a can of ginger ale. Popping open the can, I walk back into the living room, surveying the room, taking in all the memories of everyone sitting around the table on Thanksgiving. Grandma Bell used to look at me with such complete adoration that I could barely stand it by the time I was thirteen years old. I felt like I'd betrayed her; I certainly had not kept my promise to her that I'd read the Bible every day. And I shuddered to think if she knew what I was thinking and feeling half the time, all that love and hate and sorrow and fear wrapped up in a hard ball in my heart, making it so that I could not look Grandma in the eyes. Even when I got down on my knees and asked Christ to forgive me that day back when Dad had gone to the altar, and Rita followed me up there, even after that day, I felt like I had let my dear Grandma down. So I just smiled at her when she smiled at me, and spent a few minutes talking with her at the end of all our family dinners.

Somehow I managed to get to sleep around 2:00 a.m. I wrote some, watched a few old sit-coms, and laid out my clothes for the morning. Now the smell of bacon is hovering throughout the house. Even though I haven't eaten red meat for nearly twenty years, the aroma warms me. Out the little window a strong wind is blowing, with cottony puffs swirling all around. My allergies are going to make me look as though I've been crying all day. Still, I want some fresh air, so I take my Bible with me and sit down on the chair on the little patio right outside the door. The birds are already singing great symphonies: robins, their melancholy melodies; doves, their mournful harmonies; blue jays, their screeching cackles. I bubble up with thankfulness for their music, dot the tears of mixed joy and sorrow from my eyes, and turn to Psalm 139:23–24. "Search me, God, and know my heart; test me and know my anxious thoughts." For some reason, this verse had kept weaving through my flimsy dreams last night. I know very well the verse, since I think of it often when I want to hold in mind that God has a purpose for my life. So now what is God trying to show me?

One thing that TU had taught was to look at the context. Now, that is good advice. It made me uncomfortable for a very long time that they did get things right; later, I realized that in order for a phony church to reel in weak believers is precisely to speak the honest-to-God truth—about some things. And then question God about other things. Serpent-style as in Genesis.

I read aloud Psalm 139:19–22. "If only you, God, would slay the wicked! Away from me, you who are bloodthirsty! They speak of you with evil intent; your adversaries misuse your name. Do not I hate those who hate You, Lord, and abhor those who are in rebellion against You? I have nothing but hatred for them; I count them my enemies." And then immediately after this wish for punishment of David's enemies were his sweet words of submissiveness to God. I look over at the trees across the street where decades ago a cornfield had been by which I walked to get to Grandma Bell's house. A sparrow flutters in front of me and lands on the railing. "Why do you suppose David wrote that way about his enemies? Do you think God would really want him to feel that way?" I ask the sparrow. As soon as I ask the question, I have an answer. Of course, God does not want us to think hateful about any people, not even our enemies. No matter how much they have hurt us.

The door opens, and Aunt Sophia walks out with a wooden spatula and looks me up and down. "Well, hello there. You talkin' to the birds again?"

I laugh and clutch my Bible to my chest. "You know it. I'm starved. Breakfast smells wonderful." We hug and then walk through the little garage-room. Aunt Sophia stops to adjust a ceramic chicken on a shelf above the washing machine in her laundry nook. She started collecting chickens when one person gave her a chicken for a birthday present and everyone assumed she had a collection. She always smiled when somebody gave her a new chicken to add to her collection. "I need a bigger kitchen just to hold all my chickens," she told me a few years ago.

Albert is already pouring coffee for me as I pull up a stool at the breakfast counter. It is still the beautiful red tiled counter that held the twenty-pound turkey of our holiday dinners. Mom would always pick pieces of meat from the bird after we were already done eating. I wanted to do the same, preferring more turkey than even the pecan pie that Mom had made, the best I would ever find anywhere. Aunt Sophia busies herself now with setting out platters of bacon and eggs and toast. She made oatmeal just for me, too, since she knows I don't eat red meat. She comes to sit across from me. I can smell her Desert Rose perfume. "Okay, before we say grace, Renee, I need to say something," she says, her eyes boring into mine. I put my coffee cup down, my heart pounding. What now?

"I just wanted to tell you I'm very sorry for my outburst last night," she says, looking at me. "To be honest, I was more upset about what Albert said that our dad had said about me and Albert than what he'd said about you and Renee." She laughs, waves it away. "That was a tongue twister. Honey"—she takes my hand—"I was selfish and feeling guilty about something that God has forgiven me for a long time ago."

"Aunt"—I clear my throat—"Aunt Sophia, no hard feelings on my part." Tears jump to my eyes; I brush them away. "I can't thank you enough for letting me stay here, and—and for all those years of praying for me and Rita."

"Okay, time for grace. I'm starved," Albert says. Aunt Sophia and I keep holding hands as Albert thanks God for our food and for salvation and asks for mercy in our grieving.

*****

If it had been up to me, I would have just stayed in Aunt Sophia's garage-room, maybe gone for a hike up in the Sand Hills and listen for meadowlarks. I am not in the mood to be with all these people, many of whom were at the memorial service yesterday. All these pats and hugs and concerned looks and clasping of the chest is enough to make me swear off attending funerals forever, no matter for whom they might be. I keep my head down, thankful that I am wearing a hat—black with a white rose—nod, smile. Always smile, because that's what I have been taught to do from a very young age. It does come in handy.

Aunt Sophia, Albert, and I sit down in a pew in the very back of the sanctuary. First Nazarene Church is now a roundhouse structure that looks something like an opera house from the outside. The choir and the pulpit are below us, just as in a stage. No wonder Mom no longer attends here. She's never been one for stage acts. But neither has Aunt Sophia.

"Renee, there is someone here who wants to talk to you," Aunt Sophia says, taking my hand.

I look up from my reverie, weary of smiling. Then I look up to see Leroy standing in front of me. Against my own best advice, I stand up suddenly, grinning big, my heart bumping wild. Leroy beams, then something in his face changes. I remember that I am supposed to be grieving, and I lower my head. He takes my hand and grasps it gently. "Renee, I'm so sorry for your loss. Really. If there's anything I can do, let me know." Something in the tone of his voice has me looking up again, into his eyes.

"I appreciate it," I say, feeling as though I'm on a balance beam of emotions. I just want to sit down. So I do. The preacher tells us all to stand up again. So I do, along with everyone else. We sing "Rock of Ages" And "How Great Thou Art"; my heart breaks with sadness about Dad and gladness about him, too, about he and Mom and my grandparents having brought me up in church and teaching me these things. I feel lost and found all at the same time. The church choir is now singing "It Is Well with My Soul." Tears stream down my cheeks. I don't understand what I am feeling. I want to be well in my soul. Am I? Leroy turns to smile at me before he sits down in the pew in front of me.

The preacher gets up; it's time for the sermon. I look through the church bulletin at the notices of the upcoming picnics and baby showers, a funeral for someone else. I stare at the back of Leroy's head, wondering what he does on Sunday afternoons after church. But what do I care? If he asked me to go on a date with him, I would be flattered, but world-weary of the dating-until-something-happens scenario. I'd really prefer if he just talked about himself—or Amber and Rachel. How are they doing? Is Amber out of the special care facility?

My head is spinning with all these thoughts about Leroy. I'm still legally married, I realize suddenly. I sit up straight and focus on the preacher, who is pacing up and down, reading from a Bible.

"Forget the former things; do not dwell on the past. See? I am doing a new thing. Now it springs up; do you not perceive it? I am making a way in the wilderness and streams in the wasteland." I can hardly concentrate on anything else now except those words. When the preacher says it's time for the altar call, I stand again and sing with everyone else. I've been through these countless times, and always a lump in my throat begins. But this morning, it's as though Grandma Bell and Grandma Howell are both sitting beside me, smiling.

I always had thought they loved me because I was a well-behaved girl. But that wasn't it. They loved me for me, for being who I was. And while that is beautiful, it's even better that God not only sees all of what I have done and said, He sees who *I am becoming*.

The lump in my throat is now a ball of tears I can't swallow. I scurry past Aunt Sophia and Albert and go kneel at the altar. I hear and feel Aunt Sophia and Albert—and many other people come up and kneel by me.

At the altar, I ask God to show me where He wants me to be.

– 15 –

When Aunt Sophia rings the doorbell, I half expect to see Dad open the door, smiling his millionaire's smile, doing his pretend swagger. I brush tears away from my face once again. Merilee answers the door almost right away. She looks even smaller and shorter than usual, her face empty of color.

Aunt Sophia, Albert, and I take turns hugging her, short little embraces so as not to break the dam again. She smells like roses. We follow her into a room at the back of the house.

"This was your dad's office," Merilee says to me. "He did all of his bookwork here. He was such a good caretaker of our finances."

A nagging sense of betrayal starts nipping at my heart again, until I remember what we are here to do. I have to give Dad the benefit of the doubt, no matter how much more he may have done for Lara and Thomas than he did for Rita and me. I wonder if he ever challenged Lara to pay rent in the few months before she graduated from high school along with me.

I nearly jump when I hear a "hello." It's Rita, sitting in a corner at the back of the room. She is wearing a dark-blue dress, the sides of her hair pinned back, rather pretty. Merilee flips on the light switch of the room, and I see now that Rita isn't sitting so far back; it's just that the desk is so big. I follow Aunt Sophia and Albert to some dining room chairs that Merilee had put in the room. I wonder if I am sitting in the same chair that Dad used to sit in while eating his dinner every night. I wonder if people eat in heaven. I hope so; I think Dad will be very disappointed if there are no chocolate chip cookies. I don't have a proper vision of what being in heaven with Christ will be like, and I won't until I die or he returns. All I know is that when people die—when believers pass on—their souls fly straight to God.

What do they do? Hang out, be in a blissful state up there with their Creator? Dream of the chocolate chip cookies to come?

"Girl, you got that faraway look again," Rita ribs me.

I come back to earth, to Dad and Merilee's house, to this room, to see Merilee sitting beside the desk with a stack of things next to her. "Oh, dear, I forgot to offer everyone coffee," she says, almost in a whisper.

"Merilee, it's okay. We already had coffee," Albert says.

Merilee clears her throat. "Okay. Well, then, let's begin. First with you two, Rita and Renee," she says, looking at us.

"Renee, you are the oldest, so I'll start with you."

My heart is pounding in my throat. What if Dad left me his, his—ties? Or a gift certificate to Winchester's, now debunk?

"Your dad wanted you to have his Bible," Merilee says. She reaches for the Bible on top of the stack and hands it over to me. "He wanted you to know that he always loved you—and that he hoped that you keep writing. Keep writing what you know and learn about life, about people, and God. And"—Merilee smiles—"he wanted you to have the collection of his maps. Maps that he drew, of places that he made up. He told me that you always understood his affinity of maps and how you liked looking at them, too." Merilee stands up to lift up a large flat box, then walks over to me, placing it in my outstretched arms. I don't know whether to laugh or cry. She smiles at me and then turns to Rita. "To you, Rita, your dad wanted to give you much of his glass collection. He used to watch you when you didn't know he was—he told me this—when you were admiring the light shining through all the glass."

Rita stares point-blank at Merilee. "He was watching me?"

"Well, yes, in a good way. He loved both of you kids. And that's the other thing," Merilee says, reaching for a tissue. "I want you both"—she turns to me—"to understand that. He did not want to be all caught up with what your mother did and said. You know, he was always in danger of getting sick. He was that way around us, too, very guarded, very careful."

"Why are we finding this out now? Why couldn't he have told us this himself?" Rita asks, with a boxful of Dad's prettiest decanters and spires next to her elbow on the table. I would have liked a few of them myself.

Merilee blows her nose. Aunt Sophia touches her arm. "It's okay, Merilee, you don't have to explain anything."

"Sophia, I want to. And speaking of you—I have to finish what I'm doing here, giving out what your brother spelled out in his will." Merilee turns her back to us for a minute, rummaging in a box. When she turns around, she is holding a stack of small books.

"These are his journals. From the time he was ten years old," Merilee says, giving them to Aunt Sophia.

Aunt Sophia sputters. "Merilee, I—I didn't know he had these. That he wrote like this. Since he was just a kid? Why didn't he ever mention it?"

Merilee does one of her kitten-giggles, covering her mouth. "Your brother has always been somewhat of a mystery man, hasn't he?"

We are all waiting for her answer. "Even though I was married to Grady for twenty years, he still did not tell me much," Merilee says. "Just little things here and there. You know how we were together. We were so content to just be together. Sometimes we'd just spend an afternoon window-shopping."

I do remember a time when I visited with her and Dad and we had a pleasant afternoon during Christmastime having lunch in a mall somewhere in Wichita, afterward shopping at Dillard's. I still have the pretty tin I bought, use it to store jewelry I find in antique shops.

"Well, what did he leave you guys?" Rita doesn't miss a step.

All eyes are on Merilee. "Nothing," she said. "Just some family photos of all of us together."

*****

We all leave Merilee's house with our boxes and books left behind from Dad's life. The sun is way too bright, blinding us all, me blinking like a mole. Merilee does keep it awfully dark in that house, always has. I can't help but wonder if a little more sun would have helped my dad live longer. It was as if he had been afraid to let any of life's messiness get close to him. I get a sudden image of the Ken doll. My dad was like Ken—perfectly groomed, unwrinkled, and distant even when Barbie was in the same room with him. I picked up on that when I used to play with my Barbie and Ken doll—in an elaborate dollhouse that Mom and Dad had bought me one year for Christmas.

Albert walks up to us to get the boxes and put them in his truck. "No, let me take this to my car," Rita says.

I follow Rita to the run-down maroon Buick that she and Zach have owned for twenty-five years. The paint is peeling on the car just as badly as it is on their house. We load the box of glass into the backseat. I let my fingers linger at the purple and gold decanters; they were always my favorite, reminding me of one particular day out in the country on a Sunday drive way back when Rita and I were kids.

"Hey, Rita, remember that time when we all went into the glass-blowing place? It was the first time I'd ever seen such a thing. I was so impressed with it then that I decided when I grew up and had a house of my own, I'd have a room in it with nothing but glass, with the sun shining through it all," I say.

Rita shakes her head. "No, don't remember. Sometimes it's like you and I lived in a completely different house with totally different parents. I don't remember things that you do remember and same with you," she says.

I nod, sad again, start to walk away and then stop, turn around. "Rita, did you really like all this glass?" I ask, pointing to the treasure in her backseat.

She shrugs. "Sure. I suppose. Ain't half bad. It's probably worth something. I don't know what Merilee was talking about, though, about me standing and staring at it."

"Because that was me," I say.

*****

At Aunt Sophia's house, neither she nor Albert feels like talking much after the memorial service. That's fine with me. Albert excuses himself to go work with his construction crew on a pre-fab house up the street. Aunt Sophia plots around outside, filling the bird baths and watering the yard. From my dolled-up bed, I can see the resident robins alternately scold and praise, flying to the bird bath and scooping up large beaks full of water, fluffing up and flirting with each other.

Mom and I have always shared such a love for birds. On thinking of her, I sit up straight in the bed. Today was supposed to be our lunch date.

She answers on the first ring when I call her. I tell her that the will-reading took a little longer than I thought it would. So I'll be there in half an hour. For the times I need a dose of bird cuteness—or as Rita and I coined very early on, "boiyds"—Mom's is the place to be. Birds literally flock around her. She's a Disney vision now as she sweeps the porch, birds appearing out of nowhere to be near her. They fuss and fight, fluff and flurry around the bird bath and the window bird feeders. Mom must have some kind of magic, too, with the bird feeders, because I've never figured out how to make those things stick on my own windows in San Diego. Humidity. It's got to be the humidity—or lack of it, I realize.

I jump when I hear a noise. Mom is rapping on my window, waving at me. I get out of the car.

Mom laughs. "You were just sitting in there, staring in space. Are you okay?"

"Yeah, I am. You know me. I just do that."

"I've never known why," Mom says as I follow her up onto the two-step porch. I still think of the house as old Mrs. O'Malley's.

Mom's remark makes me feel feisty, like I want to kick her. It's a familiar feeling, one I definitely don't want to feel right now.

"I just made some brownies," Mom says, walking into the tiny kitchen. Her brownies have some kind of peace-making power, always have. Depression and despair often crowded around me and my sister growing up. But with Mom's brownies, even Rita was happy. The best breakfast in town was when Mom had her platter of brownies out for us to eat. Rita and I never even thought it strange to be eating chewy, luscious triple chocolate brownies with nuts for our first meal of the day.

Now Mom cuts into the pan of brownies. "Want one?"

Yes, I do. "Not now, Mom. Save me a piece for later. So where do you want to go for lunch?"

*****

It's an antique lovers' paradise here at Yesterday's Treasures, part antique store, part restaurant. The host—Mom had told me his name was Lenny—greets us with a big smile, commenting on our clothes and jewelry as if we were the town's best-dressed divas. He leads us toward the back of the shop where the restaurant is. Several other pairs and trios of women are seated, leaned in toward each other, whispering things. After Lenny seats us, he walks over to the next table where the women get all fluttery in his presence.

"The soup is just heavenly, Lenny. You have such talent," I hear the lady next to me say.

"Oh, you are too kind," Lenny says.

Lenny comes to our table with a pitcher of water. "You'll love this water, ladies. Flavored with lemons and cucumbers." The water and ice pouring into our glasses makes a loud, chinking sound.

"I highly recommend the special of the day for lunch, our spinach and bacon quiche paired with a cranberry pecan salad. And for dessert, you absolutely have to have the raspberry lemon bar," Lenny says, bring his right hand to his mouth in a mock kiss.

After Mom orders the special for both of us, I sip my cucumber-lemon water, which is true to his claims, very refreshing. Makes me think of long-ago bike rides in the summer with my mother.

"Yes, Lenny is…you know."

I mouth *gay.* She nods. I lean in and whisper, "How do you know?"

"You remember a girl from school named Tara?"

I nod. "What about her?"

Mom whispers, "Lenny is her brother. He is married. His wife is wonderful, very elegant, wonderful with the customers here, too. A marriage of convenience. They don't try to hide that from everyone. It seems to be working."

"So…that was it. That was why Tara was so angry," I say, remembering Tara when she was in the first and second grade with me.

"What do you mean about Tara?" Mom asks.

"Oh, Mom, I don't want to talk about that right now. It was just kid stuff, you know how kids are with each other—"

"Okay, ladies, here is your delicious lunch," Lenny announces carrying platters of food. So he's the owner and the host—and the waiter? I stare at him as he places our quiche and salad in front of us.

"I'll be right back with more water. Anything else for you, ladies?" he says.

"Um, my mother told me that you are Tara's brother—she was a friend of mine from elementary and middle school."

"Oh, that's wonderful," Lenny says, clapping his hands together. "Well, Tara is married, a mother of three boys. Living in Chicago."

"Married," I say, staring up at him. "Three boys. That's a lot of living."

Lenny laughs, nods his head. "You're right. I've never heard it put quite that way."

"Please tell her that I—Renee—said hello."

Lenny smiles, promises that he will. "You were good friends?"

"Um, well, not at first, later we were, then we separated in our ways, you know how high school is."

"You have kids, too?"

"No." I stagger around for my story. "I'm a writer. A journalist. Travel a lot. No time for kids."

"Oh, so you're a famous journalist, someone I should know?" I look at Mom for help.

"Lenny, she writes for several newspapers—how many?" she looks at me.

"Five or six. Community newspapers. Features and profiles of people and places."

"Oh, so you do human interest stories, like about people with their pets," Lenny says.

I laugh, way too loud. My mind is racing, trying to remember what I wrote just last week. I've written hundreds of stories over the years, and once they are printed, I go onto the next, so I rarely have time to lavish in my work well done. "Usually, it's more important stuff. Like about people helping out orphans or foster children, that kind of thing," I tell Lenny, my voice cracking.

Lenny finally leaves us alone with our lunch, and I stab at my quiche before I remember something.

"Mom, let me say grace."

After lunch, we decided to go to Newton for dessert at the Train Café just to have the time to talk between ourselves without interruption of anyone else. Somewhere along the Highway 50 between Wheaton and Newton, I gathered enough courage to ask Mom why she did what she did to Rita and me at 2206 Sherman Street.

Now she is staring straight ahead at the road, unblinking.

It seems lately like I can only ask important questions of people when I am in the car. Maybe it's because I know they can't go anywhere. I think about this as I frame my question. In the past twenty years, I have forgiven a lot, even forgotten on purpose, but there are things that I need to know. Dad's dying and even in his last month of living made that imperative. The things he told me, confided in me, I wished he'd told me years ago. It seemed there was always some kind of stop-gap between Mom and Dad, as if neither one of them were saying what they really thought.

The few times I did hear them say what they thought without us around to hear—or so they thought—it was like hearing a bad movie. My bedroom was on the other side of the wall separating it from the kitchen. Normally I couldn't hear anything except Mom happily clanging and banging on pots and pans as she cooked and baked. Comforting sounds, they were. But after Rita and I were supposedly asleep, agonizingly early for us, often with the sun still up in the summertime when the sun did not set until 9:00 p.m., I heard things. My bedroom closet was made of very thin wood, and there were slats through which I could see some things, but mostly hear, loud and clear. Like that one night when I heard the rise and fall of my parents' voices. I was lying in bed wide awake, daydreaming about Devon, hoping that the curlers in my hair would do their magic for the next day, causing him to notice me. I was deep into that fantasy, imagining Devon looking at me close, when I realized that my parents were arguing. I skittered out of bed, carefully opened my closet door and walked over to the slat through which I could see my mother leaning over the kitchen sink. She was crying.

"Grady, why don't you ever look at me anymore?"

I heard a deep groan. "Oh, for heaven's sake, Margot, stop all this. I can't stand it."

"You can't stand me. I know."

"Did I say that?"

Through the slat, I saw Mom leaning over the sink as if she were going to be sick.

"Why are you eating all these tomatoes?"

Mom wiped a towel over her face, moaning as she continued to lean over the sink.

"I don't know. I was craving them." Her voice echoed into the sink.

"I am so tired of this, Margot. I am going to bed."

Mom stood up, suddenly. I could see that her face and eyes were swollen. "Grady, just hold me." I heard the soft scamper of her house shoes against the linoleum floor.

"I'm going to bed. Good night."

And that was that. I went back to bed. By then, the sun was down, but I still could not fall asleep. In a weird way—I could not admit this to myself at the time, and still have a hard time doing so now—I was hoping that Dad would continue to be irritated with Mom so that it would somehow defuse her power over me and Rita. Of course, the opposite happened.

But this afternoon, I do not want to ask Mom about that scene of that long-ago night. I need to know something much more basic.

Mom finally speaks. "Why do you want to know this? I apologized to both you and Rita."

I look out the window at the wheat fields and cows lazing about in ponds. "Mom, yes, I know, and I am very glad you did. But that still does not explain why you did what you did." I turn to look at her profile and feel tears come to my eyes. "I still love you, Mom. I just want to know what happened. Did you even want us? I mean, me and Rita, did you want us?"

Tears are running down Mom's face. She puts the right-hand signal on and pulls over to the side of the highway. I am nervous now. Have I crossed over some line separating Mom and me forever? I look over at the sweet moon-eyed cows bunched up just behind the barbed wire fence.

Mom turns to me, her face scrunched up, her eyes brimming with tears. I dig around in my purse for some Kleenex and give them to her. "Renee, I wanted both you and Rita. It was your dad who did not want you." I've heard this before, but I remain silent, waiting, as Mom blows her nose.

She reaches out for my hand and holds it. Mom's never been a hand-holder, so I feel a little odd here. For a moment, I look back at the cows for comfort.

Mom lifts my hand in hers, pats it. "Oh, Renee, you do not have a clue how horrible it was in my marriage. I loved Grady so much, but he had so many, so many problems."

My shoulder is hurting from Mom holding my hand at a weird angle. I let go and dig around in my purse for another tissue. "I already know all that. You've talked about it a hundred times. Rita can't forgive you, but I have, you know I have. But Mom. Why were you that way?"

Mom stares out the window shield and smiles. I turn to see what she is looking at. It's the cows. "They're so cute, aren't they?" Mom says.

I sigh. "Yes. But talk to me."

She takes the tissue from me. "Remember that time I got sick in Eureka Springs?" I nod. "And the doctors said I had hypoglycemia?" I can't believe she would use this as an excuse.

"And?" I prod her.

"When we got back home and I went to my own doctor, I told him about what had happened. And he said that I'd suffered from this, this—hypoglycemia for a long time. It's why I always craved candy bars."

I am beside myself. "Is craving candy bars the reason why you treated Rita and me the way you did?"

"Renee, I know it's hard for you to understand." I turn away from her to look at the cows again. They really do chew their cud. I wish I could hang out with this vision for a while. "But hypoglycemia causes personality changes."

"What—were you hooked on drugs, too?" I am shocked that I say this. Because even as I do, I remember that she was. I'd learned that from Aunt Sophia. "Well, no."

I thrash about in my mind. "Mom. What was it about tomatoes?

Her eyebrows lift over her big brown eyes. "Tomatoes?"

I tell her about what I heard and saw that night though the crack in my bedroom closet. "I can't believe you would eavesdrop like that," Mom says. "You made it difficult to not hear. But there was this one night when I guess you were eating tomatoes at the kitchen sink and Dad came in and you started arguing. I remember him getting mad because there was tomato juice all over the floor."

"You saw all this from your bedroom closet?"

I sigh. "I only saw pieces of it—your hands, the sink—but it was what I heard that was just bizarre. Dad was getting all angry about you eating tomatoes. And you were crying and sounding, uh, weak. Or sick. What was going on?"

Mom turns to face me, nodding. She's so close I can smell on her breath the coffee she drank this morning. "I don't know, don't remember that particular night. I probably ran out of candy and was craving something sweet. But I can tell you I was crying for your dad's attention. He hardly even touched me when you girls were in your teens."

I blush, look away to the cows again. *I'm your friend. I don't eat beef,* I telepathically tell the cows.

"Sorry, Mom." She settles back into her seat. "But that still doesn't answer my question. What was it about Rita and me that made you so mad? Why did you, you hit us?" *And all those other things? Like nearly kill Rita?*

This was not the conversation to have in a car pulled off onto the shoulder of a highway. Mom suggested that we go on as planned and have coffee at the Train Café. "But let's sit outside so that we can talk better," she said.

I was at once relieved and disappointed. What if she were going to smile it all away like she did so much of the time? Or what if I do? So easy it would be to drink our coffee and let everything go.

But we didn't. The trains probably made it better. Mom and I were both moist-eyed, remembering the days when a bunch of us would come out here and watch the trains come and go, people walking with their destinations in mind. These days, the trains are not passenger trains; they carry freight, instead. The weird, wonderful comingled odor of smoke and steam and tar and bread baking at the café gave me a strange high. I think it did for Mom, too.

By the time our server came by with our coffee and apple pie, both Mom and I had had enough time to collect our thoughts. I decided not to bring up my question again; it was too embarrassing, anyway. Sometimes it is just a lot less complicated to ignore the skeletons hanging around. Trouble is, they make a lot of loud clattering sounds and they can drop in anytime, scaring the living daylights out of you.

We both pick up our forks and cut into our pie. I pick away at the pastry, going for the apples.

"You do that, too?" Mom says, laughing.

"I think I got it from you," I say.

"Don't you like the dough?"

"I love it. That's the problem. I do this little pick-and-eat game with pie. Pick away a little of the pastry, eat the fruit that is supposed to be good for me first, then have a little bite of the pastry as a treat for myself."

Mom stares at me. "Huh. You know something? I guess I do it too, for the same reason."

We sound like girlfriends laughing together. Then a shadow crosses over Mom's face. She picks up her coffee cup.

"Okay. So I don't know if you will understand or accept all what I am going to say. But, Renee? Hear me out?" Mom says, her brown eyes wide as saucers. Who wouldn't listen with those eyes of hers imploring you?

"I actually went to get counseling when you kids were really young," she says.

Mom in counseling? I just can't picture it. "Oh. Okay. When was this?"

"Well, you were really little. You and Rita. And I had to go away for a while. To a special place to get well." I remember something

Mom had said long ago about Dad putting her away. "Was it some kind of mental hospital?"

*****

Mental hospital was too kind of a term. Mom told me the whole story about the "looney bin" she got thrown into. I always had wondered why Mom referred to everything in the world that wasn't skewed quite right to her she called a loony bin. In the Train Café, one of our family's favorite gathering spots, I learned why.

Mom and Dad were as happy as any newlywed couple in their first year of being married, even though they were very different in so many ways. Dad was fastidious, while Mom was frivolous. Mom blossomed among people; Dad retreated to his armchair. For Mom, the whole world was an artist's palette; Dad, a matter of mathematical analysis. Everything about them was opposite; she was a petite brunette; he was tall with ash-blond curly hair. But they were in love, completely.

Mom tells me now as we drink our coffee that the problems started when she became pregnant. With me. They had talked about having children, but Dad had always said he wanted to wait. But within a year of being married, Mom had the happy news about me.

When Mom told Dad that she was pregnant, he had a conniption fit, as she called it. Mom tried to talk to him about it, reminding him that they were planning to have children eventually anyway.

And that's when he said, no, he never wanted any kids at all. Ever.

That's the kind of comment that kills a marriage, and the kid, too. But Mom held her own. For the nine months that she carried me, she bustled about in her cheery way, cooking and cleaning. Dad was hospitable to Mom, but distant and polite as if they were friends rather than husband and wife.

He spent all his free time on the weekends golfing with his friends from work or his father. When he was home, he spent hours with his maps and books. Sundays? He rarely went to church with Mom but would spend afternoons parked in his easy chair watching the game.

"I'd bring him his Sunday dinner on a TV tray in the living room, such a tiny space it was in that first house—and then I'd sit there and try to watch the game with him, but it was as if I was not even in the room," Mom says now.

I smile at her and sip my coffee. Mom's eyes dart around as she struggles to find words.

"What are you thinking?" I ask her.

"I used to talk to you. When you were still in my belly," she says, her face breaking up into a half smile, half cry. I picture Mom back then, all pretty with her hair fluffed up and soft, and sweet on me when I was still inside her. Tears come to my eyes. I take her hand. "What did you talk to me about?"

"About how good God was in giving you to me. I talked about how you and I would go to church together," Mom tells me.

She tells me that one Saturday, the day before Mother's day, Mom had her first labor pains. Dad was out—golfing. Neither her grandmother-in-law nor her mother-in-law drove, and Aunt Sophia was out with Uncle Jerry to watch my cousin Myra in a school play. So Mom called her own mother to take her to the hospital.

"Oh, Renee, she was so stiff, so quiet, the whole way to the hospital. I was in agony from labor pains with you, but she never tried to reassure me. I think it was because she did not like your father," Mom says now.

"But I thought that she approved of Dad because he was attending business school and he had a promise of a job with the Bank of Wheaton," I say.

Mom nods. "She did. But she grew cold on him—and me—after we got married. Strangest thing in the world."

"So when did Dad show up at the hospital?

"He never did, Renee. He never did."

Neither did he hold me, except once or twice for family photos. And when he did, he held me out far away from his body as if he were going to be soiled. "And he rarely touched me," Mom says.

The loud whistle of the next train arriving at the depot makes both Mom and me jump. We turn to watch it coming in. People hold their kids against them when the train blasts its horn again. As the train lumbers to a stop, the kids scream and laugh and clamp their hands over their ears. Watching the people and the train, I wonder where everyone is going and why. And again I ask myself, will I ever arrive to where I really want to go?

*****

Mom's and my hands touch as we pull apart the inner rings of the cinnamon bun. "It's getting cool," I say, shivering.

"Yes. My favorite time of year, though."

Mine, too, although my hands are turning ice cold. San Diego weather has spoiled me. But I need to hear the rest of Mom's story.

"So, Mom? What does all this, um, all your story, have to do with, uh, you know—why you were so mad at Rita and me?"

I know the question is stupid. Anyone could connect the dots and spell out why Mom was so angry all the time. I just need to hear her tell me, though the little kid still living in my soul does not want to hear it. Mom pulls her sweater closer around her. I do the same.

"After you were born, your father never came to church with me. I was in it all alone. Except for Sophia. I don't know what I would have done without her. We sang in the choir together, and we went to the women's ministry luncheons together.

"But we also fought. She and I. We fought all the time. About you, and how Grady and I were raising you. And Rita."

I wait. This is the crux of the matter.

"When Rita came along, your father completely turned away from me. I was starving, Renee. Just starving. I loved you girls so much. But Grady would not share in that, at all. He did not care what I did all day long, except that I had dinner waiting for him."

I can't stand this anymore. It's too old a story, too much the problem of so many women from the '50s and '60s. Doesn't she— did not she realize that she had it made?

I remember how horrible it was to grow up as a teenager in the sexual revolution. Women's libbers killed the freedom to think along the old lines that worked. Throw in some racy TV shows, some heart-and-moral-breaking movies—like *The Graduate*—and for a finishing touch, the birth control pill. Stir it all up along with a women's mixed-up emotions and we've had a cocktail of confusion. Everybody's been acting like it's been one big party, but in reality, we women have been hoodwinked. Me, probably the most hoodwinked of them all.

"I was so lonely, Renee. And I felt so inadequate. I know, I know. It was no excuse. I'm so sorry."

"Let's go. It's just getting too cold out here," I say.

*****

I have always known Mom was starving for affection from Dad. So have I most of my life, for heaven's sake. I rev up my rental car to speed down West Fourth Avenue, thinking of all the things Mom had said this afternoon.

But I can't stay mad for long, not with all this beauty around me, the winter wheat fields moving to an invisible baton. I can practically hear my friends from California saying, "Beauty? You call a place as flat as a pancake beautiful?"

Oh, yes. I like that I can see from here to forever. So I slow down and watch the pink come up in the sky, moving from the deep indigo of an autumn day toward evening. Autumn is the time I associate most with Dad because that was when he and I both would always look up at the sky. We would sit eating apples at the kitchen table on Saturday afternoons and looking at the sky as if it were a lover. He and I shared a fascination for storms and colors in the clouds and banner of sky. It was almost like our own secret apart from Mom, who was always fussing and fuming about something or other.

A part of me feels guilty about that now. If I were just a kid or a teenager, or even a young woman in her twenties, it would be understandable. But at thirty-nine? Shouldn't I have outgrown all this free-floating guilt?

Memorial Park Cemetery is up just a mile ahead. It's where Dad is supposed to be. I don't want to stop, but I do anyway. What if he's not even in the ground yet? My heart racing, stomach twisting, I turn the car into the cemetery; the sign in the office says it closes at 6:30 p.m., an hour from now.

Mom had said Dad was in grave number C3 in row J. My rental car purrs as I drive slowly toward the back of the cemetery. Near the huge angel statue, I turn off the ignition, and get out of the car. The wind blows my hair all around as if it is speaking to me. Tiptoeing around the gravestones. Don't want to be rude. But I am scared and sad. What if?

Below my feet I see the gravestone of an old friend Nellie, cousin of Amber. I cannot believe this. I'd heard she was not doing well, had cancer of some kind, but Nellie was immortal to me. She was one of those "perfect" Christian friends I had as I was growing up in the Nazarene church. Sweet-tempered, a little mousy-looking but only because she wore plain clothes and did not do much to her hair—we were Nazarenes, after all—Nellie ended up marrying Ron. Every girl in the church had a crush on Ron because of his "almost Woody Allen" looks but taller and with more hair and a better outlook on life. He'd crack up all of us girls so much with his jokes and funny little skits. Sometimes he'd even drop by our house, just to say hello. I remember one afternoon in particular when he came by. Rita and I were banished off to our rooms as usual, but when Ron knocked on the front door and Mom let him in, it was as if the Holy Spirit had entered our house with sunlight and fresh air. My heart danced.

Mom invited Ron to go to the grocery store with her. For some reason, she let Rita and me go along for the ride. My sister and I begged Ron to give us his mosquito skit. Mom said, yes, please, Ron, looking in the rearview mirror at him sitting in the backseat. And me back there right beside him. Mom had told me I could sit in the back seat with him. So there I was sitting by one of the most sought-after guys in our youth group—and Mom allowed it. Not only that, she egged Ron on to do his famous little skit.

Ron obliged. All smiles, Rita turned around to watch and listen. He pursed his lips and made a perfect flying mosquito noise, complete with bumps and hums to indicate where and when it was going to land, and when it did land, he slapped his own hand hard. Mom,

Rita and I laughed and begged for him to do it again. It was so silly but refreshing. Mom hardly ever laughed except with Aunt Sophia.

All of us girls in the church youth group, Rita included, watched and waited to see who Ron would go for. He was so sweet and funny, a good guy, that he would have made good husband material.

One summer, I joined the youth group of First Nazarene on a summer camping trip at Lake Scott State Park. I never liked church camping trips all that much, mostly because I could barely tolerate the hassle of undressing and changing clothes in front of other girls my age and figuring out where to put my things; what's more, the sleeping accommodations in the cabins were always lumpy and scratchy. Rita and I had gotten so used to having our own space, retreating to our rooms whenever any situation at home got uncomfortable that the idea of sharing space with ten or fifteen other kids, with everyone snoring and slapping each other on the back and sharing secret jokes—oh, the whispering and the looks exchanged among girls sent me into private hell—that I was usually in a tizzy the weeks before such a trip for all the anxiety. But this time, I was more relaxed. Besides, my mother was nowhere around. I'd also gained some respect among kids my age—maybe because I already did have a boyfriend, although he did not come on the trip—that I could finally be one of them.

The lake was calm and sparkling, and we were all in a good mood, splashing around under the sky and huge white clouds bruised with blue. Maybe it's because I didn't want to have to deal with the entire get-out-of-my-swimsuit-and-change-clothes ordeal, but I lazed about all day in the water into the late afternoon. When suppertime came, I just wrapped a towel around myself and chowed down a hamburger with everyone else at the barbecue. The clouds were getting fuller and lower, but we were all used to the way the sky lived and moved. Besides, our youth pastor was in the water with us.

Summer days move and breathe in Kansas like a capricious child. One minute, there is a wind, the next minute, not a leaf moves. That late afternoon at Lake Scott, the air was so thick with humidity, I did not feel the usual chill when I came up out of the water to sit for a spell. The water in the air wrapped around me so that I did not even need a towel even though the wind was picking up. I looked out on the water and saw Ron and Nellie swimming very close to each other—and kissing. I burned with a secret embarrassment and a strange mix of jealousy and joy for them. And that was when I heard the youth pastor yell.

"Get out of the water now!" he said. I thought that he was over-reacting horribly, although a part of me did indeed want Ron and Nellie to stop.

"Everyone, now get out of the water!" he yelled. And that was when I saw the lightning strike down.

You don't want to be in the water when lightning strikes.

We all scrambled around gathering up towels. The rain was coming down in sheets, thunder booming all around. A part of me wondered if God was angry at Ron and Nellie for kissing. But they were two of the sweetest, most loving friends I had. I'm sure they were friends of God, and He of them. Sure of it.

Everything after that is a blur, except a gauzy memory of some of us sitting in the bus for shelter from the rain, shivering, watching the wind and the lightning. There was also a buzz of gossip going around: Ron and Nellie are engaged now.

I never saw much of Ron or Nellie after that; they continued with First Church of the Nazarene, while Mom and my sister went to Heartland Community Church. We left our Nazarene friends behind.

But just a few years after we all had graduated from high school and I'd flown the coop, I came back home for a visit and met with Nellie and Ron, now married. They were the perfect couple, Nellie short and sweet and rather quiet, Ron boisterous and tall, life of the party. Nellie had settled into her wife-and-mother role, while Ron donned his uniform every day as police officer at the Wheaton Police Department. They already had two little boys, whom they'd left with the babysitter the night that Nellie and Ron went with me to the movies to see *The Gauntlet*. So much violence and taking the Lord's name in vain that I cringed at nearly every scene. But later at dinner, as we talked, neither of them made any crass judgments about the movie. Ron made a few jokes about never seeing a school bus the same again, and we laughed and ate burritos and tacos at the only Mexican restaurant on Main Street. But when Nellie asked about my future plans, I just said I was waiting.

"For what?" Nellie asked me.

"For the old tapes to quiet down," I said, pointing to my forehead.

Nellie nodded. She had seen the interactions between me and my mother at the very worst. In fact, she was probably the only friend who had ever witnessed my mother's complete outrage. My mother and other adults had traveled with the youth group on a mission trip to a Native American reservation in North Dakota. We rode up together on a bus. Mom sat with Aunt Sophia; me with Rita, and Ron and Nellie side by side, since they were already a bona fide couple.

The problems started when we arrived at the school on the reservation. "Stand up straight and get that smirk off your face," Mom told me as we got off the bus.

She continued berating me as all of us stood around under the hot sun waiting to be escorted to our rooms for the night. Nellie shot me puzzled glances once in a while. Mom was leaving Rita completely alone, not bothering her a bit, even though Rita was the one doing the smirking. All she wanted on this trip was a chance to flirt with the boys her age, while I simply wanted to be with people, to work and eat and talk with them—and see the scenery.

It was ugly, though, the scenery, flat and hot, barely a tree around, not at all like central Kansas. The sun baked down on all of us. Finally, Shilah, a beautiful Sioux woman with long thick braids, arrived in a bus. Shilah drove all of us to the school cabin where we would stay.

As I unpacked my things at the cabin, Mom's eyes flashed at me. I vaguely wondered if she was having one of her hypoglycemic attacks. Whatever it was, the devil was in her. She criticized the clothes I had brought, told me to stand up straight and stop glaring at her and everyone else, and said I stank to high heaven.

Nellie was in the same room with me and Mom, and she heard every single thing. After Mom finally had her fill of putting me down, she left the room. Maybe she went to get a candy bar.

Nellie came to my side. "What is going on? What did you do?"

I looked at her. "It's never a matter of what I do. It's the fact that I exist."

Nellie looked as though I'd slapped her. "You can't say that about your mother."

"Do you live with her? Do you know what goes on day after day with her and me and Rita, too? Please. Just let me be alone for a while." I sank down on the bed, my clothes scattered about me like thrift store throwaways.

Now the sky is turning orange, the sunset sending angels of light all around among the tree branches. I want to stay looking up toward the sky and see what the light is doing, but the cemetery will close soon.

"Love you, Nellie." I turn to go back to my car and that is where I see my father's own headstone: Beloved husband, father, Grady Howell, 1935–1996. God Smiles on You.

And I cry over him, kick at his headstone, cry over the guilt about doing that and the shooting pain in my big toe. Who was this man Grady Howell, really? I pray, dear God, who was he? Did he truly love me? Do You love me, God?

I let the questions sit in the evening air.

– 16 –

THE SUN IS TOO much, just too much. I squint and rub my eyes and sit up straight up in bed, disoriented. Where am I? I look at the dolls in the corner, the pictures on the wall. Out the window, I see the house where I grew up.

I can hardly breathe. Where am I? Why am I?

"Hey, girlie, I hear you're up now," Aunt Sophia says, brushing into the room.

"I'm an alcoholic," I hear myself say.

Aunt Sophia stops stirring the pancake batter in the bowl she's holding. "Well, I knew that, sweetie. But you stopped, right? Years ago?"

Tears come to my eyes. I turn to look at Aunt Sophia, shake my head. "I started again just three years later. Been drinking ever since. Except here. Not here. But I'm sick now. I can't keep my stomach from jumping out of my throat."

The tears are nonstop now. I can't hold anything down, nothing. "I need something."

Aunt Sophia stops me in my pacing. "Renee, are you going through withdrawals?"

She freezes me in that question. Of course, she would know what addiction and withdrawal looked like. She's seen Mom go through it.

"I guess so. I am so scared. I can't catch my breath." I look around me as the walls cave in and move out away from me. It reminds me of the nightmare I used to have when I was a kid. Ghouls were out to get my soul.

Aunt Sophia moves her with me to sit on the bed. "Okay, okay. Let me ask you. How much have you been drinking?"

"You mean lately?"

"Just tell me."

"Six glasses of wine. Every night. Maybe more. Yes, more." I stare down at the batter in the bowl that Aunt Sophia is holding. I can't bear to look at her face.

She puts the bowl down on the night stand and shudders with a huge sigh. I start crying.

"Renee, where is the wine now?"

I shake my head in my tears. "Don't have any."

"Don't lie to me, hon. I won't have it."

God. I could really use a drink right now. And I don't even drink in the mornings. How gross that would be. There was once a time I did, though. So maybe I don't have a problem now? What have I done in telling Aunt Sophia my struggles? I feel like there are two people living inside me right now. The one who wants a drink every night is jumping up and down on my chest, making my heart speed up and impossible for me to breathe.

I get up and pace again. "You know, it really makes me mad that you don't trust me. Believe me, I wanted to drink. But I love you, Aunt Sophia. I couldn't do that to you."

"Renee, I'd love to believe that"—she puts out her hand—"I mean, I know that you love me. But I know how addiction is. People don't tell the truth. So you've been drinking here in this room. Isn't that right?"

I let out a scream. "No! No! No!" And I run out the door into the driveway. What have I done? I ask the sky and double over staring at the pavement. I envy the red ants going about their business. They don't have the endless need to ask questions. They don't doubt themselves; neither do they doubt God. But then again they don't even know He exists.

*****

That morning, I got my first ride in an ambulance. Aunt Sophia had planned to drive me to ER, but when I had another episode that felt like my heart was going to beat out of my chest and I couldn't catch my breath, she called 911. The walls were vibrating and the room humming by the time the paramedics got there. Just like in the movies, Aunt Sophia climbed up in the back of the ambulance and sat beside me holding my hand while one of the guys adjusted some fluid hanging in a bag over me. I had an oxygen mask clamped over my nose and mouth; it made me feel like as though an alien had taken over me. I hate to think what was going through Aunt Sophia's mind.

But she stayed at the hospital while the doctors stabilized me. And Mom came. That shocked me. She'd always told me she wanted to give me the space to breathe as an adult and would not interfere or get involved with anything in my life. It sounded like a compliment when she said it, but somewhere in the back of my mind, it lurked like another reminder of abandonment. I almost did not want her there at the hospital while the doctors showed her and Aunt Sophia my chart. They all whispered and consorted, looked at me again and then Mom signed something. I wanted to yell out but was so groggy from the medicines given me. One thing for sure, I did not crave a drink of any kind. But I might as well be dead, as I had no fight left.

The doctor came over to my bed along with Aunt Sophia and Mom. "So we've designed a treatment plan for you," he said.

What? My eyes must have said it all, because the doctor grinned. Mom got a look in her eyes that scared me—a mix of the old Mom's-got-it-in-for-me stare and something resembling sympathy. Aunt Sophia reached for my hand and just smiled at me in that way she has, when I know she still thinks I'm sweet as peach pie.

"You are to go to an AA meeting once a day for at least ninety days. You won't like it so much at first, but I am willing to bet you will love it, by the end of the ninety days. It saves lives. I've seen it among other patients," he said.

"Isn't that for old men?" I asked.

The doctor laughed. "I'll let your mother or your aunt explain it to you later. In the meantime, you will get a vitamin B shot and the nurses will check your vitals. I recommend you stay here for another day. Six glasses of wine a day is a lot of alcohol for a lightweight woman like you, and you may be in for some intense withdrawal. But we will be keeping watch over you," the doctor said. He showed

Aunt Sophia and Mom a few more things from my chart and then left the room.

What was on my chart? I mumbled in thick half sleep as soon as the doctor left.

When I finally woke up the next morning, I was ravenous and I wanted to go home. To San Diego.

*****

The first time I'd ever heard of AA was a conversation that Mom and Dad were having at dinner one night when I was about twelve years old. They often talked about things and people that neither Rita nor I knew anything about, and that one night, they were going on about someone who was an alcoholic. I remember Mom telling Dad in sort of a hushed voice that the person had to go to AA meetings. For some reason, I pictured men in torn trench coats meeting in dark places and swearing to a secret code.

So when I walked into my first AA meeting in Wheaton, Kansas, I was filled with dread—and Librium. The doctor had explained to my mother and Aunt Sophia that the Librium would take the place of drinks for a few days, ensuring that I would not have any more life-endangering withdrawal symptoms. I felt a little woozy walking into the back room of a church. For some reason that I still don't understand, I asked Mom to come with me to my first meeting.

I should not have been surprised when every single man turned to look at her when we both walked into a room. The room was, just as I had imagined, dark and smelly, and the guys all seemed to be smoking. I just about gagged on the fumes.

But I did learn two things: first, don't bring my mother with me, and second, go to a women's only meeting.

I never realized how much the several hours by myself at night just to drink for a few hours was such a huge roadblock in my life. It was more than a craving; it had settled into the corners of my mind as an end-all. Shame and guilt dogged me all day along with the nagging craving. The Librium helped me keep equilibrium mentally and emotionally, but I still felt alone, confused and somehow betrayed.

Because I did feel so alone, I did not want to go to my next meeting by myself. But I knew I couldn't ask Mom again. There was just too much history there. It was awkward because I knew she had had a problem with prescription drugs, yet she still tended to look at drinking anything as one of the biggest sins anyone could commit. When not too long ago I had asked about the time that Rita and I found beer cans in the house, she did admit that she had drunk beer with the guy up the street—it had been a terrible time between Mom and Dad, worse than usual, and shortly after, they got divorced. Mom said that being with the guy had been wrong, very wrong, and so had been drinking the beer. Ever since, drinking alcohol at any time, any place was a big no-no in her mind.

Not that Aunt Sophia considered drinking any less of a no-no— she has been a complete teetotaler all her life. I did ask her to accompany me to an AA meeting the next day. It was an open meeting, one that anyone could attend. It was also a dinner meeting. Now, I could live with that. I liked the idea of having something to eat while listening to people talk, since that was a normal thing to do. Otherwise, simply sitting around in shabby rooms listening to people tell stories about themselves made me crazy with boredom.

But when Aunt Sophia and I walked into the back dining room at IHOP, my stomach went topsy-turvy for all the women in the room. Funny how it seemed easier in some way to deal with guys than it was with women. We sat near the end of the table across from a woman who introduced herself as Lexie. Pretty and cute, reminding me of Sally Field, Lexie put me at ease while Aunt Sophia and I ordered our dinner.

By the time we finished our dinner, I was completely filled with the Holy Spirit. I have never in my life—not in any church, nor in any of the other pseudo-Christian groups I'd ever been a part of, not even in any genuine revival tent—experienced the warmth and welcome of the presence of God as I did that evening eating grilled chicken sandwiches and fries with women who drank and thought like I did. They talked about acceptance being the key to peace, even when they were facing things like health problems, financial difficulties or just plain blah days. I cried and laughed right along with them as they told their stories—sometimes Aunt Sophia did, too—and that fidgety feeling that I always walk around with melted away.

I felt closer to God than at any other time in my life, and I wanted it to last. I knew that it would take some action on my part. At least for now.

*****

Several days later, I knew I had to return to San Diego, but there were still things to do in Wheaton. I had an afterglow from the AA meetings, along with a squeaky-clean feeling, similar to what I felt when I went up to the altar as a young girl and gave my life to Christ. Except this felt forever. Like I had made some kind of contract with God. It was binding yet freeing.

The old drinker part of me knew it would be hard; it would be impossible without God. The squeaky-clean part of me sensed that I was in some kind of honeymoon phase with God—even with AA— and that it would not last forever. But it was a beautiful starting point for my return home to San Diego.

I had to go see the kids and my sister. After having coffee with Aunt Sophia the morning after the women's AA meeting, I had headed over to Rita's house. When I'd called earlier, Rita was still asleep, but Heather answered the phone. She said, sure, come on over.

The plan was I'd take them to Crystal Park. Autumn has painted the trees brilliant hues of red and orange, the air so crisp that I stopped to buy apples at a grocery store for everyone before picking the kids up.

They were waiting on the porch when I got to the house. I wrapped my arms around every one of them, all of them having gotten bigger, it seemed. After my father died, it felt like I was going in slow motion while everything else sped up, as if I were in outer space. Maybe it did the same thing to the kids. Suddenly, the front door opened, and Rita stepped out onto the porch. She had that half smirk, half smile on her face again, making me feel like she was the older sister.

"Hey, I gotta ask you a favor," Rita said. "Can I talk to you later? Just you and me maybe go to the mall?"

I said I'd love that. Still, I wondered what she was up to. My sister could speak two languages at the same time.

At a sandwich shop, I had the kids order whatever they wanted. Half an hour later, armed with our lunch, we drove through the park.

Now the trees in the park are in all their splendor. "Oh, you guys, don't you just love these trees!"

"What, you don't get this in California?" Heather says.

"Well, we do, but in much smaller doses. I get autumn hunger big time there."

"You get what?"

"I mean, Evan, that I miss all these beautiful trees."

"You don't have trees in California?" asks Gemma

"We do. A lot, actually. Everything grows in California, because the weather is so good all the time."

"Wow. Sounds like heaven," Heather says.

"You know, a lot of people would say that. And think that. And on a good day it does seem like it. But heaven will be a lot better, right?" I say, looking at Heather in the rear-view mirror. She pretends not to see me and stares out the window, hiding her half-smile.

At the children's play area, Camille, Evan, and Gemma scramble around on the jungle gym. Derrick digs around in the sand, excited about some bug he had found. Heather hangs upside down from a tree nearby.

When I call out that it is lunchtime, they come scrambling to the concrete picnic table where I had everything laid out for them. Maybe it was the promise of homemade chocolate chip cookies that got them over quick. Yeah, that was the other thing. I'd actually baked cookies the night before. One of the things that drove me home— here—was the idea of feeding my family, the kids. I had visions of wearing an apron in a warm kitchen and baking batches of cookies. Yesterday, I actually got to do that in Aunt Sophia's kitchen. Like me, she had been so warmed in her spirit at the meeting yesterday that she wanted to celebrate, too.

Between the two of us, last night Aunt Sophia and I finished off half a dozen cookies in one sitting, the cookies still so warm that the chocolate chips dribbled when we broke the cookies apart. We groaned and moaned so loud that Albert came in from watching his football game to make sure we were okay. When Aunt Sophia and I recovered from laughing after convincing Albert that we were fine, it was girl stuff we were talking about, Aunt Sophia took my hand in hers. "So proud of you. Besides, who needs a drink when you can have all the chocolate chip cookies you want—and all this fun?"

She was right, I knew, but I could feel the snarky drinker in me stomping out of the room. I have to be on guard all the time to let joy reign, not sourness.

"Wait, wait, before we eat, let's join hands and say grace," I tell the kids now. They moan and roll their eyes, good-naturedly, bow their heads, take each other's hands. Out loud, I say the "Lord's Prayer."

*****

Just as the sun was going down, I pulled up at Rita's. She and Zach are sitting now in the darkened living room, with the blue light of the TV throwing ghosts on the walls. The kids burst into the house like puppies, falling over each other, racing to get first dibs on something to drink from the fridge. Maybe I should not have let them have so many cookies.

I sit gingerly by Rita on the couch. One of the lumps on the couch moves. I scream.

Rita bursts out laughing. "Uh-huh, Cary got you," she says, picking up their giant tabby cat. She and Zach named him after Cary Grant. Why, I don't know. Wiping the palms of my hands on my jeans, I feel hot and cold at the same time. Something is just out of synch.

"Want a beer?" Rita asks me.

Tears jump to my eyes. I should have known. "Uh, no, I really don't. Didn't you say earlier today that you wanted to go to the mall or something?"

Rita looks at Zach and laughs. "Changed my mind. We are in the mood to play some Frampton and get down. Please stay and join us, please?"

My heart skips a beat. It's that arrhythmia thing. The doctor had told me to make sure that I don't get too stressed because it could set off a trigger to drink as harm my heart. Good grief. Oh, help me, God.

I take a deep breath and stand up. "Rita, I don't drink anymore."

Rita laughs. "Whaddya mean? You never did drink beer. Why would you say that?"

"Beer is booze. I gave up booze ten days ago. I'm sober."

Zach and Rita laugh. "Girl, you crack me up. Ten days? Whooopee! Who's been brainwashing you?"

Before she even finishes talking, I'm out the door, my heart pounding.

*****

I never knew that there could be such a thing as an emotional hangover. Because I sure have one now. After I'd stalked out of Rita and Zach's house, I got in the car and drove in a fury to the tiny municipal airport, rehearsing in my mind a thousand things I could have said, should have said to Rita and Zach. I parked and turned off the engine, listening to the radio station that my dad loved. When "Caribbean Blue" by Enya came on, my heart bumped wildly. Enya! I had given my dad a cassette tape of her music, and he was so impressed by it, that he handed it over to the radio station for them to play. Now I turn the music up as loud as I can in the car, get out and run in the wind with my arms out wide, just like the plane that was taking off.

It's the day before I have to leave home. To go home. I will miss Aunt Sophia's vintage kitchen with its red wallpaper, red low-pile carpet, glass canisters of candy and treats, a dozen pictures on the refrigerator, a thousand memories of voices and scenes from Thanksgivings, Christmases, and New Year celebrations. Ground Hog Day with take-out burgers.

My bags are packed. Aunt Sophia and Mom are driving me to the airport tomorrow. There is just one more thing that I have to do before I leave.

Back at my room at Aunt Sophia's, the room that I had come to love as my own—how was I ever going to leave this home, this place, my family?—I opened my dad's Bible. I had so many questions about what Dad thought in his private life.

Riffling through the pages, I find tucked between the Old Testament and the Old Testament a letter from Merilee to me.

Dear Renee,

I will always love you. You are a part of Grady that lives on. Grady always stood in awe of the world around him. You possess some of the same character-istics that he had.

Many times he would call me out in the yard on a dark night to show me an awesome phenom-enon in the sky. Like a sliver of a moon with a star suspended on the end. A beautiful sunset that seemed to reach around the entire sky. An ominous thunderstorm looming in the distance. Lightning that danced from cloud to cloud, and to earth and back, like angels playing catch with the stars.

At night, I look at the heavens, and know that Grady is there reveling in all the wonders that God created. All of the questions he wondered about here on earth is revealed to him now. Sometimes, I can feel him smiling down at me, encouraging me to go on. But I miss him so much! He loved you, Renee. I'm sure you know that. Just look at the pictures you took of him at Wagoner's. He was smiling and happy. Thank you so much for the pictures. You will never know how much I treasure them. I hope in some way this gift will encourage you to press on in your journey toward heaven.

Love, Merilee

*****

After I cried for what seemed like forever, burying my face into the pillow as if I were a little girl again, I decided to call a woman whose phone number I had taken down in one of the AA meetings. Newcomers like me are told to do so because there will be a time when the urge to drink comes along, or maybe the day so sours my outlook that only the voice of another alcoholic—I cringe here, still creeped out by the word, but it's better than drunk, of which I am also, a woman who has drunk enough in her life for probably fifty people. Yet I know that it is only another person who, just like me, has looked to drink to be the answer to emotional problems and can now help me walk through this fog.

I call a lady named Peg, don't know her last name. That's also typical of AA. During the last week since I got out of the hospital, I have marveled over how I can so easily become fast friends with women who I probably would not even have talked to if I'd passed them on the sidewalk. Yet we remain anonymous in meetings and meetings after meetings, first names only, among each other. I like it because in a lot of ways that is how a big city works. You might shake hands and hug and shake hands and eat dinner together quite a few times before you even find out what their last name is.

Peg intrigues me; she's in her fifties, reminds me of a pioneer woman, wearing her long brown hair in braids, and always crocheting something. When I asked her what she was crocheting at a recent meeting, she said it was a prayer shawl for a friend who was fighting cancer. When she handed me a copy of the pattern she was working, I asked her for her phone number, too.

On the phone, Peg is friendly and thankful I had called. When she asks me how things are, though, I burst into tears and stammer out that I'll be leaving town. "Because I need to go home. I live in San Diego, but home is here. But there, too. I'm so confused." Peg is quiet on the other end. For a moment I think our connection is broken. "Hello?"

"I'm still here. Okay, what do you want to do? Do you want to leave, or stay?"

"That's the problem. I don't know."

"Put your sobriety first. Then make your decision from that."

I look around at the dolls and pillows and platitudes in pretty frames in the little room and think about my family and the run-in with my sister, how I have the strings of my heart and gut constantly tied to this town, to these people, my family. How I want to bake cookies and have the kids over, invite Mom over for tea, go with her and Aunt Sophia for a drive to wherever we want. To have Thanksgivings and Christmases together, all of us.

"Renee, do you want sobriety, really want it?"

I sit up. "Yes. Of course."

"No, no, that was too fast an answer. I want you to tell me why you want sobriety. Why it is important to you."

I pace the little room, fighting tears, winding my hair around my hands.

"I want sobriety because…because I can think straight. I can be true to my own Christian faith, I can be content knowing that I am following God's will—"

"Renee, that's wonderful. But dig deeper. I feel like you are reading from a script. Be honest with me, with yourself. Why do you want sobriety?" By now I am feeling irritated. Peg suggesting that my sobriety is not founded on real need gets to me. But I sit down and close my eyes.

"I want sobriety because I am tired of living the double life. I go to church but I am always sensing that I am somehow being torn in half. I love God but I always loved wine, depended on it far more than I did God. I want…I want sobriety because I believe that if I keep drinking, I will die. Not just my body, but my spirit. I will have no reason to get up in the morning."

The faces of my nieces and nephews float up to my mind. "Peg, I don't want to be two-faced anymore with my family, with the kids. It makes me sick in my soul and in my heart to talk to them about spiritual matters knowing full well I am going to go back to wherever I'm staying and drink six or seven glasses of wine."

Peg laughs. "Renee, if I'd had enough at six or seven glasses, I would have walked into the program years ago. I commend you on making a commitment to sobriety when you are still salvageable. And that's what you are—salvageable. If you had waited, only God knows what would have happened."

When Peg asks where I have been staying, I tell her I've been at my aunt's house. Peg asks if I drank at the house.

"No. I don't know why except that I was so tired of trying to figure out the how and when of bringing in a bottle or box of wine, hated the idea of hiding it. Besides, I have been here because of my dad's funeral. He died last week."

Peg says she is sorry. Then she asks me how I felt when I did not drink.

"Actually, not too bad. I had so much other stuff to focus on, you know, my family, Dad's funeral."

"How did you feel, I mean, really feel?" Peg asks me again.

I start pulling my hair again. "Scattered. Jumpy. Lonely. Yes, lonely."

"All right, Renee. And how have you been feeling now, since you quit?"

I pace the room, thinking. "Some of the same stuff actually. Scattered, lonely, but not as much. Is that even normal?"

Peg laughs. "Yes, it is. Your jumpiness and tendency to not be able to focus would be far worse right now while mourning your Dad's passing if you were drinking. I admire you, Renee."

I feel all proud like a little kid. But I know she has something more to tell me—or ask me.

"But you never really told me why you drink. What is the reason you picked up that glass of wine every night for the last ten years?

The little bed looks comfortable to me right now. I check to make sure that neither Aunt Sophia nor Albert is in the kitchen, then close the door and lie on the bed.

"Let me think for a moment, okay, Peg?"

"Take your time. You know me, I always have something to crochet."

I close my eyes and see the kids' faces: Heather, Derrick, Evan, Camille, and Gemma. The vision makes me happy, makes me sad. If only…

"It's because of the kids," I say. "My nieces and nephews."

I hear Peg breathing. "Did you ever have any children?"

"No. Never did. I was messed up, too messed up to have any kids."

"Who said so?"

"Me. I did." Oh, I don't want to go there.

"Oh. So you've never been married? I mean, in this day and age, women have babies whether or not they are married, but usually—"

"Yes, I've been married. I am now. In the middle of getting a divorce right now."

I hear running water on Peg's side. "But how did you manage not to not ever get pregnant? Was he sterile?"

Do I really have to do this? I ask God silently, looking up to the ceiling. Yes, I feel Him say. You're going to get better.

The tears start backing up in my throat, so I have to sit up. "No, Peg, he was not sterile. Neither one of us wanted any kids. But I'd been married before. For three years. To Kevin."

– 17 –

KEVIN WAS A GEOLOGIST I'd met in Denver when I lived there for a couple of years. I met Kevin at a Christmas party, had fallen heels over head in love with the guy, his dark hair and expressive eyes mesmerizing me. He liked to drink, too. When we got married, neither one of us was religious. He'd been brought up Catholic but rarely went to Mass; I'd long abandoned Nazarene theology, mostly because I figured God had thrown me away for all the twists and turns I'd taken in life. In our first year and a half of marriage, I went along with Kevin to the small towns in Arizona, Utah, and New Mexico where he worked in the field; a few times, I even had the chance to work alongside him. When he was away from home, he captivated my heart by writing long love letters to me, rambling on about dreams for both of us. We both talked and dreamed, but there was nothing to hold on to. He also smoked pot, getting goofy-eyed and dreamy; I preferred my jug of wine, waxing poetic and dramatic in the late-night hours.

Kevin's restlessness got him into arguments with his supervisors. He always was thinking of the bigger picture in geology, frustrated that he had to dig in the dirt like a common laborer. He grew weary of always trying to find temporary work through an agency and the hard, cold winter wore us both down. After someone smashed the windows of my car to steal the stereo and I had to drive around town with freezing rain and sleet pelting me, I reached the end of my rope, drinking much more heavily. Kevin went through one job after another, never latching on to anything.

In March of 1981, Kevin snapped up my suggestion to move to sunny San Diego. We made the drive safely, found a cute little one-bedroom house in the Middletown neighborhood with astounding views of jet planes making their descent over the skyline onto the runway. As the months went by and Kevin still could barely hold on to a job, we had so little money that I cooked big pots of beans and black-eyed peas and served them with sour cream.

Depression hung around me even though I could giggle myself silly with glee over all the mourning doves that hung around on our patio. I would lie out on the patio, letting the mourning doves walk over my legs as they puttered around eating the bird seed I put out for them.

On one of my trips to the local liquor store, I saw an ad for an astrologer who promised to help me find the answers I needed. One day I called the astrologer, a lady named Victoria, and I went to meet with her.

I have had a black cloud over me for so long, I told Victoria. She immediately drew up an intricate chart of all my planets and moons circling around me. The exotic fragrance of incense tickled my nose and my fancy as I listened to how she could help "channel my energies."

I'd been down for so long that looking to the sky seemed the best answer. Kevin went to her for help, too.

One afternoon when Kevin and I were just enjoying the sunshine on our patio, our landlord paid us a visit. Told us he was tearing down the cute little house we were living in to make a bigger one that he could live in and rent out at a higher price. Sorry, kids, but you've got to be out of here in thirty days, he said.

We would have been out in the street had it not been for Victoria inviting us to stay at her house. But I always wonder if we would have been better off admitting defeat and heading back home to Denver, or Wheaton, Kansas—because I sank even deeper into depression and alcoholism. While living at her house, Kevin drank up Victoria's litanies about his wonderful moon in Pisces. She called him an extraordinary creature. He lapped it up while I retreated to Victoria's garage—is my destiny to be played out in garages?—to pour myself another glass of wine to drink in secret. I turned up the radio to drown out the voices of people who were always dropping into the house for parties, such as new moon gatherings when they did strange things like levitations. A couple of times, I got the nerve to sneak into the back of the crowd in the living room to try and catch a glimpse of what they were doing. I just couldn't see what all the fuss was about; people carrying on as if it were better than the appearance of God Himself gave me the creeps.

The worst was when Victoria said that I needed to go with Kevin to a spirit guide. You aren't getting any better, just loafing around here all day long, so you would benefit from this, she said, taking off her glasses and coming up close to me. You need to listen to Kevin. He is the spiritual one, she said.

More out of sheer curiosity, I went with Kevin, even though my stomach was roiling with disgust at him—and at the spirit guide lady who reminded me of a toad. My skin crawled when the toad-lady's eyes rolled up in her head and began talking to the dead to counsel me and Kevin.

After that, I stayed drunk for a week. But I also had started looking for work and went for an interview the next day at the St. Thomas University, a beautiful college overlooking the bay. I applied for a job as a secretary, nothing thrilling, but the idea of getting out and working with real people who had real jobs gave me hope. When I awoke one morning from a vivid dream of the Lord smiling on me and telling me to take the job, it was the first time I felt sunshine in my soul in years. A couple of weeks later, I got the job and the power to tell Kevin we were going to move out—immediately—from Victoria's.

We were fortunate to find something in our old neighborhood, a charming apartment tucked behind a playhouse. On mornings, I'd sleep late, and throw together a sandwich or Kevin and I would go across the street to El Indio, one of San Diego's oldest and most popular Mexican eateries. Afternoons, I'd go to work, grateful for the diversion of being with other people, only mildly bored with the typing I had to do. I often found myself staring out the window at the buildings, which my supervisor told me were built in the sixteenth-century Spanish Renaissance architecture style. Once I snuck inside the cathedral on campus, slipping into a pew in the back. I'm here, Father, I whispered. The security guard opened the door, found me in there, and said I needed to get out.

When I came home from work each afternoon, I'd walk to the liquor across the street and buy giant cans of malt liquor because they were cheap and gave me a buzz. The Nazarene girl from Kansas in me shuddered each time I guzzled from the sweating can. I felt so far from God that I felt I had to keep pouring the stuff down my throat to drown out the cries. Kevin continued to smoke pot and pretend to look for work. I knew that he was still going to see Victoria for her to do his astrological charts. I wanted to tell Kevin a thing or two about what to do with his moon in Pisces. But I did my wifely duties as much as I could because I wanted to keep the peace. One late autumn afternoon, flat on my back under him, I counted the water stains on the ceiling as he moved inside me. He was so ecstatic, huffing and puffing and carrying on that I knew without a doubt that something had happened deep inside me. That evening, I drank quite a bit more than usual and followed the actors walking by our apartment dressed as characters from "Midsummer Night's Dream" to backstage of the theater. I figured they would be annoyed with me, but I wanted to do something that felt daring. Instead, they introduced me to the director. He shook my hand and told me to come for an audition sometime. You do act, right? he asked me.

Yes, I act every day.

In the meantime, Kevin continued his pleas with me to go once more to the spirit guide. He was getting into this, he told me.

Finally, one Saturday afternoon, I said no, I wasn't interested at all, never would be. He became furious, his deep brown eyes getting a devilish look I'd never seen before. He said, you need to read about Buddha and other spiritual figures. That's all that Jesus was.

If I've ever been more defensive of Christ, I don't remember when it was. A strange rage began in my stomach and reached out to my fingertips. "Jesus Christ was not just a man. He was—He is—the Son of God," I said, my whole body shaking.

Not too long after that day, I found out that, yes, I was pregnant.

*****

"So what did you do?" Peg asks me now.

"Kevin did not want kids. Neither did I. I knew I was a total mess. Besides, I figured my childhood had wrecked me. And I am ashamed of this, but I did not want to spend my time raising a kid because—" I break into tears.

Peg waits while I blow my nose. "Because you didn't want the responsibility?" she asks.

"Ha. Yeah, I guess you could say that. But it was more like me thinking that I deserved having a life of whatever I wanted to do because of the childhood and teenage years I had. I figured God owed me something." I clutch my heart and lie down on the small bed. "Oh my god. I cannot believe I actually said that." The tears start to flood my nose and throat, making it hard for me to breathe, so I have to sit up again.

After a moment, Peg talks to me. "Honey, what happened with the baby?"

"I didn't have it."

"You gave it up for adoption."

"No. I did not have the baby. I had an abortion." The words feel like sharp pieces of metal in my mouth. I hang up the phone and open the door to the night air to walk out into the street, staring next door at the house where Rita and I had grown up. All those beatings, those harsh words, the looks from Mom that shriveled me in an instant. The endless nights early to bed when the sun was still up and all the neighborhood kids were still out playing. The slaps across the face, the insults, the threats to throw us both into a foster home. The poundings by the preacher at the pulpit and his warnings that all of us in the congregation were backsliding and we would go to hell.

I could have lived with all that. As a kid, I sensed that I would grow up and away from the nightmare. I was looking forward to the days when something bigger and better would be in store for me. But when I turned thirteen years old and fell in love with Devon, I did expect things to fall into place, for God to open the doors and windows. My devotion to Devon was white-hot. He would become the man whom I would marry—and bear his children without so much a second thought. I would love the babies from this man.

But babies from Kevin? Not a chance. My heart had grown cruel and cold, and I was frightened beyond words that I would do something horrid to a little baby, the same way that my own mother had treated me. I look up at the stars in the sky now. They sparkle and twinkle, reminding me of cheery little kids prancing about with not one worry to weigh them down. How enviable.

The door to my room opens, and Aunt Sophia walks out to me in her pajamas and robe. "Renee, what are you doing out here?"

"Wondering where God is right now," I say.

"He's right here. With me," Aunt Sophia says. She links my arm into hers, and we walk back to the room. I need to call Peg back.

*****

"I'm sorry," I tell Peg as soon as she answers. "It was getting a little too intense for me."

Peg reassures me that everything is okay. "I might have been rushing you. But I wanted you to see how you are thinking, what maybe you are hiding, and what your emotional trigger is." She pauses; I hear her take a sip of something. I reach for my bottle of water. "I'm going to suggest something to you as your unofficial sponsor. Okay?"

I almost cry with a sigh of relief. I need for somebody who's been down this road to show me, to tell me what to do. These last few days, just trying to decide what I want to eat has been like a national crisis.

"Renee, you need to go back home. To San Diego." My heart falls. And lifts again. Good heavens. I'm a neurotic, too. Another *-ic* disease. "I'm leaving tomorrow."

"But don't look back," Peg says.

Who's crazier, she or I? "What, I can't come back here?"

"Of course, you can. But you have your life in San Diego. Friends. Family—"

"No, I don't," I interrupt her. "I have absolutely no family there. My husband and I are getting divorced."

"You know what I mean. You have friends, a well-established community there, a good job. I've listened to you talk about all that in the meetings. That's important, Renee. Especially in early recovery, you don't want big change. It's the fastest way to a drink. Besides, you're still getting to know yourself."

Egad. I'm thirty-nine years old. Don't I know myself by now? And yet, I have to admit Peg is right. It scares me, this not knowing who I am.

"If you don't drink, one day at a time, if you talk with your sponsor regularly, do the steps, all that stuff you hear in meetings, you'll do fine. You'll love the person you are becoming.

"If you drink, though, you will end up hiding from yourself again and being dishonest to everyone around you."

She is right again. I no longer want to live a lie to my nieces and nephews, not to my sister, either, or my mother. Nor to me.

I have a feeling I'll never see Peg again, but I have a sense of peace about it. Still, I look around the little room where I am staying—how was I ever going to leave this place, my hometown with Mom, Aunt Sophia, Rita, and her kids? Especially the kids?

All of a sudden, I miss Dad terribly. I want to ask him questions about what he really believed. His Bible. I retrieve it from the bottom of my suitcase.

Riffling through the pages, I look for Dad's handwriting on the pages. Nothing. But I do find a long strip of paper that has November 12 Baptism written on the side, and a typewritten note: Some scriptures (for example, Acts 22:16) do not make clear whether baptism is a part of salvation or is simply "sacrament signifying acceptance of the atonement of Jesus Christ," but the entire scope of scripture placed in balance seems to support the latter." On the other side of the paper strip were handwritten notes about Bible verses on baptism.

Further back is a faded blue Father's Day bookmark. "The man who leads his family in prayer leads his family everywhere," said the inscription.

It makes me wonder if this bookmark was what set Dad off in a period of gathering me, Rita and Mom with him in a family devotional time. It did not last long, that time of us all reading the Bible together, kneeling down and Dad saying a prayer. But it did make me fall more for the man in Dad who loved God, no matter that it was uncomfortable. We were all fumbling toward God.

Toward the back of the Bible, I find the letter from Merilee and unfold it to read it over again. I meditate on her words "journey toward heaven." Is that where I'm going? How can I be sure? Was Dad sure?

*****

On the drive out to the Mid-Continent Airport in Wichita, Aunt Sophia and Mom let me drive while I take the back roads to the airport so that I can soak up all the autumn scenery as much as possible before leaving for perpetually sunny southern California. The trees are bathed in gold, red, and orange under puffy white clouds and an azure sky, so beautiful my heart breaks. I remember how Dad and I would both look at the sky through the window while having a sandwich and soup on a Saturday afternoon in October. He'd tap his foot on the floor, smile at me, and we'd be starry-eyed together.

Now I put in a cassette of Vivaldi's "Autumn" and the music seems to spiral around us. Tears well up in my eyes and I breathe a little easier. It's one of the gifts that Dad has left me, this enjoying classical music. Funny thing is, Mom and I and Rita all used to complain about it. In secret, though, I'd swoon in my bedroom when Dad put on his Montovani record. I'd pretend I was dancing with Devon.

At the airport, Mom and Aunt Sophia help me check in, then we go to the little airport café to have coffee and pastries. "This is just too huge. Everything just happened so fast. And I miss Dad," I say.

Aunt Sophia and Mom nod. "We do, too, Renee. But we are so very proud of you for taking such a huge step in your own life," Aunt Sophia says.

"I sure wish Rita would do something about her own problem," she says.

"But I feel so bad about leaving the house like I did."

Mom starts to say something, then her eyes get even bigger looking at something behind me and Aunt Sophia. I turn and see Rita. And the kids.

*****

Rita surprises us all even more when she orders food for the kids and for herself. She rarely spends a dime on them outside of the house. So when Rita begins taking large bites of her club sandwich, followed by sips of a smoothie, Mom, Aunt Sophia and I can barely stop staring.

Rita has confided in me that eating around other people nauseates her, probably a hangover from the trauma she suffered when she was nine years old, I was ten. I was trying to eat my peanut butter sandwich as best as I could while Rita had to stand at the table with her pants down. Our mother was lashing into Rita with her words and smacking her with a switch made from a branch of one of the elm trees in the backyard. Mom had made me go and choose a branch to cut down. I chose a skinny one with the least twigs, hoping it would hurt Rita less. To this day, Rita cannot stand peanut butter.

I close my eyes now against that memory. In my mind, I recite one of my favorite verses: *His mercies never come to an end; they are new every morning.* When I open my eyes again, I see the kids blissfully chowing down on grilled cheese sandwiches and potato chips.

Rita puts down her sandwich. "Okay, here's the thing," she says, looking at me. "I owe you an apology. And we don't want you to go. We want you to stay. You're good for us. Me. Zach. And the kids. Especially the kids."

Gemma gets up and squeezes me around the stomach. I caress Gemma's hair and turn to Rita. "I'm flattered that you think that way. And I will miss you when I go to San Diego. But I do have to. Go. And stay. I have so many things to take care of."

"Like what?" Rita asks.

"Yeah, like what?" Evan says. I'm surprised by that. He never speaks up.

"I don't want to discuss things in front of you guys. It's just too personal," I say, gently unwrapping Gemma's arms from around me.

"Kids, she's right," Aunt Sophia says. "Renee has her own life back in San Diego. She can't just walk away."

"Is it the sobriety thing?" Rita asks me point-blank.

I feel all the kids' eyes on me. "What's so-righty?" Gemma asks me.

"Sobriety. It's when a person doesn't drink anymore," Heather answers. I just want to slink under the table.

"Kids, let your Aunt Renee be," Aunt Sophia says. "She's got a flight to take in half an hour. Let's go walk her up and see her off."

Rita and the kids shower me with gifts of stuffed animals and hugs. I practically choke on the tears backing up in my throat.

Last call to board for Flight 3421," the ticket lady says. When I hand my airline ticket to her, Mom and Aunt Sophia grab me. Rita joins in with the kids for a group hug, all of us. I cry like a baby, then straighten up and walk down the tunnel going to the plane.

Halfway, I turn to wave good-bye to them. But they have already left.

Home

– 18 –

DURING THE WEEKEND AFTER I got back to San Diego, I was still oozy with emotion, crying myself to sleep every night, going for walks and meetings in the day, another one at night, then making a beeline for bed, not daring to think of all I wanted, all I didn't have.

Walking into my own cute little condo after the long flight from Kansas was a lot harder than I thought it would be. The first thing I wanted to do was pour myself a glass of wine. Instead, I poured the rest of the box of wine I had in the refrigerator down the drain. Then I walked to an AA meeting, half out of my mind that someone from the business district office would come across me.

I haven't said a word about any of this to Wendy. For the past week, she has been up to her knees in paperwork and budget concerns over the Spring Swing Festival that we're going to put on in a few weeks. Having special events like this is supposed to get people onto Gateway Boulevard, bringing them into the shops and restaurants. It is an untold amount of work to pull something like this together.

But I am grateful for it. For once, when Wendy asks me to stay at the office and type and file and make calls, I don't complain. Sometimes when I'm out there in the world, mixed in with freedom and adventure is a breathless anxiety. So many decisions, so many thoughts in my head all the time.

Thoughts of Rita's kids. How I still want to be back there baking cookies for them and driving them over to the big corn maze during autumn in Buhler, Kansas, and then warming our cold fingers on cups of hot cocoa. My whole body hurts craving this, craving the kids' funny words and ways, remembering the afternoon we all listened to Enya in my rental car waiting for the train to pass.

Now I open the refrigerator and find olives, cheeses, some nuts, and flat bread that I'd bought at the Mediterranean store across the street. A silver crescent moon hangs in the east. I sit and eat at my little dining room table that I had bought just half a mile away at a discount furniture store. The pink-tinged sky changes from twilight to early evening; passing cars switch on their lights.

I have everything I need. But the restlessness stirs up in me and I rummage around in the refrigerator looking for something to pound down. Nothing but some yogurt drink and sparkling water. I need something stronger.

But it would take so much energy to walk to the liquor store four blocks away, decide what I want to drink, whether or not I really want to drink, all the while fighting off the anxiety that I'd run into somebody I know. Or that I wouldn't run into anybody I know. Loneliness gnaws at my stomach.

Breathless, I get into my Ford Ranger and open the glove compartment to get the AA meeting schedule; tonight's line-up includes a meeting in Hillcrest, a neighborhood just over a mile from me.

A hard ball has settled into my gut, a too-familiar sensation. I used to be able to soften it with several glasses of wine. The feeling now calls up a visual reminder of my Grandpa Howell. He loved to golf, and he always seemed to have a golf ball in his pocket. Once he took the ball out and showed me the stuff inside it—a brown, thin ribbon-like thread. If you pulled out the ribbon, it would go for miles, he used to say.

That's how I feel: spread out over miles. I can't find my center.

I drive fast, breathe fast, too, then relax a little when I park near the meeting place and fall into step with others going to the meeting. I recognize only a few people at this meeting, but the warmth and noise of everyone gathering comforts me, along with the smell of coffee that rarely tastes good, and most of all, the drone of people reading the Twelve Steps and meeting rules. Then comes the leader's turn to introduce the topic. By the time almost everyone in the room has spoken, there are still ten minutes left, and I realize people are looking back at me.

The speaker has called on me to share. In this meeting, you have to get up to the podium to speak, so I walk woodenly up to the front.

I have no idea what I am going to say on the topic—serenity—until the faces of everyone peer up at me, waiting.

"I'm Renee, an alcoholic."

Each time I say this, it still sends a shudder down through my body, as if I've committed the worst sin possible. But I know that it is not.

I tell the story of how I went back home for my dad's funeral and did not drink while I stayed at my aunt's house. I tell them that I am still uncertain of where my home really is. Then I break into tears and tell them that what I regret the most is that I've never had any children.

*****

The waves at South Mission Beach crest high and crash against the jetty. The thunder of the ocean against the jetty knocks the waves up so high that they curl up before splashing down.

It is late February now, almost nesting season for western snowy plovers. The stubby-bodied birds run fast on short little legs, making it a real challenge for me to try to capture their portrait with my Canon Rebel. The birds dash into the water to nab up a morsel, then they skedaddle out of the water along with the rest of the flock. I half run trying to catch up with them, snapping the shutter as I go. The sun has already sunk below the horizon and twilight has begun pushing in with ribbons of pink and orange arching across the sky, bluish clouds bubbling up above the ocean. Yellow light swirls through portions of the clouds. I move up further onto the beach to get a better look at the colors, careful where I step, knowing that plovers bed down for the evening in the beach.

Sure enough, I come across a family of them fluffed up against the cold, burrowed partly into hollows they've carved into the sand. Sleep makes their eyes heavy, but they keep one eye open, wary of me.

Moments like these it seems God Himself has reached down and shown me His own little diorama of the great span of life. Some people might say that these moments are better shared with someone else. That may be true if the other person swoons from the sunset colors as much as I do or delights in the discovery of a bunch of plump little birds. For right now, I am glad to have this time by myself, saying little breath-prayers of thanks to God.

The thunder of the ocean against the jetty knocks the waves up so high that they curl up before splashing down. Toward the end of the jetty is a concrete structure with a large opening, reminding me of a kind of portal between this world and another. A young couple are way out on the jetty, grabbing each other's hands as they tee-ter-totter on the rocks. The young woman's hair whips in the wind. I watch all this through my camera, snapping pictures as they get closer to the structure and step through it. The couple's figures get smaller and smaller as they advance further on the other side. They took the high road. I whisper to the wind: *Pilgrim's Progress.*

On my way home, I stop at Ralph's to buy some of their pre-pared tuna salad, tomato and cucumber salad, and Greek pasta salad and put it all into a plastic container. I'm all alone again tonight, but I don't mind. In an odd way, my brain is quieter here in San Diego. I think about this as I get a fork from the drawer and pour myself a cold glass of sparkling grape juice. It feels good taking care of myself.

I turn off the lights except for one in my tiny living room and sit at the dining room table, watching the cars pull into the Mid-City Market parking lot. What is everyone going to the store for at this hour? It does not sell booze. Maybe people are on a mad dash for cheese? Or cereal for the next morning's breakfast?

In the eastern sky gleams a nearly full moon. I look at it, won-dering if anyone from my family is doing the same. I feel so far away from them, yet now that I'm here I can't imagine being there. It takes too much energy. To be there, it does. I ponder this as I turn on the radio to the classical station and walk over to my typewriter to write in my journal. Last night, I'd finished reading "Mere Christianity" by C. S. Lewis and my heart burns with a sense of renewed hope.

I type tonight's entry to my journal: *I cannot erase from my mind Lewis's challenge that if Christ is not Lord as he said He was, he was a lunatic or a liar. I can bank on that. Can sit on that, make it home. But I don't have family here.*

I begin looking around at the stuff I have. There's the blond oak china cabinet with some of my thrift store and antique shop finds. Photographs hang pell-mell around the place—some photos from a trip to Yosemite with walkabout friends, others of the ocean and snapshots of the kids and me in Wheaton. Rita is missing from most of the pictures; she never really liked to come along on our daytrips out. "Go, have fun with them. They need you," she'd said. As if they didn't need her.

The typewriter sits on the desk I've had since my twenties when I travelled back and forth between Colorado, Hawaii, and my home-town. Even then I couldn't settle down, my heart and mind divided all the time. My marriage to Mark had been an artificial sweetener leaving an aftertaste in my mouth. I had been ushered in on his coat-tails all the accoutrements of his life, his religion, his god—a false interpretation of the Holy Almighty.

In the last several months, I have created my own tradition of attending Ridgeview Baptist Church every Sunday. My friend Molly Sullivan and her husband and their girls invite me to go to lunch with them after church. Molly also has made me be part of her crew in the church kitchen for the Wednesday night dinners. Me, I still don't cook much, but the camaraderie in the kitchen saves my soul. I chop, peel, layer ingredients to lasagna and I wash and dry the dishes and pots and pans. Those moments I feel home, even though it seems as though I am just putting a Band-Aid on my pain.

Molly and my other new friends from church helped me make it through Thanksgiving, Christmas, and New Year's. A flurry of cel-ebrations with food and presents and lunches out with friends and parties out with the group made the holidays bearable. That and all the meetings I went to. If I hadn't gone to nearly a meeting a day, I would have caved with all the booze-soaked celebrations. I have learned that even "normal" church people are fond of the grape. I looked longingly at the full glasses of rich deep red wine—just as Proverbs warns its readers not to do so, for the snakebite the lovely liquid would eventually give—but something in me did not want to go back to the lie I used to live all the time. *Used to.*

I need to talk to Pastor Alan.

That old expression of my Grandma's, "The Lord works in mysterious ways," used to bug me, but I am finding that it is true. One Sunday in January, a speaker from a pregnancy clinic came and gave us a special presentation on the sanctity of life. My stomach tightened, my fists clenched, I ducked my head as the speaker, a pretty dark-haired lady named Janna, talked about the damage that abortion does. "It kills not just the baby's body, but the woman's spirit, too," she had said.

My heart was pounding hard. Molly saw my face and asked if I were okay. I nodded yes and mumbled that I had to go to the bathroom. Behind the locked stall door, I took my pulse, counting thirty-two pulses in just fifteen seconds. I sat down on the toilet and tried to calm my breathing. Could I still be detoxing?

The whole experience scared me. Still does.

My heads hurts. Time to go to bed. I cover Spunky's cage and look out the window at the lights on the street before I get in bed. All is calm.

*****

The groan of the produce truck wakes me up at 7:00 a.m. Though it is Saturday, I do not mind. I feel glad to be alive, glad to be clearheaded.

God? I want to set some goals. Open my eyes and my heart. Show me the right road to travel.

I pad into the kitchen and load coffee and a teaspoon of cinnamon into the coffee machine, pour fresh water into the coffeepot and turn it on. While I watch the produce truck guys unload boxes and cart them into the store, I think about what I have just prayed: show me the way. How do I know what God wants me to do?

Something from the countless Bible lessons and studies in Truth Universal came to my mind: To know God's will, know God's Word. Funny how I'd always taken that for granted. I hate to admit it, but I'm a little bored with my own Bible, my own notes scrawled all over it.

I wish I could read someone else's Bible for the newness of it. And then I remember: *Dad's Bible.*

Scrounging around in the boxes I brought back from Kansas, I find it. With my cup of Vanilla Bean coffee on the desk, I carefully thumb through each book of the Bible, looking again for any scribbles or notes my dad had left. But the pages are empty through all of the Old Testament. Makes me wonder if he even read much of it.

I look again at the thin paper strip tucked into the book of Matthew with *November 12 Baptism* written on it. I don't remember at all Dad's being baptized. Did it happen before I was born, or when I was just a toddler? I read the verses on baptism, caressing the pages that Dad had touched. A warm peacefulness fills me as I picture him in my mind, picture him reading and pondering. I wonder if my dad was looking for the same sense of home reading his Bible as I do now.

Grandma Howell's Bible, that's what I need, retrieving it now from the built-in bookcase. Aunt Sophia had given the Bible to me when Grandma died ten years ago. Grandma's Bible is chock-full or checkmarks, and some of the pages are even wrinkled and torn, I see now. It's obvious she had a relationship with God, a daily one, finding home in Him.

Home. My mind staggers around for something that I have forgotten about. From my father. And then I remember his maps. The long box of maps that Merilee had given me. When I got back to San Diego, I had stashed the box up high in my mirrored closet.

Now I stand on my bed and get the box down from the closet and bring it back to my little living room in front of the futon couch. My heart is beating fast as if I'm going to find buried treasure. The idea of having something so personal—so created—by my father fills my eyes with tears. *Thank you, God, for this gift.*

Carefully I lift the lid and put it aside. And I sit staring.

Dad's maps are works of art, penciled drawings of imaginary small towns with parks and hills and railroad tracks. I sit and pull each one of them out, staring at them, tracing his pencil marks, careful to not let my tears stain the paper.

After a long while, I grab my jacket, my camera, and some cash.

*****

So grateful I am for my group of Walkabout friends on a Saturday night. We are meeting this time in front of the County Administration Building downtown. As usual we are a happy bunch talking about everything under the sun as we make our way down the waterfront, the sun making stars through the sails of the Star of India. I fall into step with my friends Jeanie and Dennis. They are not a couple; she is twenty years older than he, but they are friends who argue almost as much as they enjoy sitting together at the Monday night concerts at the Spreckels Organ Pavilion. They both have become friends of mine.

On this walk, I can talk as much as I want with everyone or fall back and think on my own while we walk along the waterfront. I came early this evening so that I could talk with Jeanie and Dennis and the other walkers. Dennis has a crush on me; in some ways, I do on him, too. Big and burly, he has the heart of a kid, working at the County of San Diego as a children's escort. Dennis has told me stories of the times he's had to take children away from their homes because they were unsafe for them. Dennis gets tears in his eyes talking about how he reads to the kids on the plane as they travel to the family who will adopt or take them in for a while. Dennis reminds me of a giant teddy bear and at times it is impossible to resist hugging him. He also happens to be a camera nut like me.

As we wait for the walk to start, Dennis and I both snap pictures of the sun sliding below the line of the ocean. Jeanie comes up beside us when the walk leader pushes off. I talk to them about my homesickness.

"What about you, Dennis, don't you ever get homesick?" I ask him.

"Yeah, it happens every time I go visit my parents and I eat dinner with them and my brother. I get very sick," he says, laughing. When he sees my face, he touches my arm gently. "But, yeah, I do get homesick. For the old days. In my mind, I keep going back home to the time before things got bad between my brother and me and my parents." A pedicab driver rings his bell behind us and Dennis and I swerve to get out of his way. "Share the walk," Dennis calls out.

I fall back to think and walk, tailing the end. Dennis waves back at me. "Don't get too far behind," he says.

I want to stay awhile and watch the colors change in the sky at the G Street Mole where the tuna boats dock. A few deck hands are hosing down the boats. A flock of seagulls float in the ocean breeze, keeping an eye out for any extra bait hanging around.

The guys on the boats wave at me as I shoot pictures of the boats, the gulls and the intricate wire lacing of the cage traps. Though the smells of fish and sea salt make my eyes water, I could stay here for hours. But I do want to catch up with Dennis and Jeanie. I'd promised to have dinner with them at the sandwich place in Seaport Village.

*****

Next day, I walk alone at Sunset Cliffs. There are so many questions in my head, so many paths I need to ponder. The heavens have scrubbed clean the air this week. The rain, usually so rare in San Diego, fell from the skies like baptismal water. The view from Sunset Cliffs, with the rolling white foam on the waves and puffy white clouds in the crystal blue sky make my heart ache.

It reminds me of the song "Fall Afresh on Me," which has been running through my mind since last Sunday when I attended the service at San Diego United Methodist Church. When I stood up to sing with everyone, I could feel a peace in knowing I was where God wanted me to be, if even for just that moment.

And I knew I wanted to be baptized.

But the Methodist church does not do adult baptisms, the kind where you go under the water. They only sprinkle on the head. I need a whole-body-and-soul immersion. But it's not just about getting doused with water. It is a covenant, a promise of entering into a life with God and the church.

A pair of sea gulls soar by me standing on the cliff.

*****

It's a beautiful day to be reborn. I check how I look in the mirror: my hair is layered and fluffed out pretty, I have on a white puffed-sleeve blouse and ruffled turquoise skirt, white ballet shoes. No makeup.

The sun is bright, there's a light breeze and birds are singing as I step outside and lock my door. Walking down the stairs of the condo building, I'm as nervous and shaky as a bride. I hear a cat whistle from the courtyard. Alicia is sitting at the wrought-iron table with Hank, my neighbor who has the condo across from me. They are having coffee and pastries.

Alicia lets out another cat whistle. I smile and open my arms wide to her for a hug.

"Mmm, you smell good. Adonde vas?"

"To church. You stayed home this morning?"

"Already went! Soy early bird."

I laugh.

"You look bonita, Renee. Doesn't she, Hank?"

Hank nods. I smile at him, do a little curtsy.

"Pero espera un minuto. You see la nota last night? From the HOA treasurer?"

"What note?"

Alicia gets a piece of paper from her purse and unfolds it. "Es some kind of mandato."

"The treasurer says that our dues have gone up $50 and we all need to pay now. But we don't know where he is," Hank says, biting into a cheese Danish.

"What do you mean, you don't know where he is?"

"No tenemos su direccion. Se fue. Gone," Alicia says.

"Oh, you guys, I am sure it will be fine. But I have to go to church now. You see, I'm getting baptized," I say, beaming.

Alicia clasps her hands together. Hank puts down his cheese Danish. "Congratulations," they say together in one voice.

I laugh. "Thanks. And I would really like it if you guys came with me. I'll drive."

Alicia and Hank look at each other, back at me. "Si, senorita, we go."

I'm so happy I could dance a jig. All of a sudden, the door to the second-story condo in the wing across from me opens. Cheryl comes out of her condo and scowls down at us, like she so often does. But I am full of light and love.

"Good morning, Cheryl. Come with us to church this morning. I'm getting baptized. I'd love for you to come along. I'll drive," I say, peering up at her.

Alicia grabs my hand. "*Que haces*? No can do *esto*. Cheryl mean."

I continue looking up at Cheryl smoking a cigarette, tapping the ashes down onto the floor by our feet. "Come with us, it's a beautiful morning," I say.

Cheryl screws up her face and takes another hit off the cigarette. "You guys are pathetic. And soon you will all be in big trouble," she says, then turns on her heel and retreats into the black hole of her condo. Alicia and Hank and I must look like Dorothy, the tin man and the scarecrow quavering, peering up at the mean old witch. When Cheryl slams her door shut, it takes a while for me to stop shaking.

I turn to look at Alicia and Hank. "I'm going to have a good morning. Especially since you guys are coming with me." I say.

*****

I can hear the choir singing in the sanctuary as I sit in the empty choir room waiting for Pastor Alan to come talk with me for a few minutes before my baptism. I can't help but think of it as the big plunge.

Pastor Alan had assigned me a deacon's wife named Sandy as my baptism assistant. She ties the strings on my robe. "You scared of going under?" she asks me.

"No, it's just for a few seconds. But I don't like being underwater."

"Me neither. I was nervous on the day I got baptized, even though I was quite young," Sandy says, sitting beside me. "But you know something? I rather liked the fact that I was nervous. I recognized that it was a small price to pay for what my Lord and Savior did on the cross for me. And for you."

251

Pastor Alan emerges from the little bathroom in his own white robe. He thanks Sandy for her assistance and then comes to sit across from me. "Do you have any questions?" he asks me.

Oh yes, a hundred. I shake my head. "Not really. I wanted to say, though, that I feel as if this is almost like a closure."

"Closure?"

"Well, yeah, kind of like a contract. I mean, I say that I will love Him forever and ever, and I do this baptism ritual as a kind of proof. And a witness."

Pastor Alan laughs. It is a kind one. "I've never heard it put that way before. Yes, I guess it is kind of a closure. But try to think of it more as a beginning. And remember that nothing you do will ever separate you from the love of God."

I think about this. "I don't see how that can be."

"Do you have kids?"

Eck, the cutting question. I shake my head no.

"Okay. Well, you had parents that loved you…"

I bite my lip. "They say now they do, that they did back when I was a kid, but…I never was sure. Neither was my sister. They hurt us horribly." I really don't want to talk about this now. I want to think about God. Pastor Alan looks at his watch. "What? Am I holding everything up?"

He smiles at me. "Absolutely not. We have plenty of time. All right, now let's talk about this. Regardless of how your parents—and particularly your father—treated you or talked about you or *to* you—your parents, your father are not like your Heavenly Father. We were made in His image, but this world is messed up because of sin and none of us is perfect. We get a sham deal a lot of the time."

I look down at my shredded Kleenex. "What about you? Did you have good parents?"

"Yes," Pastor Alan answers without hesitation. "I wish all people had parents like mine. Only thing is, I can't blame things on my parents if I mess up," he says, laughing again, the lock of hair on his forehead jiggling a little. That makes me smile.

"I have to tell you something, and then I'm ready to do this."

Pastor Alan nods, waiting.

"Sometimes I feel as though I already paid big dues from my childhood and teenage years at home."

"Well, I can assure you that God was with you in your pain. He doesn't take it away from us all the time, but He was—and is there all the time with us. And it's not about us paying our dues. Where did you get that idea?" Pastor Alan asks me, brushing the stubborn lock of hair off his forehead. He is sitting very close to me, so close I am afraid he can smell my breath.

I turn away a little and look down at my torn tissue. "Well, I suppose it was from my parents. They were always punishing me and my sister for things we did and sometimes did not do." All of a sudden, I have the painful memory of my mother spanking me and Rita brutally before we lay down to take our prescribed naps because she suspected that we would talk and giggle before we finally went to sleep. I'd crawl under the blankets with my backside burning and my heart hurting. Mom spanking us before she thought we would do anything bad made me think that God was the same way, even after I went to the altar to ask for God's forgiveness way back.

"Um, I need another tissue."

Sandy pokes her head into the choir room. "Choir started, so you have five minutes," she says.

Pastor Alan asks Sandy to get some tissues for me. Then he tells me that I am a huge miracle. "That's what my Aunt Sophia always says to me. That me wanting to love God in spite of everything I was told about God by my parents, in the way they treated me."

"She was right," Pastor Alan says.

The tears are flowing down my face like a river. Sandy comes to me with a box of tissue.

"Are you ready to be baptized?" Pastor Alan asks me.

In spite of myself, I half laugh. "I think I already am with all this water on my face," I say blowing my nose. "I can hardly breathe."

Pastor Alan and Sandy smile at me. "All right, if you are ready, I would like to say this prayer for you. And it's for all of us," he says, joining my and Sandy's hand together. I nod.

"Lord, I praise and thank You with my heart for the liberation You have given me from the clutches of sin and Satan. By your death on the cross of Calvary and your resurrection, You have put my old life with its sin and judgment to death forever, and endowed me with a new life that is abounding with joy. Amen."

When I open my eyes, I am beaming. "Amen. I am so ready," I say. Pastor Alan laughs and leads me into the baptistery.

*****

It's dark in the baptistery, like a womb. The water is tepid as I step into it, my white robe billowing about me, with Pastor Alan guiding me with his hands on my shoulders. We stop and turn to face the congregation in the sanctuary. I can't see anything except a blur without my glasses, a good thing. Pastor Alan explains to the congregation that I have agreed to be baptized into the family. Then he turns to me, says, "I baptize you in the name of the Father, the Son, and the Holy Spirit," I pinch my nose and he gently lays me back under the water.

When I come up, I hear clapping and cheering, and Pastor Alan nods me in the direction toward the stairs leading me up, out of the baptistery. Sandy is there waiting for me with a towel.

I feel as light as air as I take the towel. And I hear this in my mind: I cannot, I do not want to sin against my Lord.

– 19 –

THE PINK CLOUD OF baptism has been beautiful. That Sunday, Alicia and Hank joined me and Molly and my group of friends for lunch at Pablo's, all of us sitting on the back deck overlooking a sprawling green golf course. A few of my church friends, including Molly and Pat had margaritas, but Hank and Alicia did not, for which I was grateful. We all had a good time, eating noisily and watching the antics of the golfers below us. We all nearly died laughing when a golfer got stuck in his cart over a sprinkler and he ended up getting sprayed with water while sitting in the cart. We cheered when he finally got out of the cart and his wife came over to rescue him. They heard our cheers, looked up, hugged each other, and waved at us.

Life continued to be grand for a while, lunches with friends, dinner out with my Walkabout friends. People said I glowed. To everyone who was willing to listen, I told the story about my recommitment to Christ. Most of the time, though, people looked away or asked for a refill on their coffee or shoo-shooed away my story, telling me that they outgrew church. I could understand that.

But there was a part of me that expected the worst to happen. Look at what Jesus went through. After he was baptized and his Father in heaven said He was well pleased with him, Jesus went off to the wilderness to be alone. And that's where He met his archenemy.

*****

At work, Wendy and I have been spending almost every minute together planning for the big Spring Swing Festival. Preserving the past while honoring the future is what the banners say. I'm nervous and excited about the whole thing. Particularly because it will involve a free series of swing dance lessons. I've always wanted to dance. Mark was never into it like I was.

Mark. What a problem it has been trying to untie the knot. My attorney, Mr. Pritchard, seems to be having a lot of fun stringing me along. Maybe he is disappointed that I did not want to demand spousal support. He never answers my phone calls or even my letters to him. It's as if the case has been dropped—and I already paid hundreds in retainer fees. He must be out having coffee in the mornings with his lawyer buddies and cocktails with his secretary after hours. I chew gum constantly to drive away the nagging worries. My prayers while I drive, type, walk, and go to the bathroom are "Dear God" with nothing following except a whimpering "Help me."

What I want to be as a Christian and what I actually do are so often different. That just adds more anxiety. So I walk more, I work more and I pray that God hears my prayers more.

And of course, I always wish I were really home. Wherever that might be.

*****

I can hardly believe spring is showing its pretty face again. Can hardly remember the last time I looked forward to spring as much as this year. It's been a roller coaster ride.

I'm back to just thirty days of no wine. Two months ago, I walked to the liquor store just three blocks away and bought myself two slim, elegant bottles of Chardonnay wine, I don't even remember what the label was. I just wanted to drink and I wanted to look pretty while I did. During what I call my "real drinking" days, I would buy one of those ugly five-liter boxes with a plastic bladder that I would squeeze the wine out of. What had set me off two months ago was the ups and downs of living. Mr. Pritchard was still dragging on with the divorce proceedings, and I was paying him $1,000 a month as a retainer. I was starting to think maybe it would have been a good idea to get the spousal support he thought I should. But I just didn't want to give in to letting Mark get the upper hand. If I took his money, that would be saying that, yes, he was right: I couldn't survive on my own. Still, a nagging worry ate away at my peace. What if God really wanted me to take the money? I'd shake away the thought, remembering what Pastor Alan had said in one of his sermons: err on the side of love—God's love, that is. Any chance for romance with Mark had flown out the window long ago; besides, I no longer wanted to bank on him. I needed to trust in God, not Mark.

When I was married to Mark, my continual desire was just to have peace at home. Yet alone in my cute little condo, even that hasn't been the case. Turned out that Jeff, our HOA treasurer, had made off with all of our HOA money. But that wasn't before I came home one afternoon from work and caught him buzz-sawing the lantana bush, the branches with its little candy-shaped blossoms lying about like broken bones in the courtyard.

I stood and stared at Jeff until he turned off the buzz-saw. He flipped up his goggles and flashed me a grin. "Aren't you glad I'm getting rid of this thing? It's a sight for sore eyes."

I was so angry that I could not even make sense to myself. I screamed at him to stop, he screamed at me to shut up, I flailed my arms around as if I were having a seizure and stormed up the stairs. For the evening, I hid upstairs and called Alicia. "Ayayayay, what do we do?" she asked me.

"Call the police?"

"Ay, la policia no can do anything."

Turned out Alicia was right. Even when Jeff made off with thousands of dollars of the HOA money and she and I and Hank went to the community police station in City Heights and met Clyde, the officer assigned to us. He listened to us kindly and looked at the papers and records I'd put together from our HOA meetings. Then he rubbed his neck and turned to face us.

Clyde told us there was nothing that he could do. Until Jeff commits some kind of crime outside of the HOA, the police couldn't go after him because the HOA was like a closed society. I stood there shaking, crying. I was doing that a lot lately. Alicia put her arms around me, and the three of us walked out, a small wounded family.

Jeff is still pestering us, leaving notes on our doors at night that we need to pay the increase in HOA fees or else we will be evicted.

Really? Evicted? I wanted to laugh, but I was actually scared out of my mind. So Alicia, Hank, and I trotted back to the police station again, but Clyde told us the same thing he had before: find Jeff, find evidence of a crime he committed outside of the HOA and he would be theirs.

Who has the time and energy and wherewithal to do all that? What I did, instead, was call Vivian. I called her the night I'd had four glasses of wine from the pretty bottles. Even though I did not think I was slurring my words, I confessed to her that I'd been drinking, that I was scared out of my mind. Rather than hang up, she offered to pray for me. I could not help but wonder if God would help me in spite of my being stumbly drunk.

I think they helped, Vivian's prayers. Because Jeff stopped coming around and Cheryl, who had a crush on him and was his hopeful cohort in crime, stopped sniggering at me and Alicia and Hank. She used to pace her balcony, smoking a cigarette, narrowing her eyes at us. Her cat would slink out onto the balcony, and Cheryl would swoop it up into her arms and walk back into the darkness of her condo. Lately, she has stayed inside, although I can hear her sometimes when she talks on the phone. She always sounds like she is upset or trying to get a point across. I often wonder if she is talking to Jeff.

Even in the hellishness of those two months when I drank again and felt like everything about my newfound peace in my own life had vanished, I noticed something changing within myself. It was the holiest of times in many ways for me. After turning off the light and snuggling into my made-for-one daybed right next to the window, I'd turn and face Cheryl's condo which was directly across from me and say a prayer for her. I imagined being who she was, and I understood her. I did not like Cheryl at all, but I could feel the depth of love that Christ had for her. I could see me in Cheryl. I'd say a prayer for her, feel the light breeze on my face from the open window, a kiss from God.

Just before I'd fall asleep, the image of my grandma and great-grandma would float across my mind. They sat in their lawn chairs out in the backyard, and Rita and I would ask them if we could eat some of the mulberries from the bushes. We'd bring them back some and they'd fawn over us and touch our hair, our faces. Rita always squirmed, but I'd bask in their affection. Grandma Howell would get up and go into the house and bring back two kittens, placing one each in our arms. Grandma Howell and Grandma Bell would ask us how we were doing; I'd always say "Fine," because that's what I knew to say. Rita never said much, just kept caressing the mewling kitten in her arms. When I said we had to get on home, Rita and I would put down the kittens. Grandma Howell and Grandma Bell, their faces crinkled with smile and worry lines, took our hands and said they loved us, they prayed for us. Rita always let go first, but I held on a little longer, before I pulled away and walked home with Rita alongside our grandparents' small cornfield.

I knew my grandparents were in God's inner sanctum. Because He loved them, and they continually took their prayers for me and Rita to God, I knew I could do anything. Eventually.

*****

Powerful moments they were, those falling-asleep-while-praying, along with my quiet-no-radio-no-TV times while eating at my dining room table—mine! I'd never before had my own furniture, much less my own living space. Sunday mornings in church also saved me. They helped keep me from going over the deep end to full-scale drink-dom, I do believe.

There's a saying in AA about how you need to accept life on life's terms. I've never been good at that. When I was a little girl trying to be good enough for my parents, I would dream of some kind of paradise where I would get rewarded for every good thing I did. When I was a teenager, all I wanted was one true love and living on my own. When I was in my twenties, living on my own, I dreamed of finding the paradise I'd dreamed of as a little girl. Now I have an insane urge to grab my camera, get into my car, and drive anywhere and wherever I want. And on and on it goes.

I went back to AA meetings, but I felt like I was wasting time since I had found my spiritual home in church. Why do I have to go to meetings? I asked my sponsor many times. Think of it as replacement therapy, she said. <u>You take away something, you got to fill in the hole with something else</u>. And it's got to be with people who drank like you did.

But I didn't. Drink like they did, never wanted to. In the meetings, I tried to listen for the things that people said, hoping to get back to that beautiful place when I attended my first meetings back in Kansas.

So I just tried to get through the emotions I felt each day. I would have my morning coffee while I read my Bible or daily devotional, then go to work, spending most of my time in the office with Wendy because that's where she wanted me.

This last week, I sweat it out with Wendy preparing for the Spring Swing Festival. On Saturday, we signed in and scheduled couples for the swing dance competition and dished out food. I took pictures of the swing dancers and tried to answer all the questions everyone had about the competition. Then, of course, we had to tear it all down at the end of the day, picking up trash off the street. I did not know that I could have knee pain at my age, but I did. Vacation Village, one of the sponsors for the Spring Swing Festival, donated a free stay in a hotel for the festival organizers. Wendy gave me one of the vouchers. "You'll need it," she'd told me the day before the festival.

So right she was. After Wendy and I carried the last trash bag to the dumpster, I stumbled inside the office to get my purse and then Dennis drove me to the hotel, helped me find my room, and for a while held me on the cute little sofa. I was tired in places I didn't know I could be. Dennis never liked the idea of spending too much on a meal, but he bought me dinner that night at the Baleen, an upscale place with views of the twinkling lights on the bay. I was vaguely aware that something was off-kilter in my body, not just being tired, but I ate my chilled gazpacho and buttered a piece of the sourdough bread. Dennis watched every move I made, which was not so unusual, but it made me uncomfortable. He never suspected anything because I smiled and chatted like I usually do.

So badly I craved a glass of wine that it turned my stomach. Instead, I stuffed my face with the seafood pasta dish we ordered and drank big gulps of the lemon-flavored water. By the time dinner was over, I could barely keep my eyes open. Dennis walked me over to my room and just hugged me for a long time before I finally put the key in the door and crashed onto the bed. *Thank You, God,* I whispered, *thank You for Dennis. And You. And...*I'd never before woken up with the sun directly in my eyes until my first morning spent at Vacation Village. There was a tiny crack between the heavy drapes and a ray of sun was streaming in on my dreams. I tossed and turned, murmuring about Byron, about Dennis; Mark, too. I need women friends, I said into my pillow. And that's when I woke up. My heart was pounding as if I'd just run a race. Famished I was, too.

I did not feel like paying a lot of money for room service, nor did I want to eat an expensive breakfast all myself, so I made coffee in the miniscule coffee maker and rummaged through my suitcase to find a bag of trail mix. Brushed my teeth and hair, washed my face, and headed out the door with my small New Testament, trail mix and mug of coffee. Found a bench underneath a small grove of palm trees by a brook, closed my eyes, and said a quick prayer asking God to show me what to read. Opened Ephesians and began reading the long line of blessings that Paul the Apostle had written. A cool breeze wafted through the little palm oasis, and I closed my eyes. When I opened them, there was a fairy-like egret standing at the side of the brook, its gossamer feathers hanging down like a veil from its body. A warm peace spread throughout my body, and the words of Ephesians rang out in my mind: *Blessed be the God and Father of our Lord Jesus Christ, who has blessed us with every spiritual blessing in the heavenly places in Christ.*

The egret crept closer to me, my heart sped up, and then everything went white.

*****

Another hotel guest at Vacation Village had seen me collapse and called an ambulance. I was lying in a hospital bed at Mission Hospital ER for what seemed forever when finally Doctor Jameson came in and sat down next to me. Doctor Jemeson looked at my chart. I tried to sit up straighter in the ER bed and fluffed out my hair. He asked me if I often had a feeling as though my heart were fluttering or that I couldn't catch my breath.

I was simultaneously relieved and saddened when I told him, yes, I did. He told me that I had a heart murmur caused by mitral valve prolapse and regurgitation, premature heartbeat, too.

So this is what's been going on with me.

"Am I going to die?" I was thinking of my father.

"Absolutely not. Many people have these same issues and live a long life. But be careful of what you do, don't get over-tired and don't drink alcohol. No coffee or caffeine of any kind or sugar and cut down on the red meat."

I stared at him. "I don't drink anymore, but there's no way I'm going to give up coffee or chocolate. Just no way." My heart sped up just thinking about a day without my two favorite treats.

He smiled at me; I seethed inside. "You must. If you want to live longer and better, you have to give up those things."

"Well, I don't eat red meat anyway. Doesn't that count for something?"

He laughed; I wanted to hit him. "Of course it does. But look. You were over-tired. Didn't you tell me that?" I nodded. "And you had been drinking some coffee and eating some trail mix with chocolate. Put it all together and that adds stress to your heart. You're still young. But like I said, if you want a good healthy life, you have to cut out those things."

"But what if I don't?" He shook his head, smiled. "You need to see your regular doctor. I recommend that he get a sonogram ordered for you. And I'm sure he will tell you that if you don't do these things—give up caffeine, alcohol, all the things you love, I know—you're setting yourself up for need of a heart surgery."

Oh my Lord. "Wait. Just wait. I'm just forty. I'm too young for this."

Doctor Jameson looked at me. "Actually, no, you're not."

"So I'm going to write you a prescription for Atenolol. It helps to slow your heartbeat. But you absolutely can't drink alcohol with this. And remember, no caffeine," he said.

As if that weren't enough, the ER doc told me that I needed to up my exercise. I said I do walk about three times a week. He gave me a thumbs-up and told me to walk more and lift weights. Swim. Dance.

*****

In my mind, there was nothing to dance for. I was so depressed when I went home today. Took the bus. I called Molly, but as usual, she did not answer her phone. Wendy no way I was going to call. Besides, she lived clear out in Blossom Valley, was probably brushing down her beloved horses. I remembered the dream I'd had last night about needing more girlfriends. It's always been so easy for guys to like me, but women? It's like they ignore me or something. They never call me; I've always called them.

I needed my mother. Or Aunt Sophia. Or even Rita. But what good would it do to call them? Mom would be self-absorbed; Aunt Sophia, clucking like a hen over me, making me cry; Rita, making me crave a glass of wine. Talking to them would just have made me more confused, unsure of where I was going with my life.

I could call Dennis, but he doesn't have a car, and all he would have done was meet me at the bus stop. So I caught the bus just a block away from Mission Bay Hospital, got a seat by the window, and took out my little New Testament to read. But instead of opening it, I watched the people in their cars waiting for the traffic light to change. Some people were eating, some holding hands with their boyfriend or girlfriend, others were jamming to the music on the radio. I idly wondered what God saw when he watched us; I began to hum Bette Midler's "From a Distance" until a nice-looking Hispanic guy plopped into the seat next to me. I peered out the window again as the bus moved to the next stop along Grand Street. I was glad that the bus route was long; I needed the time to think.

I glanced at the guy next to me who was reading a small bound book with handwriting inside. He saw me looking at the book. "It's my poetry."

"*Que bueno*," I said.

"*Hablas espanol muy bien.*"

"*Mas o menos. Eres poet?*"

"*Mas o menos.*" We laughed.

"*Quieres te lea un poema?*"

"In English, please."

Jose was his name, and he read his beautiful little poem about how the sound of the ocean reminded him of all things he was grateful for: the long luxurious kiss of his young wife, the sloppy, furry love of his dog, having a good meal with family on a Sunday afternoon. "Y todo esta bien conmigo y mi Dios," he read the last line, then turned to me. "Sorry, couldn't help it. It means, 'And all is well with me and my God.'"

I felt like a silly old woman for the tears that were spilling out my eyes. Jose gave me a tissue, which made me cry. We both laughed as I blew my nose hard.

"Your poem reminds me of a song called 'All Is Well with My Soul.'" I say. "It's one of my favorites. You know something? You should read in one of the coffeehouses in San Diego."

"*De verdad?*"

"*Si, de verdad.*"

I jotted down the name of a coffeehouse in the South Park neighborhood. It was a place that welcomed any and all people. Except maybe me. In the few times that I read my own poetry years ago, I received nothing but blank stares and a few claps that sounded like someone popping their gum. I have always felt on the outside. But I love bringing people to the inside.

*****

On my lunch break on my fortieth birthday, exactly six months after I handed over retaining fees to Mr. Pritchard for him to set in motion the divorce from Mark, I found a thick package in the mail.

It was the divorce agreement, ready to be signed by me.

I tossed the thing onto my Futon couch. It seemed dirty—the agreement—lawless in nature. I really had wanted this marriage to work; I had believed that if I tried to love God with all my heart, I would find greater love in the man I married. But Mark's god was not the one I had wanted to love or respect. The rhetoric of Truth Universal sounded good, all those Bible verses they spouted; their gain, however, was not God the Creator of the Earth and me and other people and the animals and trees and birds—their idea of a relationship with a higher being was a binding contract initiated by we the people to be signed by the god of our liking.

I didn't like thinking about all this. It led me down a road of confusion and despair, especially because I felt like my own relationship with the Creator of this earth was still tremulous—not on His part, so much, but my part. I had lost a belief system that I had relied on for eleven years yet had always secretly distrusted. In the same year that I walked away from my husband and my religion, I lost my father. I needed my Father in heaven.

I poured myself a cup of coffee, picked up the divorce papers from the couch, plucked a pen from my desk drawer, and sat down. I had fifteen minutes before I had to go back to work. I closed my eyes, said a soundless prayer, opened my eyes, and signed my name.

*****

Giving up caffeine has been a piece of cake. All I did was switch to decaf and have about a cup less of the java than I used to. Chocolate, another matter. I'd almost have to be dead in bed before I gave that up. Still, I was careful, switching to See's instead of the cheap M&M's. Spending five dollars on a small box of chocolates I hand-picked myself made it easier to pass up the cheap stuff. If I really crave something tasty and have already reached my daily limit of chocolate and decaf, I brew cups of Good Earth tea. I swear, I could become addicted to that stuff, too.

Spunky helps keep me grounded. That I have this little lavender and gray parakeet waiting for me at home gives me a focus at home. Alicia, Hank, and I did finally get down the license number of one of Jeff's cars, so Officer Clyde and his team from the community police station tracked him down and nailed him on several counts of fraud and robbery he'd committed at his job.

It still isn't perfect here on Williams Street. I'm somewhat of a night owl and at around 10:00 or 11:00 p.m. I often see johns in their vans dropping off an entire band of prostitutes in our driveway to walk the streets. In the mornings, I find used rolled-up condoms and empty airplane bottles of whiskey on the sidewalk and street. Countless times I've called the information number of the police when I see the johns pull up in their vans. I've told them about the activity on the street. Often within minutes of my calling, a patrol car will pull up and arrest the prostitutes along with the john. I feel bad about that, about the prostitutes being rounded up. It's not their fault.

At work, I have fallen into a good rhythm with Wendy. We order in lunch from Etna Pizza or try out the different restaurants on the boulevard. Our latest noon on the town treat is Everest Café. I have never smelled anything as delicious as the aromas and spices of Himalayan food. Wendy and I have become experts at scooping up saag aloo and chicken vindaloo with pieces of garlic naan.

"Do they have anything like this in Wheaton?"

"No, they don't. Maybe in another ten years. Every time I go back there, I see yet another restaurant." I take a sip of the tea.

Wendy puts down her slice of naan. "Hey, I got an idea. I need to get away from Tim this weekend. You want to drive out to the desert with me? I hear the wildflowers are incredible."

I could just hug her now. Tears spring to my eyes. "Holy cow, these spices!" I sniff, blot my eyes, then look at her. "I would love that. But is it—I mean, should I?"

"Enjoy a day with your boss?" Wendy laughs. "Why not?"

– 20 –

THAT FEELING OF DANCING I got last summer back in Kansas when I looked out over the fields of wheat waving in the sun is back. But this time I am in the Anza Borrego Desert with Wendy, and we are running about under ocotillo trees with their bright red blossoms. "It's a lipstick tree," I shout, running around the thin spiny branches.

"Stop!" Wendy yells. I stop. She points down. "Have you ever seen so many tiny flowers?"

Hundreds of purple flowers on vine-like stems dot the sand. Sand Verbena is what the brochure said from the Visitors Center. Wendy and I crouch down and look closely at them. I put my camera right next to their flower faces, aiming up to catch Indian Head Mountain in the background.

The air is fragrant, a light breeze lifting my hair. Wendy and I watch the honey bees darting about in dizzy bliss from flower to flower. The sand is warm, not hot, in our hands.

I have never been to the desert before, just never got around to it. Wendy was shocked when I told her that at lunch in the mountain town of Julian. The chicken pot pie and garlic mashed potatoes made me homesick, it was so good.

"How was it that you never visited the desert? Didn't you tell me that you moved to San Diego in 1981?" Wendy asked, as we sat lingering over coffee and a slice of Julian's trademark apple pie.

"I just never got past the Laguna Mountains or the Cuyamaca Forest. I always loved the mountains," I said, thinking of the times that Mark and I had hiked the Paso Picacho Trail.

Now sitting on the desert floor with Wendy, I remember something I'd learned recently about the children who live in the area around Gateway Boulevard: most of them had never even been to the beach, much less the desert, because their families did not have the transportation, the money or the time for such a leisure.

I turn to Wendy, watch her sifting sand through her fingers. "Guess what?"

"What?" she says, looking up at me. "Hey, are you all right?"

I nod, wiping the tears out of my eyes. "Yes. I just had a revelation. I know what I'm supposed to do."

"About what?"

"With my life. With—what I have," I say, sweeping my arm across the view of the desert.

"You want to live in the desert?" Wendy asks me.

I laugh. "No. But I want to bring kids from the neighborhood—the Gateway Boulevard area—to the desert here, the beach, or anywhere. I want to show them there's a world they haven't seen. I guess it's important to me because I felt trapped in my own way, you know, at home, all the strictness, the abuse, the fears. We—my sister and I—were safe from the outside, but not from the inside."

I don't know why or what or how I feel the need to keep going with this idea, but I do. "My sister and I never felt safe at home. And we never could go anywhere either, except church or school, which I loved." Wendy raises her eyebrows. "Yes. Church and school. Loved being in both those places because I could be with other people, other kids, even if they did torment us much of the time," I say, touching my hair. "They teased us so bad, especially fat, little Ricky Hunt and the pair of brothers Perry and Jerry, their last name Cherry. Can you believe it? No wonder they tormented me and my sister. Who wouldn't with names like that?" I laugh.

Wendy looks at me, still listening. I pick a tiny white wildflower from the sand and twirl it in my fingers. I keep talking. "My sister and I rarely went anywhere else except church and school. We were prisoners at home. I know it sounds dramatic, but it's true. If it hadn't been for my aunt and uncle next door or my grandparents across the street behind the cornfield, and knowing that I would be at my aunt's house with all of them there for Christmas and Easter and birthday celebrations and even Groundhog Day, I don't think I would have survived," I say, picking up handfuls of sand and letting it fall.

"Now that I'm grown up, ha, if I can call myself that, I can be grateful for my parents and everything they gave me: food, shelter, and the most wonderful birthday celebrations, Christmases and Easters imaginable. My mother lavished me and my sister with gifts and candy on those days. It was like she turned into Mrs. Santa Claus then.

"But I was still so shut off from everything. Even from myself. I didn't know what I could do and why I was here in this world."

Wendy brushes her fingers against some of the tiny white and yellow wildflowers in the sand. "But who does? And why is it that you always want to go back to your hometown if you had it so bad there?"

"I've asked myself that question, too, many times. Basically, it's my reaching back and with God's help reconciling with the past. And I think I've done that."

Wendy sighs, brushes the sand off her legs. "I have to get up. But you may have to help me."

I laugh. "Same here." We start trudging through the sand, trying our best to avoid stepping on the flowers.

"So what does this story you told me about your past have to do with wanting to show kids the desert?" Wendy asks as we approach her car.

I stop under an ocotillo tree, looking close at its bright red blossoms. "You know our motto for the Blast to the Past event we had? Honoring our past, embracing the future?"

Wendy puts her hand on her hip. "Yes?"

"Well, that explains it perfectly," I say, pulling an ocotillo blossom close to me, peering into its petals. "I want to help a child, a girl, a teenager embrace her future. I have honored my past, and now I want to go forward." I touch the dainty parts of the flower; Georgia O'Keefe would have had a field day with this flower. I let it go and turn to Wendy. We begin walking together toward her car. "I want to show a young girl how to take pictures, I want to take her to the desert, treat her to apple pie in Julian. I want to take her to the beach where we can collect shells. We could go to the zoo. She could come to my place and make cookies. We'd have our own little Christmas."

Wendy opens the passenger door for me. "But you don't have any kids."

"I've got a whole world of kids," I say. "Right in City Heights."

Wendy gets in the car, smiles, and shakes her head before she turns on the ignition. "What, you think I'm crazy?" I tease her.

"Why don't you just go back to your hometown more often and see your nieces and nephews?" she asks me, both of us slamming the visors down against the blinding sun in the windshield.

"I'll still go to see them. But my life is here now."

Here. Now. Under God.

*****

I found a girl. Rather, she found me. I had decided on Foster Friends to begin a mentoring program there. I'd signed up for the program deciding that was the best way to begin mentoring. I had to fill out a profile, pay for a background check complete with finger-printing, and get a TB test. There was no reason for me to be worried about it—I'd never committed a crime, and I knew my family members would speak highly of me, even Rita who could hold a grudge forever—even so, I nearly fainted when I got the notice in the mail from Foster Friends that I was in. Something about passing all those tests validated me as a good person, a woman decent enough to love up a little girl who needs attention.

Why Foster Friends was my first choice for a mentoring organization had to do with a long-buried memory. One summer Saturday afternoon when I was about eleven years old, Rita had not been able to finish her peanut butter sandwich—as usual, her eyes watered and her gag reflex kicked in, during which I, like usual, looked around her out the window as I ate my own sandwich and dreamed of the big wide blue yonder, sometimes glaring at Rita as a silent begging for her to please just eat and be normal. Mom had watched Rita's gagging and went off somewhere else in the house. After Rita gave up on trying to finish her sandwich and I had eaten every bite I could of my own, washing it down with a glass of milk, we found that Mom had thrown all of Rita's clothes into the hallway.

"Pick which clothes you want to keep because you are going to a foster home," Mom screamed to Rita, her eyes like a lunatic's. Rita just stood there and bawled. Scared out of my mind, I skittered back to my room, peering around every so often at the scene. Mom kept throwing more clothes onto the floor while Rita stood and cried like a big baby. I was suddenly so furious. At Rita for not liking food. At Mom for not liking us. At the preacher for always telling us that we were going to hell. I was already living in it. Why did Big God have it in for us?

Rita refused to choose any clothes, just stood there with tears running down her face, wailing. Mom became even angrier, pushing her all the way down the hallway, through the living room and out onto the front porch. "Just leave. Keep walking and don't come back. I don't care where you go. I don't want you here anymore," Mom yelled and then slammed the door.

I shook with embarrassment at Rita standing on our front porch crying her eyes out. "Mama, please, please let me stay. I don't wanna go," she wailed.

What would the neighbors think? But maybe that would be a good thing; Aunt Sophia would come running over.

Mom ignored Rita's pleas, went into the bathroom, and came out with a bottle of shampoo and a towel. She walked into the kitchen, ignoring me still standing in the living room. I curled my hand into a fist and chewed on my knuckles, pacing back and forth, staring at Dad's fancy glass spires until I had the courage to go into the kitchen.

Mom had already rubbed shampoo into her hair and was dowsing her head with water. I ignored the thumping of my heart and went to stand beside her.

"Mama." She either did not hear me or she was ignoring me. "Mama."

"What?" she said into the sink.

"Um, I know that Rita makes you mad. She does me too, sometimes."

At this, Mom shut off the faucet and turned her head to look at me, the whites of her eyes red.

"But I want her here. I don't want you to send Rita away. Would you please let her back in? Please?"

So after Mom finished washing her hair and wrapping her head in a towel, she let Rita back into the house.

Home had become a prison for both me and Rita, one in which we were both willing to live until the day came when we would escape. For now, we would get our bread and a bed. Half the time, though, Rita could not even eat her bread. But Mom never threatened to throw either one of us out of the house again until one evening at dinnertime when I was seventeen, Rita sixteen. Then both she and Dad gave the edict: graduate from high school, leave home. Forever.

"Don't expect a penny from us," Dad said, his foot making a heavy thud on the floor.

*****

About a week after I'd signed on with Foster Friends, Sharyn, a nine-year-old girl with blond hair, blue eyes, and a funny little laugh, had come with her social service manager to help her pick out her very own foster friend.

Sharyn still loves to tell the story of how she decided on me as her Foster Friend. "I saw your picture and I liked how your hair kind of stood all around your face. It looked like you knew how to have fun," she says.

I tell her that is the best compliment I have ever received in my life. She just beams at me. She lives in a house with a married couple who have four other foster children. It's been a way to make money for the couple, but they have been kind and generous to the children as they could be on their work-horse salaries. They never had children of their own; the foster kids filled a hole in their hearts. I had trouble holding back my tears when they told me that; they might as well have been telling my own story.

The first time I came to meet Sharyn I was as nervous as if I were meeting a blind date. When I stepped foot inside after the social worker with me knocked on the door and Sharyn's foster mom invited us in, I almost fell back from the odor of cat litter, old dirty clothes and rotting wood. I felt awkward in my flowered three-quarter angel-sleeve blouse and clean jeans, smelling pretty with Avon's Candid perfume.

Mr. and Mrs. Emerson were kind to me, happy for Sharyn to have someone who could go run and play and laugh with her. I felt almost unworthy in their presence. Though they were just a few years older than I was, they had run into unfortunate circumstances years ago when their former house in North Park burned down because of a garage fire. Mrs. Emerson's mother, who was an epileptic and had been living with them under their care, died from smoke inhalation. Their home insurance did not cover the damages from the fire, they had had no money built up because every cent had been gone to doctors and medicines for the old woman, and neither of them had any living family members. Neither Mr. nor Mrs. Emerson had stable incomes—he had heart problems, so he could not do any physical work, and he ended up low on the totem pole of workers at any company he worked for. These days he worked at a small Mexican restaurant in City Heights, he told me, and at least he got his meals free. Mrs. Emerson was a caregiver for seniors in their homes, working all hours of the day and night, making just over the minimum wage.

They were content, though, the Emersons, all their foster kids, too. The kids clamored for a hug from me when I met them all that first day. I ended up with all of them—Sharyn included—on the floor coloring a picture of unicorns dancing in flower fields. That day in the dim little house began my love story with Sharyn.

But it hasn't all been sunlight and poppies with her. She gets in moods that sink her so badly she hardly talks. I just let her sit quietly in the passenger seat while I drive us someplace, to the zoo, the beach, the park. She had told me a little of her short life story on our first day together. Her natural mother had been addicted to heroin and had to give her up. Sharyn still goes to see her mother when she happens to be in a rehab place, but it's under strict supervision, always with her social worker hovering within a few feet in the rehab hospital's ugly little courtyard of plastic chairs and tables and some scruffy hedges. She and her mother never really talk about things that matter. Sharyn always gives her mother something she made at school, and then her mother hugs her and asks her questions about school.

"And she always apologizes, all the time. I don't know who my mother really is," she said one day when we were having ice cream at the mall. I put my arm around her, and she scooted up next to me on the bench while we licked the ice cream running down our cones and fingers.

We've developed a way of talking and being together. Lucky for me, Sharyn is nearly as crazy about birds as I am. We perk up at the sight of them, especially near the ocean with the herons and egrets, ducks and geese. We are hypnotized by the egrets sleuthing through the water, looking for food, keeping one eye trained on us, their feathers hanging down like a gossamer veil.

We give them names like Queenie and Prince, Shelley and Crabby. "Oh, dear," I drawl out in a faux Brit accent of Queenie, "I just can't imagine anyone acting like that."

Sharyn puts her nose up in the air. "Dahling, you are just too beautiful to bother with these common ducks and geese," she says, for Prince.

But we love the ducks and geese, too. I bring bread and crackers for them on our trips to the beach. Sharyn likes to throw the food all at once to them so that she can watch the flurry and fussing of the birds, some of them walking over her shoes to get to the food. I take a gazillion photos. Then we will walk together sometimes for a mile and a half on the beach, stopping to pick up shells and stones.

One day at the zoo, which Sharyn calls her favorite place on earth, we had exhausted ourselves walking all around the perimeter of the zoo. "Lions, tigers, and bears, oh my," Sharyn could not resist singing. I joined in with her. People looked at us, smiling, shaking their heads, at the two of us holding hands, singing and skipping. I would have looked, too, had I been them.

*****

Falling into step with a young girl has helped me fill the shoes of being a more responsible adult. It's been good for Sharyn, too.

The more times and ways that she got to be a girl out having fun, she more eagerly accepted responsibility at home. That's what the Emersons told me a few months ago.

The cookie-baking-with-my-nieces fantasy I've lived out with Sharyn. This spring has been cool, sometimes downright chilly, so turning the oven on has been a boon. Sharyn helped me beat up some chocolate cookie dough, and we took turns placing the baking sheets in the oven and slipping the just-baked ones onto a cooling rack. We ate many of the cookies, sticky warm with melted chocolate, guzzling glasses of cold milk. I'd forgotten how good milk actually tastes.

Sharyn has become good friends with Spunky, who perks up as soon as she walks into the door. "Hey, I'm jealous," I have said more than once. She just giggles and carefully opens the cage door and Spunky jumps onto her finger, easy as pie. She deftly brings her finger with him sitting on it through the door and there he is looking at us both, fluffing up, chirping so loud that Sharyn has to clamp her hands over her ears, which makes Spunky so excited that he starts jumping back and forth between us, landing on our heads.

– 21 –

WE ARE BOTH GROWING up, Sharyn and I. Especially after the incident that we call "The Hanging."

As the afternoon sun fell behind the tall eucalyptus trees yesterday on another trip to the zoo, we decided to take the ZooView ride back to the entrance. We were both bone-tired from having walked endlessly, often standing for long periods of time to gawk at gorillas and grizzly bears. I went ahead and paid some money to get on the ZooView, since it wasn't included in my membership.

Sharyn was unusually antsy as we waited in line to get into our own swaying bucket. She stared bullet-eyes at the group of noisy kids ahead of us. "They are going to be trouble," she told me. I laughed. She glared at me. "You just watch," she said.

I squeezed her hand and offered her a baggie of the trail mix I'd bought along. Finally, it was our turn, and the ZooView ride attendant barely glanced at us as he opened the door for us to get in. He clanged down the security bar in front of us hard and then clamped shut our door. Off we went up into the air. We heard the ZooView guy yell, "Hey, you up there!" Sharyn and I turned to look. He was pointing to the kids in the bucket just above us.

"Quit swinging the ride! Now!" the attendant yelled.

Sharyn clung to the pole in the center. "Told you," she moaned.

I looked above us, and Sharyn was right—the kids were swinging and kicking their legs. We moved slowly in our bucket hanging high above the zoo. I held Sharyn's hand, pointed out the California Tower rising above the thick filmy brush of trees of the park. The tower gleamed in the late afternoon sun.

"Pretty, huh?" I said.

She squeezed her stomach. "I don't feel good." She didn't look good, either, her face empty of color.

And then our bucket hiccupped and bumped and came to a stop, us swinging directly above the lion cages. Sharyn screamed. I pulled her in tight next to me.

The kids in the bucket in front of us turned and looked at us, laughing, still swinging and kicking their legs.

"Don't worry. This is normal, I'm sure. They're probably just waiting for the people down below to get on the ride," I said.

But I knew it wasn't so. So did Sharyn. She started pulling on her hair. "I've got to go to the bathroom," she said.

Awful thing was, so did I.

"We're going to die," she said.

"Sharyn. We are not. I promise you. We are not. The zoo is a good place run by good people. They want us to come back and enjoy this place again. They care about the animals and us. I promise you, it'll be okay," I said all these things just as much to myself as to her. I was fighting off a panic attack, a floating sense of doom that grabbed me at the bottom of my spine and worked its way up to my heart making it hard to breathe. I imagined Sharyn and me hanging for hours on end, long past the setting sun, into the night with nothing but our flimsy sweaters to protect us against the cold.

"I'm cold. I have to go to the bathroom," Sharyn said.

I held on to her, smoothing her hair. "Me, too. But I got an idea. Let's sing."

"Whaaat?"

"Sing with me. You know "Amazing Grace?"" I started humming. Sharyn nodded, and almost without missing a beat, she started humming, too.

"Amazing grace, how sweet the sound…" I sang the words, and Sharyn joined in, softly. "I once was lost, but now am found, was blind, but now I see."

The sun was getting lower, the breeze getting stronger, but Sharyn and I held on to each other. And then our bucket hiccupped and lurched forward, and we were on our way gliding smoothly once again. The kids in the cable car ahead of us had calmed down.

As soon as our feet touched the ground, a ZooView ride attendant pressed something into our hands. "Free zoo passes for your trouble," he said.

Sharyn and I squealed and hugged each other, then ran for the restroom.

*****

One day not long after "The Hanging," Sharyn and I went to have a picnic on the huge grassy area of Colina del Sol Park in City Heights. People who had come to America from all places in the world were here, people from Somalia, Nigeria, Columbia, Iraq, and Venezuela.

While we lay on our backs watching the clouds, I asked Sharyn where she had learned to sing, "Amazing Grace."

She shrugged. "At church once with my foster parents. I didn't really understand what the preacher was saying, but I remember singing that song. And people around me blew their noses. They were crying. But it was like they were happy. It made me cry, too."

"So you believe in God?" I asked her.

"Oh, yeah, I mean who else could make flowers? And trees? And Queenie and Prince?"

"What do you think God is like?" Sharyn asked.

I pointed to the clouds. "See that?"

We watched the clouds move along, some of them bumping into each other and becoming completely different shapes, others breaking off and wisping away.

"I think I just saw a cow become an angel," Sharyn said.

"Yeah, and how does that happen?"

Sharyn turned to face me on the blanket. "What, you mean turn a cow into an angel?"

I laughed and turned on my side to look at her. "Why do these clouds move?"

"Oh, that's easy. The wind," Sharyn said.

"But where does the wind come from?"

Sharyn thought for a moment, turned over on her back, and looked at the sky. "I have no idea."

"Where does the wind go?" I asked her.

"Everywhere?" Sharyn whispered. "Yeah, everywhere. Like God. He's everywhere."

"But is God the wind? No, God created the wind. He can't be what He created."

Sharyn thought about that for a minute. "Oh, that hurts my head," she said.

"Just think of him as the Great Artist who created the wind and these clouds and trees and birds—and you".

Sharyn smiled. "And you. And my foster parents. And my cat."

"Yes. Now let's eat."

Moments like those with Sharyn make me feel as if I am lifted .up on a cloud where I can see forever. And I remember the days when I sang "On a Clear Day" with Aunt Sophia and Grandma Howell and Grandma Bell with all of us bumping along in the bed of the pick-up truck on our jaunts out into the country.

Even after all the wonderful times with Sharyn, the contentment I get from work and having my own place, I go about my days now with a pang in my soul, a deep hunger that feels as though even God cannot satisfy. I pray at night in my bed, turned toward the window so that I can feel the breeze on my face, asking for a grateful heart.

*****

The air smells sweet from the wild daisies and San Diego sunflowers in the biggest bloom in a decade. Sharyn and I are sitting on a picnic blanket at Country Goods Farm in Valley Center listening to a band play '80s and '90s covers. We are both silent, sad together. Her mother had died two months ago from a massive heart attack after she had left rehab and gotten high on heroin again. I haven't even tried to rationalize with Sharyn why her mother died. Who, what Christian would even do that? Sharyn still has so much little-girlness in her.

And yet, I've just asked Sharyn if any family has come forward and asked to adopt her. I could just die because a dark shadow crossed her face. She fiddles now with a feather she'd found near the little barnyard of goats, turkeys, and llamas.

"Sorry I asked, sweetheart," I say, shoving toward her the bag of licorice allsorts that I'd bought in the store. Sharyn and I both go crazy over licorice.

She shrugs and takes a handful of licorice.

"You still happy with the Emersons, though?" I shove licorice into my mouth, willing myself to stop asking Sharyn questions. What am I thinking?

Sharyn nods. "They are good to me. To all of us. Always. I think of them as my aunt and uncle. Because I know they'll never adopt me," Sharyn goes on. "They can't afford me or anyone else they have. I know they make money with us being there. But it's okay. I know they love us."

I scramble over on my hands and knees to give Sharyn a hug. "You are so smart, so wise. I love you. And I hope you will always be my friend."

Sharyn gives me a little smile. "I hope so, too."

"Well, things might change between us," I say.

"What do you mean?"

"You turn thirteen, you'll see. You may not ever want to hang out with me again."

"Huh-uh, no way," she says, popping more licorice pastels in her mouth.

And then the band starts playing a cover of Seal's "Don't Cry." Goosebumps jump up on my skin. I look up at the sky, sway back and forth, and sing softly along with the band.

Sometimes music voices exactly what is in my heart what yet I hadn't even known lived there. Such is "Don't Cry."

I sing until the band plays its last note. Quiet, I cry. For me. For Sharyn. For the people I love and can't be with. For the ones I've loved and never could be with. For the loss of my father. For the love of my Heavenly Father. For not always being who God made me to be.

And yet. And yet it's all good, by the hand of God. That God makes it all good in the end is partly my doing. He can't do His work if I sit idly by and wait for some kind of miracle.

"It's true, Sharyn. You're not alone. You'll always be loved," I say as we stand up to leave. We stop at a flower vendor where I buy Sharyn a bunch of daisies and myself a white basket filled with ever-lasting flowers. I will keep this basket as long as I can in memory of my father—and this moment of clarity I have in knowing what I need to let go of, what I need to do, whom I need to love.

Epilogue

October 1997

THE CUMULUS CLOUDS ARE like giant white bubbles in an azure sky as I head east on US-56 through the Cimarron Grasslands in western Kansas. I've got my Enya cassette tape playing; the radio picks up only mariachi music. Sharyn is humming and playing with a Native American doll I'd bought for her in the gift shop where we went to church this morning in Santa Fe, New Mexico.

When we had stepped inside the cool dim of the Cathedral Basilico of St. Francis, I dipped my hands into the holy water and made the sign of the "Father, Son, and Holy Spirit." Sharyn did the same, her little voice in a whisper.

Sharyn is mine now; I am hers. Adopting Sharyn and leaving the Golden State is the wildest, most wonderful thing I have ever done. I sold my condo in just two weeks, earning $80,000 in capital gains, then wired a check to the real estate agent in Wheaton to buy the little one-bedroom house next to Aunt Sophia's for $30,000. Ironically, the people who used to live there had also been members of TU. They'd sold out completely to TU, their lives pulled up by the roots with promises of grand prosperity and new life—pairing up with different partners.

"They weren't smart like you, Renee." Aunt Sophia told me on the phone. "They were fooled by all the smoke and mirrors."

Sharyn and I had our tearful goodbye yesterday with the Emersons. We stood around in the little house, awkward with all our love, the mix of emotions twisting our mouths. Mrs. Emerson handed Sharyn and me a huge basket of fruit.

"For the long drive home," she told me.

I could barely see for all my tears, presenting them with a photo album of the times I've had with Sharyn. We hugged, all of us, shaking and sobbing, until Sharyn and I pulled away.

"I will always love all of you," Sharyn said.

It was just as difficult letting go of Spunky. Sharyn shed as many tears as I did as we took my lavender and gray puffball friend in his cage downstairs to Alicia. But she was thrilled to adopt him. "I take good care of the little keeto. Por favor, write to me. Bueno?" she said. Sharyn and I nodded. We hugged for a long time before we said good-bye with Spunky chirping at us. We made sure not to turn around to look.

We will come back for a visit sometime. The call of San Diego has always been strong, beckoning me to its shores like the foghorns on misty mornings at Ocean Beach. It has been good to be away from my hometown to become who God intended me to be. But now I must leave or the hope for something more will elude me, like a butterfly, teasing me, brushing against my skin and hair, then winging away the moment I get too close.

After I signed the official adoption papers for Sharyn last month, I took her to get a milkshake to celebrate. As we slurped and sipped the chocolatey mix, we talked nonstop about all the things we would do together and with her new cousins—and grandmother.

"I can't wait to make sugar cookies and decorate them for Christmas," I said.

Sharyn licked fudge sauce off her spoon. "Does it snow there?"

"Oh, yes, every winter. We can make snowmen."

"What do people do in the summer?"

I laughed. "It'll be hot. When my sister and I were little, we used to run around and play in the water from the sprinkler."

At this, Sharyn stopped eating. "You can run around in the water in your yard there?"

"That's right. Because there's no limit to water use. They don't have to worry about droughts back there. Cool, huh?"

"Can we get another cat?" she asked.

"Oh yes. And a bird, too, if you want one. And we'll have squirrels to feed."

"At the park?"

"Yes. But in our yard, too. The squirrels and rabbits will come around, and cardinals, too. Ever seen a cardinal? The bright red bird?"

Sharyn shook her head, spooning the last of the ice cream into her mouth. "Can't wait to be there, can't wait," she said.

Neither can I. But I'm going to savor every moment of the journey.

This returning home is a risk worth taking—all about family and keeping good memories alive, letting the bad ones melt away just like the Wicked Witch of the West. It is quite the out-of-the-body, in-the-spirit experience. This morning while browsing through the devotional my mother had given me a year and a half ago, I came across Romans 12:1 that summed things up for me: "And we know that God causes all things to work together for good to those who love God, to those who are called according to His purpose."

I think on those words now as we drive through the vast sea of the Cimarron National Grassland over which you can see forever. The grass ripples and shimmers in the wind.

Sharyn taps my arm and points out her window. "Look, Renee! The grass is dancing," she says.

It is indeed. I pray that my new life with Sharyn will be as a dance of joy unto the Lord.

Discussion Questions

1. If a child enjoys going to church for the social interaction, how and why might that be good in developing spiritual growth?

2. When are family secrets detrimental? What kind of family secrets are fine to keep as such?

3. Could Mr. and Mrs. Howell (Renee and Rita's parents) truly have been Christians, even though they often did not act that way towards their daughters? Why or why not do you think so?

4. How could Renee have responded differently when she came face-to-face with now grown-up Delores, her childhood tormentor and teaser?

5. Should older children and tweens be counted on to report to authorities any kind of parental abuse? If so, what should they expect?

6. In what ways do you think Renee should have acted differently toward her adult sister?

7. How does having an extended family nearby help with the emotional, mental, and spiritual health of a child?

8. In what ways do you think Renee was more concerned with her earthly home than her eternal one—and how could she have changed her perspective?

9. How important is it for a woman to remain connected to her family of origin, especially if there had been abuse of any kind?

10. In what ways do you think Renee could be a better witness of the Lord's help in her troubled childhood and adult life?

About the Author

CYNTHIA G. ROBERTSON, A long-time journalist and photographer, likes to say that she was born with a pen in one hand and a camera in the other. In more than three decades of freelance writing, she has written hundreds of articles and taken photographs for newspapers and magazines about the people, places, and events in the Southern California region. The splendor of nature and the wonderful things that people do to help each other have been the source of inspiration for her writing, which she began at the University of San Diego. She has a heart for those who need a sense of family, particularly in the family of God, even with all the conflicts that sometimes occurs. *Where You See Forever* is Cynthia's first novel. She also authors a blog called Shutterbug-Angel, featuring her photographs of the wonders she finds in the great outdoors and meditations on God's Word. Cynthia lives with her husband in San Diego.